Richard Laymon was born in Chicago in 1947. He grew up in California and took a BA in English Literature from Willamette University, Oregon, and an MA from Loyola University, Los Angeles. He worked as a schoolteacher, a librarian, a mystery magazine editor and a report writer for a law firm before becoming a full-time writer. His novel FLESH was named Best Horror Novel of 1988 by *Science Fiction Chronicle* and also shortlisted for the prestigious Bram Stoker Award, as were FUNLAND and his short story collection, A GOOD, SECRET PLACE. Richard Laymon wrote many acclaimed works of horror and suspense, including THE STAKE, SAVAGE, AFTER MIDNIGHT and the three novels in the Beast House Chronicles: THE CELLAR, THE BEAST HOUSE and THE MIDNIGHT TOUR. He died in February 2001.

For up-to-date cyberspace news of Richard Laymon's books, contact Richard Laymon Kills! at: http://rlk.cjb.net

'An uncanny grasp of just what makes characters work . . . readers turn the pages so fast they leave burn marks on the paper' *Horrorstruck*

'If you've missed Laymon you've missed a treat' *Stephen King*

'A brilliant writer' *Sunday Express*

'Once again, Laymon offers unexpected, well-rounded characters blown about in a narrative that moves like the wind' *Publishers Weekly*

'Laymon's biggest strength is that he is able to provide lighthearted fun and disturb at the same time' *Fear*

Dreadful Tales

Richard Laymon

headline

First published in 2000
by HEADLINE BOOK PUBLISHING

First published in paperback in 2001
by HEADLINE BOOK PUBLISHING

15

ISBN 978 0 7472 6463 7

Typeset by Palimpsest Book Production Limited,
Polmont, Stirlingshire

Printed and bound in Great Britain by
CPI Group (UK) Ltd, Croydon, CR0 4YY

HEADLINE BOOK PUBLISHING
A division of Hodder Headline
338 Euston Road
London NW1 3BH

www.headline.co.uk
www.hodderheadline.com

Table of Contents

Bibliographic Information

'Invitation to Murder' – c.1991. First appeared in *Invitation to Murder* edited by Ed Gorman and Martin H. Greenberg, published by Dark Harvest, 1991, published by Diamond, 1993.

'The Grab' – c.1982. First appeared in *Gallery* magazine, January, 1982. Reprinted in the anthology, *The Year's Best Horror Stories: Series XI*, edited by Karl Edward Wagner, published by DAW Books, 1983. Reprinted in *100 Hair-Raising Little Horror Stories*, edited by Al Sarrantonio and Martin H. Greenberg, published by Marboro Books, 1993. Reprinted in my collection, *A Good, Secret Place*, published by Deadline Press, 1993. Performed by the New Hampshire Radio Theater group on Halloween, 1997. To be reprinted in 8th grade Australian textbook, *English Magic 2*, published by Addison Wesley Longman.

'Saving Grace' – c.1991. First appeared in *Cold Blood*, edited by Richard Chizmar, published by Mark Zeising, 1991.

'Barney's Bigfoot Museum' – c.1981. First appeared in *Creature*, edited by Bill Pronzini, published by Arbor House, 1981. Reprinted in *A Good, Secret Place*, 1993.

'Herman' – c.1996. First appeared in *Cemetery Dance* magazine, edited by Richard Chizmar, Fall, 1996.

'The Champion' – c.1978. First appeared in *Cavalier* magazine, October, 1978. Reprinted in the anthology, *Modern Masters of Horror*, edited by Frank Coffey, published by Coward, McCann & Geoghegan, 1981. Paperback reprints by Ace, 1982 and Berkeley, 1988. Reprinted in *A Good, Secret Place*, 1993. Reprinted in *100 Fiendish Little*

Frightmares, edited by Stefan Dziemianowicz, Robert Weinberg and Martin H. Greenberg, published by Barnes & Noble, 1997.

'The Maiden' – c.1994. First appeared in *Dark Love*, edited by Nancy Collins & Edward Kramer, published by New American Library, ROC, 1995.

'A Good Cigar is a Smoke' – c.1976. First appeared in *Ellery Queen's Mystery Magazine*, February, 1976. Reprinted in *A Good, Secret Place*, 1993.

'I'm Not a Criminal' – c.1993. First appeared in *After the Darkness*, edited by Stanley Wiater, published by Maclay, 1993. Belgium (French language) translation published in PHENIX, 1997.

'Oscar's Audition' – c.1975. First appeared in *The Executioner Mystery Magazine*, June, 1975 under the pseudonym, Dick Kelly. Reprinted in *A Good, Secret Place,* 1993.

'Into the Pit' – is original to this collection.

'Spooked' – c.1981. First appeared in *Mike Shayne's Mystery Magazine*, October, 1981. Reprinted in *A Good, Secret Place*, 1993.

'The Good Deed' – c.1993. First appeared in *A Good, Secret Place*, 1993.

'The Direct Approach' – c.1977. First appeared in *Alfred Hitchcock's Mystery Magazine*, January, 1977. Reprinted in *A Good, Secret Place*, 1993.

'Good Vibrations' – c.1996. First appeared in *Night Screams*, edited by Ed Gorman and Martin H. Greenberg, published by ROC, 1996.

'Phil the Vampire' – c.1995. First appeared in *Vampire Detectives*, edited by Ed Gorman and Martin H. Greenberg, published by DAW Books, 1995.

'Paying Joe Back' – c.1975. First appeared in *Ellery Queen's Mystery Magazine*, September, 1975. Reprinted in *Masters of Suspense*, edited by Ellery Queen and Eleanor Sullivan, 1992. Reprinted in *A Good, Secret Place*, 1993.

'The Fur Coat' – c.1994. First appeared in *The Earth Strikes Back*, edited by Richard Chizmar, published by Mark Zeising, 1994.

'Blarney' – c.1981. First appeared in *Mike Shayne's Mystery Magazine*, September, 1981. Reprinted in *A Good, Secret Place*, 1993.

'Dracuson's Driver' – c.1992. First appeared in *Dracula, Prince of Darkness*, edited by Ed Gorman and Martin H. Greenberg, published by DAW Books, 1992.

'Roadside Pickup' – c.1974. First appeared in *Ellery Queen's Mystery Magazine*, December, 1974. Reprinted in *A Good, Secret Place*, 1993. Reprinted in *100 Tiny Little Terror Tales*, edited by Robert Weinberg, Stefan Dziemianowicz and Martin H. Greenberg, 1996.

'Wishbone' – c.1989. First appeared in *Night Visions 7*, edited by Stanley Wiater, published by Dark Harvest, 1989.

'First Date' – c.1997. First appeared in *Love in Vein II*, edited by Poppy Z. Brite, published by HarperCollins, 1997.

'Stickman' – c.1993. First appeared in *A Good, Secret Place*, 1993.

'Mop Up' – c.1989. First appeared in *Night Visions 7*, edited by Stanley Wiater, 1989.

Preface

Me, I don't read prefaces, forewords or introductions. Not until *after* I've read the book. I'm always afraid that the writers of such pre-story material might give away details about what awaits me in the body of the book.

In many cases, they do.

I hate to know anything in advance about a story I'm about to read – or watch on the television or at the movies. As audiences, we're not *meant* to know what happens until we encounter it in the course of the story. For that reason, I avoid reading book covers or dustjackets. When movie previews start to roll, I often shut my eyes and plug my ears.

You may, therefore, feel free to read this Preface without fear that I'll spoil the stories for you. Not me. No way.

You may prefer to avoid it, anyway, and get straight to the stories. (If so, of course, you probably haven't read this far.) I find it perfectly understandable to leap-frog such introductory material and 'skip to the chase'. After all, you're here for the stories, not for authorial observations and assorted blather.

You may wish to return and peruse this material *after* you've read the stories. That's what I do. When finished with a novel or a collection of stories, I usually sit back and check out the details: the cover design, the blurbs, the plot description, the introductory material (if any), the interesting assortment of information to be found on the back of the title page, and so on. By then, none of it can hurt me. I may even find it to be edifying or entertaining.

So why am I writing a 'Preface'? Wouldn't it be more sensible, considering my own habits, to write an 'Afterward' or nothing at all?

Providing an 'Afterward' is like introducing a guest at the end of a party.

And I couldn't simply write *nothing*. Readers of story collections *expect* some sort of additional material. (As do agents and publishers.) The piece needs to be written by the author himself or by a *guest* author – someone with clout. Well, Dean Koontz wrote the introduction for my other collection, *Fiends*. I can't do better than Dean, so I'm stuck writing my own introductory material.

And you're stuck reading it.

(You've gone this far, so you might as well see it through to the end.)

Don't worry. It'll soon be over and you'll be able to move along to the actual stories.

They're *Dreadful Tales*.

I looked up 'dreadful' in my *Webster's Seventh New Collegiate Dictionary*. According to the definitions I found there, you might expect my tales to 'inspire awe or reverance' (reverance?), to be 'extremely distasteful, unpleasant or shocking' (more like it), or perhaps to be 'cheap and sensational' (humph).

Pretty much the sort of thing you might expect from a guy like me.

The twenty-five stories collected in this book – some more dreadful than others – were written over a period of more than twenty years. The earliest, 'Roadside Pickup', was published in *Ellery Queen's Mystery Magazine* in 1974. The most recent, 'First Date', was published in *Love in Vein II* in 1997.

2

When combined with the Headline editions of *Out are the Lights* (the title novel and five pieces of my short fiction) and *Fiends* (the title novella and twelve short stories), *Dreadful Tales* offers *all* of the adult short stories and novellas that I've had professionally published from the start of my career until 1997.

These stories have seen print in a variety of American magazines and anthologies and in my own limited edition collection, *A Good, Secret Place*, which was short-listed for a Bram Stoker award in 1993. To my knowledge, nothing in this volume has ever been published in the United Kingdom. Every dreadful tale will be new to anyone who has not had access to the US publications. Many will be new to American readers as well, because they've appeared in magazines and books that are difficult to find.

Hope you like them.

You'll be able to start in on the first tale very shortly, because my Preface is almost over.

It's 'Invitation to Murder', about an author trying to write a short story about . . .

Never mind. I'll let you find out for yourself.

Ready to read it?

My Preface is almost over.

It *is* over.

Now.

Richard Laymon
April, 1999

Invitation to Murder

A story. Gotta have a story. Time's running out.

The week in Hawaii wouldn't be any vacation at all with a deadline looming.

You've got tonight and tomorrow, pal. Otherwise, you'll be scowling into your Mai Tais, worrying your damn head off.

Shane booted up the word processor, typed the date, and got started.

'Ed wants a story for his *Invitation to Murder* anthology. Every story in the book must have something to do with a twenty-two-year-old female being found dead in her apartment. That's the anthology's unifying premise.'

Oughta be a cinch. A million ways you can go with that.

Has to be tricky, though. I need a nifty reversal for it.

Can't be a whodunit. Not from me. He'll probably get plenty of those from the mystery writers. From me, he'll expect horror or a thriller. It has to be a grabber. There'll be names a lot bigger than mine in that book. I don't want to look like a slouch.

Gotta come up with something hot.

Hot. Christ, it's hot in here.

West LA usually cooled off at night. But this was one of those periods that seemed to come around a couple of weeks each summer when the daytime temperatures hit the upper nineties, the cooling sea breeze took a hike, and the heat lingered on through the night. Even with the windows open, the still air in the apartment felt stifling. Shane's T-shirt and shorts were already damp and clinging with sweat.

A long, cool shower would feel great.

Come up with a plot first. A shower can be your reward.

All right. Shouldn't be all that difficult.

Shane stared out the window and tried to concentrate. A gimmick. A reversal. Okay.

'Idea. A guy picks out this gal. She's twenty-two, of course. And a knockout. He's got the hots to mess around with her. One fine night, intending to rape her, he breaks into the gal's apartment. Only to find her stretched out on the floor, dead. Murdered. Neat. But then what? Is the killer still in the apartment?'

Shane stared at the computer screen, read the amber lines again and again.

How does it end? What's the twist?

Nothing came.

Forget it.

'I like the idea of a guy obsessed with a woman. Maybe he's alone in his hot apartment. Goes out on the fire escape for some fresh air.'

I wish I had a fire escape. Or a balcony, for godsake.

'Just across from his building is an old, abandoned apartment house. Condemned, maybe. But while he's out there trying to get cool, a beautiful young woman appears in a window of that creepy old place. The most beautiful woman he has ever seen.'

All right! Now we're cooking!

A sudden blare of raucous music shattered Shane's thoughts.

Shit!

Was it coming from outside? Yeah, but it also seemed to be driving straight through the wall.

Standing, Shane leaned over the computer screen and touched the wall. It *vibrated* like the head of a drum.

Goddam modern cheap apartment houses!

Calm down, calm down. Just ignore it.

What if it goes on all night?

It won't.

Forget about it.

Guy on fire escape trying to get cool. Gal appears in window across the alley. 'The lighting is bad,' Shane typed. 'No electricity, of course, since the building is condemned. He sees her by firelight. Candles. Can't make her out very well. In fact, all he can really see is her gorgeous face, her shimmering blonde hair. They talk. She has sultry voice. Invites him over. He's reluctant to go. Worried. Who is she? What's she doing there? He REALLY wants her, but he's hesitant about venturing over there. It's a lousy neighborhood. Weirdos around. Only that evening, he'd run into a bag lady at the mouth of the alley between the two buildings. A real hag.

'Reluctantly, he declines to go over. He's about to go back inside his apartment to avoid further temptation when the woman lifts a couple of candles onto the windowsill. She is visible from the waist up. She is naked. She fondles her breasts and again asks him to come over.

'He goes. Spooky stuff while he searches the alley, finds a broken door, and enters. Makes his way through the dark corridor, up a creepy staircase. (Give him a flashlight.) Goes along the second story corridor to the door of the apartment across from his. The door is ajar. A glow of candles from inside. He enters.

'And finds a body sprawled in a corner of the

6

room. He shines his flashlight on it. The body is that of a female (twenty-two, of course). Her clothes are strewn around the floor. She has no face, no hair. From shoulders to waist, she is a mass of gore.

'Out of the shadows steps another woman. Naked. Wearing a mask of the dead gal's face. Withered old arms and legs. But with a fresh, young torso tied in place with a harness of twine. She hobbles toward the guy, caressing the full, perfect breasts she's taken from the corpse.

'She cackles, tells him he's such a hunk. Tells him that she knew, from the way he'd reacted in the alley earlier, that she couldn't hope to have him – he's too picky to be interested in someone like her. So she borrowed good looks from a gal she caught walking past the alley.

'He stands there stunned as she comes closer. "Ain't I pretty now? Ain't I a knockout?"'

Shane grinned at the screen.

Terrific! That story'll be prime Shane Malone: creepy, perverse, sexy, with a touch of black humor. And nice thematic touches about loneliness, desperation, the dubious merits of physical beauty. It'll blow Ed's socks off.

But what if it's too much? Ed had explained that he didn't want stories that were too extreme.

This is pretty damn extreme. That old babe's wearing a dead gal's tits.

A vest of tits.

Shit! Harris used that in *Silence of the Lambs*. A goddam best-seller! Everyone'll think I stole it from him. He got the idea from Gein, no doubt. Gein really did it. But still, they'd figure I copied Harris's gimmick.

Shane sank back in the chair and gazed at the computer screen.

And gazed at it.

That idea's dead in the water. Gotta come up with something else.

The music was still blaring.

It hadn't really gotten in the way, though. Shane had hardly been aware of it once the story idea began to flow. But now . . .

What kind of cretin plays music that loud?

Who the hell *is* playing it? The noise was obviously coming from 210. That apartment had been empty for the past month.

Somebody must've moved in while I was at work.

Some fucking lunatic.

Just block it out. Ignore it.

A twenty-two-year-old gal is found dead in her apartment. Need a twist.

How about something from the point of view of a young woman?

Damn that racket!

'Open with gal walking alone through city streets. Nervous about being out so late. Maybe she thinks someone is following her. She's spooked, quickens her pace. At last, she gets to her apartment building. Unlocks the foyer door, enters. She's safe at last. Relieved, she climbs the stairs to the second floor. The door of her apartment is ajar. She looks in. Her room-mate, a twenty-two-year-old gal (of course), is dead on the floor. And the killer, crouching over the body, grins over his shoulder at the main gal, lurches up and rushes her.'

Rushes her. Then what?

'She whirls away and runs . . .'

Shane glared at the wall. That music!

Am I the only person in the whole damn place it's driving nuts?

This *is* Saturday night. Maybe everyone's out –

8

gone to the movies, gone to visit friends, gone to parties.

Was the creep in the next apartment having a party? Didn't sound that way. No voices, no laughter, no sounds of anyone moving around. Just that blasting music.

Shane stood up, leaned over the computer screen, and pounded the wall. 'Hey! Could you please hold it down in there? I'm trying to work.'

The volume of the music lowered.

'Thank you.'

'Get fucked!' shouted a female voice from the other side of the wall. Then the music blared, even louder than before.

Shane's heart thudded.

Calm down, calm down.

I oughta go over and clean that bitch's clock for her!

What I oughta do is calm down.

What about complaining to the landlord? Right. That moron. Dudley. A dud, all right. I'd get nothing but grief from him. If he's even home. Saturday night. Probably out somewhere, pursuing his hobby – 'bagging babes' as he liked to put it.

What about calling the cops?

Oh, that'd be a neat move. If they do come over and give that bitch a warning, I'll have a real enemy on my hands. No telling what kind of shit she might start pulling.

What about taking the shower?

Come up with a story first. That was the deal.

Shane blinked away some sweat and read the last few sentences on the computer screen.

Okay. The gal finds her room-mate dead. The killer leaps at her and she whirls away and runs 'through the doorway. Runs down the corridor, shouting for help.

Nobody comes out to help. The killer races after her with his knife.'

What next?

That bitch! Told me to get fucked!

Pound on the wall again? Lot of good that would do. She'd probably turn the music up even louder – if that's possible.

'The guy hot on her tail, she pounds on an apartment door. It swings open. She rushes in. Trips over a body. Sees another body slumped against a wall.

'Neat idea. Suppose the . . .'

Sweat stung Shane's eyes. Nothing within reach to wipe them dry.

My shirt.

The T-shirt came off. Though damp, it did a fine job mopping the sweat away. There *was* a breeze from the window. Very slight. But it felt good. Shane tossed the shirt to the floor, sighed, and studied the computer screen.

'. . . killer has murdered everyone in the whole building? But why would he do something like that? Just because he's nuts? Suppose he's the owner and there's rent control and he wants to get rid of all his tenants so he can convert the place into a condo?'

Stupid.

'Forget him killing any other people in the building. His targets are the two gals, nobody else. He lived in the apartment next to theirs. He decided to knock them off because he just couldn't stand them always playing their fucking stereo too damn loud!'

Oh, man, I'm getting nowhere fast.

Too noisy! Too hot!

The breeze was better than nothing, but hardly cool enough to stop sweat from running down Shane's face and sides and chest.

This might easily qualify as the most miserable

night of my life. Thanks a lot, Ed. And *you*, you bitch!

Shane kicked the wall, then hunched down sideways and picked up the T-shirt and attacked some tickling runnels of sweat.

I'll *never* come up with a decent idea. Not with all this racket. Not with all this heat making the sweat pop out as fast as I can wipe it off.

So take the shower.

Yeah!

Feeling better already, Shane hurried to the bathroom. Its shut door muffled the maddening beat of the music. And the sounds of water splashing into the tub obliterated the noise completely.

Maybe I'll just stay in here. Never come out again.

You left the computer on, stupid. Good move. Hope it doesn't explode or something. That'd be a fitting finale for this misbegotten night.

Hey, I'd have a good excuse for Ed. Sorry, afraid I can't do that story for you. My computer blew up.

Peeling the shorts down, Shane scowled at a haggard twin in the full-length mirror: short hair clinging in wet points; specks of sweat under the eyes, above the upper lip; tanned skin gleaming as if it had been slicked with oil; untanned skin, hidden from the sun by swimsuits, that looked white and felt clammy.

Oughta get some air conditioning in this dump. Maybe buy one of those window units.

Sure. With what?

With the $5,000 advance I got for *The Black Room*?

That was reserved for Hawaii.

In two days, I'll be soaring out over the Pacific. Away from all this. Hawaii. Beaches. Soft breezes. Mai Tais. Maybe meet someone nice . . .

11

The bod's not half bad. Trim and firm. The tan looks pretty good, and nobody'll see the white. Not unless I get lucky.

Shane smirked at the face in the mirror, then stepped to the tub, climbed in, swept the curtain shut and turned on the water. It gushed from the spout. Nice and cool. A tug at the little knob on top of the spout sent it raining down.

Wonderful!

Maybe I can pick up some kind of air-conditioning unit with the money I get from Ed.

Have to write the story, first.

Have to think of *an idea* first.

How about a twenty-two-year-old babe gets offed in the shower? Some kind of a twist on the *Psycho* thing. Maybe the gal in the shower turns out to be a guy. Right. Only then we've got a *male* dead. Has to be a female.

Besides, it's stupid. Everybody would say I was ripping off Bloch. I could say it's not a rip-off, it's a *homage*. That's what everyone else calls it when they swipe somebody's stuff.

Shane sat down on the tub's cool, slick enamel.

Think think think.

Eyes shut, legs crossed, the deliciously cool water pattering, sliding, caressing.

I could almost fall asleep.

You can't.

Think! Twenty-two-year-old gal found dead in her apartment.

What if she's a bitch who deserved to die? A nag. Always at her husband. And her husband's a cripple in a wheelchair. Totally at her mercy. One fine night, she steps out of the bathroom after taking a shower and he zaps her.

How does he zap her?

With darts. That's his only fun in life, throwing darts. And she's always giving him shit because he misses the target sometimes and puts little holes in the wall.

Maybe the bitch hid his dart board. And that was the last straw. She steps out of the bathroom, maybe onto a sheet of plastic he's spread on the carpet to catch the blood, and whammo! Nails her with some darts in the face.

Not half bad.

Smiling, Shane stretched out along the bottom of the tub.

Now we're getting someplace!

Could you kill someone with a dart? Probably. A good hard shot right to the forehead. Penetrates the skull. Pokes the brain. And maybe he puts one in her eye.

Bull's-eye!

Make her a lesbian, you'd have a nifty play on words: bull's-eye, bull dyke.

No. The pun's going too far. Pushing the ludicrous.

But nice and sickening, a dart jabbing into her eyeball.

Anyway, she winds up dead. Twenty-two-year-old gal dead in her apartment.

And the perp is a cripple in a wheelchair. So he needs help disposing of her body. So he phones his best friend, and invites the guy to come over for a game of darts. The friend is reluctant to come. Doesn't want to face the guy's shrew of a wife. Guy says, 'That's okay, she's out.'

Out, all right.

This is great.

So the friend shows up, finds the bitch dead on the floor. He's shocked, but not especially upset. He

13

needs some convincing, but finally agrees to help get rid of the body. He's afraid he might be seen if he tries to carry it out through the apartment building, but there's a balcony over the alley. So he and the crippled guy lower the body with a rope.

How about giving it a toss, instead? More fun that way.

Either way, it ends up in the alley. And the friend goes down, planning to drive it away. But the body isn't there. He can't find it anywhere. He goes back up to the apartment.

The two guys are discussing what to do, when suddenly they hear voices. Shouts. They go to the balcony and look down. Half a dozen creepy, ragged derelicts are gathered in the alley, all of them gazing up at these fellows. 'Give us another one! We want another!'

What did they do with her? Eat her? And they're still hungry, and if the boys don't throw down seconds for them, they might just come up and help themselves.

So then what?

Shane sat up, shivering.

Too much time under the cold shower? Or am I shivering with excitement because of the story?

Hell, it's not that good. But it's not that bad.

Is it good enough?

Shane turned off the water, groaned at the muffled sound of the music, but climbed out of the tub and pulled a towel off its bar.

Just don't think about the damn noise or that slimy scum-sucking bitch next door. Think about the story.

Is it really the end of the story when we figure the bums want more? Maybe the guy in the wheelchair could push his friend off the balcony. But then what? It would sure be the end if I tell the story from the friend's point of view. But that way, how would I work in the neat business of the cripple darting his wife to death?

Dry, Shane draped the towel over its bar and opened the bathroom door. The music pounded in.

'Shit!'

At least the apartment no longer felt like an oven. Probably as hot as before, *I'm* just cool. Won't be for long, though, especially if I let that music get to me.

Shane put on a fresh pair of running shorts and a short-sleeved shirt, left the shirt unbuttoned so air could get in, and sat down in front of the computer.

Stick with the idea of the wheelchair guy? Cannibalism. Derelicts. I've used both those things a lot lately. And the ending isn't all that terrific.

The story seems okay until the bums show up in the alley. But if I get rid of them, where did the body go?

Walked away? She's dead, for Christsake. Make it a zombie story, and she comes stumbling back up, seeking vengence.

Crapola.

Damn it! The story hadn't seemed half bad while I was under the shower – and couldn't hear that bitch's music. With that noise messing up my head, maybe *nothing* will seem any good.

I oughta go over there and break her face. Or break her stereo, even better.

No, just be polite. Explain the situation. Ask her nicely to turn the volume down.

The thought of it made Shane's heart pound.

Chicken.

You've gotta do it. Otherwise, you'll just sit here getting more and more steamed and you'll never accomplish anything.

15

Do it!

Heart hammering, mouth dry, Shane got up from the chair and walked to the door. Paused to button up.

Shit. I don't want to do this.

Opened the door.

She might be nice. Who knows? Nice, sure. She told me to get fucked.

Stepped into the corridor, left the door open, and walked on shaky legs to the neighbor's door. Knocked.

Bitch probably can't hear me through all that noise.

Knocked again.

The volume of the music dropped. 'Yeah? Who's there?'

'It's me from next door.'

'What do you want?'

'I'd just like to talk to you for a second.'

'Yeah?'

Shane heard a metallic click.

'If you came over here to give me shit about . . .' The door swung open. The woman's glower softened. So did the tone of her voice as she said, 'Well, now. So you're my new neighbor, huh?' She made a little toasting gesture with her cocktail glass, and said, 'Pleased to meet you, neighbor.'

Shane managed a nervous smile.

Jeez, the gal was practically naked. All she wore was a black negligée. It had spaghetti straps. Its low front exposed the tops of her breasts. Its skirt was hardly long enough to reach her thighs. And Shane could see right through the gauzy fabric.

Any gal who would open the door in an outfit like that must be weird or half-polluted. Maybe both. Her eyes looked a little red. From the booze, or had she been crying?

'I'm Francine,' she said, holding out her hand.

16

Reluctantly, Shane shook it. 'I'm Shane.'

'Nice to meet you. Come on in, why don't you?'

'Oh, I don't want to intrude.'

'Please?' A smile twitched on her heavy lips. 'Come on in and have a drink, okay? Hey, it's my birthday. Nobody oughta have to be alone on her birthday, huh?'

Shane suddenly felt a little sorry for the woman. 'I guess I can come in for a minute. But no booze. I'm trying to work.'

'Sure, sure. How about a Pepsi?'

'That'd be fine, thank you.'

Francine shut the door, gestured with her glass toward a sofa, and headed for the kitchen area.

Shane sat at one end of the sofa.

This is not bright. Francine's obviously a bit mental. But not really a bitch. After this, she might be willing to cooperate and keep the music down.

The stereo and its twin speakers were on the floor, right up against the same wall that Shane faced when sitting at the word processor.

If the wall weren't there, I could've knocked them over with my feet.

No wonder the noise had been so bad.

The turntable was empty. In front of the stereo were stacks of cassette cases.

'How do you like this heat?' Francine called.

'I don't.'

'My last place was air conditioned.'

'This close to the ocean, you usually don't need one. Just for a couple of weeks each summer . . .'

'Makes me wanta scream.'

She came back, a full glass in each hand. A strap had slipped off her shoulder. When she bent down to hand the soda to Shane, that side of her negligée drooped, exposing her entire breast.

17

On purpose?

What've I gotten myself into here?

She stepped by, and lowered herself next to Shane. Turning sideways, she rested an arm across the back of the sofa, brought up one leg and hooked its foot behind her other knee.

Shane glanced down. The negligée was hardly long enough to conceal Francine's groin.

Man oh man.

'Here's how,' Francine said, and gulped some of her drink.

'Happy birthday.'

'Happy. It's been the shits till now.'

'Birthday's can be that way.'

'See how *you* feel when you hit the big two-two.'

'Already did,' Shane said.

This gal is twenty-two! Talk about your coincidences and ironies of life!

'You don't look any older than nineteen,' Francine said.

'Neither do you,' Shane lied. The gal looked closer to thirty.

'You're just saying that.'

'No, it's true.'

A corner of Francine's mouth curled up. 'Do you think I'm attractive?'

Her dark hair was mussed, her face a little puffy and red. Though she looked older than her age, she was beautiful. No denying that. And she certainly had a body.

'Sure,' Shane said. 'Of course you're attractive.'

The other corner of her mouth trembled upward. 'You're not bad, yourself. I'm so glad you came over. I was feeling so down in the dumps you just wouldn't believe it.'

'It hasn't been a banner night for me, either.'

18

'I guess I'm partly to blame, huh?'

'Well, it's all right.'

She took another drink, then set her glass on the table. 'I'm sorry I yelled at you.' She leaned a little closer. Her fingers began to caress the back of Shane's neck. 'Can you forgive me?'

'Sure. No problem. But I'd better . . .'

Her other hand, wet and chilly from the glass, squeezed Shane's thigh. 'Doesn't that feel good? Nice and cold?'

'Look, Francine . . .'

'You have such lovely blue eyes.'

'I'm really busy tonight. I have to get back to my work.'

'Do you? Do you really?' The hand crept higher, fingertips slipping under the leg hole of Shane's shorts.

'Hey!'

The hand retreated. Staring into Shane's eyes, Francine said, 'You want me. I know you want me.'

'I don't. Really. Thanks all the same.'

There was pain in the woman's eyes. Loneliness. Despair.

'I'm sorry, Francine, but . . .'

With a noise that seemed partly growl, partly whimper, she hurled herself onto Shane. The Pepsi glass went flying.

'No! Get off!'

Lips. Wet, sloppy lips. A sour reak of gin. Hands plucking feverishly at buttons, yanking open Shane's shirt. Grabbing, caressing, squeezing.

I don't believe this. God, I don't believe this!

The mouth and hands suddenly went away. Shane, slumped on the sofa, hips pinned down by Francine's weight, gasped for breath as the frenzied woman arched her back and peeled off her negligée.

19

'Don't. Please.'

'You love it.' Hunching down, she pushed a breast against Shane's mouth.

And tumbled off as Shane bucked and twisted.

Her back struck the edge of the coffee table. Her head pounded it. The table skidded, capsizing her glass. Then she flopped off and dropped to the floor.

She lay there face-down, sprawled between the table and the front of the sofa.

Shane scurried over the end of the sofa. Stood. Stared down at Francine. Felt a hot surge of shame and revulsion. Whirled away, doubled over and vomited.

Shouldn't have shoved her. Oh, God, shouldn't have shoved her.

Why didn't I just let her do what she wanted?

Shane backed away from the mess on the carpet, and gazed at Francine.

What if she's dead and I killed her?

Who says she's dead? Probably just unconscious. That's cheap movie stuff, people getting shoved during a struggle, falling, dying from a little bump on the head. She'll probably wake up in a few seconds.

When she does, I don't want to be here.

Watching the body, Shane knelt beside the coffee table and picked up the Pepsi glass.

Anything else with my fingerprints?

Probably just this glass.

Don't take it! Jesus! That's like admitting she's dead, admitting your guilt.

But Shane kept the glass. Rushed to the door. Wrapped a hand in a shirt-tail before turning the knob. Checked the corridor.

Empty. Silent.

Stepped out, swung the door shut, and walked fast.

She can't be dead. But if she is, there's no way they can pin it on me. No physical evidence. The vomit! They'll know somebody else was there. But they won't know who. They'll end up deciding it was an accident. She was drunk, she fell and hit her head. They'll check her blood alcohol level during the autopsy, realize she was polluted, and . . .

There won't be an autopsy! She's okay.

What if I'm locked out?

But the door was still open. Shane lunged in, locked the door and leaned against it, gasping.

Safe.

God, *why* did I have to go over there!

She's all right. Just a little knock on the head.

Shane pushed away from the door, staggered over to the desk, and dropped onto the chair. The music came softly through the wall.

Turn it up, Francine. Come on, make it blast.

On the computer screen was Shane's last sentence. 'He decided to knock them off because he couldn't stand them always playing their fucking stereo too damn loud!'

No no no no no!

'Shane?'

Little more than a whisper through the wall.

'Francine?' Rising from the seat. Heart thumping. Relief like a flowing warmth. 'Francine, are you okay?'

'Fuck you.'

'I'm sorry you got hurt, but—'

A blast pounded Shane's ears. White dust and flecks exploded from the wall a foot to the right. Something zipped by.

In the wall was a hole the size of a dime.

She shot at me!

'Francine!'

The next shot punched Shane in the chest.

Twenty-two-year-old female found dead in her apartment.

Oh, shit.

Shane dropped onto the chair, saw blood hit the computer screen, the keyboard – then stared down at the spurting hole between her breasts.

The Grab

My old college roomie, Clark Addison, pulled into town at sundown with a pickup truck, a brand-new stetson, and a bad case of cowboy fever.

'What kind of nightlife you got in this one-hearse town?' he asked, after polishing off a hamburger at my place.

'I see by your outfit you don't want another go at the Glass Palace.'

'Disco's out, pardner. Where you been?'

With that, we piled into his pickup and started scouting for an appropriate watering hole. We passed the four blocks of downtown Barnesdale without spotting a single bar that boasted of country music or a mechanical bull. 'Guess we're out of luck,' I said, trying to sound disappointed.

'Never say die,' Clark said.

At that moment, we bumped over the railroad tracks and Clark punched a forefinger against the windshield. Ahead, on the far side of the grain elevator, stood a shabby little clapboard joint with a blue neon sign: THE BAR NONE SALOON.

Short of a bucking machine, the Bar None had all the trappings needed to warm the heart of any yearning cowpoke: sawdust heaped on the floor, Merle Haggard on the jukebox, Coors on tap, and skintight jeans on the lower half of every gal. We mosied up to the bar.

'Two Coors,' Clark said.

The bartender tipped back his hat and turned away. When the mugs were full, he pushed them toward us. 'That's one-eighty.'

'I'll get this round,' Clark told me. Taking out his wallet, he leaned against the bar. 'What kind of action you got here?' he asked.

'We got drinking, dancing, carousing, and The Grab.'

'The Grab?' Clark asked. 'What's that?'

The bartender stroked his handlebar mustache as if giving the matter lots of thought. Then he pointed down the bar at a rectangular metal box. The side I could see, painted with yellow letters, read, TEST YER GUTS.

'What's it do?' Clark asked.

'Stick around,' the bartender said. With that advice, he moved on.

Clark and I wandered over to the metal box. It stood more than two feet high, its sides about half as wide as its height. THE GRAB was painted on its front in sloppy red letters intended, no doubt, to suggest dripping blood. Its far side was printed with green: PAY $10 AND WIN.

'Wonder what you win,' Clark said.

I shrugged. Leaning over the bar, I took a peek at the rear of the box. It was outfitted with a pound of hardware and padlocked to the counter.

While I checked out the lock, Clark was busy hopping and splashing beer. 'No opening on top,' he concluded.

'The only way in is from the bottom,' I said.

''Twas ever thus,' he said, forgetting to be a cowboy. He quickly recovered. 'Reckon we oughta grab a couple of fillies and raise some dust.'

As we started across the room toward a pair of unescorted females, the jukebox stopped. There were

24

a few hushed voices as everyone looked toward the bartender.

'Yep!' he cried, raising his arms. 'It's time! Step on over and face The Grab. But let me warn you, this ain't for the faint of heart, it ain't for the weak of stomach. It ain't a roller coaster or a tilt-a-whirl you get off, laughing, and forget. This is a genu-wine test of grit, and any that ain't up to it are welcome to vamoose. Any that stay to watch or participate are honor bound to hold their peace about the doings here tonight. Alf's curse goes on the head of any who spill the beans.'

I heard Clark laugh softly. A pale girl, beside him, looked up at Clark as if he were a curiosity.

'Any that ain't up to it, hit the trail,' the bartender said.

He lowered his arms and remained silent while two couples headed for the door. When they were gone, he removed a thin chain from around his neck. He held it up for all to see. A diamond ring and a small key hung from it. He slid them free, and raised the ring.

'This here's the prize. Give it to your best gal, or trade it in for a thousand bucks if you're man enough to take it. So far, we've gone three weeks with The Grab, and not a soul's shown the gumption to make the ring his own. Pretty thing, ain't it? Okay, now gather 'round. Move on in here and haul out your cash, folks. Ten dollars is all it takes.'

We stepped closer to the metal box at the end of the bar, and several men reached for their wallets – Clark included.

'You going to do it?' I whispered to him.

'Sure.'

'You don't even know what it is.'

'Can't be that bad. *They're* all gonna try.'

Looking around at the others as they took out their money, I saw a few eager faces, some wild

25

grinning ones, and several that appeared pale and scared.

The bartender used his key to open the padlock at the rear of the metal box. He held up the lock, and somebody moaned in the silence.

'Dal,' a woman whispered. She was off to my left, tugging on the elbow of a burly, bearded fellow. He jerked his arm free and sneered at her. 'Then go ahead, fool,' she said, and ran. The muffled thud of her cowboy boots was the only sound in the room. Near the door, she slipped on the sawdust and fell, landing on her rump. A few people laughed.

'Perverts!' she yelled as she scurried to her feet. She yanked open the door and slammed it behind her.

'Gal's got a nervous stomach,' Dal said, grinning around at the rest of us. To the bartender, he said, 'Let's get to it, Jerry!'

Jerry set aside the padlock. He climbed onto the bar and stood over the metal container. Then he raised it. The cover slid slowly upward, revealing a glass tank like a tall, narrow aquarium. All around me, people gasped and moaned as they saw what lay at the bottom, barely visible through the gray, murky liquid. A stench of formaldehyde filled my nostrils, and I gagged.

Face up at the bottom of the tank was a severed head, its black hair and mustache moving as if stirred by a breeze, its skin wrinkled and yellow, its eyes wide, its mouth agape, its neck full of ragged pulp.

'Well, well,' Clark muttered.

Jerry, kneeling beside the glass tank, picked up a straight-bent coat hanger with one end turned up slightly to form a hook. He slipped the diamond ring over it. Standing, he lowered the wire into the tank. The ring descended slowly, the brilliance of its diamond a dim glow in the cloudy solution. Then it vanished inside the open mouth. Jerry flicked the hanger a bit, and raised it. The ring no longer hung from its hook.

I let out a long-held breath, and looked at Clark. He was grinning.

'All you gotta do for that pretty diamond ring is to reach down with your hand and take it out of the feller's mouth. Who'll go first?'

'That's me!' said Dal, the bearded one whose girl had just run off. He handed a ten-dollar bill to Jerry, then swung himself onto the bar. Standing over the tank, he unbuttoned his plaid shirt.

'Let me just say,' Jerry continued, 'nobody's a loser at the Bar None Saloon. Every man with grit enough to try The Grab gets a free beer afterwards, compliments of the house.'

Throwing down his shirt, Dal knelt beside the tank. Jerry tied a black blindfold over his eyes.

'All set?'

Dal nodded. He lowered his head and took a few deep breaths, psyching himself up like a basketball player on the free-throw line. Nobody cheered or urged him on. There was dead silence. Swelling out his chest, he held his breath and dipped his right hand into the liquid. It eased lower and lower. A few inches above the face, it stopped. The thick fingers wiggled, but touched nothing. The arm reached deeper. The tip of the middle finger stroked the dead man's nose.

With a strangled yelp, Dal jerked his arm from the tank, splashing those of us nearby with the smelly fluid. Then he sighed, and shook his head as if disgusted with himself.

'Good try, good try!' Jerry cried, removing the blindfold. 'Let's give this brave fellow a hand!'

A few people clapped. Most just watched, hands at their sides or in pockets, as Jerry filled a beer mug and gave it to Dal. 'Try again later, pardner.

Everyone's welcome to try as often as he likes. It only costs ten dollars. Ten little dollars for a chance at a thousand-buck ring. Who's next?'

'Me!' called the pale girl beside Clark.

'Folks, we have us a first! What's your name, young lady?'

'Biff,' she said.

'Biff will be the very first lady ever to try her hand at The Grab.'

'Don't do it,' whispered a chubby girl nearby. 'Please.'

'Lay off, huh?'

'It's not worth it.'

'Is to me,' she muttered, and pulled out a ten-dollar bill. She handed her purse to the other girl, then stepped toward the bar.

'Thank you, Biff,' Jerry said, taking her money.

She removed her hat and tossed it onto the counter. She was wearing a T-shirt. She didn't take it off. Leaning forward, she stared down into the tank. She looked sick.

Jerry tied the blindfold in place. 'All set?' he asked.

Biff nodded. Her open hand trembled over the surface of the fluid. Then it slipped in, small and pale in the murkiness. Slowly, it eased downward. It sank closer and closer to the face, never stopping until her fingertips lit on the forehead. They stayed there, motionless. I glanced up. She was tight and shaking as if naked in an icy wind.

Her fingers moved down the face. One touched an open eye. Flinching away, her hand clutched into a fist.

Slowly, her fingers fluttered open. They stretched out, trembled along the sides of the nose, and settled in the mustache. For seconds, they didn't move. The upper lip wasn't visible, as though it had shrunken under the mustache.

28

Biff's thumb slid along the edges of the teeth. Her fingertips moved off the mustache. They pressed against the lower teeth.

Biff started to moan.

Her fingers trembled off the teeth. They spread open over the gaping mouth, and started down.

With a shriek, she jerked her hand from the tank. She tugged the blindfold off. Face twisted with horror, she shook her hand in the air and gazed at it. She rubbed it on her T-shirt and looked at it again, gasping for air.

'Good try!' Jerry said. 'The little lady made a gutsy try, didn't she, folks?'

A few of the group clapped. She stared out at us, blinking and shaking her head. Then she grabbed her hat, took the complimentary beer, and scurried off the bar.

Clark patted her shoulder. 'Good going,' he said.

'Not good enough,' she muttered. 'Got spooked.'

'Who'll be next?' Jerry asked.

'Yours truly,' Clark said, holding up a pair of fives. He winked at me. 'It's a cinch,' he said, and boosted himself onto the bar. Grinning, he tipped his hat to the small silent crowd. 'I have a little surprise for y'all,' he said in his thickest cowboy drawl. 'You see, folks . . .' he paused and beamed, '. . . not even my best friend, Steve, knows about this, but I work full-time as a mortician's assistant.'

That brought a shocked murmur from the audience, including me.

'Why, folks, I've handled more dead meat than your corner butcher. This is gonna be a pure cinch.'

With that, he skinned off his shirt and knelt behind the tank. Jerry, looking a bit amused, tied the blindfold over his eyes.

'All set?'

'Ready to lose your diamond ring?'

29

'Give it a try.'

Clark didn't hesitate. He plunged his arm into the solution and drove his open hand downward. His fingers found the dead man's hair. They patted him on the head. 'Howdy, pardner,' he said.

Then his fingers slid over the ghastly face. They tweaked the nose, they plucked the mustache. 'Say ahhhh.'

He slipped his forefinger deep between the parted teeth, and his scream ripped through the silence as the mouth snapped shut. His hand shot up, a cloud of red behind it. It popped from the surface, spraying us with formaldehyde and blood.

Clark jerked the blindfold down and stared at his hand. The forefinger was gone.

'My *finger*!' he shrieked. 'My God, my *finger*! It bit . . . it . . .'

Cheers and applause interrupted him, but they weren't for Clark.

'Look at him go!' Dal yelled, pointing at the head.

'Go, Alf, go!' cried another.

'Alf?' I asked Biff.

'Alf Packer,' she said without looking away from the head. 'The famous Rocky Mountain cannibal.'

The head seemed to grin as it chewed.

I turned to Biff. 'You knew?'

'Sure. Any wimp'll make The Grab if he doesn't know. When you know, it takes real guts.'

'Who's next?' Jerry asked.

'Here's a volunteer,' Biff called out, clutching my arm. I jerked away from her, but was restrained by half a dozen mutilated hands. 'Maybe you'll get lucky,' she said. 'Alf's a lot more tame after a good meal.'

30

Saving Grace

At the top of the hill, Jim stopped his bike, planted a foot on the pavement and twisted around. Mike was far back, red-faced and huffing, fat bouncing as he pumped his way up the slope.

While he waited for his friend, Jim took off his shirt. He wiped his sweaty face with it, then stuffed it into the basket on the rack behind his seat.

'It's all downhill from here,' he said.

Mike rolled to a halt beside him. He draped himself over the handlebars, gasping. 'Shit on a stick,' he muttered. Sweat dripped off his nose and chin. 'Gonna have a heart attack.'

'Beans. Nobody fifteen has a heart attack.'

'Oh yeah?'

'Just think how neat it'll be at the lake.'

'If we ever get there. You and your great ideas. I bet there won't even *be* any babes there.'

'You'll see.' Yesterday, when trying to talk Mike into a bike trip to Indian Lake, he'd told all about the girls who'd been there last Saturday when he picnicked on the shore with his family. 'There were some real yucks,' he'd said, 'but some were fantastic. This one, she had on a white suit you could see right through. You could see *everything*. Everything! And some had on these bikinis you wouldn't believe. It was just incredible. We'll take our binoculars, you know?' Mike had listened, nodding, his

31

lips pursed, and readily agreed to make the twelve-mile trip.

'Man,' Mike said, 'if you're wrong . . .'

'Trust me. Your eyes are gonna fall out.'

'They better.'

'Let's get going.' A shove at the pavement started Jim's bike rolling. He pedaled a few times, picking up speed. Then the road slanted downward through the dense forest. He coasted faster and faster, sighing as the summer air rushed against him. It was better than standing in front of a big fan, the way it blew his hair and buffeted his face and rubbed his arms and chest and belly and sides. It felt really wonderful against the heat of his armpits. It felt best where it slid up inside a leghole of his swimming trunks, cool on his hot groin.

With a glance back at Mike, he saw a car come over the crest of the hill. 'Watch out behind you!' he called.

Mike looked around, then steered toward the edge of the road. The car swung out and crossed the center line a bit, giving him a wide berth. As it sped down, Jim eased his bike over. The car stayed far to the side. It shot past him, and quickly returned to its own lane before disappearing around a curve to the right.

'Did you see that babe?' Mike called.

Jim looked over his shoulder. 'Huh?'

'The gal driving. Hope *she's* on her way to the lake.'

'Hot stuff?'

'Didn't you . . . look out!'

Jim snapped his head forward. Just in time to see a black van straight in front of him. Parked. Its rear jutting into the road. He braked and swerved to the left. Missed it. But his bike was skidding sideways, tires sliding out, dropping him toward the pavement.

32

He shot his foot down, swung his other leg clear and hopped a couple of times as the bike flew out from under him. From the feel of things, he knew that dismounting hadn't solved his problem. A twister suddenly seemed to grab him. It whirled him, whipped him down, tumbled him.

He lay there.

Mike came to a stop and grimaced down at him. 'Are you okay?'

'Shit fuck damn hell.'

'Should've watched where you were going.'

Groaning, Jim sat up. The side of his left knee was filthy, scuffed and bloody. So was a patch of his left forearm, just below the elbow. He tried to brush some of the grit out of the wounds, and winced. I'll wash up when we get to the lake, he thought. He struggled to his feet and limped to his bike.

His shirt and towel were still in the basket. His lunch bag and binoculars had fallen out.

'Oh, man,' he muttered, picking up the binoculars. He pulled them out of the case, glanced at the lenses.

'They okay?'

'Yeah, I guess so.' He stuffed them back into the case. 'Asshole. Why didn't he pull *all* the way off the road?'

'Well, there's a ditch.'

'The bastard.' He hobbled close to the van and kicked its side.

'Jeez! Don't! What if someone's in there?'

That hadn't occurred to Jim. With a grimace, he hurried over to his bike. Mike was already starting off. 'Hey, wait up.' He jammed his binoculars and lunch back into the basket and lifted his bike by the handlebars. Giving the van a nervous glance, he planted a foot on the lower pedal, gave himself a push and swung up his other leg.

33

And heard a high-pitched shriek.

It seemed to come from somewhere nearby in the woods.

Mike stopped and looked back at him. 'Jeez!'

Jim rolled past him, then steered to the roadside in front of the van and braced a foot against the pavement. He stared into the thick, shadowy woods.

Mike glided over and stopped. 'It was a scream, wasn't it?'

'Sure was.'

'A gal.'

'Yeah. But I don't know.'

'Don't know what?' Mike asked.

'You know girls. They scream all the time just for the fun of it. I mean, it doesn't mean she's in trouble, or anything. She might've just been messing around.'

'Yeah, or she saw a spider.'

They stopped talking and listened. Jim heard a soft breeze stirring the treetops, birds squawking and twittering, insects buzzing.

Then, '*Please!*'

'God,' he muttered, 'maybe she *is* in trouble.'

Mike's eyes widened. 'Maybe she's *screwing.*'

Jim felt his heartbeat quicken. 'Yeah,' he said. 'I bet that's it.' He dismounted and lowered the kick stand. 'Let's check it out.'

'Are you kidding?'

'No, I'm not kidding. Besides, what if she *is* in trouble?' He plucked his binoculars out of the basket, removed them from the case, and slipped the strap over his head.

'Oh man, oh man,' Mike muttered, propping up his bike. He took out his own binoculars.

Jim led the way, Mike close behind him as he hurried to the bottom of the shallow ditch and climbed its other side. He entered the shadows of the forest.

He walked slowly, weaving around bushes and trees, setting his feet down as softly as possible, cringing at the quiet sounds of leaves and twigs crunching under his shoes.

Flies buzzed around the scrapes on his knee and arm. Mosquitos settled on him. He wished he were wearing more clothes. But this was neat, in a way. Exciting. Creeping through the woods like an Indian, nearly naked.

What if there really *is* a gal getting screwed?

It'd be like a dream coming true, getting to watch something like that.

As long as we don't get spotted.

What if the guy sees us and comes after us?

God, he'd kill us.

Jim stopped and looked around at Mike.

'What?' Mike whispered.

'Maybe we'd better not.'

'Oh, man.'

'I mean, what if we get caught?'

As if stabbed with pain, Mike bared his upper teeth. The expression pushed his cheeks so high they seemed to squeeze his eyes shut. 'We've gotta at least take a peek,' he whispered. 'This is our big chance.'

Jim nodded. He knew Mike was right. They'd seen naked women in movies and skin magazines, but never in the flesh. If he should turn back now, he would want to kick himself later.

Probably won't see much, anyway, he thought as he turned away from Mike and began walking deeper into the forest.

Probably won't even be able to find her.

Less than a minute later, he glimpsed movement beyond some trees far to the right. His heart gave a lurch. Halting, he pointed.

'Yeah,' Mike whispered.

They made their way slowly in that direction. Jim couldn't see much. The trees were too close together, offering only glimpses of someone through the tiny spaces between their trunks. Soon, however, he began to hear a rustle of dead leaves and twigs. There were also a few muffled moans and squeals.

Crouching low, he crept up to a tree that he hoped might be near enough so he could get a good view. He squatted, one hand on its trunk. Mike came up behind him. He felt Mike's knees push against his back.

Hearing a soft intake of air, he realized that Mike was already looking.

Jim eased his face past the side of the trunk.

And gasped.

And felt his bowels shrivel.

The girl in the clearing ahead was naked, just as he'd hoped. She was slim and beautiful, probably no older than eighteen. Sunlight slanting down through the trees made her hair shine golden, her damp skin gleam. She was sweaty, dripping. She had a dusky tan except for where a skimpy bikini must've hidden her skin from the sun. Her breasts were creamy mounds. The darker flesh of her nipples jutted. Lowering his eyes, Jim gazed at sunlit hair so fine and meager that he could see right through it, see the soft edges of the split between her legs.

This was so much better than he'd ever hoped.

But so much worse.

Worse because the girl was suspended from a tree branch by a rope looped around her neck, because she was writhing and weeping, because her mouth was stuffed with cloth to stifle her noises and the man behind her was doing something that must be hurting her terribly.

As Jim watched, stunned and breathless, the man stepped around to the front. He was not very old, maybe

36

twenty. He was very handsome. He was grinning. He was naked except for his socks and sneakers. He had a huge boner. He had a hunting knife in one hand, pliers in the other.

He turned toward the girl. Crouching slightly, he put his face against one of her breasts. She jerked her head from side to side, a wild look in her eyes. She made whimpery noises through the gag. She tried to kick him, but lost her balance. The rope yanked at her neck. Her eyes bulged. She made choking sounds. Then she found her footing and shut her eyes.

The guy moved his face to her other breast. The one he'd left behind was no longer creamy. It had a reddish hue. Above the nipple was a curving row of dents – teeth marks.

When he sank to his knees, both her breasts looked that way.

His face pushed against her groin.

Though the girl twisted and squirmed and shook her head, she didn't try to kick him away. Nor did she reach for him. Obviously, her hands were bound behind her back.

He tilted his head back. Then he reached up with the pliers.

He shut their jaws on her right nipple.

As the girl let out a muffled shriek, Jim leaped up and ran, raced at the man, swinging his binoculars by their strap.

The guy looked over his shoulder.

Started to turn around.

But he was on his knees. Not quick enough.

The binoculars smashed against the side of his face. His head jumped as if he wanted another quick look at the girl's crotch. Her knee pumped up. Jim heard teeth crash together. He leaped out of the way. The man flopped backward and slammed the ground. His head

37

struck with a quiet thump. He had landed with both knees up. Now, one slowly sank sideways. The other leg straightened out, his sneaker sliding in between the girl's bare feet. She stomped on his ankle and he let out a groggy groan.

He groaned again when Mike stomped on the wrist of his right hand. Bending over, Mike took the knife away. The pliers, Jim noticed, had already fallen from the other hand.

The man raised his head off the ground.

'Get him again,' Mike gasped.

Jim twirled the binoculars by their strap. Faster and faster. Then he whipped his arm down and crashed the binoculars against the man's temple. The head jerked sideways, sweat and spit spraying.

He lay motionless.

'Out like a light,' Mike said.

Jim and Mike both faced the girl. She had tears in her eyes. Her chest was heaving as she sucked air through her nose. Jim glanced at her rising, falling breasts. Saw their redness, the marks left by the bastard's teeth. Her right nipple was bright red and looked as if it were swelling up because of what the pliers had done.

He felt no desire. He felt only weak and shaky and nauseous.

'You'll be all right,' he told the girl. Stepping over the man's legs, he pulled the cloth from her mouth. Red, lace panties, moist with her saliva. As he tossed aside the wadded garment, the girl gasped air through her mouth. 'We'll get you down,' he said.

Mike, using the assailant's knife, cut through the rope above her head.

She slumped forward. Jim caught her. He wrapped his arms around her and held her up. Her face rested against the side of his neck. He felt her slick, hot skin against his bare chest. The soft push of her breasts.

38

And something warm running down the backs of his hands.

Mike stepped behind the girl. He winced. 'God, the guy cut her.'

Moments later, her arms went around Jim. She clung to him, gasping and sobbing. Mike raised the severed ropes for Jim to see, then tossed them down.

'You'll be all right,' Jim whispered.

And realized that, in spite of his shock and revulsion, he was starting to get hard. The feel of the naked girl was just too much. Embarrassed, afraid she might notice his arousal, he eased her away.

'Maybe you'd better sit down.'

She sniffed, nodded, wiped her eyes.

Holding onto her upper arms, Jim guided her sideways. He watched her head turn as she tried to look past him at the man.

'It's all right. He's out cold.'

'He . . . he might wake up.'

'Don't worry,' Mike told her. 'We'll take care of him.'

She started to sag. Jim lowered her gently. When her knees met the ground, he released her. She hunched over and braced herself up with straight arms.

He saw her back.

It was slick with blood.

Mike stepped up beside her. He'd found a T-shirt. He wadded it and patted the bloody mess. When he lifted the rag, Jim saw a design carved into the girl's skin.

'My God,' he murmured.

'A face,' Mike whispered.

'It's a *skull*. It's a goddam *skull*.'

As he stared at the skull, its lines of blood thickened and began to trickle down the slopes of her back.

'We oughta kill the bastard,' Mike said.

'I'll kill him,' said the girl.

'Just take it easy. Mike, why don't you pull down that rope and tie him up? I'll take care of the girl.'

Mike lowered the bloody cloth to her back, then hurried away. Jim gently mopped the cuts. Sidestepping, he rubbed the crimson mounds of her buttocks, then the backs of her legs. He returned to the skull, blotted it, and left the rag there. 'I'll get your clothes.'

She stayed on her hands and knees, her head drooping.

The man was still sprawled flat, motionless.

Mike, face to the tree, was busy working at the knot that bound the rope to its trunk.

The girl's clothes were scattered on the ground. Jim picked up the damp ball of her panties. Pulling them open, he found that their sides had been severed. The man must've cut them off her. He dropped them and saw a red bra nearby. Sliced apart the way it was, it would be of no more use than her panties.

Her skirt and blouse were not far from the bra. Jim went to them. The short, denim skirt appeared to be all right. The plaid blouse was pretty much intact, though one sleeve hung loose from its shoulder and all its buttons were gone.

He glanced around, but couldn't find her shoes and socks.

The T-shirt used to clean her back, Jim realized, must belong to the man. A pair of jeans were neatly folded on top of a boulder near the edge of the clearing. No shirt. Just jeans.

'Want to help me tie him up?' Mike asked, dragging the rope down from the limb.

'Okay. Just a second.' He returned to the girl. She raised her head and watched him approach. Crouching, he set down the skirt and blouse in front of her. 'Here, you can put these on.'

40

'Thanks.'

'Your other stuff's wrecked.'

She reached out a shaky hand and lifted the blouse. Then she pushed herself back and settled onto her haunches. She seemed much calmer now. She rubbed her face with the blouse.

'How are you feeling?'

'I guess I'll live. Thanks to you and your friend.'

'Jim,' he said. 'I'm Jim. That's Mike over there.' He nodded toward Mike, who had already managed to roll the man over. Knife clamped between his teeth, he was straddling the guy's rump and tying one of the hands.

'I'm Grace,' the girl said. 'I owe you two my life, I really do.' She gave him a sweet, trembling smile. 'Could you help me with this?' She held the blouse toward him.

He took it, and tried not to look at her breasts as he slid a sleeve up her outstretched arm. He remembered how they'd felt, pushing against his chest. He wondered how they would feel in his hands.

Don't even think about it, he warned himself. After what she's been through . . .

Embarrassed, he leaned forward and pulled the blouse across her back. He held it while she struggled to get her other arm in.

'Thanks.'

'That's all right. I'd better go and help Mike.'

She nodded.

Jim stood up and hurried over to his friend.

Now, both wrists were bound together behind the man's back. Knife in hand, Mike was climbing off.

'Looks like you've got him taken care of.'

'Yeah. But what about his feet? We don't want him running off.'

'I don't know.'

41

'What are we gonna do with him?'

'I wonder if that was his van.'

'Probably.'

Jim turned around. Grace was on her feet, bent over and stepping into her skirt. She straightened, pulling it up her legs. Jim caught a last glimpse of her downy pubic hair before the denim ruined his view.

'That van by the road, is it his?'

'Yeah.' Grace raised the zipper and fastened the button at her waist. Then she came toward them, walking a little stiffly, making no attempt to close her blouse. She halted in front of Mike. 'I'm Grace,' she said, and held out her hand.

'Nice to meet you. I'm Mike.' He blushed fiercely as he shook her hand.

'You two saved my life.'

Mike shrugged. 'Glad we did.'

'We're trying to figure out what to do with him,' Jim said. 'If that's his van, I guess we should try to get him into it. We could drive him into town and turn him over to the cops.'

She stared down at the man, and said nothing.

'Or we could stay here with him,' Mike suggested, 'and she could go for the cops.'

'I'll stay,' Grace said. 'You guys go for help.'

'Are you kidding?' Mike blurted.

'Yeah, you don't want to do that. He's bound to wake up.'

'I'll be okay. He's tied. Just leave me the knife.'

'But we're on bikes,' Mike pointed out. 'It'd take us a long time to reach town.'

'We could take the guy's van,' Jim said, though he thought it was crazy to let Grace stay behind. 'Maybe just one of us should go.'

'Meaning me,' Mike said, looking a little sour. 'You're the one with the learner's permit.'

'This is an emergency. The cops aren't gonna worry about whether you've got a driver's license.'

'Why don't you just take your bikes?' Grace suggested. 'I don't think anybody oughta use the van. When the cops come, they'll want to search it for evidence. It shouldn't be . . . you know, tampered with. I think he's had other girls in there besides just me.'

'Really?' Mike sounded surprised.

'Yeah. There were some clothes in the back. And I saw stains. I think he's one of those guys who goes around . . . getting a lot of people.'

'A serial killer?' Jim asked.

'Yeah, something like that.'

'Geez,' Mike said.

'How'd he get you?' Jim asked.

She pressed her lips together hard. She looked as if she were struggling not to cry. After a few moments, she said, 'He just grabbed me.' Her voice sounded way too high. 'I was going to my car.' She sniffed. 'He came up behind me and . . . gave me a jab. With his knife. And he said, "Come with me. I wanta show you something." And he made me go to his van. And he pushed me in. He didn't even know me. I never did anything to him.'

Jim's throat had gone tight while he listened and watched her painful struggle to communicate. Now, he reached out and put a hand on her shoulder. She sniffed. She wiped her nose.

'I've never been so . . . scared. And then . . .' Her breath hitched. 'The things he did to me.'

The way she looked at Jim, the way she leaned toward him, he knew she needed to be held. He took her into his arms. The back of her blouse felt sodden and sticky. She squeezed herself against him. He wished her blouse were open wider so her breasts would be bare against him like last time.

43

Mike was watching. Frowning. 'Come on. We'd better do something about this guy.'

'Why don't you go for the cops?' Jim told him. 'I'll stay with Grace.'

'Thanks but no thanks.'

'You should both go,' Grace said. 'I'll be okay here.'

'We can't leave you alone with him.'

'Yes, you can.' Easing out of his arms, she wiped her eyes. 'Go. I mean it.'

He suddenly realized why she wanted them both to leave. A thick weight seemed to sink inside his stomach. 'You're gonna *do* something to him.'

'No, I'm not. Just go. Please.'

'So you can kill him.' It made Jim hurt, talking to her this way. He wanted to hold her, to kiss her, not to stand here accusing her. 'You'll kill him. Then you'll probably take his van and leave.'

'Oh, man,' Mike said. 'You're right.'

'You saw what he did to me. *Some* of what he did.' Her face was red, twisted with agony, tears spilling down her cheeks. 'He would've . . . My God, don't you think he deserves whatever he gets?'

'Yeah, but . . . you can't just murder him in cold blood.'

'That's *just* what he was gonna do to me. Once he got done torturing me. And raping me. And I bet I'm not the first. I bet he's done it to a lot of girls.'

'I don't know about killing him,' Mike said.

'You guys don't have to watch. Just go. I'll wait till you're gone.'

'We'd still *know*,' Jim said.

'So would you,' Mike told her. 'Right now, you want to make him pay for what he did. But what about later? If you kill him, you'll have to live with it for the rest of your life.'

44

'I'll always have to live with what he did to me,' she said. She took a deep, shaky breath. 'As long as he isn't dead, I'll be . . . afraid he might come after me again.'

'He won't be able to,' Jim said. 'They'll never let a guy like him out of prison.'

'Yeah, sure.'

'What if they can't prove any murders on him?' Mike said. 'He might get . . . I don't know, ten or twenty years for what he did with Grace. And they give time off for good behavior.'

'That's right,' Grace said. 'He could get out in five or ten years, and then what'd happen? Even if he doesn't come after me, he might get someone else.'

'She has a point.'

'And it'd be *our* fault.' She was no longer crying. She seemed completely focused on changing Jim's mind. 'If they let him out or he escapes or something and kills somebody, we'll be to blame. We've got a chance, right now, to get rid of him. Nobody will ever know but us. And he'll never, never be able to hurt anyone again.'

'It'd be murder,' Jim said.

'*I don't care!*' She suddenly lurched sideways, grabbed the knife from Mike, and threw herself at the tied, motionless man. His body shook as she dropped onto his rump. She raised the knife high.

'No!'

Even as the knife slashed down, Jim slammed her to the ground with a flying tackle. She rolled and squirmed under him. 'Get off me!' she gasped. 'Leave me alone!' He caught her wrists and pinned them down.

'Let go of the knife!'

'God, Jim,' Mike blurted from behind.

'We can't *let* her!'

45

She stopped struggling. She stared up into Jim's eyes. 'Let me do what I want,' she said, 'and you can have me. You both can.'

'What?' Jim gasped.

'You want to. I know you do.'

'Oh, my God,' Mike said.

Breathless, Jim gazed down at her. He was sitting across her hips. Her blouse hung open, showing her breasts. He could feel her heat through his trunks and her denim skirt. He thought about how she was wearing no panties. He started to get hard.

'I mean it. I like you both. We can make love right here. Right now. If you'll let me keep the knife and . . . take care of him.'

'Oh, man,' Mike murmured.

'Kiss me, Jim. Kiss my breasts.'

'Geez. Go for it.'

He released her left hand – the one without the knife. Gently, he caressed her breast. He thought he had never touched anything so smooth, so wonderful. Grace moaned softly. 'Am I hurting you?'

'No. No.'

He fingered the crescent of dents made by the man's teeth.

And flinched with surprise as Grace's hand rubbed his penis through the trunks. No girl had ever touched him there before.

She's only doing this so I'll let her kill the guy.

So what? Let her.

It'll be the same as if I killed him with my own hands.

He's the price.

He's a monster, anyway.

Grace's hand slipped inside his trunks. Her fingers curled around him, glided slowly up and down. He shuddered. He felt as if he might explode.

46

'No!' he shouted. He grabbed her wrist, forced her hand away and pinned it to the ground. 'We can't. We can't do this. It'd be wrong.'

'Please,' Grace said.

'No.'

'Don't be an idiot,' Mike said. 'When'll we ever get another chance like this?'

'It doesn't matter! We can't just murder the guy. I don't care what he's done, we can't just murder him. We'll take him to the cops. This is something for the law, not for us. If we kill him, we wouldn't be any better than he is.'

'Shit,' Mike muttered.

Releasing Grace's left hand, Jim reached across her body and tried to take the knife from her right hand.

She held on tightly. 'You don't know what you're doing,' she said. 'Please.'

'I'm sorry.' He pried Grace's fingers away from the handle. He picked up the knife, then scrambled off her and got to his feet.

Mike, frowning, shook his head. 'Man, we could've . . .'

'It wouldn't have been any good.'

'Oh, yeah, right. *Look* at her.'

Grace lay on her back, braced up with her elbows, looking from Jim to Mike. Her blouse was wide open. Her skirt was rumpled high around her hips. Her knees were up, and spread apart. 'Please,' she said. 'If we don't kill him . . . I don't know what I'll do. I'll always be afraid. I don't want to always be afraid. Why can't you understand that?'

'I do understand. I'm sorry. I really am. God, how I'd love to . . . but I'm not a murderer. I don't want you or Mike to be murderers, either.'

'It'd be kind of like self-defense,' Mike said. 'You know?'

47

'He's *tied up*, for godsake. And out cold.'

'We could untie him.'

'Oh, that's a neat idea. Come on, let's get going. It'd be nice if we can get him to the cops before he wakes up.'

'What're we gonna do, carry him?'

'Drag him, I don't know.' Jim walked over to the man's folded jeans. He picked them up. As he searched the pockets, he watched Grace struggle to her feet. She straightened her skirt. She closed the front of her blouse and held it shut. She stared at him. She looked betrayed.

Jim found the car keys and a wallet.

Curious, he flipped open the wallet. The driver's license identified the man as Owen Philbert Shimley. 'Shimley,' Jim said.

The man on the ground moaned as if awakened by the sound of his name.

'Oh shit,' Mike said.

'Maybe it's better this way,' Jim said. 'He can walk under his own steam.'

Mike, looking alarmed, snatched up the length of rope he'd cut away after binding Shimley's hands. He quickly made a slip knot in one end, dropped to his knees, and pulled the loop down over the man's head. A tug sent the knot skidding until it stopped against the back of his neck.

Jim let the jeans fall. He had no pockets, so he tucked the key case and wallet under the elastic waistband of his trunks. They seemed secure there. Knife clenched in his right hand, he hurried over to Mike.

Mike, standing behind the man's feet, held the rope taut.

'Get up, Shimley,' Jim ordered.

Face pushing against the ground, he struggled to his knees. A tug at the rope yanked him backward,

48

choking. Upright on his knees, he glared at Jim. Then at Grace. She hunched over and seemed to shrink as he looked at her.

Jim ducked, picked up his binoculars, and dropped their strap over his head. 'On your feet,' he said.

Shimley stood up.

'We're taking you in,' Jim said. 'Don't try any funny stuff, or you'll be sorry.' Boy, did that sound trite and dumb.

But the man didn't make any remark about it. He nodded his head.

'Let's go.'

'I want my pants.'

'Fuck you,' Mike said.

Shimley glanced around at him.

'Come on!'

Shimley started walking.

Grace stayed behind him, stayed with Mike.

She hates me, Jim thought.

But this is for the best. We're doing the right thing.

He walked backward, watching Shimley. The man really looked pitiful, stumbling along with his head down, his shoulders slumped, his limp penis wagging.

Big, tough monster.

But not so tough now.

With a roar, Shimley charged. The rope clamped his neck like a choke collar. His head jerked. His face went scarlet. But he didn't stop coming.

'Shit!' Mike yelled. Either he'd lost hold of the rope or . . .

Jim thrust his knife straight forward at Shimley's chest.

The man lurched to a halt inches from its tip. He hunched over. He bared his teeth. He growled.

'Don't move!' Jim shouted in his face.

'Abracadabra, motherfucker.' Shimley's arms came around from behind him. He dangled a knotted tangle of ropes in front of Jim's eyes.

Mike and Grace hit him at the same instant.

Mike slamming against Shimley's back.

Grace tackling him low.

They hit him hard, smashing him forward.

Jim's knife plunged into his chest.

Shimley crashed into him. As he went down backward, he knew he'd killed the man, after all.

Then his head struck something.

Jim awoke with a horrible, raging headache.

He sat up, and saw that his feet were bound together with rope.

Then he saw Mike's head. It was near enough to touch. It was upside-down. A big red ball with teeth and open eyes. Some spinal column, jutting from a ragged stump of neck, pointed at the sky.

Then he saw Grace. She had a rope around her neck. She was hanging from the limb of the tree. Her feet didn't quite touch the ground. Her tongue was sticking out. From just below her neck all the way down to her knees, she was raw and pulpy and strange. Skinless.

Shimley stepped out from behind the tree.

He was red all over. And grinning.

His left hand was pressed tight against his ribcage. His right hand held the bloody knife.

He walked toward Jim.

'Too bad you slept through the fun, asshole.'

Jim lurched forward and started to vomit on his thighs.

He was still vomiting when Shimley kicked him in the forehead.

Dazed, he dropped backward and hit the ground.

'But you didn't miss *all* of it. Get a load of this.'

Jim bucked as the knife punched deep into his belly.

Barney's Bigfoot Museum

All day long, people stopped by. Not just for a beer or a meal, or to stock up on minnows or bug spray, or to have a look at my Bigfoot Museum. That's not why. I'll tell you why.

It was the gray, lonely weather out there, the kind that makes you ache for a brightly lighted diner, a cup of chili, a familiar tune on the jukebox. You can get all that at my place. Mine's the first spot after almost fifty miles of forest so heavy and bleak you think you'll never see another human face. I call it Barney's Bigfoot Museum 'n' Diner.

My wife was working the lunch counter, late that afternoon, when this fellow came in. He climbed out of a Dodge pickup with a Pathfinder camper on the back, and came up the porch steps. At the door, he stopped and glanced around like he thought someone might be sneaking up on his back. Then he came in.

He looked lean and hard, and banged up. The sleeve of his flannel shirt was torn. His face and neck were threaded with scratches.

Turning away from the counter, he limped toward the museum entrance. He had my curiosity up, so I followed him through the door. He must've heard me. With a small sound, he spun around and grabbed under his shirt. I glimpsed black steel – the butt plate of an automatic – before he dropped his hand and the shirt-tails fell shut.

52

'Damn,' he said.

'Are you all right?'

He didn't answer. He just turned away and gazed up at the Winchester. It hung on the wall above a display case, its barrel bent toward the ceiling.

'Bigfoot did that?' he asked.

'So I'm told.'

'Where'd you get it?'

'Bought it off a fellow.'

He lowered his eyes to the display case and looked for a while at the plaster casts of giant footprints.

'Buy these, too?'

'Some. I made two of them, myself, from prints I found near Clamouth.'

'Authentic?'

'Far as I know.'

He limped to the next display case and peered through the glass at half a dozen photos.

'Ever seen one?' he asked.

'A Bigfoot?'

'Yeah.'

'No. Not yet. I keep hoping, though. There've been several sightings in the area. And I've seen the footprints, like I said. I go out searching when I get the chance.'

He stepped over to the corner and peered at the plaster bust.

'That's lifesize,' I told him. 'A sculptor over in Kalama claims he saw one, back in seventy-eight.'

'Pay much for this?'

'It wasn't cheap.'

'You got taken. It's all wrong.'

'Oh?' I'd been suspicious, at the time, but finally agreed to pay the artist's exorbitant price. Whether or not he'd actually seen the beast, the simian features conformed with other eyewitness accounts and blurred photos. 'What makes you think it's wrong?'

53

The man turned to me. He rubbed a scabbed-over scratch above his eye, as if it might be itchy.

'My God,' I gasped. 'You've seen one, haven't you?'

A grim smile creased his face. 'More than that.'

'Tell me – tell me *all* about it! I mean, what I'm doing, I'm writing a book. It'll be *the* book on Sasquatch. I've been working on it for five years, collecting artifacts and stories . . . My museum, it draws everyone who—'

He held up a hand for me to stop. He smiled as if amused by my eager babbling. 'I'll tell you about it.'

'Great! Just great! Wait and I'll get my recorder. That okay, if I record you?'

'Help yourself.' He glanced out the window at the gloomy sky. 'Make it quick.'

'Right.'

I hurried to my office and lugged my heavy reel-to-reel tape recorder back to the museum room. The man was still alone. I shut the door to keep intruders out, plugged in the machine. I put on a fresh spool of tape and ran it through.

'One thing before I start,' he said.

I glanced up, ready for bad news.

'I want something in return. Do you have a car?'

I nodded.

'What kind?'

'A seventy-nine Bushmaster, four-wheel drive.'

'Do you have the pink slip?'

'In my office.'

'I'll leave you my Dodge and Pathfinder. You sign your Bushmaster over to me.'

'I don't—'

'It'll be worth it, believe me. So far, you've paid out a lot of money for junk. Nothing but junk.' He

54

gazed at me with weary, red eyes. 'I'll let you in on something that'll put your museum on the map.'

I hesitated.

'Wait till I'm done, then decide.'

I couldn't see any objection to that. 'I guess . . .'

'Start the machine.'

I turned on the recorder, and the man began to speak. He talked swiftly, staring at the floor, often turning for a quick glance out the window.

'My name is Thomas Hodgson. I'm thirty-two. I come from Enumclaw. For the past two weeks, I've been hunting Bigfoot in the woods about thirty miles north of here.

'I had three friends with me – Charles Raider, Bob Chambers, and Armondo Ruiz – all from Enumclaw. It was Chambers's idea. He'd run into some tracks back in early June. He figured we'd all be millionaires if we could capture Bigfoot. Or kill it. Either way. I don't suppose we really figured we'd find the thing, though. Just an excuse to spend our vacation running wild. We'd all been together in the Marines – that's where we met – in Nam. We all came to Enumclaw in seventy-two and started a sporting goods . . . forget all that. The thing is, we went out looking for Bigfoot and we sure as hell found it.

'Ruiz saw tracks on the twelfth day out. He was picking up firewood and sucking on a brew. *Cerveza*, he called it. You never saw Ruiz, he didn't have a *cerveza* in his fist.

'We spent the next day and a half following the tracks. We finally lost them at a stream about twenty miles from our base camp. They just ended at the stream. Couldn't pick them up again, so we decided to stick around and see what developed.

'We camped near the stream that night. Ruiz had first watch, then Chambers. At about two in the morning, a

55

gunshot woke me up. Chambers started yelling his head off. "Hey, I bagged one! I bagged one!"

'I grabbed my rifle and got ouside just as he came running into camp. Raider and Ruiz popped out the other tent. They hit Chambers with their flashlight beams. Christ, what a . . . He stood there with his feet planted and lifted this . . . *thing* by its arms. It hung there like it was dead. Blood kept pumping out, though. You could hear it pattering on the ground.

'Chambers put the thing down.

'Ruiz shined his light on it, and we all saw it wasn't human. It was covered with bristly fur, and the shape wasn't right: the arms too long, the rump more like a bear than a man. But its face was bare and pale, and it somehow made you think of a little kid.

'"It came along for a drink at the stream," Chambers told us. He sounded pretty upset. "I figured, you know, it's Bigfoot."

'"Kind of small, don't you think?" Raider said.

'"I think it is a Sasquatch," I said. "A young one. What else could it be? Have you ever seen anything like it?" None of us had. "We've got a hell of an opportunity here," I said. "We came in after Bigfoot and by God, we got one! You're looking at the one and only specimen, guys. We'll be famous. And rich! We can sell this thing, or tour with it, or parlay it into a whopping book contract. The possibilities are staggering!"

'After that, Chambers went on about how we should dig a grave and bury the thing. Nobody bought it, though. While Ruiz and Raider were still dazed with the idea of riches, I tried another pitch on them.

'"We'd be better off, though, with a full-grown version. If this is a baby Bigfoot, its parents are probably nearby." They all looked at me as if they'd been thinking the same thing, and not liking the idea

56

much. But I went on. "We'll put out the kid as bait. When papa or mama come along, *wham*!"

'"No way," Chambers said. "Count me out."

'"What've you got against money?" I asked him.

'"There's ways and there's ways, Hodgson. I just killed this thing. That's enough for me. More than enough."

'"How about you?" I asked the others.

'Ruiz shook his head. "I don't know, man."

'"I say we get while the gettin's good," Raider said. "A bird in the hand, you know."

'Ruiz nodded. "We killed the kid, man. If its folks come looking . . ." He shook his head, fear in his eyes.

'I argued for staying, but the others wouldn't give in. Finally, we tied up the carcass, slipped it under a tent pole, and started out. Raider led the way, with Chambers and me on the pole, and Ruiz bringing up the rear. None of us talked. I guess we were listening, expecting to hear footsteps or a roar or something. None of that happened. The woods were silent except for the usual night sounds: owls and frogs, that sort of thing.

'Then Raider shrieked and left his feet. He went straight up, flapping his arms and kicking. I couldn't see anything but him. He just hung there, squirming and yelling, for a second. Then he fell. He landed right at my feet, and he didn't have a head any more.

'Yeah, his head was still up there about twelve feet above the ground. In the hands of this *thing*. This huge, dark *thing*! Bigfoot. It had to be. It threw Raider's head to the ground and stomped on it – crushed it.

'We'd dropped the pole by this time. While the creature was busy mashing Raider's head into the ground, I shouldered my rifle and fired. The thing flinched and staggered back. Then it left. It just ran off.

'The three of us stood around for a while, looking at what was left of Raider and staring off into the woods. Ruiz kept shaking his head and muttering, "Holy Jesus."

'"It's gonna get us all!" Chambers was yelling.

'"It's had its chance," I told him. "Probably going off someplace to die in peace."

'"It'll be back," Chambers said. "It'll keep coming back."

'"Since when are you psychic?" I asked him. But Chambers ignored me.

'"It wants the kid," Ruiz said. "I say we leave the kid."

'"I'm not leaving it," I told them.

'"That's your problem," Chambers said. He gestured to Ruiz, and they started away together.

'That's how I found them, an hour later. Together – their arms and legs all broken and intertwined like a terrible bloody knot.

'I kept moving. I hardly expected to survive the night, but I kept trudging along, the creature on my back, its tied hands pulling at my neck like a kid riding piggyback.

'Dawn came and I kept moving. The sun beat through the trees and the body stank and flies swarmed all around us, but I kept moving. Finally, I reached base camp. I threw the carcass in the back of my Pathfinder, then drove like hell.

'That was this afternoon,' he said.

'You mean . . . ?'

He nodded, anticipating my question. 'Yeah. The thing's in my camper.'

'My God! Can I . . . can I *see* it?'

'Just sign over your Bushmaster. I'll give you the papers on my Pathfinder and truck. Fair trade.'

I hesitated. 'Something wrong with them?'

A smile twisted his face. 'Not a thing. Just want to trade, that's all.'

'You don't think Sasquatch could follow a truck!'

'Of course not. I'd just feel better.'

'I'll be right back.'

With a nod, he turned toward the window and stared out at the dark forest.

I left him. I ran for my office, ignoring the curious looks from my wife and half a dozen customers at the lunch counter.

In the office, I searched madly through my desk. My hands trembled as I flipped through the papers, searching for the pink title slip. Finally, I found it. As I shoved the drawer shut, I heard a burst of glass out front. Then a gunshot.

I ran for the museum room ahead of the customers and shoved open the door.

Hodgson was gone.

The room reeked of a foul, musty stench that made me think of mold and dead things.

Gagging, I raced to the broken window. I looked out, but saw only the dark road and the timber on the other side of it.

I climbed out. I ran through the windy night. To the side of the diner. To the parking lot. To Hodgson's battered Pathfinder.

Its rear door lay on the gravel.

Stepping over the door, I peered into the camper and saw a dark shape on the floor. I scurried inside. On hands and knees, I picked up the thing by its hair.

Voices. Rushing footsteps.

Before the curious arrived, I had it safely concealed in a cupboard.

It's the pride of my Bigfoot Museum, but I show it to no one, not even my wife. I stuffed and mounted it myself. I keep it inside a locked case, in the corner below the twisted metal door of the Pathfinder.

Perhaps, when my Bigfoot epic is complete, I'll reveal it to the world.

Perhaps not.

It's mine, and I want to keep it that way.

Often, late at night, I lock myself in the darkness of my museum and open the case. I hold Hodgson's head on my lap as I listen to the tape of his voice. Sometimes, I half expect to feel his lips move with the words.

But they never do.

Herman

Charlotte, who went by Charlie, was thirteen and a very brave girl who thought of herself as a tomboy. She also thought of herself as an explorer of territories unknown, as a teen detective, and as a crusader against injustice. She thought of her bicycle as a stallion named Speedy, and she thought that she had an invisible friend named Herman who went everywhere with her and who would, against any and all odds, keep her from harm.

She was a very imaginative girl.

But not completely out of touch with reality.

She knew trouble when she saw it.

When the car sped toward her from the rear, she pulled way over to the edge of the road. She flinched when it raced by, engine roaring, radio blasting, guy yelling out the passenger window at her, 'Eat me!'

The car, an old blue Mustang, zoomed past her so quickly that she didn't get a chance to see who was inside.

A couple of jerks, that's all Charlie knew for sure.

Her left hand let go of Speedy's handlebar.

She jabbed at the noon sky with her upraised, stiff middle finger.

Ahead of her, the car braked.

That's when she knew she was in trouble.

She muttered, 'Uh-oh,' skidded to a stop and caught the pavement with her feet.

61

Holding Speedy between her legs, she looked over her shoulder. The road was a sunlit strip of pavement bordered by bright green forest. All the way back to the bend, its lanes were empty.

She looked forward. The only car in that direction was the Mustang.

It began backing slowly toward her.

'Oh, man,' she muttered. 'Now I've done it.'

She glanced from side to side as if checking the woods for an escape route. Then she faced the Mustang.

About twenty feet in front of her, it stopped. The doors opened and two young men stepped out. What with school, church, the band and choir and softball team and her general roamings about the town of Maplewood and the county in general, Charlie knew just about everyone who lived in the vicinity. These guys were strangers to her.

They looked the right age to be high-school dropouts. Both of them wore T-shirts, blue jeans and cowboy boots. The driver looked scrawny and mean. He had a cigarette pinched between his lips, but it wasn't lighted. The passenger looked fat and mean. He was chewing on something.

At the rear of the Mustang, they stopped. They both stared at Charlie. Then they gave each other a smirk.

Look what we got here.

The scrawny one flicked his Bic and lit up.

'Hi, guys,' Charlie said. 'What's up?'

'Your number,' the fat one said. His voice sounded mushy through the mouthful of whatever he was chewing.

'I guess that was supposed to be cute,' she said.

'What're you doing on our road?' the scrawny one asked.

62

'This isn't your road. This is a *public* road, State Highway Sixty-three as a matter of fact, and I have every right to use it.'

'Wrong.'

'Dead wrong,' added the fat guy.

Charlie looked over her shoulder again.

'Who you looking for back there?' the scrawny one asked. 'John Wayne?'

'Dead,' said the fat one.

'The Seventh Cavalry?'

'Dead.'

'Batman?'

'Dead.'

'Is not,' Charlie said.

'Might as well be,' the scrawny one said, 'for all the good he's gonna do you.'

'You're up Shit Creek,' said the fat one, 'and *we're* the shit.'

'Shut up, Tom,' the skinny one said.

Tom scowled like a kid scolded by his father. Then he started to swallow whatever he'd been chewing. The swallowing seemed to take a lot of effort.

While he worked on it, Charlie said, 'Look, I'm sorry I flipped you guys off. I mean, not that you didn't sort of have it coming. Him, anyhow. Tom. It's not exactly nice manners to shout at me like he did. I mean, *eat me*? That's a really crude thing to say to someone, especially a total stranger. So I like lost my temper. But I'm sorry. Okay?'

'Okay,' the scrawny one said.

But they didn't turn around and head for their car. They just stayed put, and kept staring at her.

'Can I go now?' Charlie asked.

'What's your name?' the skinny one asked.

'Why do you want to know?'

He darted the cigarette at her. She flinched. Before

she had a chance to dodge it, the lighted tip poked softly against the front of her pink T-shirt, just below her shoulder. It made a circle of ash the size of a pencil eraser. As the cigarette fell, she brushed at the gray dot and said, 'Nice going. Jeez. Real nice.'

'What's your name?'

'Charlie.'

'That's a boy name,' Tom said.

'You a boy?' asked the other.

'She ain't a boy,' Tom said.

'May I go now?' she asked the scrawny one. He seemed to be in charge. 'Please?'

'Say "pretty please with sugar."'

'Pretty please with sugar.'

Tom suddenly got an urgent, happy look on his face. He leaned in close to his friend's side, cupped a hand by his mouth as if he was afraid Charlie might be a lip-reader, and whispered something. At the end of his message, he faced her, folded his arms across his huge chest, and grinned.

The other one spoke. 'Tom wants you to pull up your shirt.'

For a few seconds, Charlie just stood there, staring at them and holding her bike up. Then she said, 'Tom can blow it out his kazoo.'

Tom lost his grin. 'Make her do it, Bill.'

'If you do it,' Bill said, 'maybe we'll let you go.'

She shook her head. 'I'd better warn you guys, you'd *better* let me go or you'll be really really sorry.'

'Just do like we—'

'No!' she suddenly snapped. 'Now go away and leave me alone!'

'All we wanta do is get a little look at your tits. What's the big deal?'

'Maybe she's 'shamed of 'em,' Tom said. 'Seeing as how they're so teeny.'

'You'd better just get out of here.' She glanced over her shoulder again.

'Nobody's coming,' Bill pointed out. 'Not yet. And if a car just *should* happen to come along, it won't do you any good. Nobody's gonna help you.'

'I'm warning you. Get back in your car and go away! You might think we're all by ourselves out here, but you'd be wrong. You see what kind of bike this is?'

'What about it?' Bill asked.

'It's a bicycle-built-for-two.'

'So what?'

'What does that tell you?' she asked.

'That you're some kind of a fuckin' dweeb,' fat Tom said, and grinned. 'Nobody but a dweeb goes around by herself on a bike like that.'

'That's 'cause I'm not by myself.'

'Yeah, right,' Tom said.

'Herman's with me.'

'Yeah, right.'

'Herman?' Bill asked.

'He's my best friend. And he's so big and strong you wouldn't believe it. He makes Arnold Schwarzenegger look like a weenie.'

Bill and Tom grinned at each other.

'I'm scared,' Bill said. 'Are you scared?'

'I'm petrified,' Tom said. He raised his open hands and fluttered his fingers and said, 'Ooooooo, I'm so scared! Look at me! I'm shaking!'

Bill, the skinny one, didn't seem so amused. He said, 'What's your friend's name? Helen?'

'*Her*man.'

'And he's, like, your riding companion on this two-seater?'

'That's right.'

'Well, shit. *I* don't see him.'

Tom broke out laughing. His huge belly shook and wobbled. He slapped Bill on the back a couple of times.

'Knock it off,' Bill told him. To Charlie, he said, '*How* big is this Herman of yours?'

'Real big. He's almost seven feet tall.'

'That *is* big. So how come I can't see him?'

'Because.'

'Oh, be*cause*.' He glanced at Tom. 'That explains it.'

Tom laughed some more, but he kept his hand off Bill's back.

'Nobody can see him,' Charlie explained.

'Oh, I get it. You mean he's invisible.'

'That's right.'

'Now I'm *really* scared.'

'I'm so scared I'm gonna shit!' Tom blurted, and did a little dance as if he were trying to hold it in.

'You won't think it's so funny if you try anything with me. He'll rip you guys from limb to limb.'

'Oh, yeah?' Bill looked at Tom. 'You stay here, I'll take care of him.' Then he came forward, strutted past Charlie, and halted beside the second set of handlebars. She twisted around to watch him. 'All right, Herman, give me your best shot.' He stuck out his chin.

Charlie said, 'Herman isn't there.'

Looking at her, Bill lifted his eyebrows. 'Really? You wouldn't be kidding me, would you?' He reached out and patted the leather seat. 'You're right. Darn! I was *so* looking forward to meeting him.'

'Me, too,' Tom said.

'So, where *is* this Herman of yours?'

'He got off when we stopped.'

'You mean, he *was* here but now he's not?'

66

'That's right.'

'Where *is* he?'

'Close enough to take care of you guys if you don't leave me alone.'

'How do you know that?' Tom asked. 'You can't see him.' He sounded pleased, as if he'd outsmarted her.

'I just know,' Charlie said. 'He's right here, and he's waiting for you guys to try something funny, and then he's gonna lambast you like you wouldn't believe.'

Bill shook his head slowly from side to side. 'Aren't you kind of like too *old* to have a make-believe friend?'

'He isn't make-believe.'

Behind her, Tom said, 'Betcha it's that Snuffleupagus.'

She faced Tom and said, 'His name is Herman.'

'Yeah, right.'

'And he's gonna rip us limb from limb if we try to mess with you?'

She twisted around to face Bill again. 'That's right. He's not just my best friend, he's my bodyguard. And you'd better let me go right now. All I've gotta do is give him the signal, and . . .'

'So give it,' Bill said.

'Don't make me. You'll regret it. I'm warning you. You'd better just go—'

Bill rammed his hand against the front of her left shoulder. The blow twisted her toward him and knocked her backward. She gasped, 'Yah!' and tried to hop clear of her bicycle. The saddle caught the back of her left thigh. Crying out and flapping her arms, she fell. She slammed the pavement. The bike crashed down on her right leg.

She yelled, 'Ow!'

'Ooo, nasty fall,' Bill said.

67

He hurried around to the other side of the bike, grabbed one of Charlie's arms, and dragged her clear. Then he hoisted her to her feet. 'Get rid of the bike,' he said to Tom.

'Don't you *dare*!' Charlie snapped. 'Leave it alone, you big ox!'

'Fuck you, babe.'

'You won't be needing it,' Bill told her.

'What'm I s'posed to do with it?' Tom asked.

'Take it off into the trees. Throw it someplace. Just so nobody can see it from the road here.'

'Right.' Tom hitched up his drooping jeans, then bent down and lifted the bicycle-built-for-two onto its tires. Holding the front set of handlebars, he rolled Speedy to the edge of the road and into the woods.

Charlie watched it go.

When it was out of sight, she tried to break free from Bill's grip.

'Knock it off,' he warned.

She kicked him in the shin.

He decked her.

She was still sprawled on her back, moaning, when Tom returned from concealing her bike.

'What'd you do to her?' Tom asked.

'Gave her a taste of my famous knuckle sandwich.'

Tom scowled. 'You gotta not do that sort of stuff when I can't watch.'

'Don't worry, you didn't miss much. Tell you what, I'll pull the car off the road, and you can stay with her. Maybe take her into the trees over there.'

'Hey, great.' He clapped his hands a couple of times, then headed for Charlie while Bill returned to their Mustang.

Stopping by Charlie's hip, Tom gazed down at her. 'You got a boyfriend?' he asked.

'Maybe.'

'Huh? Do you or don't you?' He tapped her with the toe of his cowboy boot.

'Maybe Herman. But—'

He kicked her. 'Don't give me this Herman shit. I mean a *real* boyfriend.'

'Herman's real,' she muttered.

'Yeah, right.'

'He is. And you guys are gonna be sorry you were ever born by the time he gets done with you.'

'Sure.'

'He's right behind you!' Charlie blurted.

Tom glanced around.

Charlie flipped from her side to her belly. As she scrambled to get up, Tom stomped her on the back. His boot slammed her against the blacktop. Her breath whooshed out. 'Think I'm an idiot?' Tom asked.

Bending over her, he grabbed the neck of her T-shirt and the waistband at the back of her shorts. He lifted her off the road. The T-shirt stretched and ripped, but its shoulders held. The waist button popped off her shorts. The zipper skidded down a little bit at a time as she was carried into the woods.

When Tom got her where he wanted her, he let go of the T-shirt and used both hands to shake Charlie out of her shorts. She fell headfirst toward the ground, but caught herself with her arms.

On hands and knees, she scurried over the forest floor.

And halted when Tom pulled the elastic waistband of her panties.

'You ain't going nowhere.'

'Leave me alone!' she gasped.

He tugged the elastic and let it go. It snapped her across the buttocks. He laughed.

At the sound of footsteps hurrying through the dry

pine needles, Charlie raised her head and saw Bill striding into the clearing.

As he approached, he pulled his T-shirt off. His jeans hung very low. The brass buckle of his belt looked like a skull. At the right side of his belt hung a knife in a brown leather sheath. Charlie hadn't noticed the knife before.

He was very skinny and bony and white. He looked as if he had never before been out in the sun without a shirt on. In the middle of his chest, directly between his nipples, was a cluster of bright red pimples.

'Let's see what we got,' he said to Tom.

Tom's broad, oily face grinned. He stepped behind Charlie and slipped his fingers under the drooping shoulders of her T-shirt.

'Don't,' she said, her voice shaking. 'I'm warning you.'

He jerked the T-shirt, stretching and tearing it. As he dragged it down to her ankles, she clutched her breasts and called out, 'Herman!'

Bill, an odd smile on his lips, helped. 'Herrr-mannn?' he called in a lilting voice. 'Yooo-hooo, Herrrr-mannnn! Where arrrrre you? Charlie neeeeeeds you.'

Tom, still behind her, tugged her panties down. He tongued her rump, and she flinched.

'Herman!' she cried out. 'Help!'

'Can I have firsties?' Tom asked.

'No way.'

'Hey, come on. You *always* get firsties.'

'That's 'cause they're too messed up by the time you get done with 'em. Just hold her for me.'

'Yeah yeah yeah. Hang on.'

Charlie stood stiff and trembling, legs tight together, hands cupping her breasts, while Bill took the knife from its sheath and clamped it between his teeth. The handle of the knife was wrapped with black tape. The blade, at least five inches long, looked sharp on both edges.

With his hands free, Bill unfastened his skull buckle and pulled down the zipper of his jeans.

He didn't have any underwear on.

Charlie looked away fast.

Then Tom's hands came around from behind her. They clutched her wrists and forced her arms high. He raised them until her shoulders hurt and she had to stand on tiptoes.

She could feel his bulging belly against her back.

Bare skin, hot and slippery.

In front of her, Bill finished taking off his boots and jeans. Then he stepped toward her, grinning behind the handle of the knife in his teeth.

'Get away from me,' she blurted.

He took the knife out of his mouth.

Charlie shook her head.

He touched the tip of the knife to the underside of her chin, then scraped it lightly down her throat and sideways.

'Please,' she murmured.

'Please? Who you talking to?' he asked. 'Me or your buddy Herman?'

'Don't hurt me.'

'Guess ol' Hermy must've deserted her,' Tom said, and writhed so his belly slid against her back.

'What's the world coming to,' Bill said, 'when you can't count on your invisible friends in a pinch? A sorry state of affairs, that's what I think.'

'Don't,' she said. 'Please.'

Gritting her teeth, she watched the tip of the knife scratch a line down the top of her left breast. She jerked when it nicked the tip of her nipple. A speck of blood, very bright red, bloomed, then disappeared.

Vanished between Bill's lips.

He licked. He sucked. He moaned and sucked harder, drawing her small breast deep into his mouth as his right hand came up and shoved the entire five-inch blade of the knife into his own right eye.

The impact shoved his head back.

Charlie's breast popped out of his mouth.

Behind her, fat Tom let out an odd, high-pitched laugh as if he figured his buddy was pulling some sort of a weird stunt with the knife.

'Hey,' he said.

Bill said nothing. Mouth wide open, he stumbled backward two steps, three, with the black-taped handle of the knife sticking out of his face.

'What're you doing?' Tom asked.

Bill fell flat on his back. As he lay twitching on the ground, Tom let go of Charlie's wrists and hooked an arm across her throat. He squeezed her tightly against him, his belly forcing her back to bend, his chin above her left ear.

'Fucking shit!' he gasped. 'Bill? What the fuck? Bill? Why'd you go and do that?'

Bill, no longer twitching, answered with a loud, moist farting noise.

'Shit!'

The knife began to rise. Its blade slid upward, pulling slowly out of the bloody mess in Bill's eye socket.

'Oh, hey,' Tom said.

The knife came the rest of the way out. It lingered motionless above Bill's face. Blood dripping from the blade made soft splashes in the socket puddle.

'Oh, hey, shit.'

'Herman,' Charlie groaned out.

'No way. Huh-uh. Bull*shit*.'

'Let . . . me . . . go.'

72

The knife drifted higher. Higher and higher as if it were being offered, pommel first, to someone on a tree branch above Bill's body.

Arm still tight across Charlie's throat, Tom started backing away. His belly shoved at her back, forcing her feet off the ground. She started to choke.

Eight or nine feet above Bill's face, the knife's rise halted.

Charlie, being hustled backward by her throat, kicked her legs and flapped her arms and choked.

The knife flew at her.

Or at Tom.

Tumbling blade over hilt, flinging off a wispy spray of blood.

It struck with a thunk above and just to the side of Charlie's left ear.

Tom went, '*Uh!*'

His arm jerked against her throat. He dropped backward. Charlie followed him down, riding the soft hill of his belly. It sank in when she landed. Air blew out of him.

Legs still kicking at the sky, Charlie shoved his arm away from her throat. Then she flung herself off his body. She crawled clear and scurried to her feet before turning around for a look.

Where the knife should have been sticking out of Tom's forehead, he had a red mark the side of a quarter.

The size of the knife's pommel.

Gasping for breath, Charlie rubbed her throat and grimaced. She stepped closer to Tom.

His big white belly moved up and down with his breathing.

His eyes were shut.

He still had his boots on, but his jeans were down around his shins. He was very white and lumpy. He looked like an effigy made from loaves of uncooked bread dough that had been basted with oil.

She glanced at his *thing*. Wrinkling her nose, she turned away fast.

'Herman?' she asked.

'Yo.'

The voice came from straight in front of Charlie, but somewhat higher than her head.

'Thanks,' she said.

'My pleasure.'

'But jeez, you sure took your time about it.'

'Well . . . Better late than never. Right?'

She shook her head. 'You let them hurt me.'

'I know. I'm awfully sorry. I truly am.'

'Why didn't you stop them? I mean, jeez!'

Herman didn't answer.

'Didn't you see that guy slug me?'

'Yes.'

'Why didn't you *destroy* him right then?'

'I . . . I was curious, I suppose.'

'Curious? What do you mean, curious?'

'I wanted to see what they had in mind.'

'Jeez, wasn't that pretty obvious? I mean, by the time fatso *stripped* me, it should've been pretty—'

'I'm afraid I was . . . rather caught up in the situation.'

'You *what*?'

He hesitated for a few seconds, then said, 'I . . . wanted to watch.'

'*Watch?*'

'I'm afraid so.'

'Oh, isn't *that* wonderful. I thought you were supposed to be a gentleman.'

'I know. I'm sorry. Oh, Charlie. I've always . . . I've *never* spied on you. I've always left the room whenever you . . . needed privacy. But . . . I don't

74

know. I'm so sorry. The thing is, you're not quite the child you used to be, and I'm afraid that I . . . I should've intervened much sooner. I know that. I just couldn't quite force myself . . . You're so beautiful, Charlie.'

'Oh, man.'

'Do you hate me?'

She scowled. 'No. Don't be dumb. I could never hate you. But . . . you let that guy actually . . . cut me.' She touched the small slit on her nipple and showed Herman the blood on her fingertip. 'See?'

'Yes. I see. Can you . . . will you forgive me?'

She licked the blood off her finger. 'Maybe.'

'Please, Charlie.'

'You've got to kiss it and make it well,' she said.

Herman hesitated. Then he murmured, 'All right.'

At the touch of his lips, Charlie gasped and stiffened. The blood smeared and swirled. Her nipple began to stretch. Trembling, she moaned. She found Herman's shoulders and held on to them and shuddered.

His mouth went away from her breast.

'How's that?' he asked.

And she saw his lips move when he asked. Phantom lips, stained by her blood.

'The other,' she said.

'But it's not cut.'

'I don't care.'

By the time he finished, she was gasping for breath and she could hardly stay on her feet. She clung to his shoulders.

'I want to see you,' she gasped. 'I want to see what *you* look like.'

'We've been through all that, Charlie.'

'I know, I know. You're naked . . . wouldn't be decent. That's . . . not hardly a problem any more, is

75

it? I mean, you let those guys strip me. Now it's only fair . . . And anyhow, I love you.'

'You do?'

'Yes. Of course. But I've gotta *see* you. I've never seen you.'

'I suppose we could go home and get some make-up.'

'No, now. I've gotta see you right now.'

'Ah. But I don't see how . . .'

'The knife,' she gasped.

'Huh?'

'Where'd it end up?' She let go of his shoulders and turned around. She glanced at Tom, still sprawled on his back. The mark on his head had become a livid lump. His eyes were still shut. She scanned the floor of the forest beyond his head, then blurted, 'There it is.' She ran, crouched, and picked up the knife.

Then she hurried back to Tom.

He opened his eyes as she knelt on the ground above his head.

He opened them very wide.

'Over here, Herman,' she said. 'Quick.'

'Hey,' Tom said, his voice groggy.

'Hey yourself,' she told him.

His belly sank and widened when Herman sat on it.

He raised his head off the ground as if he hoped to see who was there. His fat red face dripped sweat . . . and maybe a few tears. He began to make a high-pitched whimpery sound.

'That's good,' Charlie said. 'You just sit there, honey. I'll do all the work.'

Tom squealed when she tore open his throat with the knife.

Blood shot high.

76

Charlie tossed away the knife. She started to splash Herman with the blood. Then she leaned into the gushers herself, grabbed Herman by his red-splattered shoulders and pulled him toward her. She wrapped her arms around him.

Blood hosed his face.

Coated it.

Dripped.

She kissed his slippery lips.

He was slippery all over – massive and gentle and very slippery – as they tumbled off Tom's body and rolled on the grass and wrestled and kissed and made love in the sunlit clearing.

Soon, the blood began to make them itchy. They licked each other clean.

Then they lay side by side on the grass.

After a while, Charlie said, 'I hate it that I can't see you. I used to think it was great, but now . . . God, how come you have to be invisible? It isn't fair. I can't look at you.'

'It has its advantages,' Herman pointed out.

'I guess so, but . . . I know we can try make-up on you, and stuff. *Paint* you.' She wrinkled her nose. 'It's not the same, though. I want to really *see* you. How will I ever get to see what you'd look like if you were . . . like *real*?'

'I am real, Charlie.'

'I know, but . . . I mean, actual flesh and blood. With skin. What would you look like if you had skin just like . . . Hey! I've got it!'

She gave him a pat, then pushed herself up and crawled toward the knife.

'Wait, now, Charlie.'

'No, this'll be cool.'

'It'll be *hot*. Not to mention *messy*.'

'Oh, don't be a spoilsport. It'll be great.'

77

Herman groaned. 'Besides, I'm bigger than Tom. It'll never fit.'

'Hey, there's two of them, only one of you. There'll be plenty, maybe even some left over for a hat.'

The Champion

'You're not going anywhere,' said the man blocking the door.

He was smaller than Harry Barlow, with neither the bulk nor the muscle to make his words good. But he had a friend on each side. Though Harry figured he could take the three of them, he didn't want to try. Like most big men, he'd been pestered all his life by people wanting to prove their toughness. He was tired of it. He wanted never to fight again.

'Please move,' he said to the man.

'Not on your life, bud. You're staying right here. This is your big night.'

The entire restaurant erupted with cheers. Harry turned slowly, studying the faces around him. Most belonged to men. Funny, he hadn't noticed that during the meal. He hadn't noticed much of anything, really, except his dinner of top sirloin.

When he first saw Roy's Bar and Steak House, he'd been surprised by the crowd of cars in its parking lot. The town, hidden in a valley deep in northern California's timber country, seemed too small to have so many cars. Once he'd tasted the rich charbroiled steak, however, he'd realized that folks had probably driven miles for supper at Roy's. He'd been glad he'd stopped in.

Until now.

Now, he only wanted to leave. He took a step toward the three men barring his way.

'Hold up,' someone called from behind.

Harry turned around. He'd seen this man before. During supper, the fellow had wandered from table to table chatting and laughing with the customers. He'd even exchanged a few words with Harry. 'I'm Roy,' he'd said. 'This your first time here? Whereabouts are you from? How's your beef?' He'd seemed like a pleasant, amiable man.

Now he had a shotgun aimed at Harry's midsection.

'What's that for?' Harry asked.

'Can't have you leave,' Roy told him.

'Why's that?'

Except for a few scattered clinks of silverware, silence hushed the restaurant.

'You're the challenger,' Roy said.

'What am I challenging?' Harry asked. He waited, feeling a tremor of fear.

'It's not a what, it's a who.'

Harry heard some quiet laughter. Looking around, he saw that every face was turned toward him. He rubbed his hands along the soft corduroy of his pants legs. 'Okay,' he said. '*Who* am I challenging?'

'The champion.'

'Am I?'

More laughter.

'You sure are. You ever hear of the Saturday Night Fights? Well, here at Roy's Bar and Steak House, we have our own version.'

Cheers and applause roared through the restaurant. Roy held up his hands for silence. 'The first man through the door after nine on Saturday night, he's the challenger. You walked in at nine-o-three.'

Harry remembered the group of seven or eight men

80

who had been standing just outside the door, talking in quiet, eager voices. A few had looked at him oddly as he stepped by. Now he understood why they were there. They'd arrived at nine. Knowing the score, they'd been smart enough to wait for a chump to come along and enter first.

'Look,' Harry said, 'I don't want to fight anyone.'

'They hardly ever do.'

'Well, I'm not *going to*.'

'We had a guy about two years back,' Roy said. 'Some kind of chicken pacifist. He wouldn't fight the champion. Just wouldn't do it. Made a run for the door.' Roy grinned and waved the barrel of his shotgun. 'I cut him down. I'll cut you down if you make a run.'

'This is crazy,' Harry muttered.

'Just our way of having a good time.' Roy turned his attention to the crowd. 'All right, folks. For any newcomers to the Saturday Night Fight, I'll tell you how she works.'

A waitress stepped up to his side, holding a fish bowl stuffed with red tickets.

'We got a hundred tickets here in the bowl. Each ticket has a three-second time period on it, going up to five minutes. Never had a fight go more than that. You pay five bucks for each chance. Winner takes the pot. Any tickets aren't sold by fight time, they belong to the house.' He patted the arm of the woman holding the bowl. 'Julie, here, she's time-keeper. I'm referee. The fight's over when one or the other contestant's dead. Any questions?'

No questions.

'Buy your tickets at the counter. Fight starts in ten minutes.'

During the next ten minutes, as customers filed past the cash register and drew their tickets from the bowl,

Roy stood guard. Harry considered running for the door. He decided, however, that he would rather face the champion than Roy's shotgun. To pass the time, he counted the number of tickets sold.

Seventy-two.

At five dollars each, that came to $360.00.

'Fight starts in one minute,' Roy announced. 'Last call for tickets.'

The ticket buying was done.

'Elmer?'

A thin, bald old man nodded and went out the rear door.

'The champion will be right in, folks. If a couple of you could help move these tables outa the way . . . ?'

Six tables from the center of the room were moved toward the sides, leaving a clear area that seemed awfully small to Harry.

The crowd suddenly cheered and whistled. Looking toward the rear door, Harry saw Elmer enter. A tall, lean man walked behind him.

'Ladies and gentlemen!' Roy called. 'The champion!'

The champion scowled at the crowd as he hobbled toward the clear space. From his looks, he'd fought many times before. His broad forehead was creased with a scar. He wore a patch over his left eye. The tip of one ear was missing. So was the forefinger of his left hand.

Looking down, Harry saw the cause of the champion's strange, awkward gait. A three-foot length of chain dragged between his shackled feet.

'I'm not fighting this man,' Harry said.

'Sure you are,' Roy told him. 'Elmer?'

The skinny old guy knelt down. Opening a padlock, he removed the shackle from the right ankle of the champion.

Harry took a step backward.

'Stand still,' Roy ordered.

'There's no way you can make me fight this man.'

'The folks with low numbers'll be glad to hear that.'

'Right!' someone yelled from the crowd.

'Just stand there,' called another.

Others joined the shouting, some urging him to wait passively for death, some demanding that he fight.

Elmer locked the iron onto Harry's left ankle. The yard-long chain now connected him to the champion.

'Time?' Roy called.

The yelling stopped.

'Ten seconds to starting,' Julie said.

'Elmer?'

The old man scurried away. From behind the counter, he took a matching pair of knives.

'Five seconds,' Julie said.

The knives had wooden handles, brass cross guards, and eight-inch blades of polished steel.

'We won't do it,' Harry said to the champion. 'They can't make us.'

The champion sneered.

Elmer handed one knife to the champion, one to Harry. He rushed out of the way as Julie said, 'Go!'

Harry flung down his knife. Its point thunked the hardwood floor, biting deep. Its handle was still vibrating as the champion jabbed at Harry's stomach. Harry jumped away. The chain stopped his foot, and he fell backward. The champion stomped on his knee. Harry cried out as his leg exploded with pain.

With a demented shriek, the champion flung himself down on Harry. Using both hands, Harry held back the knife that the champion was driving toward his face. The blade pressed closer. He blinked, and felt his right eyelashes brush the steel tip. Turning his head, he shoved sideways. The blade ripped his ear and stabbed the floor beside his head.

He smashed a fist upward into the champion's nose. Rolling, he got out from under the stunned man. He crawled away from the grasping hands and stood.

'Enough!' he shouted. 'That's enough! It has to stop!'

The crowd booed and hissed.

The champion, tearing his knife from the floor, leaped to his feet and swung at Harry. The blade sliced the front of Harry's plaid shirt.

'Stop it!'

The champion lunged, growling. He punched the knife toward Harry's belly. Chopping down, Harry knocked the hand away. The champion stabbed again. This time, the blade slashed Harry's blocking hand. It struck at his stomach. Spinning aside, he dodged the steel.

He gripped the champion's right arm at the wrist and elbow and pumped his knee up. The forearm broke with a popping sound like snapped kindling. Screaming, the champion dropped his knife.

But he caught it with his left hand and thrust it wildly at Harry, who dodged out of the way.

Dropping to one knee, Harry grabbed the chain and tugged. The champion's leg flew high and he tumbled backward. Harry sprang onto him. With both hands, he clutched the champion's left hand and pinned it to the floor.

'Give up!' he shouted into the man's blood-smeared face.

The champion nodded. The knife dropped from his hand.

'That's it!' Harry raised his eyes to the crowd. 'He gave up! He quit!'

Abruptly, the man sat up and clamped his teeth

on Harry's throat. Blind with pain and enraged by the deception, Harry slapped the floor. He found the knife. He plunged it four times into the champion's side before the jaws loosened their grip on his neck. The champion flopped. His head hit the floor with a solid thunk.

Harry crawled aside, fingering his wounded neck. He wasn't bleeding as badly as he'd feared.

Sitting on the floor, he watched Roy kneel at the champion's side.

'Is he dead?' someone shouted from the crowd.

Roy checked the pulse in the champion's neck. 'Not yet,' he announced.

'Come on!' someone yelled.

'Hang on, champ!' shouted another.

'Give it up!' called a woman's voice.

The crowd roared for a few seconds. Then silence fell. Complete silence. All eyes were fixed on Roy kneeling beside the fallen champion.

'Gone!' Roy announced.

Julie clicked her stopwatch. 'Two minutes, twenty-eight seconds.'

'That's me!' a man cried out, waving his red ticket. 'That's me! I got it!'

'Come on up here,' Roy said. 'We'll just verify that and hand over your loot.' He turned to his skinny old assistant. 'Elmer?'

Elmer knelt between Harry and the body. He unlatched the dead man's shackle. Before Harry could move to prevent it, the iron cuff was clamped around his own right ankle. Elmer shut the padlock.

'Hey!' Harry protested. 'Take 'em off! I won! You've got to let me go!'

'Can't do that,' Roy said, smiling down at him. 'You're the champion.'

The Maiden

'I don't know about this,' I said.

'What's not to know?' Cody asked. He was driving. His car was a Jeep Cherokee and he had it in four-wheel drive. We'd been bouncing along a dirt road through a forest for about half an hour, it was dark as hell out there except for the headlights, and I didn't know how much farther it might be to our destination, a place supposedly called Lost Lake.

'What if we break down?' I asked.

'We aren't gonna break down,' Cody said.

'It sounds like the car's shaking to pieces.'

'Don't be such a weenie,' said Rudy, who sat in the passenger seat.

Rudy was Cody's best pal. They were both a couple of pretty cool guys. In a way, I felt very honored that they'd invited me to come with them. But I felt nervous, too. Maybe they'd asked me to come along because I'm the new kid in school and they just wanted to be nice and get to know me better. On the other hand, maybe they planned to screw me.

I don't mean 'screw' in the literal sense. There was nothing the least bit funny about Cody or Rudy, and they both had girlfriends.

Rudy's girl wasn't much. Her name was Alice. She looked like someone had taken hold of her by the head and feet, then stretched her out till she was way too long and skinny.

Cody's girl was Lois Garnett. Everything about Lois was perfect. Except for one thing; she *knew* that she was perfect. In other words, she was a snot.

I had a bad case of the hots for Lois, anyway. How could I *not*? All you've got to do is look at her, and she'll drive you crazy. But I made the mistake of getting caught, last week. She dropped her pencil on the floor in Chemistry. When she bent down to pick it up, I had a view straight down the front of her blouse. Even though she had a bra on, the view was pretty terrific. The problem is, she looked up and saw where my eyes were aimed. She muttered, 'What're you looking at, asshole?'

'Tit,' I answered. I can be a wiseguy, sometimes.

It's a good thing looks can't kill.

Boyfriends can, though. Which was one reason I was a little bit worried about going off into the woods in the middle of the night with Cody and Rudy.

Nobody had mentioned the incident, though.

Not so far.

Maybe Lois hadn't told Cody about it, and I had nothing to worry about.

On the other hand . . .

I figured it was worth the risk. I mean, what was the worst that could happen? It's not like they would actually try and kill me just for looking down Lois's blouse.

What they *said* they wanted to do was set me up with some gal.

I was eating my lunch in the quad, just that afternoon, when Cody and Rudy came over and started talking to me.

'You doing anything tonight?' Cody asked.

'What do you mean?'

'He means,' Rudy said, 'we know this babe that

thinks you're hot stuff. She wants to *see* you, know what I mean? Tonight.'

'Tonight? Me?'

'Midnight,' Cody said.

'You sure you've got the right guy?'

'We're sure.'

'Elmo Baine?'

'You think we're morons?' Rudy asked, sounding steamed. 'We *know* your name. *Everybody* knows your name.'

'You're the one she wants,' Cody said. 'How about it?'

'Gosh, I don't know.'

'What's not to know?' Rudy asked.

'Well . . . Who is she?'

'What do you care?' Rudy asked. 'She *wants* you, man. How many babes *want* you?'

'Well . . . I'd sort of like to know who she is before I make up my mind.'

'She told us not to tell you,' Cody explained.

'Wants it to be a surprise,' Rudy added.

'Yeah, but I mean . . . How do I know she isn't some sort of a . . . you know . . .'

'A dog?' Rudy suggested.

'Well . . . yeah.'

Cody and Rudy looked at each other and shook their heads. Then Cody said, 'She's hot stuff, take my word on it. This might be the best offer you ever get, Elmo. You don't wanta blow it.'

'Well . . . Can't you tell me who she is?'

'Nope.'

'Is she someone I know?'

'She knows you,' Rudy pointed out. 'And she *wants* to know you a lot better.'

'Don't blow it,' Cody told me again.

'Well,' I said. 'I guess . . . okay.'

After that, we made plans about where and when I would meet their car.

I didn't ask if 'anyone else' would be going with us, but I figured there was a chance they might show up with Alice and Lois. The possibility had me really excited. As the day went on, I got myself so sure Lois would come along that I pretty much forgot all about the mystery girl.

I fixed myself up and snuck out of the house in plenty of time to meet the car. When it showed up, though, it didn't have anyone in it except Cody and Rudy. I guess my disappointment must've showed.

'Something wrong?' Cody asked.

'No. Nothing. I'm just a little nervous.'

Rudy grinned at me over his shoulder. 'You sure smell good.'

'Just some Old Spice.'

'You'll have her licking you.'

'Cut it out,' Cody told him.

'So,' I said, 'where are we going? I mean, I know you're not supposed to tell me *who* she is, but I'm sort of curious about exactly *where* you're taking me.'

'Can we tell him?' Rudy asked.

'I guess so. Have you ever been out to Lost Lake, Elmo?'

'Lost Lake? Never heard of it.'

'You have, now,' Rudy told me.

'Is that where she lives?' I asked.

'It's where she wants to meet you,' Cody said.

'She's sort of a "nature girl",' Rudy explained.

'Besides,' Cody said, 'it's a great place for fooling around. Way out in the woods, a nice little lake, and you've got all the privacy in the world.'

That crummy dirt road seemed to go on forever.

The Jeep shook and rattled. Branches or something squeaked against the sides. And talk about dark.

There's nothing like a forest when it comes to darkness. Maybe that's because the trees block out the moonlight. It was like driving through a tunnel. The headlights lit up the stuff just in front of us, and the tail lights made a red glow out the back window. Everything else was black.

I was okay for a while, but I started to get more and more nervous. The deeper into the forest we went, the worse I felt. They'd told me that the car wouldn't break down, and Rudy had called me a weenie for even asking. A while later, though, I went ahead and said, 'Are you sure we aren't lost?'

'I don't get lost,' Cody said.

'How are we doing on gas?'

'We're fine.'

'What a pussy,' Rudy said.

What a shithead, I thought. But I didn't say it. I didn't say anything. I mean, we were out in the boonies and nobody knew I was with these guys. If I made them mad, things might get pretty drastic.

Of course, I realized that things might take a turn for the ugly, anyway. This whole deal could be a set-up. I hoped not, but you just never know.

The trouble is, you can't make any friends at all if you don't take a chance. Whether or not a friendship with Cody and Rudy was worth this much of a risk – and I was having some real doubts about that – an 'in' with them would mean an 'in' with Lois.

I could just see it. There might be triple dates: Cody and Lois, Rudy and Alice, Elmo and Mystery Girl. We would travel crowded in the Jeep. We'd sit together at the movies. We'd go on picnics, have swimming parties, maybe take camping trips – and fool around. My actual partner would be Mystery Girl, but Lois would be right there where I could watch her, listen to her, and maybe more. Maybe we would trade partners sometimes. Maybe we would even have orgies.

No telling what might happen if they accepted me.

I guess I would do just about anything to find out – even take a ride into the middle of nowhere with these guys, where they might be planning to leave me stranded, or beat me up, or worse.

I was pretty scared. The deeper we got into the woods, the more I suspected a bad time from these two. But I kept my mouth shut after Rudy called me a pussy. I just sat there in the back seat and worried and kept telling myself that they didn't have a good enough reason to really *demolish* me. All I'd done was take a look down Lois's front.

'Here we are,' Cody said.

We had come to the end of the road.

Ahead, lit by the white beams of the headlights, was a cleared place big enough for half a dozen cars to park. There were logs on the ground to show you where to stop. Off beyond the parking area, I saw a trash barrel, a couple of picnic tables, and a brick fireplace for barbecues.

Ours was the only car.

We were the only people.

'I guess she isn't here yet,' I said.

'You never know,' Cody told me.

'There aren't any other cars.'

'Who says she drove?' Rudy said.

Cody steered toward one of the logs, stopped and shut off the engine.

I couldn't see any lake. I almost made a crack about it being lost, but didn't feel much like joking around at that moment.

Cody shut off the headlights. Blackness dropped on us, but only for a second. Then both the front

91

doors swung open, making the overhead light come on.

'Let's go,' Cody said.

They both climbed out. I did, too.

When they shut their doors, the light inside the Jeep died. But we were standing in the open. The sky was spread above us. The moon was almost full and the stars were out.

Shadows were black, but everything else was lit up, almost like a dirty white powder had been sprinkled around.

That was one extremely bright moon.

'This way,' Cody said.

We walked through the picnic area. I've got to tell you, my legs were shaking.

Just past the tables, the ground slanted down to a pale area that reminded me of how snow looks at night – only this seemed dimmer than snow. A sand beach? It had to be.

Beyond the curve of the beach, the lake was black. It looked beautiful, the way the moon made a silvery path on the water. The silver came straight at us from the far end of the lake. It stretched past the side of a small, wooded island and came all the way to the beach.

Cody had said that this place had 'all the privacy in the world', and he was right. Except for the moon and stars, there were no lights in sight: none from boats on the water, or from docks along the shores, or from cabins in the dark woods around the lake. The way things looked, we might've been the only three people for miles around.

I wished I wasn't feeling so nervous. This could be a great place if you weren't here with a couple of guys possibly planning to mess you over. A great place to be alone with a really terrific babe, for instance.

'I don't think she's here,' I said.

92

'Don't be so sure,' Rudy told me.

'Maybe she changed her mind about coming. I mean, it's a school night, and everything.'

'It's gotta be a school night,' Cody explained. 'Too many people here, weekends. Look at this, we've got the whole place to ourselves.'

'But where's the girl?'

'Jeez,' Rudy said, 'will you knock off the whining?'

'Yeah,' Cody said. 'Relax and enjoy yourself.'

Just then, we walked out onto the sand. After a few steps, both the guys stopped. They took off their shoes and socks. I took off mine, too. Even though it was a warm night, the sand felt cool with my feet bare.

Next, they took their shirts off. There was nothing wrong with doing that; they're guys and the night was warm and a soft breeze was blowing. But it made me so nervous, I got a cold wad in the pit of my stomach. Cody and Rudy had really fine physiques. And even in the *moonlight*, you could see they had good tans.

I untucked my shirt and unfastened the buttons.

They left their shirts on the beach with the shoes and socks. I kept mine on. Nobody said anything about it. As we walked down the sand toward the water, I almost decided to go ahead and take my shirt off. I wanted to be like them. And I sure liked the way the breeze felt. I just couldn't do it, though.

We stopped at the water's edge.

'This is great,' Cody said. He raised his arms and stretched. 'Feel that breeze.'

Rudy stretched, flexed his muscles, and groaned. 'Man,' he said, 'I sure wish the babes were here.'

'Maybe we'll come back Friday, bring 'em. You can come, too, Elmo. Bring your new honey and we'll have ourselves a big ol' party.'

'Really?'

'Sure.'

'Wow! That'd be . . . really neat.'

It was *exactly* what I wanted to hear! My worries had been stupid. These two were the greatest pals a guy could have.

A few more nights, and I'd be right here at the beach with Lois.

I suddenly felt terrific!

'Maybe we oughta just, you know, put off everything till then,' I said. 'My . . . uh, date . . . she isn't here anyway. Maybe we should just leave, and we can *all* come Friday night. I wouldn't mind waiting till then to meet her.'

'That'd be okay with me,' Cody said.

'Same here,' said Rudy.

'Great!'

Smiling, Cody tilted his head sideways. 'Wouldn't be okay with *her*, though. She wants you tonight.'

'Lucky bastard,' Rudy said, and slugged my arm.

Rubbing my arm, I explained, 'But she isn't here.'

Cody nodded. 'You're right. She's not here. She's *there*.' He pointed at the lake.

'What?' I asked.

'On the island.'

'On the *island*?' I'm no expert on judging distances, but the island looked pretty far out. A couple of hundred yards, at least. 'What's she doing *there*?'

'Waiting for you, lover boy.' Rudy punched my arm again.

'Quit it.'

'Sorry.' He gave me another slug.

'Cut it out,' Cody told him. To me, he said, 'That's where she wants to meet you.'

'*There?*'

'It's perfect. You won't have to worry about anyone barging in on you.'

94

'She's on the *island*?' I was having a fairly difficult time believing it.

'That's right.'

'How'd she get there?'

'She swam.'

'She's sort of a "nature girl",' Rudy said. He'd pointed that out once before.

'How am *I* supposed to get there?'

'Same way she did,' Cody said.

'Swim?'

'You know how to swim, don't you?'

'Yeah. Sort of.'

'Sort of?'

'I mean, I'm not exactly the world's greatest swimmer.'

'Can you make it that far?'

'I don't know.'

'Shit,' Rudy said. 'I *knew* he was a pussy.'

Screw you, I thought. I felt like slamming him in the face, but all I did was stand there.

'We don't want him drowning on us,' Cody said.

'He won't drown. Shit, his *fat*'ll keep him up.'

Part of me wanted to pound Rudy for saying that, and part of me wanted to cry.

'I can swim to that island if I want to,' I blurted out. 'Maybe I don't want to, that's all. I bet there isn't even any girl there.'

'What do you mean?' Cody asked.

'It's just a trick,' I said. 'There isn't any girl, and you know it. It's just a trick to make me try and swim to the island. Then you'll probably drive off and leave me, or something.'

Cody stared at me. 'It's no wonder you don't have any friends.'

Rudy nudged him with an elbow. 'Elmo here thinks we're a couple of *assholes*.'

95

'I didn't say that.'

'Yeah, right,' Cody said. 'We try to do you a favor, and you think we're out to screw you. Fuck it. Let's go.'

'What?' I asked.

'Let's go.'

They both turned their backs to the lake and started walking up the beach toward the place where they'd left their stuff.

'We're leaving?' I asked.

Cody glanced back at me. 'That's what you want, isn't it? Come on, we'll take you home.'

'To your mommy,' Rudy added.

I stood my ground. 'Wait!' I called. 'Hold on, okay? Just a second. Let's talk this over, okay?'

'Forget it,' Cody said. 'You're a loser.'

'I am not!'

They crouched and picked up their shirts.

'Hey look, I'm sorry. I'll do it. Okay? I believe you. I'll swim to the island.' Cody and Rudy looked at each other. Cody shook his head.

'Please!' I yelled. 'Give me another chance!'

'You think we're a couple of liars.'

'No, I don't. Honest. I was just confused, that's all. It's just strange. I've never had a girl . . . like *send* for me. Okay? I'll go. I'll do it.'

'Yeah, all right,' Cody said. He sounded reluctant, though.

They tossed their shirts down. As they walked back to where I was standing, they kept shaking their heads and looking at each other.

'We don't wanta be here all night,' Cody said to me. He checked his wristwatch. 'What we'll do, we'll give you an hour.'

'And then leave without me?'

'Did I say that? We're not gonna leave without you.'

96

'He *does* think we're assholes,' Rudy said.

'I do not.'

'If you're not back,' Cody said, 'we'll yell or toot the horn or something. Just figure you'll have about an hour with her.'

'Don't keep us waiting,' Rudy warned. 'You wanta screw her till dawn, do it some time when we ain't your chauffeurs.'

Screw her till dawn?

'Okay,' I said. I faced the water, and took a deep breath. 'Here goes. Anything else I need to know?'

'Are you planning to keep your jeans on?' Cody asked.

'Yeah.'

'I wouldn't.'

'They'll drag you down,' Rudy pointed out.

'You'd better leave them here.'

I didn't like the sound of that, at all.

'I don't know,' I said.

Cody shook his head. 'We aren't gonna take them.'

'Who'd wanta *touch* 'em?'

'The thing is,' Cody went on, 'those jeans'll soak up a lot of water. They'll get damned heavy.'

'You'll never make it to the island in 'em,' Rudy said.

'They'll sink you.'

'Or *she* will.'

'*What?*'

'Don't listen to Rudy. He's full of crap.'

'The Maiden,' Rudy said. 'She'll get you if you don't swim fast enough. You gotta lose the jeans.'

'He's just trying to scare you.'

'The *Maiden*? There's a *maiden* who's gonna *get* me or drown me or something?'

'No no no,' Cody said. He scowled at Rudy. 'Did you have to go and mention her? You idiot!'

97

'Hey, man. He wants to keep his jeans on. He keeps 'em on, he'll *never* stand a chance of out-swimming her. She'll nail him, for sure.'

'There's no such *thing* as the Maiden.'

'Is, too.'

'What are you two *talking* about?' I blurted.

Cody faced me, shaking his head. 'The Maiden of Lost Lake. It's some bullshit legend.'

'She got Willy Glitten last summer,' Rudy said.

'Willy got a cramp, that's all.'

'That's what you think.'

'That's what I know. He ate that damn pepperoni pizza just before he went in. That's what killed him, not some stupid ghost.'

'The Maiden ain't a *ghost*. That shows how much you know. Ghosts can't grab you and . . .'

'Neither can gals who've been dead for forty years.'

'*She* can.'

'Bull.'

'*What are you two talking about?*' I snapped.

They both looked at me.

'You wanta tell him?' Cody asked Rudy.

'You go ahead.'

'You're the one that brought it up,' Cody said.

'And you're telling me I'm full of shit. So you tell it *your* way. I'm not saying another word about her.'

'Would *some*body please tell me?'

'All right, all right,' Cody said. 'Here's the deal. There's this story about the Maiden of Lost Lake. Part of it's true, and part of it's bull.'

Rudy made a snorty noise.

'The true part is that a gal drowned out there one night about forty years ago.'

'The night of her senior prom,' Rudy added. He'd broken his word about keeping his mouth shut, but Cody didn't call him on it.

'Yeah,' Cody said. 'It was Prom Night, and after the dance was over, her date drove her out here. The whole idea was to fool around, you know? So they park in the lot back there, and start in. Things get going pretty good. Too good for the gal.'

'She was a virgin,' Rudy pointed out. 'That's how come they call her "the Maiden".'

'Yeah. Anyway, it's all getting out of hand, as far as she's concerned. So to slow things down, she says they oughta go and take a swim in the lake. The guy figures she means a skinny-dip, so he's all for it.'

'Nobody else was around,' Rudy said.

'That's what she thinks, anyway,' Cody said. 'So they climb out of the car and start stripping. The guy takes off everything. Not her, though. She insists on keeping her underwear on.'

'Her panties and bra,' Rudy explained.

'So they throw their clothes in the car and run down here to the beach and go in the lake. They swim around for a while. Play games. Splash each other. That sort of thing. Then they get hold of each other and, you know . . . things start getting hot again.'

'They were still in the water?' I asked.

'Yeah. Out where it isn't very deep.'

I wondered how he knew all this.

'Pretty soon, she lets him unhook her bra. It was the first time he'd ever gotten that far.'

'Finally got to feel her titties,' Rudy said.

'He figures he's died and gone to heaven. And he figures he's finally gonna score. So then he tries to pull her panties down.'

'He was gonna put it to her, right there in the lake,' Rudy explained.

'Yeah. But then she tells him to stop. He doesn't listen, though. He just goes ahead and tries to pull her panties down. So she starts fighting him. I mean,

99

this guy is bare-ass naked and probably has a boner to beat the band, so she *knows* what's gonna happen if he gets her panties down. And she isn't about to let it. She pounds on him and scratches him and kicks him until she finally manages to get loose and head for shore. Then, just when she's wading out of the lake, her boyfriend starts shouting. He yells, "Guys! Quick! She's getting away!" And all of a sudden, these five other guys come running down the beach at her.'

'They're his buddies,' Rudy explained.

'A bunch of losers who hadn't even *gone* to the prom. The guy, the Maiden's date? He'd collected five bucks from each of them, and set up the whole deal. They'd driven out earlier that night, hidden their car in the woods, then waited around, drinking beer. By the time the guy showed up with the Maiden, they were plastered out of their minds . . .'

'And horny enough,' Rudy added, 'to fuck the crack of dawn.'

'The Maiden never had a chance,' Cody said. 'They caught her while she was running up the beach, and they held her down while her prom date banged her. That was part of the deal, that he'd get to go first.'

'Didn't want no sloppy seconds,' Rudy explained.

'After him, all the rest of them took turns.'

'Two or *three* turns each,' Rudy said. 'Some of 'em nailed her in the butt, too.'

'That's . . . awful,' I muttered. It *was* cruel and terrible – which made me feel guilty about how the story made me sort of hard.

'She was messed up pretty good by the time they were finished with her,' Cody explained. 'They hadn't *beaten* on her, though. There were four or five of them holding her down, the whole time, so they never had to punch her out or anything like that. They figured she'd look all right, once she'd washed up and gotten dressed. The plan was for the boyfriend to drive her back home, just as if nothing had happened. They figured she wouldn't dare tell on them. Back in those days, you looked like the town slut if you got yourself gang-raped. She'd be ruined if she tried to get them in trouble.

'So they tell her to go in the lake and clean herself up, and while they're thinking everything's gonna turn out great, she goes stumbling into the water and wades out farther and farther. Next thing they know, she's swimming hell-bent for the island. They don't know if she's trying to escape or wants to drown herself. Either way, they can't let it happen. So they go and swim out after her.'

'All but one,' Rudy said.

'One of the guys didn't know how to swim,' Cody explained. 'So he stayed on shore and watched. What happened is, the Maiden never reached the island.'

'She *almost* made it,' Rudy said.

'Had about fifty yards to go, and then she went under.'

'God,' I muttered.

'Then the *guys* went under,' Cody said. 'Some were faster swimmers than others, and they were spread out pretty good. The guy on shore, he could see them in the moonlight. One by one, they each sort of let out a quick little cry and splashed around for a few seconds, and vanished under the water. The gal's prom date was the last to go. When he saw his buddies were going down all around him, he turned tail and tried for shore. He made it about halfway. Then he yelled out, "No! No! Let *go* of me! Please! I'm sorry! Please!" Then, down he went.'

'Wow,' I muttered.

'The guy who'd seen it all, he jumped in one of the cars and went speeding for town. He was so drunk and shook up, he crashed after he got out to the main road. He thought he was dying, so he confessed while they were taking him to the hospital. Told everything.

'It was a couple of hours before a search party made it back here to the lake. And you know what they found?'

I shook my head.

'The guys. The boyfriend and his four buddies. They were stretched out side by side, right here on the beach. They were all naked. They were lying on their backs with their eyes wide open, gazing up at the sky.'

'Dead?' I asked.

'Dead as carp,' Rudy said.

'Drowned,' Cody said.

'Jeez,' I said. 'And it's supposed to be the Maiden who did it? She actually drowned *all* those guys?'

'You couldn't exactly call them guys anymore,' Cody said.

Rudy grinned, then chomped his teeth together a couple of times.

'She *bit* off their . . . ?' I couldn't bring myself to say it.

'Nobody knows for sure *who* did it,' Cody said. 'Someone or some*thing* did. I'd say she was the most likely candidate, wouldn't you?'

'I guess.'

'Anyway, they never found the Maiden.'

'Or the missing weenies,' Rudy added.

'People say she drowned out there on her way to the island, and it was her ghost that took vengeance on those guys.'

'It's not her *ghost*,' Rudy said. 'Ghosts can't do shit. It's *her*. She's, you know, like "the living dead". A zombie.'

'Bull,' Cody said.

'She just sort of hangs around out there under the

water and waits till a guy tries to swim by. Then she goes for him. Like she did Willy Glitten and all those others. She gets 'em by the dingus with her teeth . . .'

Cody elbowed him. 'She does not.'

'Does, too! And pulls 'em down by it.'

I suddenly laughed. I couldn't help it. I'd been pretty wrapped up in the story, and actually *believing* most of it, up till Rudy said that about the Maiden turning into some sort of a dick-hungry zombie. Maybe I can be a little gullible sometimes, but I'm not a complete dope.

'You think it's funny?' Rudy asked.

I quit laughing.

'You wouldn't think it's so funny if you knew how many guys have *drowned* trying to swim out to the island.'

'If they drowned,' I said, 'I'll bet it wasn't because the Maiden got them.'

'That's what *I* say,' Cody said. 'Like I told you, only part of the story's true. I mean, I'm willing to believe the business about the girl getting raped, and then drowning. But the rest of it, I think somebody made it up. I don't think it's true about the guys getting *picked off* when they went after her. Much less that she bit off their cocks. I mean, that's complete bull. It's just somebody's idea of poetic justice, you know?'

'You can believe whatever you want,' Rudy said. 'My gramps was there with the bunch that found the guys that night. And he told my dad about it, and my dad told me.'

'I know, I know,' Cody said.

'And he *didn't* just tell me it to scare me.'

'Sure, he did. 'Cause he knows you're just the kind of guy that might pull a stunt like those jerks.'

'I never raped nobody in my life.'

103

'That's 'cause you're scared you'll get your whang bit off.'

'I sure won't go swimming in *there*,' Rudy said. He stuck an arm out and pointed at the lake. 'No way. You believe what you want, the Maiden's in there and she's just waiting.'

Cody, looking at me, shook his head. 'She *is* out there, I guess. I mean, I think she *did* drown that night. But that was forty years ago. There's probably nothing much left of her by now. And she doesn't have anything to do with the drownings we've had. People just drown sometimes. It happens. They get muscle cramps . . .' He shrugged. 'But I sure won't hold it against you if you've changed your mind about swimming out to the island.'

'I don't know.' I stared out at it. There was a lot of black water between me and that patch of wooded land. 'If so many people have drowned . . .'

'It's not *that* many. Only one guy last year. And he'd just finished wolfing down a pepperoni pizza.'

'The Maiden got him,' Rudy muttered.

'Did they find his body?' I asked.

'No,' Cody said.

'So you don't know if he'd been . . . eaten.'

'I'd bet on it,' Rudy said.

I looked Cody in the eyes. They were in shadows, actually, so I couldn't see them. 'But *you* don't believe any of the stuff about the Maiden . . . you know, waiting around in the lake to . . . uh, do that to guys who swim by?'

'You've gotta be kidding me. Only dorks like Rudy believe in crap like that.'

'Thanks, pal,' Rudy said to him.

I took a deep breath, and sighed. I looked once more toward the island, and saw all that blackness along the

104

way. 'I guess maybe I'd better skip it,' I said.

Cody gave Rudy an elbow in the side. 'See what you did? Why didn't you keep your big mouth shut?'

'*You* told him the story!'

'*You* brought it up in the first place!'

'He had a right to know! You can't just send a guy out like that without warning him! And he was gonna wear his *jeans*! Your only chance is if you can outswim her, and you can't do that with *jeans* on.'

'Okay, okay,' Cody said. 'Anyway, it doesn't matter. He's not going.'

'We shouldn't have tried to make him in the first place,' Rudy said. 'The whole idea was dumb. I mean, you-know-who's as hot as they come, but she ain't worth *dying* for.'

'Well,' Cody said, 'that's what she wanted to find out, isn't it?' He turned to me. 'That's the main reason she picked the island. It was supposed to be a test. What she told me, if you aren't man enough to make the swim, you aren't man enough to deserve her. The thing is, she didn't figure on Bozo here shooting off his mouth about the Maiden.'

'It's not that,' I said. 'You don't think I believe that stuff, do you? But, you know, I'm really not such a great swimmer.'

'It's all right,' Cody said. 'You don't have to explain.'

Rudy said, 'We just gonna leave now?'

'Guess so.' Cody turned toward the lake, cupped his hands to the sides of his mouth, and yelled, 'Ashley!'

'Shit!' Rudy blurted. 'You said her name!'

'Ooops.'

Ashley?

I knew of only one Ashley.

'Ashley Brooks?' I asked.

Cody nodded and shrugged. 'It was supposed to be a surprise. And you weren't supposed to find out, at all, if you didn't make the swim.'

My heart was slamming.

Not that I believed a word of it. Ashley Brooks could not possibly have the hots for me and be waiting for me on that island. She was probably the one girl in school who was just as stupendous as Lois. Beautiful golden hair, eyes like a summer morning sky, a face to dream about, and a body . . . a body that didn't quit. Talk about *built*!

But her personality wasn't at all like Lois. She had a kind of innocence and sweetness that made her seem like she was from another world – almost too good to be true.

I couldn't come close to believing that Ashley even knew I existed.

She was too much to hope for.

'It can't be Ashley Brooks,' I said.

'She knew you'd be shocked,' Cody told me. 'That's one reason she wanted us to keep it secret. She wanted to see the surprise on your face.'

'Oh, sure.'

Facing the island again, Cody called out, 'ASHLEY! Might as well show yourself! Elmo's not interested!'

'I didn't say that!' I gasped.

'ASHLEY!' Cody called again.

We waited.

Maybe half a minute later, a white glow appeared through the trees and bushes near the tip of the island. The glow seemed to be moving. It was very bright. It probably came from one of those propane lanterns people use on camping trips.

'She's gonna be awfully disappointed,' Cody muttered.

A few more seconds passed. Then she stepped out

106

onto the rocky shore, the lantern held off away from her side – probably to avoid burning herself.

'And you thought we was liars,' Rudy said.

'My God,' I muttered, staring at her. She was awfully far away. I could only make out vague things. Like the goldness of her hair. And her shape. Her shape *really* caught my eye. At first, I thought she was wearing some sort of skintight garment – tights or a leotard, maybe. If that's what she had on, though, it must've been the same color as her face. And it must've had a couple of dark spots where her nipples belonged, and a golden arrowhead pointing down at . . .

'Holy shit,' Rudy said. 'She's butt naked.'

'Nah,' Cody said. 'I don't think—'

'Sure is!'

She raised the lantern high. Then her voice drifted over the lake. 'Elll-mo? Aren't you coming?'

'Yes!' I shouted.

'I'm waiting,' she called. Then she turned around and walked toward the woods.

'She *is* naked,' Cody said. 'Man, I don't believe it.'

'*I* do,' I said. She was out of sight by the time I got my jeans off. I kept my boxers on. They were a little limp in the elastic, so I hitched them up as I headed for the water. I glanced back at the guys. 'See you later.'

'Yeah,' Cody muttered. He seemed distracted. Maybe *he* wanted to be the one going to the island.

'Swim fast,' Rudy said. 'Don't let the Maiden get you.'

'Sure,' I said.

As I waded into the lake, I could still see the pale light from Ashley's lantern and knew she was in the woods, just out of sight, naked and waiting for me.

107

The night was pale with moonlight and stars. A warm breeze drifted against my skin. The water around my ankles felt even warmer than the breeze. It made soft lapping sounds, and climbed my legs. In my loose boxer shorts, I felt almost naked.

I trembled as if I were freezing, but I wasn't cold at all.

It was just from too much excitement.

This can't be happening, I thought. This sort of thing just doesn't happen to guys like me. It's too fabulous.

But it is happening!

I'd seen her with my own eyes.

As the warm water wrapped my thighs and I imagined how she would look *close up*, I could feel myself rise hard and slide out through the fly of my boxers.

Nobody can see, I told myself. It's too dark, and my back's to the guys.

A couple more steps, and the lake water took me in. It was all soft, sliding warmth. I shivered with the pleasure of it.

'Better get *moving*!' Rudy yelled. 'The Maiden's homing in on you.'

I scowled over my shoulder at him, angry because he'd shouted and ruined the mood. He and Cody were still standing beside each other on the beach.

'You can quit trying to scare me,' I called. 'You just want to make me chicken out.'

'She's too good for you, barf-bag.'

'Ha! Guess *she* doesn't think so.'

The water was up to my shoulders by then, so I shoved at the bottom and started to swim. Like I said before, I'm not the greatest swimmer in the world. My 'crawl' pretty much stinks. I've got an okay breaststroke, though. It's not fast like the crawl, but it gets you where you're going. And it doesn't wear you out. Also, you can see where you're going if you keep your head up.

I like the name, breaststroke. But most of all, I like how it feels to be gliding softly through the water that way. The warm fluid just slides and rubs against you, all over.

Or would, if you didn't have anything on.

Like boxer shorts. They were down low on my hips, clinging, trapping me. They wouldn't even let me spread my legs enough for good kicks.

I thought about taking them off, but didn't dare.

Anyway, they didn't have me *completely* trapped. I was still sticking out the fly, and I loved having it out and feeling the caress of the water.

This was all the more exciting because of the Maiden.

The risk.

Offering her bait.

Taunting her with it.

Not that I believed for one minute in all that garbage about the Maiden drowning guys and devouring their whangs. It was like Cody said: bull. But the *idea* of it turned me on.

You know?

I didn't believe in her, but I could picture her. In my mind, she was sort of suspended in the darkness maybe ten feet below me, her head about even with my waist. She was naked and beautiful. In fact, she looked sort of like Ashley or Lois. She was down there, drifting on her back, not swimming but keeping pace with me, anyhow.

The darkness didn't matter; we could see each other through it. Her skin was so pale that it seemed to glow. She was grinning up at me.

Slowly, she began to rise.

Rising to the bait.

109

I could see her gliding closer. And I knew she wasn't going to bite. The guys had it all wrong. She was going to suck.

I kept breaststroking along, imagining the Maiden coming up and latching on. The guys had meant the story to scare me. It *had* scared me. But the mind is a great thing. You can turn things around. With a bit of mental legerdemain, I'd changed their dong-chomping zombie into a seductive water nymph.

But I told myself to stop thinking about her. What with everything else – the sexy Prom Night story, seeing Ashley naked, the feel of the warm water – I was so excited that the last thing I needed was to imagine the Maiden underneath me, naked and ready to start sucking.

I had to think about something else.

What'll I say to Ashley?

That gave me a quick scare, until I realized there wouldn't be much need to say anything. Not at first, anyway. You swim to an island for a rendezvous with a naked girl, the last thing you do is chit-chat.

I raised my head a little higher and saw the glow of the lantern. It was still among the trees, just in from shore.

I'd been making good progress. I was past the halfway mark.

Getting into Maiden territory.

Yeah, right.

Come and get it, honey.

'You better quit dawdling and get your ass in gear!' Rudy shouted.

Yeah, right.

'She's gonna get you! I'm not kidding!'

'You'd better swim faster!' Cody yelled.

Cody?

110

But he doesn't believe in the Maiden. Why's he telling me to swim faster?

'Move it!' Cody shouted. 'Go!'

They're just trying to scare me, I told myself.

It worked.

Suddenly, the water no longer felt like a warm caress; it gave me chills. I was all alone on the surface of a black lake where people had drowned, where rotting bodies lurked, where the Maiden might not really be dead after forty years and where she might be a sharp-toothed, decayed huntress with nothing in her head except revenge and a taste for penis.

Mine shrank like it wanted to hide.

Even though I *knew* there was no Maiden coming after me.

I started swimming hard. No more breaststroke. I churned up a storm, kicking like a madman, windmilling my arms, slapping the water. There were shouts from behind me, but I couldn't make out the words through the noise of my wild splashing.

Head up, I blinked water out of my eyes.

Not much farther to go.

I'll make it! I'm gonna make it!

Then she touched me.

I think I screamed.

As I tried to twist away from her hands, they scurried down from my shoulders, fingernails scraping my chest and belly. They didn't hurt me. But they made me tingle and squirm. I quit swimming and reached down to get them away from me. But I wasn't fast enough. Gouging some skin, they clawed at the band of my shorts. I felt a rough tug. My head went under. Choking, I quit trying to grab the Maiden. I reached up as if trying to find the rungs of a ladder that would lead me to the surface, and air. My lungs burned.

The Maiden dragged me lower and lower.

111

Dragged me down by my boxer shorts.

They were around my knees, then around my ankles, then gone.

For a moment, I was free.

I kicked for the surface. And got there. Gasping, I sucked at the night air. It took both hands to tread water. I swiveled around. Spotted Cody and Rudy standing on the beach in the moonlight. 'Help!' I yelled. 'Help! It's the Maiden!'

'Told you so!' Rudy called.

'Tough luck,' called Cody.

'Please! *Do* something!'

What they did, it looked like they each raised a hand into the moonlight and flipped me off.

Then a pair of hands underneath the water grabbed my ankles. I wanted to scream. But I took a deep breath, instead. An instant later, they yanked me down.

This is it! She's got me! Oh, God!

I clutched my genitals.

Any second, her teeth . . .

Bubbles came up.

I heard the gurgling sound they made, and felt sort of a tickle as some of them brushed against my skin.

For a second, I thought the bubbles might be gas escaping from the Maiden's rotting carcass. She'd been dead forty years, though. The rotting should've been over and done with, long ago.

My next thought was *air tanks*.

Scuba gear!

I stopped kicking. I squatted, reached down between my feet, made a sudden lunge with both hands and caught hold of some equipment that I think turned out to be her mouthpiece. I gave it a tug for all I was worth.

She must've taken in a mouthful when I did that,

because the rest was fairly easy. She hardly fought back, at all.

From the feel of things, she was naked except for her face mask, scuba tank and weight belt. And she wasn't any corpse, either. Her skin was slick and cool, and she had wonderful tits with big, rubbery nipples.

I hurt her pretty bad, right there in the lake.

Then, I towed her ashore at the side of the island, so the guys wouldn't be able to see us. From there, I dragged her a few yards to the clearing where she'd left her lantern.

In the lantern light, I saw who she was.

Though, of course, I'd already guessed.

After doing her Ashley routine to lure me over, Lois must've gotten into her scuba gear real fast and snuck into the lake for her Maiden routine.

She looked great in the lantern light. All shiny and pale, her breasts sticking out between straps. She'd already lost the face mask. I took off her tank and belt so she was naked.

She was sprawled on her back, coughing and choking and having spasms, which made her body twitch and shake in ways that were very neat to watch.

I enjoyed the show for a while. Then I started in on her.

This was *the best*.

For a while, she was too out of breath to make much noise. Pretty soon, though, I had her screaming.

I knew her screaming would bring Cody and Rudy to the rescue, so I started swinging her weight belt. It caved her head in nicely, and finished her off.

Then I hurried to the tip of the island. Cody and Rudy were already in the lake and swimming fast.

I planned to take them by surprise and bash their heads in, but guess what? I was spared the trouble.

113

They got about halfway to the island. Then, one at a time, they let out squeals and went down.

I couldn't believe it.

Still can't.

But they never showed up.

I guess the Maiden got them.

Why them, but not me?

Maybe the Maiden felt sorry for me, the way I was being abused by my supposed 'friends'. After all, we'd both gotten betrayed by guys we'd trusted.

Who knows? Hell, maybe Cody and Rudy suddenly got cramps, and the Maiden had nothing to do with it.

Anyway, my little excursion to Lost Lake turned out way better than I ever would've dreamed.

Lois was stupendous.

It's no wonder people like sex so much.

Anyway, I eventually sank Lois and her gear in the lake. I found the canoe she must've come over in, so then I climbed aboard and paddled back to the beach. I took Cody's Cherokee most of the way home.

I wiped it to get rid of fingerprints. Then, for good measure, I set it on fire. I made it home just fine, with a while to spare before dawn.

A Good Cigar is a Smoke

Just before 10:00 p.m. the stench came. Beth shut her eyes and breathed deeply through her mouth, but it wouldn't go away. Bourbon always helped, so she got to her feet, turned off the television, and went into the kitchen.

She took a half-empty bottle from the top of the refrigerator. Her glass, resting upside-down over the bottle's neck, clinked quietly as she returned to the living room. She sat on the couch and put up her feet.

Then, holding the bottle beneath her nose, she twisted off the cap. The bourbon fumes mixed with the terrible odor, masking it.

'Damned cigars,' she muttered into the silence.

Randy had never smoked before their marriage. The smoking started seven months later, on a mild June evening. The Eden Street apartment was windy with blowing fans. Randy came in and tossed his necktie over the back of a chair. His upper lip was moist with sweat when he kissed her.

'How were things at the office?' she asked.

'Hey, we got the Harrison account!'

'Wonderful.'

'Quite a coup.'

'That's just wonderful.'

'And Jim Blake had twins. A boy and a girl.' Smiling and roguishly wiggling his eyebrows, Randy withdrew a pair of cigars from the breast pocket of his shirt. Each cigar was long, as slender as a finger, and brown beneath its cellophane wrapper.

'Twins, huh?' Beth sat on his lap and put an arm around his shoulders. 'We've got a lot of catching up to do.'

'We'd better get started.'

Beth kissed him and whispered, 'Dinner first, before it wilts.'

They ate Crab Louis by candlelight. Afterward, as Beth sipped her coffee, she heard a filmy crinkling sound. She looked up. Randy was peeling the wrapper off a cigar.

'You wouldn't dare,' she said.

'Join me?'

'Are you kidding? I wouldn't *touch* one of those vile . . .' She went silent and her smile withered as Randy's shadowy, distorted face loomed above one of the candles. The flame wavered toward the tip of his cigar. 'Please, Randy, don't. I can't stand the smell of those things.'

The face above the candles, bruised with moving shadows, grinned. Its lips blew smoke toward her. 'Doesn't smell so bad, does it?'

'It smells awful.'

The cuckoo clock began to strike ten, startling Beth from her memories. She watched the plastic bird bow down to 'ku-ku' each of the hours. Then she waited for the tiny Balkan villagers to start their cheerful dance below the clock face. They didn't move. And she remembered. They hadn't danced since the old apartment on Eden Street.

Such a shame. She and Randy had bought the clock in Solvang on their honeymoon – the cuckoo clock and the kerosene lamp they always kept on the bedroom

116

dresser to light when they wanted the room rosy with a romantic glow.

She gripped her glass tightly as the terrible smell seemed to grow stronger. A wave of nausea rolled through her. She gulped down the bourbon, then refilled her glass.

Somehow, she had withstood the stink of Randy's first cigar. 'Thank God you're done with *that*!'

'Hey, these are really great. Quite a revelation. If I'd known how good they are, I'd have—'

'You can't mean it.'

'*Quite* a revelation. Now I know what Kipling was talking about. "A woman is only a woman, but a good cigar is a smoke." That guy knew his stuff.'

'Thanks a bunch.'

Grinning, he opened the cellophane wrapper of the second cigar.

'Randy, don't.'

'It's all right.' He lighted it.

'Please. Put it out.'

'Why?'

'Please? Because I ask you to. The smell makes me sick.'

'You'll get used to it.'

'Will I? Oh, will I? Think so?' She sprang up. Her chair skidded backward and crashed to the floor.

'Elizabeth!'

She slammed the front door behind her.

On the balcony, she gazed through tears at the swimming pool in the courtyard a story below.

Then Randy was behind her, his hand warm on the back of her neck. 'Hey, honey, it's no big deal.'

'No?' She faced him. The cigar was tilted sideways from his mouth. She snatched it away and threw it from the balcony.

117

'*Loo*-kout!' yelled a voice from below. 'What's going on?' Cleo, a downstairs tenant, grinned up at them from the pool's apron. She held a bag of groceries in her arms. 'Trying to burn my supper?' Her husky laugh floated up to them.

'Sorry,' Randy called. Then he clutched Beth's collar, jerked her into the apartment, and kicked the door shut. 'That was quite a display,' he snapped. His open hand smacked her cheek. 'Don't you *ever*' – another slap – 'do *that*' – another slap – 'again.'

That night in bed, he held her gently and said, 'I'm sorry, honey. I shouldn't have hit you. But you shouldn't have taken my cigar. You had no right to do that.' When she began to cry, he cradled her head against the side of his neck and whispered, 'It's all right, honey. Everything's all right.'

'Think so?'

'Sure. Hey, what say we give the Blakes a run for their money?'

'Why not?' Beth said.

To her it was a mourning rite for what was lost.

The awful smell grew stronger. Beth lifted her glass. She stared at the comforter covering the high slope of her belly, then put down the glass without drinking.

Poor kid. He would have enough strikes against him. He didn't need bourbon in his veins before he could even see the light of day.

'Where's dinner?' Randy demanded three weeks and three dozen cigars after the first.

'In the fridge, I guess.'

'What?' He set down his briefcase and stared at her.

'I fixed myself a lamb chop.'

'That'll be fine.'

118

'Nobody's stopping you.'

'Hey, what *is* this?'

'Around here, we eat by seven. It is now nine.'

'So?'

'So I don't know where you've been – and I don't think I want to know – but you weren't here where you belonged. Here with me. It's part of the bargain. If you can't keep your part, you can damn well fix your own supper.'

'That's quite enough. Now, please get me a couple of lamb chops and—'

The front door slammed off his sentence.

Beth went downstairs to Cleo's apartment. The door stood open. 'Don't be bashful, sweetheart.'

Cleo was reclining on a couch, her carrot-colored hair disarrayed. She wore a bright, glossy kimono. The way the clinging fabric showed her body, Beth had little doubt that she wore nothing beneath it.

'If this isn't a good time . . .' she started.

'Hey, it's always a good time for a friendly visit.' Cleo twisted a cigarette into the tip of a long holder. 'You look like a woman with Randy trouble.'

'That's me.' Beth had to smile.

'Well, sit yourself down, sweetheart. I'm all ears.'

'I just don't know what to do,' Beth began.

Cleo listened, often nodding agreement, sometimes shaking her head in sympathy, twice lighting new cigarettes.

'Maybe I should ask him for a divorce,' Beth finally said.

'Mistake, sweetheart. Don't ask. File first, then tell him. Take it from an old hand who's been there and back, don't ask. That is, if a divorce is really what you're after.'

'It's *not*! I want Randy back the old way, the way he used to be. That's what I want. But I guess we can't

119

ever go back . . .' She trailed off, thinking about how good it used to be.

'Might as well bail out then, sweetie. You know what they say about sinking ships? Rats leave first? Let me tell you, it's not just the rats. It's the survivors, too.'

'But I . . .' Beth began to cry.

'Aw, now don't . . .' The ringing telephone interrupted. Cleo said, 'Damn,' and got to her feet.

Beth needed a tissue.

'Hi back, big fella,' she heard Cleo say.

Heading toward the bathroom, Beth passed the bedroom doorway. She glanced inside. On a lamp table beside the bed was a Kleenex dispenser. She went to it and plucked out a tissue. She wiped her eyes and blew her nose . . .

Then she noticed the odor.

A faint lingering smell, bitter and disgusting.

From the wastebasket. She reached inside, pushed aside a wadded tissue, and found the butt of a dead cigar.

She picked it up. It was soggy and cold where his mouth had been.

'I'm sorry, sweetheart.' Cleo stood in the doorway, shaking her head sadly. 'I could tell you it isn't Randy's, but . . .'

Beth shoved past Cleo, ran outside and dashed upstairs to her own apartment. Randy's quiet, hurried voice came from the bedroom. He hung up the extension when he saw her.

'So you know,' he said, gray smoke pouring from his mouth. He was lying on the bed, the telephone resting on his belly, a freshly lit cigar clenched in his teeth.

She flung the wet cigar butt at him. It thumped against the headboard.

'That's quite enough,' he said. 'Knock it off.'

On the dresser was the lamp, the honeymoon lamp from Solvang, its red chimney dusty from disuse. She grabbed it and threw. The glass shattered above Randy's head, splattering kerosene onto his hair. Into his eyes and his open, startled mouth. Onto his shoulders and chest. Onto his cigar.

It made a quiet *whuh!*

Beth's shaking hand lifted the glass to her lips. She held it there, wanting to drink away the foul, wretched odor. But that wouldn't be fair to little Randy. The poor kid would have enough problems: no father, a murdering mother – manslaughter, they'd called it.

The smell of the bourbon helped, but not enough.

Leaning forward, she took a cigar from the box on the lamp table. She tore off the wrapper and wadded it into a ball. The crinkling cellophane sounded like fire.

She struck a match. Soon the cigar was smoldering. Beth sucked and gratefully breathed in the smoke.

Not such an awful odor, really. So much better than the other, the stench of burning flesh.

I'm Not a Criminal

'Of *course* he's not,' Wade said.

'You've gotta give him points for originality,' said Karen.

'Wanta pick him up?'

'Oh, sure.'

They both turned their heads to watch the hitch hiker as they sped past him. He stood motionless by the side of the road. His hair was slicked down by the rain, his cheeks ruddy. The way his dripping poncho bulged behind him, Wade figured he was lugging a backpack. The letters on the wet cardboard sign held at his chest looked as if they'd been printed with a black crayon.

This wasn't the first hitch hiker they'd spotted since embarking on their journey up the California coast four days ago. Nor was this the first carrying a cardboard sign. But the other signs had announced destinations: Crescent City, Eureka, Portland.

Not on this trip, and never before in his life, had Wade seen a hitch hiker bearing a placard that read, 'I'M NOT A CRIMINAL.'

Karen twisted around and peered back. In the rearview mirror, Wade saw the young man resume walking.

'Second thoughts?' he asked.

She faced Wade and smirked. 'Oh, let's rush right back and pick him up. After all, he's not a criminal.'

'That's what he says.'

'And it's gotta be the truth, right? Could anybody actually fall for something like that?'

'He's probably *not* a criminal.' Wade rounded a curve and glanced again at the rearview mirror. All he saw through the rain was empty road bordered by Redwoods. 'Probably a student, or something.'

'Something, all right. Like a serial killer.'

'Whatever he is, he's clever.'

'I don't know about that. The sign's sure an attention-grabber, all right, but the first thing you've gotta think is that it might be a lie. I can't imagine *anybody* being stupid enough to give him a lift.'

'You wouldn't necessarily have to be stupid.'

'No, you might just have a death wish.'

'I can imagine some people taking pity on him. Clean-cut young man stuck out in the rain in the middle of nowhere. A good, decent person might stop for him just to be kind. Or someone lonely might do it for companionship. Or a serial killer who prefers guys.'

Karen chuckled a bit at that one.

The rain came down harder. Wade twisted the knob at the end of the turn signal to speed up the wipers. 'You might even pick him up just out of curiosity. Hell, I'm tempted, myself. Find out what his story is.'

'If you do that, you can let me out and *I'll* hitch-hike.'

'Maybe he'd let you have his sign.'

'I wouldn't need it.' With a grin and a wink, Karen hoisted her skirt a few inches up her thighs.

Wade reached over and stroked her smooth, warm skin.

'That'd be really safe,' he said.

A few minutes later, they followed signs up a side road, paid a woman at a ticket booth, and made their way slowly through the forest to the Chandelier Tree. Though they hadn't seen another car since passing the hitch hiker, there were several here. Lined up. Each waiting its turn to drive through the mammoth Redwood that had a tunnel through its trunk. There were even more cars – maybe twenty or thirty – scattered about the unpaved parking area near the gift shop.

In spite of the rain, people wandered about with cameras and bags of souvenirs.

Wade stopped behind a Porsche. Three cars waited ahead of it while a Mazda rolled into the Redwood.

'Will we fit?' Karen asked.

'Hope so.'

'It'd be neat to get a picture.'

'If we'd picked up "I'm not a criminal", we could've had *him* run out and take a snapshot.'

'He might've run off with the camera.'

'But we'd stay dry.'

'I don't mind. Just try not to crash.' Karen unbuckled, reached between the seatbacks for the camera, then swung open the door and hopped out. The door thumped shut. Hunched over, she rushed for the other side of the tree. The wind blew her long brown hair. Her white blouse looked very bright in the gloom. Her skirt whipped against her legs.

She's getting drenched, Wade thought.

In front of the Porsche, a station wagon tried to enter the tree. Its driver changed his mind, backed out and circled around to the other side. Then a man leaped from the passenger seat of the Porsche and reached inside for a video camcorder. He walked backward into the trunk, taping while his friend steered.

Finally, Wade eased his Cherokee forward.

Gonna be a tight squeeze.

When his front bumper entered the gap, he stopped. No more than a couple of inches to spare on each side.

Great.

A good chance I'll knock off the mirrors.

Squinting through the rain-splashed windshield, he saw Karen step into the light at the far end of the tunnel. Her hair was matted flat. She raised the camera to her face, then lowered it and gestured for him to come ahead.

Wade shook his head.

Frowning, she called out something he couldn't hear.

It's not worth the risk, he thought. They'd been driving a heap for years. Even their arrogant mechanic had enjoyed referring to it as 'the junk'. Only two weeks ago, after the advance from his English publisher had finally arrived and cleared the bank, were they finally able to buy their bright new Jeep Cherokee.

I'm not gonna bash it up trying to drive through a goddamn Redwood tree.

He checked the rearview mirror. The car behind him was a safe distance away. He shifted into reverse.

Karen, a look of annoyance on her face, waved him forward.

With a final shake of his head, he slowly backed clear of the tree. He turned out, then steered around the trunk. Karen came rushing up to the passenger door, yanked it open and jumped in.

'Jesus, Wade!'

'I couldn't have made it.'

'You had *plenty* of room.'

'No, I didn't.'

'Yes, you did. Jesus! *I* should've driven. I'm soaked to the bone and you didn't even *do* it!'

He crossed the parking area and stopped. 'Do you want to try? Feel free. I'll take the pictures.'

'Never mind. There's no point in *both* of us getting drenched. God, you're such a wuss sometimes.'

125

'I just didn't want to wreck the car.'

'You had plenty of room. Why did we buy the Jeep anyway if you're scared of *doing* things with it? The whole idea was to have fun with it. God, where's your sense of adventure?'

'It's no great adventure driving through a hole in a tree. But if it means that much to you, I'll go ahead and do it. Or you can. It's not worth fighting about.'

'It wouldn't be any fun now, anyway.'

Women, he thought.

Deciding it was long past time to change the subject, he said, 'Why don't we check out the gift shop?'

'Oh, that's a terrific idea. We can pick up mementos of the drive-through Redwood you wouldn't drive through.'

'Come on, honey. They've probably got some neat stuff.'

'You hate gift shops.'

'I'll make the sacrifice for you.'

A corner of her mouth turned up . . . Almost a smile. 'Let's just get going,' she said. 'There'll be plenty of other gift shops.'

'You're telling me.'

'I can't go inside anyplace looking like this, anyway.'

The pink of her skin and the white of her bra showed through her clinging blouse.

'Maybe you should get out of those wet clothes.'

'In your dreams, buster.'

But moments after their return to the main road, she asked Wade to pull over. He stopped on the muddy shoulder. Karen climbed out and got into the backseat. Wade twisted around to watch her. Kneeling on the cushion, she reached into the luggage area and unzipped her suitcase. She pulled out a towel and rubbed her hair.

126

'You can get moving again.'

'Oh, that's all right.'

'Then don't just stare at me. Keep an eye out for cars.' She dug into the suitcase, pulled out a sweatshirt, then took off her blouse and bra. She rubbed herself with the towel.

'Shouldn't you turn around to do that?'

'Ha ha ha.'

Hearing a faint engine noise, Wade faced the front. A logging truck came around a bend. 'Better cover up.' As the truck rumbled closer, he checked on Karen. She was bare-backed, holding the open towel against her breasts.

Their car shook as the truck roared by with its load of three huge Redwood trunks. Its horn blasted out a few quick toots.

'Guess he liked what he saw.'

'He didn't see anything,' Karen said.

She dropped the towel to the seat and shook open her sweatshirt and Wade saw a man through the rear window. Walking toward them, but still thirty or forty feet away. The man carried a cardboard sign.

'Company.'

'Shit!'

Karen ducked. Wade stepped on the gas pedal. The Jeep lurched forward, bouncing over the rough ground for a moment before its wheels got onto the pavement.

In the rearview, he saw Karen peer over the seatback.

'It's him,' she said.

'"I'm not a criminal"?'

'I hope he didn't see me.'

'I'm sure he didn't.'

In seconds, the hitch hiker was out of sight.

Karen struggled into her sweatshirt. She caught Wade watching the mirror. 'Keep your eyes on the road.'

He obeyed. For a while. When he glanced through the gap between the seats, she was facing forward, bent over and pulling a pair of skimpy black panties up her legs.

'*Wade!*'

'What?'

'Don't be a jerk.'

'Just looking.'

'Don't trouble yourself. You might crash your precious Jeep.'

He forced a smile, then turned away. 'This is the thanks I get for saving you from the clutches of "I'm not a criminal"?'

'If you'd been keeping a proper lookout, he never would've gotten that close.'

'Maybe I should've just waited for him. I'm sure he'd appreciate a lift. And he wouldn't be giving me a lot of grief because I committed the horrible sin of not driving my car through a fucking *tree*.'

'No, I'm sure he wouldn't. He'd be too busy cutting our throats.'

'You're so hot for adventure, you might enjoy it.'

She didn't say anything to that. Wade heard only the quiet rhythm of his wipers, the patter of raindrops on the roof, the hiss of his tires on the wet pavement.

Great. Now she's pouting. Giving me the famous silent treatment.

After a while, he looked back. She was wearing blue jeans. One knee was raised as she pulled a fresh sock onto her foot. She gave him a sullen, bitter glance. He turned away.

'Are you planning to stay back there?' he asked.

She didn't answer.

'Geez, what did I do? I didn't drive through a tree. I'm sorry, all right? Are you going to screw up the whole day pouting about it?'

'I'm not pouting.'

'That's a good one.'

'How am I supposed to get into the front seat without getting wet?'

She could squeeze through the space between the backs of the bucket seats. An awkward maneuver, but it could be done. If she wanted to. Obviously, she preferred staying in the back, away from the wuss.

Wade drove on in silence. More than an hour passed before his stomach began to grumble. He looked back. Karen was slumped in the seat, her eyes shut.

He hoped she was asleep. Maybe she would wake up in a better mood.

There was no point in disturbing her right now, anyway. They'd been eating picnic lunches during the trip, but they certainly wouldn't be doing that today. Not with the rain pouring down. And he didn't much like the idea of eating in the car.

We'll just wait, he decided. There's bound to be a restaurant sooner or later.

Half an hour later, he came to an area with pullouts on both sides of the road, cars and vans and RVs parked near various gift shops, a gas station, a general store and the Big Trees Cafe.

As Wade swung onto the gravel in front of the cafe, Karen's groggy voice asked, 'What're we doing?'

'I thought we might stop for lunch. Are you hungry?'

'I guess so.'

'We could eat in the car if you don't want to get out in the rain, but . . .'

'No, this is fine.'

No argument. Not even a hint of annoyance in her voice. Maybe things are all right now.

Wade felt optimistic as he parked the Jeep. They both leaped out and ran through the rain. They met

129

beneath the roof of the cafe's porch, and walked side by side to the entrance.

Though the place wasn't crowded, they chose to sit at the counter so they could watch the cook in action. He wore a floppy chef's cap. He whistled 'Listen to the Mockingbird.' He was a master of the spatula. Karen seemed to get a kick out of the show he put on.

They drank Pepsi, ate cheeseburgers, and shared an order of chili fries.

They didn't talk much. Wade knew she was still annoyed with him, but at least she was making an effort to act friendly.

He let her eat most of the chili fries.

By the time they left the cafe, the rain had stopped. The heavy clouds were off to the east, letting the sun glare down.

They crossed the road. They explored a gift shop. Karen picked out a refrigerator magnet and a Christmas tree ornament, both depicting Redwoods. She kept eyeing a vase made of polished Redwood burl. It cost sixty bucks, but Wade insisted they buy it.

On their way back to the Jeep, Wade said, 'I'll bet Reagan had just finished a trip like this when he made his infamous comment.'

'"You've seen one Redwood tree, you've seen them all"?'

'Yeah. Puts it in a different light, I think.'

Karen laughed and nudged him with her elbow.

We're almost back to normal, Wade thought.

He opened the door for her.

They were on the road less than five minutes when they spotted a hitch hiker, a young man striding along under the weight of a backpack.

He didn't wear a blue poncho, so Wade assumed he wasn't 'their' hitch hiker.

Then the man turned to face them, smiled, and raised his 'I'm not a criminal' sign.

'My God,' Karen said. 'I don't believe it. How the hell did he get *ahead* of us?'

'Obviously, he got a lift.'

They sped past him.

Wade eased off the accelerator. 'I guess the guy's not a criminal, after all.'

'What makes you think so?'

'Elementary, my dear Karen. Someone gave him a ride, and now he's on foot again. Which means he didn't slit their throats and steal their car. Should we stop for him?'

'Are you kidding?'

He slowed the Jeep and eased it off the edge of the road.

'Wade. Come on.'

'Chicken?' *Now* who's the wuss? he thought, and smiled.

'We *never* pick up hitch hikers.'

'This will be the exception. Hey, consider it an adventure.'

In the rearview, he saw the young man jogging toward them.

'It's not a good idea.'

'He's proven he's not a criminal,' Wade explained. 'But he's gotta be an interesting character. And this *is* supposed to be a research trip, you know. I'd bet anything I'll get a story out of him.'

'Jesus,' Karen muttered.

The door behind her swung open. The stranger stuck his head inside. He had a friendly, boyish smile. Wade doubted that he was much older then eighteen.

'Can you use a lift?'

'Thanks. Sure can.' He shoved his pack across the

backseat, climbed in after it with his cardboard sign, and shut the door.

Wade checked for traffic, waited for an RV to pass, then steered onto the road. Karen was sitting up very straight, very stiff, face forward, hands gripping her thighs.

She probably thinks I did this to get back at her, Wade thought.

He smiled at the young man. 'We don't usually pick up hitch hikers.'

'Well, I sure appreciate it.'

'That's quite a sign you've got.'

'"I'm not a criminal"? Yeah, it works real fine for me. The way I see it, you know, most people are pretty good-hearted and the only reason they don't stop for a fellow is because they're scared. And I don't blame them. Not a bit. I mean, they don't know me. They're scared I might be one of those homicidal maniacs you're always hearing about. So I figure if I put their minds at ease on that score, maybe they'll give me a try.'

'It sure caught our interest,' Wade told him. 'Let's say we were *intrigued*. But we didn't necessarily believe it. In fact, it made us think you actually *might* be a criminal.'

'Then how come you stopped for me?'

'Well, we didn't. Not at first. But you obviously got a ride with someone after that, because you managed to get ahead of us while we were stopped for lunch.'

'Ah.'

'That convinced us that your sign wasn't a . . . fabrication.'

'Those folks were only going up to some diner back there.'

Wade grinned at the cheerful face in the rearview. 'The way we saw it, you would've taken *their* car if

132

you were the type who does away with people who stop for you.'

A soft laugh came from the backseat. 'Glad I didn't, then. But they were a couple of old farts driving a goddamn piece of junk. Now, if they'd been tooling along in a brand new Cherokee and one of them had been a juicy babe . . . might've turned out different.'

Wade's bowels went ice cold.

'Oh, Jesus,' Karen murmured.

'This is my lucky day, huh?' Leaning forward, he reached through the space between the seats and scraped the blade of a pocket knife against Wade's neck. 'My name's Chip. And you are?'

'Wade.'

The blade went away. With the back of his hand, Chip caressed Karen's cheek. 'And you?'

'Karen,' she murmured. She was staring straight ahead. She was squeezing her legs. Wade could see her shaking.

'You can have the car,' Wade blurted. 'Just let us out, okay?'

'Oh, I don't think so.'

'Come on, man. We picked you up, for godsake.'

'Big mistake, Wade. Not a bright move.' He prodded Wade's shoulder with the knife point, but not hard enough to hurt. 'You should've known better. Just asking for trouble, you pick up a stranger.' He laughed. 'You two apparently don't believe in playing safe. Look at you, not even wearing your seatbelts. Put them on now, why don't you? Come on, buckle up for safety.'

Buckle up so we can't jump out and run for it, Wade thought.

Karen reached over her shoulder. She pulled the harness down across her chest and lap. She tried to latch it. Her hand was shaking too much. Chip took hold of her hand and guided the buckle down onto the steel tongue.

Wade wondered what he'd done with the knife.

Probably just switched it into his left hand.

'Don't you feel a whole lot safer now?' Chip asked. 'How about you, Wadeboy? What are you waiting for?'

Wade drew down his harness and latched it.

'Now all we need is a little privacy. Once the party starts, we wouldn't want any interruptions. Let's find a nice, secluded road.' He let go of Karen's hand. Then he stretched forward, knocked the rearview mirror upward, and dropped back out of sight. 'I'll tell you when to turn,' he said.

Karen looked at Wade. Her eyes were frantic.

I'm sorry, he thought. God, I'm sorry.

This can't be happening. Not to us.

There must be a way out!

Two of us, only one of him. But we're strapped in, and he's behind us and he's got the knife.

As soon as we stop, he'll slit my throat.

Then it'll be just him and Karen.

Wade felt like throwing up.

'Okay. Coming up on the right. Take it.'

Wade saw a narrow road ahead. He checked the rearview mirror. It showed only ceiling. He glanced at the side mirrors and saw a logging truck. It seemed to be about a hundred yards behind them. But he wasn't used to side mirrors, didn't trust them, so he looked over his shoulder.

Chip, in the backseat, had the pocket knife clenched between his teeth. His shirt was gone. With both hands, he was pulling down his jeans. He didn't have underwear on.

He grinned around the knife. Then he plucked it from his teeth. 'Don't miss the turn, pal.'

134

Wade twisted around, hit the brake and swung onto the one-lane road. Its asphalt surface was rough with ridges and potholes. He drove slowly, hands tight on the wheel.

'We'll find a nice, sunny clearing,' Chip said.

That'll be a good trick, Wade thought. Redwoods pressed in close on both sides. Only a few specks and strips of sunlight found their way down to the road.

When we do come to a clearing, he knew, that'll be it.

The bastard's already naked. So he won't get blood on his clothes. So he'll be all ready for what he plans with Karen.

Why is this happening to us?

Because I wouldn't drive through the goddamn Redwood tree, that's why. Triggered the whole thing. If only . . .

Chip leaned forward. His left arm appeared between the seats. He squeezed Karen's breast. She gasped, grabbed his wrist and shoved his hand away.

'Let go,' he told her, his voice calm.

'Damn it!' Wade blurted. 'Leave her alone!'

'Let's have some cooperation here, folks. You don't want to piss me off, do you?'

'You're gonna kill us anyway,' Karen said.

'Not if I have a really good time.'

'Yeah, sure,' she said, but she released his wrist.

'Very good.' He dragged her sweatshirt up until it was bunched above her breasts, the bulk of fabric mashed flat in the middle by the safety harness. He leaned forward for a view. 'Nice,' he said. 'Very nice.' He curled his hand beneath her left breast.

The breast, bouncing with the motions of the car, slapped softly against his open hand.

Karen began to sob.

'You bastard,' Wade said.

135

As if to punish Wade for the remark, he pinched Karen's nipple. She yelped and flinched and jerked his hand away.

'Let go!' Chip snapped.

'No!'

'I'll cut off your fuckin' tits and make you eat 'em!'

She let go.

He squeezed her breast. Karen squealed.

The engine roared as Wade punched the gas pedal to the floor.

'Slow down, you . . . !'

He jerked the wheel. The Jeep swerved toward the broad trunk of a Redwood.

'Shit!' Chip yelled.

Then the Jeep slammed the trunk, hurling Wade hard against his safety harness, throwing Chip forward between the seatbacks and crashing his head against the windshield. The glass didn't break. Chip's head rebounded off it. He dropped limp across the control console.

Wade and Karen sat motionless, looking down at him. Karen gasped out quiet whimpery sounds.

After a while, Wade realized the engine was still roaring. He took his foot off the gas pedal. He looked toward the front. The left side of the Jeep was crushed against the tree, but he saw no steam or smoke rising from under the hood. He turned off the engine.

'It wasn't exactly a drive-through Redwood,' he said.

Karen said nothing. She was gently rubbing her left breast as she stared down at the body. Her eyes were red and wet. Her nose was running. She sniffed.

'Are you all right?' Wade asked.

She shook her head a bit from side to side, and muttered, 'He's . . . naked.'

'Yeah.'

'God.' She pulled her sweatshirt down.

Wade unfastened his seatbelt. Twisting sideways, he grabbed Chip's bare shoulders, lifted and shoved.

Chip fell in a slump into the backseat, head drooping. His hair was matted with blood. His face was shiny red. Bloody drool hung in strings from his open mouth. Blood dripped from his face, splashed his chest and trickled down.

Karen, free of her harness, looked around at the body. 'Is he dead?'

'I don't know. But he's gonna get blood all over the upholstery.'

Wade didn't think that was funny, but apparently Karen did. She let out a strange, high laugh.

'I'm getting him out of here.'

Wade climbed out, opened the back door, tossed the pack to the ground, then leaned inside and dragged Chip from the car.

Chip groaned when his head bumped the earth.

'Was that him?' Karen asked from inside.

'Yeah.'

'Good.'

Wade didn't know what was so good about it. The groan meant Chip was still alive, probably meant he was regaining consciousness. What could possibly be good about *that*?

He looked up and saw Karen crawling across the front seats. Hair hung in front of her eyes. Her chin was thrust forward, the edges of her lower teeth against her upper lip. Her sweatshirt drooped away from her body. Through its loose neck hole, he could see her breasts swaying.

She looked . . . wild.

Wade felt a sudden hot surge in his groin.

He half expected her to spring down from the Jeep

137

on all fours like a panther. But she didn't do that. She grabbed the steering wheel and knelt on the driver's seat and came out feet first. Wade gripped her forearm and helped her down.

He wanted to pull her against him. For starters.

That's crazy, he told himself. We've got a maniac here.

They turned to Chip. He was sprawled motionless on his back, head to one side. His eyes were shut. The lids had blood on them. His chest rose and fell slightly, its bright red dribbles shimmering in the sunlight.

Karen stepped close to his side.

'He might be playing possum,' Wade warned.

As if to test that theory, Karen nudged his hip with the toe of her sneaker. He shook a little. His penis, limp against his thigh, wobbled.

'We'd better tie him up, or something,' Wade suggested.

'Or something,' Karen muttered. She lifted her sweatshirt, pulled it up over her head, and started folding it.

'What are you doing?' Wade asked. He felt light-headed, breathless.

'Don't want to ruin my clothes,' she answered. She carried her sweatshirt to the Jeep and tossed it onto the driver's seat. She shut the back door. Rump against it, she started taking off her shoes and socks. She kept her eyes on Chip.

'You're . . . taking off everything?'

'You, too.'

'Jeez.'

'He wanted a party. That's what he's going to get.'

Wade shook his head. He didn't understand. But watching Karen pull down her skirt and panties was like watching a stranger – a very exotic, exciting

138

stranger. He wanted very much to please her. He wanted to have her.

She's my *wife* for godsake. She's Karen.

But she hardly seemed like Karen, at all.

Wade began to take off his clothes.

He glanced at Chip, who still appeared to be unconscious. Then he watched Karen open the back door and crawl onto the rear seat. Her buttocks looked pink and smooth. When she reached down to the floor, he could see the folds between her legs and he wanted to hurry over to her and mount her and thrust himself in.

Chip moaned again.

Wade whirled around.

The guy's eyes were squeezed shut as if trying to pinch out the pain in his head. But he wasn't moving.

Karen came up beside Wade. In her hand was Chip's pocket knife.

'Use your belt,' she said. Her voice was low and husky. 'Bind his feet.'

Wade crouched over his jeans and pulled his belt from the loops.

This is too far out, he thought. This is wild. What the hell is she up to?

Every muscle in his body seemed to be trembling as he knelt at Chip's feet, pulled at them to straighten the legs, and wrapped his belt around the ankles.

He hadn't been shaking like this, he realized, even when Chip had been holding the knife to his throat. His heart hadn't been thundering like this, either. Nor had he been so breathless. He most certainly hadn't felt any sexual arousal, much less this incredible hard-on.

He'd *never* felt this way before.

When he finished strapping Chip's ankles together, Karen said, 'Go to the other end and grab his hands.'

He scurried past the body, knelt at Chip's head and leaned forward, pinning his wrists to the ground.

And watched Karen.

Watched her straddle Chip, watched her squat, watched her sit down on his pelvis.

Her skin was flushed. It was shiny with sweat. Her left breast looked as if it had been scorched by a hot glove.

She leaned forward. The knife was in her right hand. With her left hand, she slapped Chip's face. The sweep of her arm made her breasts lurch. The impact rocked Chip's head and splashed out a spray of blood and spittle. He groaned. One of his eyes opened. Then the other. He blinked up at her.

'It's your party,' she said. 'Are you having fun yet?'

He squirmed a bit. He made a feeble effort to move his hands, but Wade had no trouble keeping them down.

'This is pretty much what you had in mind, isn't it, Chip? A get-naked-and-fool-around kinda party? In a nice, sunny clearing in the woods? Wishes *can* come true.'

She grinned down at Chip.

'Do you still feel up to cutting my tits off? Making me eat them?'

His lips moved, but no words came out.

'Is that a yes or a no, Chipper?' She cupped the underside of her left breast. She slowly scraped the top of it with the blunt edge of the knife. Wade saw goosebumps rise on her skin. The blade slid down over the front. Her nipple bent beneath it, then sprang up. 'Wanta slice it off for me?' she whispered.

'No.' The word came out quiet and whiny.

'How about fucking me? Huh?' Her hips shifted. She was rubbing herself against him.

140

Wade wondered vaguely if he ought to feel jealous about that. But all he felt was excited. As if she were doing it to him.

Chip's face contorted, and he started to sob as he shook his head from side to side.

'Isn't that what it's all about, really?' Karen asked. 'Fucking me? Torturing me and fucking me and killing me?'

'Don' hurt me!' he blurted. 'Please.'

'Not even to mention killing Wade, huh? Just to get him out of the way.'

Wade felt strangely pleased that she had remembered that aspect of the situation.

'I . . . I wasn't gonna . . . hurt anyone.'

'Oh, we know. We know that. You're not a criminal.'

'*Please.*'

'You just wanted to have a little party, didn't you?'

'Y . . . yeah.'

'I like parties. Do you know what I like to do at parties?'

He shook his head wildly. He didn't know. He didn't want to know.

'I like to have a *drink*,' Karen said, and swept the knife across his throat. Her breasts lurched, just as when she'd slapped him. Then blood shot up and splashed them and splashed her face and she leaned into the geyser with her mouth.

Chip gurgled and thrashed. He jerked one hand from Wade's grip, but didn't go for Karen with it. Instead, he clutched his throat. The hand didn't stop the blood, just made it fly in different directions.

Karen, sheathed in blood, sank down on top of him and scurried backward.

Scurried until her face was between his thighs.

Her eyes looked very white in the red mask of her

141

face. 'I like to drink at parties,' she said. 'And I like to eat chips.'

She chomped.

By the time Wade was done with Karen, he was bloody all over.

They went to the stream and washed off.

Then they got dressed and climbed into the Jeep. Karen tossed the 'I'm not a criminal' sign out the window.

The Jeep, though bashed up a bit in front, seemed to work fine.

They drove back to the main road.

'This is turning out to be quite a vacation,' Wade said.

Karen reached over and squeezed his thigh.

Soon, they came upon a hitch hiker. He was a young man with a beard. He walked backward along the roadside, watching their approach. He carried a sign that read, 'Coos Bay.'

Wade and Karen looked at each other.

Oscar's Audition

I came out of the Blue Light Bar just short of midnight with a head that felt like it'd run into the business end of a buzz saw. The fresh air helped. I fired up a cigar, zipped my coat, and was starting to feel like a human being when I rounded a corner and walked into a fight.

Three on one.

Since the single guy was a shrimp and didn't have command of judo, Karate, Kung Fu or sprint, he was getting trounced.

'Knock it off, guys!' I shouted.

They tried, but the shrimp's neck was stronger than it looked.

I walked right up to the scuffling quartet, took a long draw on my cigar, and tapped the ash off. A big, meaty character was holding the shrimp's arms. He let go as soon as he felt the hot end of my cigar inside his ear. He also screamed.

His buddies got indignant. One lunged at me, bellowing like a maniac. I almost lost my glasses as I deflated him with a knee. The other guy pulled out an eight-inch blade, and grinned. I pulled out a .357 magnum, and grinned bigger. He was smart enough to run like hell. His buddies joined him.

The shrimp, who'd been sitting on the sidewalk in the middle of everything, smiled up at me thankfully. He didn't smile too well, though – only half his face was working right.

I touched my head to make sure my new rug was still in place. The thing took some getting used to. 'Want an ambulance?' I asked.

'Nah, I'm okay.'

He probably was, too. These young people heal up so fast they're good as new before they know they've been hurt.

I holstered my magnum, reached down, and helped the shrimp to his feet. While I still had a grip on his hand, I introduced myself. 'The name's Clare,' I said. Just like I thought, the shrimp gave a lopsided grin. A real funny name, Clare. I gave his hand a bone-crusher. 'Something amusing?'

'Nothing,' he gasped. 'Not a thing.' His voice had the tight, choky sound you get when you talk and groan at the same time.

'What's your name?' I asked, not letting go of his hand.

'Oscar.'

'Aren't you gonna thank me, Oscar, for saving your tail?'

'Sure, sure. Thanks, Clare.'

'Sure.'

He looked plenty thankful when I finally let go of his hand.

I wasn't happy about returning to the Blue Light Bar. Awful booze, too much noise and smoke, and a couple of topless dancers that kept looking up at the ceiling. They hoped it would fall in, I think, to relieve their boredom. But what the hell – I had business to conduct, and the Blue Light was handy.

I wiped the steam off my glasses as Oscar and me walked to a corner table. It was a stubby little table, made so lovers can sit close and play kneesies. I didn't love Oscar the shrimp, so I stretched my legs out sideways. When the barmaid came with our beers, I pulled in. Once she was gone, I stuck them out again.

'How long have you been out?' I asked.

'Huh? What d'ya mean?'

'Outside the joint. You just got your walking papers, it's written all over you.'

His eyes narrowed. One did, anyway. The other was puffed up and shiny, and already as narrow as it could get. 'Are you a cop?' he asked.

'Not hardly.'

'Then why're you carrying?'

'Makes me feel good,' I said, and took a swallow of beer. It had a sour taste. 'You oughta be glad I do, pal. If I'd been clean when I saw those three jerks follow you outa here, I might've let them have you.'

'Why'd you help me, anyway?'

''Cause I got a heart of gold. Also, 'cause I got a good eye, and my good eye tells me that you're the kind of guy I'm looking for. Now, how long you been out?'

'Two days. After nine big ones at Q.'

'I called Soledad home for twelve. But that was a long time back – the only time they ever made one stick.'

'Yeah?' His good eye looked plenty interested.

'That's right. What'd they get you on?'

'They said I put it to some chick.'

'What, rape?'

'That's what *they* called it.'

'Is that what *you* call it?'

'Hell, no. What d'ya think, I gotta rape some chick to get what I want? She was willing and eager.'

'Eager, huh? And they shipped you off to Q for nine years?'

'So I had a knife. Big deal.'

'Cut her?'

'No way!' He looked insulted.

'Why not? You ever see the DA put a corpse on the stand?'

'Hey, man, you're talking Murder One. That's not for me. No thanks.'

'So you've never iced anyone?'

'Me? Hey, not a chance.'

I grinned through my cigar and said, 'That's good, Oscar. I don't like working with guys that might change a simple armed robbery into murder.'

'What're you talking about?' His voice sounded suspicious, but real interested.

'Maybe I can use you.'

'What for?' He leaned forward. He back-handed some beer foam off his upper lip and folded his arms on the table. The centerpiece, a candle with a red chimney, made Oscar's swollen face look wet and sticky.

'Ever knock over a liquor store?' I asked.

'Maybe.'

'We'll hit one together,' I said. 'Call it an audition. I want to see how you handle yourself. If you do good, maybe I'll let you in on something bigger.'

'Yeah? Like what, for instance?'

'Something bigger,' I said again, and took a long time sucking on my cigar. Oscar spent the time staring at me. He looked like he might be thinking, or maybe just trying to remember how many green ones he'd seen in his billfold the last time he looked. He finally nodded. 'Meet me here tomorrow night at ten,' I said. 'I'll bring you a clean piece.'

'What about wheels?'

'I'll take care of it. I'll take care of everything, Oscar, my friend.'

* * *

The next night, Oscar showed up at the Blue Light on time. 'That's a point in your favor,' I told him, and lit up a cigar to mask the cigarette stench of the place.

'If I'm one thing, I'm prompt.' He grinned proudly with the working half of his face. Over night, the broken half had turned purple.

'It's good in this business, being prompt. But it's even better being something else.'

'Like what?' he asked.

'Like obedient.'

'Sure, sure. I'll do whatever you say. I mean, you know, as long as . . .'

'Let's get going.'

Oscar wasn't overly impressed by the '68 Buick out front. We got into it anyway, and I pulled onto the street. 'Don't worry,' I said, 'your girlfriend won't see you in it. The thing's hotter than a hundred-watt bulb. We'll dump it two minutes after we hit the store.'

'What girlfriend? I haven't got a girlfriend.'

'Not even what's-her-face? Old Willing and Eager?'

'Her? After what she done to me? You gotta be kidding.'

'Yeah. Which reminds me. If there's a chick in the store, don't touch her. This is business, understand?'

'Sure.'

'See that sack on the floor? Take the stuff out of it.'

He picked up the cloth bag and took out a snub-nosed .38.

'A mean-lookin' sucker, isn't it?' I asked.

'Wicked.'

'That's the point. If you scare them bad enough, you won't have to shoot. And you'd better *not* shoot, Oscar. This is for peanuts, remember that. Anyone gets hurt, it's your tail. Understand?'

'Sure,' he muttered. He was plenty scared. He set the revolver down on his lap and grabbed a deep breath. Then he pulled a wool ski mask out of the sack, then a pair of rubber gloves.

'We're almost there. When you get inside, stick the muzzle up the owner's nose. Make him empty his cash register into the bag. There won't be much. They empty the register all the time into a floor safe. Don't worry about what's in the safe. We just want the ready cash. We're not greedy. Like I said, it's your audition. The bigger stuff's for later, if everything goes smooth.'

'Sure.'

'I'll wait for you in the car.'

'Hey!' He didn't like that. Not a bit.

'Yeah?' I asked.

'I mean, aren't . . . ? What if there's customers or something? You want me to go in there alone? Is that it? Geez! I don't know, man.'

'Okay,' I said. 'It's off. Easy as that.'

'I mean . . .'

'I know what you mean. You don't want to go in there alone. Fine. Fine and dandy. So you're not the kind of guy I need. You're a real hot-shot with a knife and a woman, but when it comes to a .38 and hard cash, you turn into cold spaghetti.' I pulled over to the curb. 'You can get out.'

'Now wait. Just a minute . . .'

'Forget it. I thought I was a good judge of character. I saw you lapping up brew in the Blue Light and I said to myself, "This guy's fresh outa the joint and has enough guts to get into something big." So I followed you out and gave you a hand with those mugs. So I wasted my time. Get outa my car.'

'WAIT JUST A GODDAMN MINUTE!'

'Yeah?'

'I'll do it.'

'Yeah?'

'I will. I'll do it. Take me to the store, you'll see.'

I grinned real big. 'I don't have to take you there, Oscar, my friend.' I aimed my finger at a neon sign halfway up the block. It read, 'Barney's Liquor.'

'That's it?'

'That's it.'

'Okay.' He was breathing real hard while he pulled the gloves on.

'You can walk from here. Don't put on the mask till you're ready to step inside.'

'Sure.'

'Once you're in, I'll pull up in front of the place. I'll have the door open for you when you come out. Just climb in, and we're off like a shot. My own car's parked six blocks from here. We'll pile into it, and we're home free.'

'Sure. Sounds okay.'

'Remember what I said about plugging someone.'

'Yeah.' He nodded with quick, nervous jerks.

'Go.'

'Right.' He nodded some more, like a goddamn woodpecker whacking at concrete.

'Now!'

He threw open the door, bailed out, and went rushing up the sidewalk real fast, like he wanted to get it over with before his guts melted. At the store's entrance, he stopped long enough to pull the ski mask over his head. Then he charged inside.

I didn't pull up to the door. Nope. Instead, I climbed out of my trusty Buick and headed for the door on foot. Real slow. Taking off my glasses so I could see better. Unzipping my coat.

I was thirty feet from the entrance when two things

149

happened: a gal in a yellow windbreaker stepped out of a doorway in front of me, and Oscar backed out of the store with the money bag in one fist and the pistol in the other.

'Out of the way!' I gasped, grabbing for my cannon. The gal jumped sideways and crouched in the doorway. 'Hold it!' I yelled at Oscar.

He swung around, snapping off a couple of shots. With a snub-nose, most guys can't shoot their way out of a wet popsickle bag. Oscar wasn't an exception. His bullets hit nothing but air.

I fingered my trigger. The piece jumped. Through the tail end of its roar, I heard my slug thump Oscar. Before he went down, I put a second one on top of it. Then I ran toward him.

Barney O'Hara, the liquor-store owner, got to the body at the same time as me. Our eyes met. 'Clare?'

'Hi, Barn.'

'I didn't recognize you. New hair, huh?' He shook his own bald head, grinning. 'Say, I guess I owe you for this one.'

'You owe me nothing, pal. Pay your debt to Lady Luck. I was just dropping by for a six-pack.' I reached down and pulled the ski mask off Oscar. Then I muttered, 'My God, I don't believe it!'

'What's a trouble?' Barney asked.

'This guy . . . It's Oscar Morton. I'd heard he was in town, but . . .' I shook my head, trying to look confused and shocked.

'So who's Oscar Morton?'

'The guy that raped Peggy.'

'Peggy? Your kid, Peggy? *Cheese-Louise*, talk about Lady Luck!'

'Luck, nothing,' I said. 'I've got some mighty fancy explaining to do. The shooting board's gonna ride my tail like . . .'

Barney clapped me on the shoulder. 'Hell. That was a righteous shoot if I ever saw one. You—'

'Shouldn't somebody call the police?' asked the gal in the yellow windbreaker.

I flashed her my shield.

Into the Pit

1.

In the year 1926, William Brook's father traveled to Egypt for the purpose of lending his expert assistance to the famed Howard Carter, who had recently unearthed the tomb of the child king, Tutankhamen. William accompanied his father on that journey.

In Luxor, they met Mr Carter. He welcomed William's father heartily, for they had worked together several years earlier with Theodore Davis at the tomb of Mentuhotep I. He was not so enthusiastic, however, about the presence of William. He must have felt that a youth of eighteen years, no matter how mature, would prove a hindrance. William was pleased to note that Mr Carter's attitude in this matter changed remarkably once he saw how the young man aided his father in the intricate details of the work. His copious, exact notes soon earned the archaeologist's respect.

It was his bravery, however, that won the respect of the Egyptian youth, Maged. They met on a December night. Suffering from the oppressive heat, William had wandered beyond the boundaries of the encampment in hopes of chancing upon a stray breeze. He longed for the winters of his Wisconsin childhood: to be sledding down a slope, a chill wind battering his face, snowflakes blowing, the night lit by a full moon. He was near weeping with frustration when suddenly an urgent cry startled him.

Never one to flee in the face of a crisis, he rushed forward and discovered half a dozen youths engaged in beating a young fellow senseless. He attacked. In the brief affray that followed, he struck several telling blows on the bullies and sent them scurrying for safety.

The victim introduced himself as Maged, using passable English. (His father, William later learned, had served with the British during the Great War.) He offered William his gratitude and his friendship.

At first, he explained that the boys had fallen upon him for the purpose of committing robbery. After the friendship had grown, however, he finally confided in William. It seems that Maged, no innocent victim, had made vile suggestions to the sister of one of the boys. When she refused him, the young Maged had shown his hostility by defecating on the family's doorstep. The brother, together with several friends, had reacted with violence.

Over the weeks, Maged proved to be an invaluable companion. The little Egyptian led William about in the night. They fought his enemies. They drank stolen raki. On regular occasions, they whiled away the nights in the arms of tawny, lusting women who showed William delights he had never known.

On a warm January night, after saying goodnight to his father, William met Maged at their usual rendezvous point. From there, they traveled a long distance on foot until they reached a village of mud huts. In one of these, Maged assured him, they would find a pair of twin sisters whose beauty and sexual talents would spoil him for all other women.

William waited outside while Maged entered one of the huts to fetch them. Soon, the Egyptian reappeared.

153

The two girls behind him were beautiful indeed, though no older than sixteen. For long moments, William stared at them in the moonlight, struck with awe. He greeted them in Arabic. They smiled lasciviously, but spoke not a word. Maged quickly informed him that they were deaf-mutes. At first, William was troubled by this revelation. He soothed his conscience, however, by reminding himself that the five piasters (amounting to twenty-five cents) he intended to pay the girls was a handsome amount for such peasants. The fellahin who worked at the tomb, after all, received only three piasters for an entire day's labor.

Taking the hand of one girl, William followed Maged into the desert beyond the village. There, they spread blankets on the earth. The girls disrobed. William was ready to take his at once, but Maged restrained him and indicated that he should be seated.

The girls stepped away from the young men. With olive oil cupped in their hands, they caressed one another until their skin had a glossy sheen in the moonlight. Then they danced.

Never had William seen such a dance. He watched the flow of their bodies moving as if to a wonderfully haunting, erotic melody. But there was no music. The only sound was the distant barking of pariah dogs.

He saw the naked girls caressing themselves, hands rubbing pointed breasts, sliding over bellies and thighs, stroking the darkness between their legs while they turned and writhed as if spitted on great phalluses.

He saw them move closer to one another. Reaching out, their fingers met. Then they were drawn together like lovers long apart, lovers starved for the touch of one another, starved for the taste.

How long they continued, William didn't know.

He wanted them to go on forever; he wanted them

154

to stop instantly so that he might satiate the appetite that strained his entire being.

At last, their bodies slid apart. They stepped toward William and Maged, chests heaving, hair wild. They had, no doubt, expended themselves several times in the course of their strange dance, but their half-shut eyes held a promise of boundless delights.

William stood motionless as one of the twins slowly removed his clothing. She smelled of blowing sand, and olive oil, and woman. A moonlit droplet of sweat or oil slid to the tip of her nipple and shimmered there. William longed to lick it off, and did so once his clothing was removed.

Had he been cheated out of the next minutes, he should have counted his life a waste. But whispers of the girls' departure from the village were tardy in reaching Kemwese, their father. Before his arrival, William found time to gratify himself with both of the girls. He was standing, a twin upside-down in his embrace, his head hugged by her slick thighs, his tongue darting into her hot depths, his phallus throbbing within the tight constriction of her sucking mouth, when a sharp blow to the back of his leg toppled him.

As he rolled in the sand, he glimpsed Maged making a dash for freedom. A sandaled foot kicked his breath away. Hearing a struggle behind him, he managed to look around. The naked girls were at their father, clutching his legs and arms, fighting to save William.

They proved no match for the enraged monster. He battered them aside and rushed at William, roaring.

His foot lashed out. Catching it in both hands, William twisted it, throwing Kemwese down. At this moment, he might have chosen to run and save himself. This, however, was against the young man's nature.

Never one to abandon a fight, he attacked the growling savage. He fell upon the man, fists pommeling the face. He heard a satisfying, gristly crunch as his knuckles smashed the bulbous nose. No sooner did blood begin to gout from the nostrils than an arm swung up and struck William's head with the force of a club.

Dazed, William tumbled away.

He was only vaguely aware of the huge man lifting him. Kemwese raised him high, then tipped his head downward and drove him toward the sand. The blow shocked every inch of William's body.

Kemwese lifted him again. William knew, in what remained of his conscious mind, that he would soon be dead.

Rather than throwing him down again, however, the man began to carry him. Where he was being taken, William had no idea. Nor did he care. He only hoped, in a fogged and dreamy way, that if he were carried far enough, some of his strength might return and he might yet save himself.

At length, Kemwese reached his destination. He flung William to the ground.

Though William hadn't the power to raise his head, he could see that they were near the ruins of the Temple of Mentuhotep. Grunting, Kemwese pushed aside a large block of stone.

The young man immediately recognized his intentions. Horror coursed through him, clearing his mind and giving him new strength. Raising his head, he saw a small, black patch in the sand beneath where the rock had rested.

Just as he'd feared. A hole.

When Kemwese came for him, he threw a handful of sand at the grinning face. Blinded and coughing, Kemwese groped for him. William rolled away. He got to his hands and knees. Crawling, he tried to gain his feet but his body obeyed the commands of his mind in only the slowest fashion and soon the raging man had him by the foot.

William was dragged backward, dragged toward the awful hole. His fingers clawed at the sand and gravel. All sense of manhood broken by the horrible prospect awaiting him, he cried out for forgiveness. He begged Kemwese. He offered money. At the end, he threatened the man with terrible vengeance.

It was useless.

William's feet were lifted high above him. He saw the black pit, like a tunnel to Hell, below his face. His hands dug into the debris at its edges, but to no avail.

Kemwese released him.

He plunged headfirst into the darkness, screaming.

2.

William fell, petrified by an unreasoning fear that he might plunge forever through the lightless void. He had little time, fortunately, to dwell upon the horror of that thought. Abruptly, he hit the bottom of the shaft and lost consciousness.

When his mind returned to him, the aches in every limb of his body quickly reminded him of his situation. The darkness was so intense that he blinked several times to be certain his eyes were indeed open. The lumpy pressure on his back told him that he was lying face upward.

He raised his arms. He found great relief and comfort in touching himself: his face, his chest and belly, his privates, his thighs. The hands, touching familiar places, gave him a warm feeling that he was not

157

entirely alone in this strange and frightful pit. They also confirmed that he was still whole, at least so as far as he could reach. He stirred his legs. They seemed unbroken.

As he lay there continuing to stroke his body and regain a sense of reality, he began to assess his situation. The devil, Kemwese, had undoubtedly left him here to die. That being the case, he must have covered the opening of the pit with the enormous block of stone that had originally sealed it. Even should William succeed in climbing to the top, he would be powerless to stir the rock. His best chance of survival, however, lay in that direction.

Gazing into the black space above him, he tried to determine whether Kemwese had, indeed, replaced the stone. No light came in from the stars or moon. Nothing was visible. Nothing.

William decided he must attempt to climb out, nonetheless. First, however, it would be necessary to explore the confines of his prison.

As he stirred himself to sit up, the uneven ground beneath him seemed to wobble. Lowering a hand to the lump beneath his hip, he touched a pliant surface that he immediately recognized as animal hide.

His fingers explored further. The hide felt dry, wrinkled, shrunken. Pressing it, he detected the solid roundness of a bone below its surface. With a gasp of alarm, he flung his naked body clear of the creature.

He huddled in the darkness and gazed in its direction. He could see nothing, of course. To confirm his fears, he finally ventured forward. His hands again encountered the dead flesh. He explored it briefly before realizing, with an agony of horror and revulsion, that his fall had been cushioned by the desiccated corpse of a man.

He, like William, was naked. William wondered if

this man, too, had been caught in debauchery with the daughters of Kemwese. The thought chilled him in spite of the pit's dreadful heat. Perhaps William would meet a similar end.

'No,' he said. The sound of his voice was horribly loud. Silly, of course, but he feared for a moment that he might have startled his companion awake. He listened, half expecting the man to speak.

From that point on, William took pains to remain silent.

Starting at the feet of the dead man, he began to inch his way along the boundary of his cell. He crawled on hands and knees, and let his shoulder brush along the stone wall to keep his orientation. After proceeding in this manner for a short time, he set his hand down on someone's face and screamed.

Petrified, he crouched against the wall, panting the hot air, and struggled to regain his composure.

Finally, he ventured forward. With hesitant hands, he familiarized himself with his new neighbor. The flesh felt more stiff than that of the other man, leading William to the assumption that his residence here had been more prolonged.

He left the body behind and continued his exploration. His reaction to the next body was more easily controlled. He didn't scream. He merely removed his hand rapidly from the foot.

This man was fully clothed. William checked the pockets. In the shirt, he found a pack of cigarettes and a small box of matches.

He slid open the box. It contained eight matches. He struck one.

Its head sparked in the darkness, then burst alight with such brilliance that pain shot through his eyes. In a moment, however, the pain passed. He gazed upon the awful scene and groaned.

Gathered around him in the bottom of the shaft no larger than a dozen feet in diameter were the dried corpses of five men. The one in front of him, the clothed one, still held a revolver in his shrunken hand. William saw a hole in his right temple.

Another corpse, across the floor, had gaping wounds on his thigh. William had little doubt how they had gotten there. The grim thought entered his mind that he, too, might soon be driven by extremes of thirst and hunger to consider partaking of his companions.

One in particular, a bald, lean man clad only in undershorts, looked more fresh than the others. Perhaps his body still retained enough moisture to quench the thirst that would shortly begin its slow torture. No. That would be . . .

The fire scorched William's fingers. He dropped the match. Darkness swallowed him and he stood motionless among the dead, considering his next course of action.

At length, he crouched beside the man who had taken his own life. Groping blindly, he found the pistol. He tried to pry it loose from the stiff fingers, and finally snapped three of them before freeing the gun.

He carefully released the cylinder catch. The cylinder swung sideways. He tipped the barrel upward. Six cartridges dropped into his palm. Among them, he found two empty shells and four live rounds. From their size and weight, he guessed them to be of .38 caliber.

He reloaded, then set the revolver by his side.

For the present, he had no need for the weapon. The fact of its presence, however, was a great comfort. He knew that, should circumstances offer no alternative, he need not be reduced to a groveling, inhuman beast. He would simply take his own life and be done with it.

With that settled, he stripped the man of his trousers. He found a penknife in one of the pockets. Using that, he cut the legs into long, narrow strips. When he had a dozen of them, he struck another match. He applied its flame to the end of a strip and found that he had created a rather satisfactory source of light. Paying out fabric as needed, he made a close inspection of the chamber.

The smooth stone walls, he noticed, sloped gradually inward above him. This ruled out the possibility of scaling the shaft.

Might there be another way out?

Certainly, his predecessors hadn't found one.

Their failure, he told himself, constituted no proof that such an exit did not exist.

Here, his knowledge of Egyptian tombs stood him in good stead. The pit, his prison, had obviously been constructed in ancient times. Its proximity to the Temple of Mentuhotep might indicate that it had been built during his reign, possibly as a secret entrance to his tomb. It was not unusual to find such passages, often designed as elaborate mazes complicated with false entries, dead ends and portals concealed in walls and ceilings for the purpose of foiling tomb robbers.

William exhausted most of his supply of makeshift wicks in a fruitless search of the walls and floor. While his flame still burned, he quickly fashioned more strips from the dead man's trousers. Then he renewed his search, looking for the slightest clue that a secret passage might lie behind the stone blocks of his cell. He found no such clue.

Allowing his light to die, he sank against one of the walls. He was sweaty and exhausted. His hopes of escape had faded to a dim prayer.

As he sat in the blackness, surrounded by his silent

companions, an idea began to form. It seemed impractical at first. It seemed less so, however, as he gave it more thought. Though the top of the shaft was higher than his frail light had carried, any project which might take him closer to it seemed worthwhile.

Perhaps, after all, the passage to the tomb had been placed partway up the shaft wall. Such a manner of concealment was not unknown to the wily priests of those times.

Thus, with the project justified in his mind, he set about constructing a platform of bodies. It was a ghoulish task. In the darkness, he dragged each from its place of rest. Their joints were stiff, their skin tough. He grew to know them apart from one another by touch: by the firmness of their flesh, by their manner of undress, by the various configurations of their limbs. Some had died prone, others sitting. He made use of these differences in constructing his platform, often sacrificing height for sturdiness.

At last, by clever stacking of four cadavers against the wall, he had a platform as high as his chest.

He lifted the last body, the one most recently dead. This one was less brittle than the others. Also, his limbs had stiffened into convenient positions.

William stood him upright on top of the others, leaning him slightly backward against the wall. When the cadaver was securely in place, William lit a strip of cloth, the upper end of which he had earlier inserted into the corpse's mouth. He adjusted the burning tip at the side of his platform so it wouldn't hinder his progress.

Then he began the awful climb.

3.

The bodies trembled precariously under William's

162

feet, but he was careful to place his weight only on the strongest of places: a hip here, a shoulder there.

At last, he reached the top of his platform. He stood motionless, gripping the wall, gathering his strength for the most strenuous part of the climb.

The flame had inched slowly up the strip of cloth, scorching flesh. As he paused, it ignited the hair of one man. The hair blazed, filling his nostrils with a terrible, acrid stench. When the fire died a few seconds later, he inspected the end of the taper.

Half the strip yet remained. William intended to use its flame, when he reached the summit, to ignite another makeshift taper which was wound around his neck. This would save him the use of a precious match. The match box was tied at his throat, however, so he wouldn't be at a loss for light should the flame of the taper expire during his climb.

Without further hesitation, he inched sideways. He swung the burning strip of cloth away from the knees of his ghastly companion and let it hang at the side, out of his way.

Pressing his body to the man, he began to climb. It was a horrible business, all the more so because of William's nudity.

He was perched upon the man's bent knees, one hand pressed to the wall, the other gripping the left shoulder of the corpse, when the light failed.

The sudden darkness unnerved him, but he knew that he would soon fall if he didn't continue upward. Sliding a foot up the dry leg, he sought the bony protuberance of a hip. Perched more precariously than ever, he leaned forward, his knees gripping the body as if he were a child shinnying up a tree.

Carefully, he straightened up, leaning full against

163

the man. He felt the face against his belly, his privates. Nightmarish images passed through his mind as he made his slow way higher.

He was almost onto the shoulders when the man moved. His hands sought purchase on the stone wall, but found none. The corpse continued to slide out from under him.

Then he was falling.

One foot struck the top body of his platform and punched through as if it were a plank of rotten wood.

From there, he tumbled backward through the darkness.

The ground struck him a terrible blow. As he lay there, stunned, a body fell on him. Then another. He flung them aside and scurried away.

Hunched against a wall, he gazed at the darkness. He listened intently. Beyond the drumming of his own heart, beyond the windy gasping of his lungs, he heard other sounds.

Muted, incoherent babbling.

The papery sounds of dry flesh dragging across the gravel floor.

'*NO!*' he shrieked.

He heard their sandy laughter.

With palsied hands, he unlooped a strip of cloth from his neck. He tore open the box of matches. Poised to strike one, he hesitated.

Better to die in the darkness, certainly, than to look upon the creatures crawling toward him.

But he *had* to see!

He struck a match. In its sudden glare, he saw a cadaver reaching for his foot. Another, sitting upright, grinned at him. The others, still in a heap, writhed as they tried to untangle their twisted limbs.

His trembling hand dropped the match.

Its light died.

'*NO!*' he cried out. '*Stay AWAY!*'

But on they came, the dry sounds of their dragging bodies quiet in the silent blackness, their clicking teeth loud.

4.

Their calls drew no response, so William's father and Mr Carter lowered Maged on a rope.

The boy heard nothing as he descended into the pit. At last, his feet found the gravel floor. Stepping away from the rope, he turned on his electric torch. He swept it around the pit. The sight of the tumbled, awkward bodies chilled him. Tight with dread, he stepped through the bodies and crouched behind the naked form of William.

He put a hand on his friend's sweaty back.

William flinched and whimpered.

'I've come for you,' Maged whispered.

William rolled onto his back. His wild eyes gazed up at Maged. 'They want to eat me,' he explained.

'No. We'll leave now.'

'They want to . . .' His eyes darted to the darkness behind Maged.

Maged looked. The bodies, sprawled in their grotesque attitudes, were motionless. He turned to his friend. 'They can't eat you, my friend. They're dead.'

'Are they?' William sat up. He stared at the bodies. 'They are, aren't they?'

'Most surely.'

With a sudden laugh, William leaped to his feet. He kicked the nearest corpse. It rolled onto its side. He bent over and gazed at it, then reached down and tore off one of its arms.

'*Dead!*' he cried out.

He cast the arm aside, then crouched and twisted off the corpse's head and flung it against a wall.

He grinned at Maged. 'He can't eat me *now*, can he!'

Giggling, he fell upon the next corpse and twisted its head off.

Maged quickly climbed the rope. At the top, the men helped him from the mouth of the pit. He gulped the fresh air.

'Is William quite all right?'

'He will come up soon, Mr Brook. Most surely.'

Spooked

Selene woke up, wondering vaguely what had disturbed her sleep. She glanced at the lighted face of the alarm clock. Nearly 3:00 a.m.

If only Alex were here. How could he leave her alone on a night like this – on Halloween, of all nights! He knew very well how nervous she got . . . Well, he would be home in the morning. Only a few hours from now.

Taking a deep breath that seemed to fill her entire body with peaceful weariness, Selene curled up on her side and snuggled her face against the pillow.

Then she heard someone else taking a deep breath.

Someone under the bed!

She went rigid.

Couldn't have been, she told herself.

She felt faint, and realized that she was holding her breath. She opened her mouth, eased air out silently, and breathed in. But not much. Too much, and her chest might expand enough to make the bedsprings creak. If the springs should creak . . .

You're acting like a fool, she thought. There is nobody under the bed. Can't be.

A drop of sweat stung her eye. She wanted to wipe it away, but that would require moving her arm. She didn't dare.

Nobody down there. Not enough room. Plenty of room for the suitcases, though. Only yesterday, she'd dragged out one of them for Alex. A man isn't much thicker than a suitcase.

Selene imagined a man on his back directly under her, his pale eyes staring upward.

Knock it off. Go to sleep.

Selene closed her eyes and rolled onto her back. From beneath her came a stifled cough.

She flung the sheet aside, flipped over, and got to her hands and knees in the center of the king-sized bed. Her nightgown stuck to her back with sweat. 'Who's down there?' Her voice was a dry rasp. She cleared her throat and said firmly, 'I know you're under there. Who are you?'

A long silence answered her question.

'Who?'

A breeze filled the curtain above her. It chilled her wet face. She heard the whisper of a distant car.

'Please! Who's down there?'

From beneath the bed came a single laugh. A shiver scurried up her back like quick, furry spiders.

'It isn't you, is it, Alex?'

What on earth made her think it could be Alex? Because he'd acted so weird before his trip? Because one minute he was gazing into space, the next acting more loving and considerate than he'd been in years? They say that's a sure sign a husband's having an affair.

Ridiculous.

'That isn't you, is it?' she asked.

Silence.

'Alex?' She began to crawl toward the edge of the mattress, trying to see over its side. In her mind, she saw an arm lash up to grab her. She retreated to the center of the bed.

Then she heard a groan.

Alex never groaned like that. *Nobody* ever groaned

168

like that. Nobody but those demented, shadowy mutes that sometimes hulked down the alleys of her nightmares.

Maybe this is a nightmare.

Don't you *wish*.

A low, whispery voice said, 'Se-leeeene.'

She heard herself whimper.

Her eyes roamed the borders of the mattress. Except for the headboard against the wall, a sea of darkness lay beyond its edges. The bedroom door stood open, but so far away!

If she could reach the door without being overtaken, a long hallway lay beyond it. Then a flight of stairs. And finally the front door, chained against burglars. But maybe, with luck . . .

She slowly stood up, the mattress giving beneath her feet.

'SELENE!'

Gasping with fright, she lost her balance and fell backward. Her shoulders hit the headboard. Her head knocked the windowsill, the curtain fluttering against her cheeks and eyelids.

The window!

A way out! She could jump to safety, avoiding the awful darkness where hands were waiting to snatch her ankles . . .

But it would be a long fall to the ground.

She remembered Alex's recent advice. 'If you're ever trapped up here by a fire or something when I'm out, jump. You might break a leg, but that's a far cry better than the alternative. Besides, the saplings will cushion your fall.'

Spinning around, she ripped the curtain off the window and smashed the screen with her fists. It dropped easily away.

She squirmed headfirst through the window. The

169

wooden framework was rough, and full of splinters. One splinter ripped her arm.

'I'LL TEAR YOU UP!' the voice shrieked.

She was halfway out, gazing fearfully at the rows of pine saplings far below, when her nightgown snagged on the sill. She tugged at it, couldn't jerk it free. She squirmed and writhed, whimpering, kicking, waiting for the rough grip to catch her ankles.

'No!' she cried out. 'Oh God, NO!'

Shortly after dawn, Alex entered the bedroom. He noticed that the screen was missing from the open window, saw the curtains piled on the bed. And he smiled.

His smile died when he saw the suitcase on the mattress.

He rushed to the window. The rows of saplings below stood upright against the wind, braced in place by the tall, iron stakes which he'd pounded into the ground last week while Selene was at the beauty parlor. The stakes were green and barely visible.

Selene was not impaled on any of them.

'Damn,' he muttered.

Something had gone wrong.

At the bed, he opened the suitcase. The timer was there. So was the tape recorder. He flicked its switch.

'I'LL TEAR YOU UP!'

He gazed at the recorder, stunned. His words. Yes, the very words he'd screamed into the microphone only a few days ago. But not *his* voice – *Selene's!*

Trembling, he turned off the recorder.

Hands gripped his right ankle and jerked, smashing his shin against the metal bed frame. Pain surged up his leg.

He fell.

Selene, on her belly, scurried from under the bed with madness in her eyes and a butcher knife clenched in her teeth.

The Good Deed

She was asleep when I spotted her. Asleep, or playing possum. Either way, she was curled on her side at the bottom of the cage, not moving.

The first thing that went through my mind was *Holy shit!*

Here I was, taking a leak in the woods, a gal no more than twenty feet away. What if she rolls over? I wished like hell that I'd noticed her before unleashing, but I couldn't stop now. Too much coffee at that diner down the road. So I turned around quick and strained to finish fast. Fast. Before she heard the splashing. Before she turned over and saw me. Before she *said* something.

What's she doing here? I kept thinking.

In a cage, no less.

Shit!

I've gotta get outa here!

I felt shocked, confused, embarrassed, spooked. And then ashamed of myself because my dick was starting to get hard. Because it was out, I suppose, in the presence of a woman. Even if she couldn't see it.

She'll see it if I turn around, I thought. If she's looking.

I didn't turn around, of course.

At last, I finished and shook off. By then, I had to really work at getting myself tucked back into my jeans.

I zipped up. I glanced over my shoulder.

The gal still lay curled on the floor of her cage, her back to me.

I hurried away. The matted dead leaves underfoot crackled and snapped, no matter how softly I tried to step. I kept expecting the gal to call out. She didn't, though. When I looked back, she and her cage were safely out of sight. I saw only thick forest, gloomy with shadows except for a few streaks of morning sunlight that slanted down through the treetops.

I made my way to the Jeep. It was parked to the side of the dirt road, the passenger door open and waiting for me. I climbed in.

'Took you long enough,' Mike said. 'Have to take a dumper?'

'Just a piss.'

'You hiked a mile just to take a piss? Could've done that right here.'

'I didn't hike any mile.'

He started the engine. 'All the traffic we had, you could've done it in the middle of the road here.'

'I like my privacy,' I said.

'Like I'm sure I'd wanta watch. Gimme a break. Do I *look* like a homo?'

'You look like a dork.'

By the way, we were sixteen years old. In case that isn't obvious from the sophisticated nature of our repartee.

Mike and I were buddies, and we'd just finished our sophomore year at Redwood High. If you're wondering what we were doing out in the boonies without adult supervision, it's because we'd begged and pleaded with our parents till they caved in.

It helped matters that the parents on both sides were intelligent, reasonable people. It also helped that Mike and I were a pair of polite, responsible

173

over-achievers. Aside from having four-point grade averages, we were Eagle Scouts. Upstanding citizens, self-reliant, experienced in the wilds. What parent could *not* trust whizzbangs like us, in spite of our youth, to spend a couple of weeks on our own?

When we proposed our plan to explore the scenic wonders of California via Mike's dad's Jeep, camping out at night and calling in every few days to assure everyone that all was well, they went for it. Eventually. None of the folks was tickled by the idea, but the dads soon came around. They admitted it might be a good experience for us, a chance to see a bit of the world and to gain some maturity. Hell, they probably wished *they* could do it. Once we had the dads on our side, the rest was easy.

Which is how we ended up out here by ourselves.

If you're wondering how come we weren't discussing my leak in the dignified manner befitting a couple of brainy, reverant Eagle Scouts, it's because we're guys and we were out here by ourselves, no adults to impress.

'You oughta know, dickhead,' Mike said. (Before embarking on the aside, I'd said he looks like a dork. Remember? We're back in the car, now.) 'It takes one to know one. Are you gonna shut the door?'

I looked at him.

'Well?' he asked.

'Maybe we'd better . . . not drive off yet.'

He grimaced. 'Oh, man. You got the runs?'

I shook my head. My face felt hot. My heart was suddenly thumping awfully hard. 'There's a girl,' I explained.

'A *what*?'

'A girl. A female. A woman. You know.'

'A *babe*?'

'Yeah.'

174

'Shit. What're you talking about? Where?'

'In there.' I pointed toward the woods.

'Bullshit. No way.'

'It's true.'

'A *babe*? Over there in the trees?'

'I saw her when I went in to take my piss.'

Mike grinned. 'She hold your dick for you?'

'She's in a cage.'

'A *what*?'

'A cage. You know. Like a zoo cage or something. With bars.'

He chuckled. 'Bullshit.'

'I'm serious.'

Mike knew me. When I said that about being serious, he knew I meant it. He narrowed his eyes. 'A babe in a cage. I'm supposed to believe that?'

'Go and take a look for yourself.'

He kept staring at me, frowning. 'What did she look like?'

'All I saw was her back.'

'You didn't talk? Like maybe ask her what the fuck she's doing in a cage in the middle of Fort Boondocks?'

'I think she was asleep.'

'Jee-zus.'

'Hey, man, I was taking a piss. All I wanted to do was get outa there. But she's in a *cage*, you know. She probably can't get out. I don't think we can just drive off and leave her. She might die, or something.'

Mike scrunched his eyes tight and gazed at me through slits. 'You'd better not be shitting me, man.'

'I swear to God.'

He shut off the engine, pulled out the ignition key and threw open his door. Leaping out, he glanced over his shoulder and said, 'This I gotta see.'

I went with him, of course.

175

I led the way. I felt nervous for a lot of reasons. Part of me hoped we wouldn't find her at all. Then we wouldn't need to deal with the situation. But she and her cage couldn't have walked off, and I'm not one to hallucinate. Besides, Mike would give me no end of crap if we failed to find the mysterious, caged babe.

My heart nearly bashed through my chest when I spotted the cage. I came to a quick halt. Mike stepped up beside me. We both stared.

'What'd I tell you?' I whispered.

'Oh, man, I don't believe it.'

The girl looked as if she hadn't stirred. She lay curled on her side, her back toward us. She was mostly in shadow, but dappled with sunlight that made her hair gleam like gold. She wore a white blouse. It was untucked, its tail hanging crooked so it showed a strip of bare skin above her cut-off jeans. The jeans, low around her hips, were cut away very high so that they really had no legs at all. They were also pretty ragged. One of the rear pockets drooped, ripped halfway off, leaving a rectanglar gap. Her skin showed there, too.

Mike nudged me with his elbow. 'Look,' he whispered. 'You can see her butt.'

'I know, I know. Big deal.'

'Man.'

'Get your mind out of the gutter.'

'Yeah. Right. Come on.' He started toward the cage, but I grabbed his arm. 'What?'

'Just hold it. What're we going to do?'

'Check her out.'

'I don't know. I don't like this. It's too damn weird.'

'I just hope she ain't a dog.'

'Would you cut it out? This is *serious*. What the

176

hell is a cage doing out here? Why's she in it? I mean, maybe this is some kind of a trap.'

'A trap, all right. And she's in it.'

'No. I mean like a trap for us.'

He smirked. 'Get real.'

'Maybe some crazy maniacs put her in there as bait.'

His smirk slipped. 'Bullshit,' he said.

'I've read about hunters doing stuff like that. Say they're after a lion? They'll stake out a lamb or something and hide. Pretty soon, along comes a lion. When it goes for the lamb, they blast it.'

'If anyone wanted to blast us, we'd be blasted by now.'

'Maybe they want us alive. There might be a pit over by the cage. You know, covered over so that when we step on it . . .'

'Knock it off, huh? Good God.'

I knocked it off. We both stood silent for a while, peering into the bushes and trees along the borders of the clearing. We even looked up into the higher limbs.

'There's nobody here,' Mike finally whispered.

'Just because we can't see them . . . I mean, *somebody* put her here.'

Mike frowned the way he does when he's concentrating. 'That's true. Or at least somebody brought the cage. *She* sure didn't lug that thing through the woods.' He nibbled his lower lip. 'Could be some guy used it to bring a wild animal out here.'

'That's possible.' I liked the idea. A nice, reasonable explanation that sapped away some of the menace.

'Maybe an environmentalist,' Mike went on. 'Brought out a bobcat or bear to return it to its natural habitat. Let it go, but left his cage behind. And this gal wandered along. Stepped inside to check it out. Shut the door, just for the hell of it. But the damn thing locked on her. Presto, she's caught.'

'Nice theory, Einstein,' I said.

'What?'

'I guess you were too busy scoping her butt to notice the padlock. She didn't fasten a *padlock* by accident, did she?'

He scowled over at the cage. 'Shit.'

'Right.'

Shrugging at me, he said, 'So somebody did put her in there. Doesn't mean she's bait.'

'So what *does* it mean?'

'I guess we'll have to ask her. Come on.'

This time, I didn't try to stop him. Nervous as I was about the whole deal, we couldn't just walk away and leave her. But I let Mike go first. I stayed a few paces behind him and kept a sharp lookout.

Mike didn't seem to be in any great hurry. He stepped along slowly, hunched over a bit, setting his feet down with great care, actually *creeping* toward the cage. I followed his example. Though we tried to be quiet, we couldn't help but make a lot of crunching sounds. Every footstep sounded like somebody balling up a sheet of paper.

The girl didn't move, though.

We got to the front of the cage without getting nailed by any sort of boobytrap. Mike stopped, and I eased over to his side. We gazed through the bars at the girl.

She still hadn't moved.

From where we stood, we could see one side of her face. Part of it, anyway. It was turned downward because of the way her head was resting on her arm. Also, most of it was hidden under a drape of

178

shiny blonde hair. We couldn't really tell what she looked like.

'Hello!' Mike blurted. It came out so loud that I flinched. The girl didn't. She lay motionless. 'Excuse me? Ma'am? Lady? Hello?'

No response.

I snapped my head this way and that, afraid a lunatic – or a family of lunatics – might suddenly come charging out of the woods. But nothing stirred.

'Jeez,' Mike whispered. 'You don't suppose she's dead?'

I quit looking around and concentrated on the girl. 'She doesn't *look* dead.'

'How many stiffs have you met?'

'I've *read* about plenty. They're supposed to have a funny color.'

We both studied her. The slight bits of face that weren't hidden by hair looked healthy enough. Her legs looked sleek and tawny. The portion of her back that showed above her cut-offs wasn't as tanned as her legs, but it had no sickly pallor. Even the creamy skin we could see through the ripped seat of her pants looked *alive*. Looked *great*.

'I don't know,' Mike whispered.

'She isn't dead.'

'Just because she hasn't started to rot yet . . .'

'They do stuff like evacuate their bowels.'

'They take a dump?' He sounded astonished and appalled.

'That's what I've read.'

'Shit! Man, that's disgusting!'

'Shhhh.'

'What do you mean, shhhh? She's out of it. If she's not dead, there's sure as hell *something* wrong with her. Let's see what she looks like from the front.'

When he said that, my heart started pounding really

179

hard. I got a hot, squirmy feeling inside as we made our way around to the opposite side of the cage.

There, we crouched and gazed in at the girl.

Still, not very much of her face showed because of all the hair hanging down across it. Maybe half of her forehead. The tip of her nose. Her lower eye, which was shut. She looked to be about the same age as us, and not at all bad looking from the little I could see.

Her head rested on her left arm, the elbow sticking out past her face. Her right arm hung across her chest. The upper part of it was pushed against the side of her breast. Her blouse was snug over the breast. Her nipple made it really jut out.

Mike nudged me.

'I know, I know.'

'Wow.'

'Shhh.' Feeling turned on and a bit raunchy, I quit looking at the breast. Her blouse was buttoned. Except for leaving a bare triangle above her hip, it covered her all the way down past the waist of her jeans. Those were cut off so high that the bottom of a pocket lining hung out. It lay flat against the front of her thigh like a pale tongue. Her legs were on top of each other, and pulled up so that they were angled toward us, her knees not very far from the bars.

'Look,' Mike said. 'She's breathing. See her hair?'

Sure enough, after studying her face for a few moments, I saw the hair stir slightly where it draped her mouth.

'I *told* you she isn't dead,' I whispered.

'She doesn't even look like she's hurt. What's the matter with her?' In a loud voice, he said, 'Hey! Hey, you!'

Nothing.

So he reached between the bars, leaning forward

until his shoulder met the cage. Before he could touch her, I said, 'Wait. Don't.'

He hesistated, his hand hovering above the top knee. 'What?'

'You'd better not.'

'Just gonna give her a little shake.'

'What if she's . . . I don't know . . . infected?'

'Are you nuts?'

'Maybe she's got something, you know? A disease. Maybe she's contageous, and that's why they put her out here. So she wouldn't spread it around. I mean, *something's* wrong with her. And she was *left* here. Maybe she was left here to die, you know?'

'What kind of asshole would do that?'

'Who knows? Somebody ignorant. Or scared. He didn't have the heart to kill her, maybe, so he just . . .'

'Hey, I bet she's a vampire.'

'I'm serious.'

'Or a werewolf. Yeah, that's the ticket. She's a werewolf. It'll be a full moon tonight. Her folks locked her up so she won't run wild and rip out the throats of innocent children.' He let out a howl.

'Cut it out.'

'Gimme a break, huh?' He lowered his hand, clasped her right knee and gave it a shake. 'Come on, girl. Wake up. What's the matter with you?' She didn't respond, so he shook her more roughly, jostling her whole body. I found myself watching her breast, the way it jiggled inside her blouse.

She moaned.

My heart gave an awful kick. Mike's arm jumped and he jerked it back outside the bars.

The girl moaned again, then slowly brought her right hand up to her face. While she rubbed her face

181

like someone waking from a heavy sleep, she rolled onto her back and stretched her legs out.

Suddenly, she froze. She lay motionless for a few moments, then bolted upright, sweeping her hair out of the way. Eyes all wide with alarm, she glanced this way and that, taking in the cage, the forest, and us. She gaped at us. Her mouth hung open. She was breathing hard.

'It's all right,' I told her.

She sprang to her feet, whirled around, and threw herself at the door. It made a clanky sound and stayed shut. The cage rocked a bit. She tugged and shoved at the bars, putting her whole body into it, struggling like a madwoman to force the door open. When that didn't work, she turned toward us. Her face was red. She was huffing for air.

Mike and I were both standing up by this time. But we hadn't moved away from our side of the cage.

'You ought to calm down,' Mike told her. 'We aren't going to hurt you.'

She thrashed her head from side to side, hair flying.

'We'll try to get you out,' I said.

She quit throwing her head, but kept on gasping. She held onto a couple of bars down low by her hips as if there was a current or something that she was afraid might drag her toward us.

Though she still had some wisps of hair in front of her face, I could see what she looked like now. She wasn't any great beauty, I guess. But better than average. Kind of pretty, but not stunning.

In a way, I was glad she'd turned out not to be gorgeous. The ones who are really great-looking make me awfully nervous. I felt shaky enough without having to deal with something like that.

182

The way she stared at us, you'd think we were a couple of Frankenstein monsters or something.

To Mike, I said, 'Why don't you go back to the car and find something we can use to bust the lock?'

'Me?'

'Just do it, huh?'

'Hey, buddy, you're the one who said she might be contagious. Maybe we'd better find out what's going on before we start trying to break her out.'

'Come on. She's scared to death. We'll both go. It'll give her a chance to calm down.' I took Mike by the arm and pulled him. When we started to move alongside the cage, the girl sidestepped toward the far corner. 'We're just going back to our car,' I explained. 'We'll be right back. We need some tools for the lock. Okay? All we want to do is let you out.'

'Yeah,' Mike added. 'We're the good guys.'

She didn't look as if she believed us. She kept lurching sideways, her back to the bars, watching us from behind swaying slips of hair with panic in her eyes.

By the time we got to the front, she was pressed against the back of the cage where we'd been crouching when she woke up.

We hurried away.

'Christ,' Mike said, 'she's like a madwoman.'

'She's just scared.'

'How do we know she *isn't* mad? Maybe she's a total nutcase. Maybe that's why they put her here.'

'Well, we can't just leave her. That's for sure.'

'I'm not saying that.'

'What are you saying?' I asked.

'We'd just better watch out.'

'Right. She might be a werewolf.'

'I don't know what she is, but we'd better find

183

out before we bust her out. Remember that "Twilight Zone"?'

Mike didn't even need to describe which episode. Right away, I knew the one he meant. For years, we'd been getting together at my house to watch an annual 'Twilight Zone' marathon where they showed reruns of the old show for twenty-four hours straight. It was funny that I hadn't thought of the story, myself, before now.

I wished he hadn't reminded me.

I shook my head and forced myself to laugh. 'You think she was caged by a bunch of monks? You think she's the Devil?'

'Don't be a jerk.'

'You're the one who brought it up.'

'The principle of the thing.'

'She was caged out here to protect the world from her evil ways?'

'Who knows? Do you know? I don't. I'm just saying we'd better find out what gives.'

'Well, I'm all for that.'

About then, we reached the Jeep. Mike dug out the tire tool. One end of the iron rod had a head for wrenching off lug nuts and the other end had a prying wedge. I pulled my old Boy Scout hatchet out of my pack, figuring we could bash the lock to pieces if it resisted the tire iron.

I decided to take along my canteen and a chocolate bar. Even if the gal wasn't thirsty or starving, the offer might help to show our good intentions.

When I stepped away from the Jeep, Mike was busy slipping the sheath of his Buck knife onto his belt.

'What the hell do you want that for?'

'You never know.'

'It might spook her.'

'And just suppose we let her out and she goes ape and attacks us?'

'Gimme a break.'

'She might.'

'I guess it's possible.'

'Fucking-A-right it's possible. I'm all for being a good Samaritan and shit, but it's not worth dying for. Besides, *you've* got a goddamn *ax.*'

'Okay, okay.'

With the knife at his hip, he buckled his belt. Then he pulled the tire tool from between his knees, and we headed into the woods.

'At least she ain't ugly,' Mike said after we'd walked a short distance. 'I'd hate to put my butt on the line for a dog.'

'She's probably harmless.'

'They always put harmless people in cages.'

Not wanting to get into another round of pointless speculation as to why she might be locked up in that thing, I changed the subject. 'I guess we might have to take her with us.'

That idea seemed to cheer Mike up. 'Only two seats. You'd better take over the driving. She can sit on my lap.'

I grinned. 'Hey, it's your car. You drive. Besides, you don't want a werewolf sitting on your lap.'

'A werewolf that looks like her? Wearing cut-offs like that? No panties? No bra? Lycanthropy, where is thy sting?'

'Horny bastard.'

'Oh, yeah, and like she doesn't turn *you* on.'

'I'm above such things.'

'Right.'

The cage came into sight. We quit talking, and stayed quiet as we approached it.

The girl was standing, her back to the bars at the

185

far side, but she didn't seem quite as rigid and jumpy as before. Hair no longer hung in front of her face. She was no longer panting for air.

'That didn't take long, did it?' I asked her.

She didn't answer.

At the door of the cage, I dropped my hatchet and Mike put down the tire iron. 'Here's some water and chocolate.' I reached through the bars with the canteen and candy bar. She stayed put. So I gave them a toss and they fell to the floor near her feet. She didn't even glance down at them. Just stared at me and Mike.

Mike started to say, 'Knows better than to take candy from stra—'

And she spoke. 'Why'd you bring me here? What do you want?'

'Huh?'

'Oh, man,' Mike said. 'She thinks *we* . . . hey, we had nothing to do with this. We *found* you here.'

'That's right,' I added. 'All we did was find you. You were already here.'

'Oh, yeah?'

'Yeah!' Mike blasted her. 'Christ on a crutch!'

'Calm down,' I told him. To the girl, I said, 'You don't *know* who did this to you?'

As she shook her head slightly from side to side, her eyes seemed to lose some of their terror. She frowned. She looked wary, confused. 'It really wasn't you guys?' she asked.

'No way,' I told her.

'We left our shining armor back at the car,' Mike said. He sounded a bit snotty.

'If you two didn't . . . what are you doing here?'

'We're just out driving around and camping and stuff,' I explained.

'Ed came over to take a leak.'

'Oh, thanks a heap.' I gave Mike a jab with my

186

elbow. But then I saw the girl crack a smile. The smile only lasted an instant, then vanished. It had looked good on her, though. 'I'm Ed, by the way. The jerk is Mike.'

'I'm Shanna.'

'Nice to meet you, Shanna.'

'Hi,' Mike said.

'He's not really a jerk.'

That brought another fleeting smile from Shanna.

'Look, we'll get you out of there and—'

'Not so fast, buddy. We had an agreement, remember?'

'She doesn't know why she's here. She thought *we* were the ones who . . .'

'So she claims.'

I gave her a smile and kind of rolled my eyes upward. 'Mike's afraid you might be a werewolf or something.'

'Hey,' he said, 'screw you.'

'Tell him you're not a werewolf.'

'Just tell me what the hell you're doing in a *cage* in the middle of the goddamn boondocks.'

Shanna frowned, shook her head some more, and took a deep breath. 'I don't know,' she said. 'I fell asleep on the beach.'

'On the beach? At the ocean?'

'Yeah. Stanley Beach. Or Stanton?'

'Stinson Beach? In Marin?'

'That's the one.'

'That's a couple of hundred *miles* from here.'

'Where are we?' she asked.

'In the mountains. The foothills, actually. A ways north of Yosemite.'

'God,' she muttered.

'Anyway, you were at the beach. Then what happened?'

187

'I woke up here.'

'If you were at the beach,' Mike said, 'then where's your swimming suit?'

Apparently, she didn't like his tone of voice. She gave him a resentful look. 'I didn't have it on.'

'What was it, a nude beach?'

'Come on, Mike. Jeez.'

'It was night. I was wearing what I've got on.'

'Must've been awfully cold,' Mike said.

'I had my sleeping bag.'

'You were spending the night on the beach?' I asked.

'Sure. I did it all the way down the coast.'

'Alone?'

'Yeah. Something wrong with that?'

'What are you,' Mike asked, 'a runaway?'

'That's my business.'

'It's our business if you want us to let you out of there.'

'Look,' I said, 'it doesn't matter. The thing is, you went to bed in your sleeping bag on the beach, and you don't know what happened after that? You just woke up here?'

She nodded. 'Yeah.'

'That's really weird. You weren't beat up, or . . . have you got a sore head or anything?'

'No, huh-uh.' She slipped the fingers of one hand through her hair and felt about as if examining her scalp. 'I do feel kind of funny, though.'

'Funny how?'

'I don't know. Heavy? Tired? Like maybe . . . maybe they drugged me.'

Mike and I looked at each other. Drugs would account for a lot: how she'd come to be here without any awareness of what led to it; how she'd gone on sleeping soundly when Mike had called out to her.

'Seems mighty convenient,' he said. 'Drugged. So she doesn't know anything.'

'I *don't* know anything!' she snapped. 'I can sure figure a few things out, though. Some creeps found me sleeping on the beach, shot me up with something, and drove me out here while I was unconscious. And locked me up.'

'Maybe, maybe not.'

'Hey, come on, Mike.'

'How do we know she isn't lying about everything?'

'It's the truth!' Shanna blurted, 'Don't be such an asshole.'

'Oh, now I'm an asshole.'

'Would you guys please just get me outa here before they come back?'

'Oh, now it's please.'

'Before *who* comes back?' I asked her.

'Whoever brought me here. What are you, retarded? You don't really think they just put me in a cage and that's it? This is just to hold me. That should be obvious even to a moron.'

'She's now called you retarded and a moron,' Mike pointed out.

I'd already noticed. And wasn't too happy about it.

'You sure aren't behaving very well for a gal who needs a favor,' I told her.

'Okay, okay. I'm sorry, okay? I didn't mean it. But they're *going* to come back. Isn't that obvious? They must wanta *do* something to me.'

'I know what *I'd* like to do to you,' Mike said.

'Cut it out,' I told him.

'If some creeps just wanted to molest me, they would've done it right there on the beach. This is . . . I don't know. Maybe there are others. Maybe

189

it's a cult or something and they want to sacrifice me. Maybe they'll be meeting here tonight.'

I turned to Mike. 'That might be it.'

'A cult? Give me a break.'

'It makes sense,' I said. 'An advance man for some weird kind of group, it's his job to provide a gal for the evening's festivities. It doesn't have to be devil worship, necessarily. But they need a gal for it.'

'Yeah. She would come in handy for a gang-bang.'

'And they'd want someone who wouldn't be missed. Like a runaway camping on the beach.'

'Might be something like that,' Mike admitted. He grinned. 'Maybe we oughta stick around and watch.'

'Damn it!' Shanna blurted. 'Get me out of here!'

'We could climb a tree, have us a bird's-eye view.'

'You bastard!'

'He's just kidding,' I told her. 'But you oughta quit calling us names.'

'You think I'm kidding?' Mike asked. 'It might be a real kick. Wouldn't you like to watch and see what they do to her?'

I actually began picturing it. Night. Mike and I in a tree, gazing down as rednecks with flashlights and Coleman lanterns gathered around the cage. Shanna terrified, weeping and pleading.

'Neat?' Mike asked.

Already, I was feeling pretty excited, and the imaginary rednecks hadn't even started to work on her. 'We can't do that,' I said.

'Why not? It's none of our business what they do with her. We'd just be innocent observers.'

'It'd be our fault.'

'Hell, no. If we hadn't come along, it would've happened to her anyway. Right? This would just be like letting nature take its course.'

190

'I don't know.'

'Maybe nothing will even happen. We don't know what's going on. Shanna might be lying through her teeth. For all we know, she might've locked *herself* in there.'

'You're nuts,' Shanna said. 'And if you guys think you're gonna hide and watch what happens . . . go ahead and try it. Whoever shows up, I'll tell 'em right where you are. Then maybe all three of us can end up getting massacred.'

'Listen to her,' Mike said. 'The bitch is threatening us.'

'Yeah. Why don't we just go on back to the car and leave her? Who needs this?' I didn't actually mean it, but she had me peeved.

'I'd rather stick around and watch the fun,' Mike said.

'You heard her. She'd tell on us. Let's just split. She's acting like a jerk.'

'I'm with you.'

I picked up my hatchet. Mike picked up his tire iron. We both turned away from the cage.

'You want your canteen?' Shanna asked.

I looked back. She'd stepped away from the bars and picked it up.

'Toss it over.'

'Huh-uh. You can have it when you let me out.'

'I'll buy you a new one,' Mike told me.

'Fine. You can have that one, Shanna. You might get thirsty while you're waiting for tonight.'

She hurled it down. It thumped against the floor of the cage. 'Get back here! You can't go!'

'Oh, really?' I asked. 'Just watch us.'

We went on walking away.

'Please!' she cried out. 'You can't just leave me! You can't! Please!'

191

We kept walking.

'We really gonna do it?' Mike whispered.

'Leave?'

'Yeah.'

'Why not? The hell with her.'

'What a bitch.'

'No!' she called. 'Don't go!'

I looked back at her. 'And why the hell shouldn't we? Give us one good reason.'

Her hands scurried down the front of her blouse, rushing from button to button. In a flash, all were unfastened. She pulled her blouse wide open.

'My God,' I muttered.

Mike and I stared. While we watched, she let her blouse fall to the floor of the cage.

'*Now* will you come back?' she asked.

We didn't need to discuss it. We headed back, our eyes pinned to her. She was watching us, standing rigid, arms hanging down at her sides, fists clenched. She was breathing hard again.

She looked great.

Her hair gleamed golden. Her skin, partly in shadows but splashed here and there with sunlight, had a soft, light brown color. Not her breasts, though. They looked pale, creamy. Their nipples were dark and pointing at us.

She was slender and bare to the waist of her cut-offs. Which wasn't at her waist, but a lot lower. Below the jeans, her legs reached down slim and tawny to her bare feet planted somewhat apart on the cage floor.

I'd never seen anything like this.

Nothing even came close.

I felt like I might faint. Or explode. Or wake up.

'Is this what you wanted?' she asked, her voice trembling.

'You didn't have to . . .' I murmured.

'Yeah, sure. Now get me out of here.'

'We'll think about it,' Mike said.

'Give me that.' I reached for the tire iron, but he swept it aside so I missed. 'Hey. Come on. Hand it over.'

'What's the big rush? Let's just relax and enjoy the scenery for a minute.'

I know. I could've wrestled him for the tire iron. Or I could've started whacking the padlock with my hatchet. But I didn't feel much like doing either of those things.

We both turned our attention to Shanna.

She glared at us. Her lips were pinched shut. Her breath hissed through her nostrils. I didn't spend much time, though, studying her face.

After a while, she said, 'Why don't you just take a picture.'

'Wish we had a Polaroid,' Mike said.

'Yeah.'

'Man.'

'You creeps!'

'Lose the shorts,' Mike told her.

She looked like she might start to cry. 'Guys,' she said. 'Hey.' Her eyes went to me as if searching for an ally.

'You don't want us to leave, do you?' I asked.

'Hey. Please. Come on.'

'What's the big deal?' Mike asked. 'We didn't even *ask* you to shuck the shirt. You thought that up all by yourself.'

'Yeah,' I said. 'You started it.'

She nibbled on her lower lip, eyes flicking from me to Mike. Finally, she said, 'If I do, will you get me out of here? No more . . . messing around?'

'Sure,' Mike said.

'Sure,' I said.

Grimacing as if it hurt, she unbuttoned the front of her cut-offs. She didn't bother to unzip, but hooked her thumbs under the sides of the shorts and tugged them down. She bent over as she lowered them. Her breasts swayed a little. When the jeans were about halfway down, she let go and they dropped around her ankles. She stood up straight. She freed her left foot. With her right, she swept the cut-offs aside. Then she pressed her legs together tight.

'Oh, man,' Mike said.

I didn't say anything.

Shanna must've spent some time under the sun in bikini pants. Very skimpy ones. Her skin had narrow pale strips slanting down from the hips toward the center, where the cords must've run into a bit of fabric not a whole lot larger than an eyepatch. Her skin there was white, stubbled with golden bristles.

'Turn around,' Mike told her.

She let out a shaky sigh, then followed orders.

I was glad she did. I couldn't have taken it, staring much longer at her front. This gave me a chance to calm down some.

Her back was tanned all the way down to the pale strips from her bikini cords. The seat must've been no more than about four inches across at the top and tapered down from there, covering the crease of her rump but not a lot more than that. The smooth, firm mounds of her buttocks were mostly tanned. I like a nice tan. But I found my eyes drawn mostly to the area that hadn't been touched by the sun.

'Okay,' Mike said. 'Face us again.'

She did.

'Now get down on your back and spread your legs.'

'No!'

194

If she did that, I'd lose it for sure. Besides, making her do that seemed really low. 'Come on, Mike,' I said.

'You wanta see her pussy, don't you?'

I could already see it. So could Mike. 'We shouldn't be doing this,' I said. 'We shouldn't be doing any of this.'

'Don't be such a wuss.'

'She's done enough.'

'You promised,' she said.

'Promised what?'

'If I took off my pants, you'd let me out. You said no more messing around.'

'Did we say that?' Mike asked.

'Yeah, we did.'

'Who's side are *you* on?'

'We gave her our word.'

'So what?'

'So plenty.'

He sneered at me. Facing Shanna, he said, 'Okay. Just come over here.'

She shook her head.

'No?'

'No.'

Mike looked at me and raised his eyebrows. 'Is that too much to ask?'

In spite of our promise, I wanted Shanna to come closer. 'I don't guess so. Come on over here,' I told her.

'No!'

'Shall we leave now?' Mike asked me.

'Sure,' I said. 'Let's go.'

'All right!' She stepped over the canteen. Her foot landed on the chocolate bar, but she didn't seem to notice. She walked slowly toward us, the patches of sunlight sliding along her skin, her breasts hardly

195

jiggling or bouncing at all. Halfway across the cage, she stopped.

'Closer,' Mike said.

'This is close enough. I'm not taking another step until you've busted that lock off.'

'Unless we start to leave, right?' I'm the one who said that.

'You won't leave,' she said.

'We will if we feel like it,' I told her. 'You'd just better do what we tell you.'

'If I come any closer, you can reach me through the bars.'

'Maybe that's the point,' Mike said.

'Yeah.'

'You guys wanta touch me.' It wasn't a question.

'I guess it's crossed *my* mind,' Mike said.

I laughed, but it came out sounding funny.

'Of course, we could always drive away,' Mike said. 'Is that what you want?'

She gave us a twitchy smile. 'There's only one way you'll ever get your hands on me. That's to open the cage.'

Mike and I glanced at each other.

'I think we'd better open it,' he said.

'What're we waiting for?'

Then he grinned at Shanna. 'You wouldn't have the key on you?'

'Oh, yeah. Sure.'

'Guess we'll have to do it the hard way.'

He started by slipping his tire iron between the shackle and the case. He braced the end of the rod against the door's steel frame for leverage, and shoved down with all his weight. The lock didn't give. But he didn't quit. He rammed the rod down again and again. Then he sat in front of the lock, feet against the bars, and jerked the rod again and again until he was huffing and drenched with sweat.

Shanna stood silent, watching. She nibbled her lower lip. She rubbed her open hands against her thighs. She looked plenty nervous. Maybe she was worried that we wouldn't be able to get the lock off. Maybe she was worried that we would.

I only looked at her once in a while. Because my eyes wouldn't stay on her face. And where they went got me too worked up. So I spent most of the time watching Mike.

Finally, he flopped backward with the tire tool across his belly and lay there, panting.

'Move,' I told him.

He scooted out of my way. I crouched and whacked the door hasp just above the padlock's shackle. I only hit it once, though. The way it rang out and my hatchet hopped off, I decided that I might have better luck dealing with the padlock. So I started bashing the lock with the blunt side of my hatchet. Sometimes I missed, but mostly I hit its case.

With each blow, the lock rebounded with a wild bounce and I had to wait for it to settle down. I must have struck fifty times before taking a breather. I stood back and wiped sweat out of my eyes. The shackle was still inside its hole, but the body of the lock looked really battered and caved in.

'I think we've almost got it,' I gasped. 'Give me the tire iron.'

Mike handed it to me.

I positioned it the same way he'd done, held it steady with my left hand, and struck it near the top with my hatchet. One hit. Another. On the third, the case dropped a bit and swiveled, loose at one side.

'My God!' Mike blurted. 'You got it!'

'Yep.'

I tossed the hatchet and tire iron aside. As I slipped the lock off the door hasp, I looked up at Shanna.

She had moved, was squatting near the other side of the cage, her back to us as she picked up her clothes.

'Me first,' Mike whispered.

He pushed me out of the way, threw open the cage door, and rushed in. Shanna only had time to glance over her shoulder before he was on her. He grabbed her from behind, hoisted her up, and rammed her straight forward. Her head pounded the bars. He swung her around and let go. She hit the floor hard, rolled a couple of times, and came to rest on her back, sprawled out and gasping.

It had happened very fast. I had watched, stunned. Now I shouted, 'Mike! Christ!'

He looked startled. He blinked at me. 'Just watch and enjoy. You're next.' He stepped between her legs, dropped to his knees and lunged forward, shoving his face into her groin.

'Don't,' Shanna muttered. Her voice was really feeble. 'No.' She tried to reach down for him, but her arm didn't make it and fell.

'Stop!' I shouted, rushing into the cage.

He raised his head and turned it toward me. He was all wet and shiny around the mouth.

I stopped right beside him.

'Leave her alone. I'm serious.'

'She wants it, man. Fuck. Don't be a wuss.' He got up to his knees and unbuckled his belt.

'You hurt her. That wasn't part of the deal.'

'What deal?'

'Damn it, Mike!'

'You wanta go first? Is that it? Okay, be my guest.' He stood up and stepped backward. 'Help yourself.'

I shook my head.

'Look at her. Look at her!'

I did. Her eyes were squeezed shut, her face contorted with pain. She was gasping for breath. Her breasts rose and fell. They were shiny with sweat. She was shiny all over, splashed with sunlight. Her legs were wide apart.

'Have at her,' Mike said.

'I can't.'

'Fuck her, man! Do it!'

'Fuck you,' I said.

'You feeling sorry for her? Shit, man, she called you a retard. Remember? A moron and a retard.'

'Yeah, I know. But . . .'

'So ream her! Ream her out!'

'I can't.'

'Forget it. I'll go first.'

He took a step toward her, but I blocked the way.

'Move.'

'No way.'

'I mean it.'

'We aren't gonna do this.'

'Like hell.' He pulled his knife. He shoved it toward my face.

'Go ahead and use it. Kill me. That's the only way you're gonna get at her.'

'You're asking for it.'

'If you're gonna kill me, do it.'

For a long time, we faced each other. I really figured he might go ahead and slash my throat. Hell, I knew how he felt. I wanted her, too. Or I *had* wanted her until Mike drove her head into the bars. It had changed, then, somehow. When I'd looked down at her, sprawled out all exposed and hurting and vulnerable, barely conscious, she'd stopped being a thing I ached to grope and fuck.

199

Stopped being a collection of sweaty breasts, jutting nipples, and pussy. Instead, she was a person, a girl named Shanna who didn't deserve any of this.

Corny, huh?

Sue me.

'This is nuts,' Mike finally said.

'Yeah. I know.'

Grimacing, he shoved his knife back inside its sheath. He said, 'Shit.'

I stuck out my hand.

He scowled at it. Then reached out and shook it. 'You're such a fucking wuss.'

All of a sudden, I felt really good. Buoyant, in fact. Have you ever been in a bad earthquake? This is how you feel after it's over and you realize the house hasn't come down on your head. You're trembling and weak, and so glad it's over that you damn near feel drunk.

'Don't know what you're grinning about,' Mike said. 'We just blew the chance of a lifetime.'

'More than likely,' I said.

He shook his head.

We stepped over beside Shanna. She blinked up at us.

'We aren't going to do anything to you,' I said.

'That's right,' Mike muttered.

'We'll leave the door open and go back to our car. You're free.'

Shanna started to weep.

We left the canteen and chocolate bar in the cage with her, picked up the hatchet and tire iron, and walked through the woods to the car.

About half an hour later, just after Mike said, 'She isn't coming,' Shanna walked out of the trees.

She'd put her clothes on. The canteen swung by

200

her side. She poked the last of the chocolate bar into her mouth, and was still chewing when she reached the car.

'You guys wanta give me a lift?' she asked.

'Where to?' I asked.

'Wherever you're going.'

'You'll have to ask Mike,' I said. 'It's his car.'

'You drive,' he told me.

We switched places. Shanna, standing by the open passenger door, stared at Mike for a second. Then she whapped the top of his head. Quite hard. 'You're still an asshole.'

'Do you want a ride or don't you?'

Shanna climbed in and sat on his lap. She pulled the door shut. 'Let's get outa here.'

And that's what we did.

We never found out who'd put Shanna in the cage, or why.

Maybe a bunch of guys showed up that night only to find themselves robbed of their fun. Maybe not. Maybe she'd been locked up for some other reason.

By someone who just wanted rid of her.

By someone with good intentions who hoped to save the world from her evil.

Maybe she *was* the Devil, or a vampire, or a werewolf.

If so, she behaved herself around Mike and me. I won't go so far as to say she was an angel. Sometimes, she could be a real pain in the butt.

Which isn't all that unusual for a girl.

But she stayed with us for eight days and nights. Not once did she sprout horns and a tail, suck our blood or grow a hairy snout and rip out our throats. Not even when the moon was full.

We bought her a lot of stuff in the first town we found. Including clothes and a pack and a sleeping

201

bag. She took all of it with her when we finally dropped her off at Half Moon Bay. But she never used the sleeping bag while she was with us.

She slept in ours. She took turns.

Somebody once said that no good deed goes unpunished. Whoever said that was nuts.

The Direct Approach

'I was about to leave.'

'I'll only take a few minutes of your time, Mrs Morton.'

'Miss,' she corrected. 'It's Miss.'

'*Miss* Morton.'

'You got my name from the mailbox, right?'

'That's very astute, Miss Morton, very astute. If I might have a few moments of your time?'

'I really should be leaving.' She started to shut the door, but the man's black case blocked it. 'Will you please remove your sample case?'

'Miss Morton, I'm offering you the opportunity of a lifetime.'

'What are you selling?'

'If I might just step inside for a moment?'

'I really don't think I'd be interested, Mr . . .'

'Snye. Marvin Snye. It'll be worth a great deal to you.'

'Just what *are* you selling?'

He smiled. His mouth was too red, his teeth too white, his hair too slick and black. 'Miss Morton, I'm in the mortality business.'

'Cemetery plots?'

'No, no. Hardly that. The firm I represent deals in discreet homicide.'

Peggy Morton's heart raced.

'Murder?'

'Precisely.'

'You're kidding me.'

'I'm quite serious, Miss Morton.'

Shutting her eyes, she rubbed her temples. 'I . . . I don't know. Murder? Okay, let's hear what you've got to say.' She opened the door wide. 'Come in.'

Marvin Snye stepped into her house. He looked slight in his gray suit. His face looked white except for the slash of his mouth. He sat on the couch. Peggy hoped he wouldn't lean back; his hair, she was certain, would leave a dark smudge on the upholstery.

'You may be wondering, Miss Morton, about the exact nature of the service I'm making available to you.'

'You might say that.' She smiled nervously, and sat on a chair facing him.

'I represent the firm Futures Unlimited. We believe that the future lies in the hands of the strong, Miss Morton, in the hands of those individuals with the courage to make it theirs. If you're that kind of person – and I think you are – then you may find our service perfectly suited to your special needs.'

She cleared her throat. 'What do you do, exactly?'

'I'm glad you asked that question. It shows you're a woman who likes the direct approach, and so do I. You believe in confronting situations head-on, don't you?'

'Usually, yes.'

He smoothed his hair, then glanced at his hand as if to see whether anything had rubbed off. 'Our firm believes,' he explained, 'that situations arise from time to time that cannot be solved by conventional means. For a modest sum, we remove those obstacles, those irritants which stand in the way of a more satisfying life for our customers – often with astounding results. If I may?'

He lifted the black case onto his lap, opened it, and took out a leaflet.

'Allow me to read you comments from a few of our satisfied customers.' From the back of the leaflet, he read, '"When I was recently passed over for a promotion, I was truly despondent. Futures Unlimited changed all that. I am now vice-president of a major manufacturing company, and have a brilliant career ahead of me. My gratitude goes to you."

'And here's another. I'm sure you'll appreciate this one. "The old goat simply wouldn't pass on. I thought he'd live for ever, and I was penniless. You did good. You're worth every red cent." We get all kinds, don't we, Miss Morton?' He grinned, and chuckled softly.

'One more? "My husband was a drunken brute. Futures Unlimited worked wonders for my peace of mind." I think that speaks for itself, doesn't it? I have many others in a similar vein, but these ought to be sufficient to indicate the positive response of our customers.

'Now, Miss Morton, tell me this: is there someone in either your personal or professional life whom you feel to be an obstacle, a nuisance, a threat?'

'Yes,' she said. 'Yes, there sure is.'

'Wonderful. I'm sure you'll be totally satisfied with our handling of the matter.'

'What will it cost?'

'Five thousand dollars. Twenty-five hundred in advance, the rest to be paid in full upon completion of the task.'

'That's an awful lot, isn't it?'

'We *do* offer a five percent discount if you agree to provide a testimonial for advertising purposes. An additional fifteen percent discount is available if you

205

purchase two disposals. That would mean, in effect, that you could purchase each for a mere $4,000.'

'I'd only want one.'

'With the testimonial?'

'I guess that'd be okay.'

'It would come to $4,750.'

'That's still awfully steep.'

'Frankly, I'm disappointed to hear you say that, Miss Morton.' He shook his head with regret.

'I'm sorry,' she said.

'If you shop around, you'll find that our fees are entirely reasonable. Certainly, you *could* have the job done for less, but you would invariably be dealing with amateurish thugs. Highly dangerous. In matters as sensitive as this, you would be unwise to settle for anything less than the very best. And we, at Futures Unlimited, *are* the best. We offer you complete confidentiality and prompt, efficient service of the highest professional quality. Naturally, the best costs a little more.'

'Naturally.'

'Now, shall we get down to basics?' He took a gold-plated pen from his shirt pocket, and a note pad from his suit coat. 'Your name?'

'Margaret Morton.'

'Address including zip code?'

She gave it to him. He scribbled in the notebook, never looking up.

'Occupation?'

'Police officer.'

The pen stopped. His lips formed a sickly smile. 'You are joking, of course.'

'Of course.'

'I'm certain you realize, if you are a police officer, that a charge of conspiracy to commit murder requires an overt act?'

'I'm not a cop.'

'All we have done so far is – fantasize.' He cleared his throat. 'Occupation?'

'Salesperson.'

'Employer?'

'Western Cosmetics.'

'Annual income?'

'Is that necessary?'

'I'm afraid so. We need to—'

'About thirty thousand.'

'Very good, Miss Morton. Now, I'll need the name of the subject.'

'Steve Hayes. H-A-Y-E-S.'

'Address?'

'This address.'

'Oh?'

'He lives here.'

'When can he be found at this location?'

'Every evening. He gets home from work at a quarter past five, and leaves at ten after seven in the morning.'

'Weekends off?'

'Yes.'

'Very good. Now, Miss Morton, what would you like me to put down as your motive?'

'What?'

'Your motive. Your reason for wanting Futures Unlimited to remove this man from your life.'

'He's been stepping out on me,' she muttered.

Marvin Snye shook his head. 'If I may say so, Miss Morton, it's difficult to believe that a man could find any woman more beautiful and alluring than you.'

'Thank you.' She squirmed under the man's watery gaze. 'You want a snapshot of him or something?'

'That would be very helpful.'

'Just a moment.' Peggy went to the front door where

she'd left her purse. She removed her wallet, opened it, and took out a color photo. 'Here's one,' she said. She brought it to the couch and handed it to him.

'Very good. Excellent. This will be of considerable help. Now, if you'll just sign here?' He held out his pen.

Peggy took it. 'What's this you want me to sign?'

'Your agreement to provide a testimonial at the completion of our task. It will mean a saving to you in the amount of $250.'

'Okay.' She scanned the document. 'I'll bet you get a lot of business.'

'We do quite well.' He smiled with pride. 'I've just been transferred from back east to handle this region, and I certainly find my hands full.'

'I guess there's lot of people around who want somebody dead.'

'Almost everyone. Of course, many can't pay the price we ask and others haven't the moral courage to deal with us. Still, I've managed to sign up half a dozen prospects within the past week.' He fondly patted his notebook. 'Now, if you'll sign right here?'

She signed.

'We'll require cash, of course, for the down payment.'

'Of course. But I don't keep that much in the house. I'll have to make a withdrawal from my savings account.'

'I'll be more than happy to pick it up at your convenience. When would that be?'

She grinned down at him.

'Miss Morton?'

'How about never?'

'Miss Morton, really, I fail to . . .'

'I won't pay you a single cent. How do you like that, sleazoid?'

His face went red. 'I fail to see . . .'

He tried to duck away as Peggy thrust the pen at his throat, but he wasn't quick enough. It punched in deep.

'Amateurish thugs, huh?'

She looked at the blood spilling onto her couch and groaned. Cutthroat competition could get *so* messy.

Good Vibrations

Kim spread her blanket on the sand. She stepped onto the middle of it, set down her beach bag and pulled off her sneakers and socks. She placed her sneakers at two corners of the blanket in case the wind should pick up.

Then she unbuttoned her blouse.

She wondered who might be watching. The beach was hardly deserted. At least a dozen guys – some playing volleyball, a few tossing Frisbees, others sunbathing alone or with friends or families or lovers – had turned their heads to inspect her as she'd made her way along the beach in search of an empty place to put down her blanket. Some would be staring at her now, eager to watch the clothes come off.

The beach was aswarm with beautiful young women in scanty swimsuits, but most of the guys within range would have their eyes on Kim. Because she was the one still wearing a blouse and shorts. And they wanted to watch her strip.

She'd come to the beach often enough to know how they were.

Right now, any number of men were staring at her back, aware that she'd unbuttoned her blouse, waiting for her to slip it off her shoulders. Most, she suspected, hoped that by some miracle of recklessness or mischance she'd left the top of her swimsuit elsewhere.

Sorry to disappoint you, fellas, she thought.

She removed her blouse, dropped it to the blanket, then quickly pulled down her shorts and stepped out of them. That should pretty much end the suspense for her audience. Now, she was just another gal in a string bikini. She hadn't forgotten to wear a suit, after all. And it wasn't transparent. And it hadn't fallen apart to give them a thrill.

The guys could turn their attention to other matters.

Some, of course, were bound to keep on watching. There were always a few of those.

It's just part of coming to the beach, Kim told herself. You know you'll be stared at and admired. You know you'll be getting some guys turned on. Like it or not, that's the way it is.

Relax and enjoy yourself.

Clasping her hands behind her head, she stretched. She shut her eyes, arched her back, rose onto tiptoe, clenched her buttocks, and moaned with the good feel of her straining muscles. She sniffed the fresh, briny air. She heard the surf roaring in and washing out, the squeals of seagulls and children, laughter and shouts, rock 'n' roll and rap and country music and the manic voices of DJs from nearby radios. She felt the heat of the sun. She relished the way the soft, cool breeze stirred her hair and roamed over her bare skin.

This is really the life, she thought. It doesn't get much better than this.

It would be better without the bikini, she thought.

And laughed softly.

The fellas would *really* have something to look at, then.

No way.

Kim opened her eyes. Even through the tinted lenses of her sunglasses, the gleam of the sunlit waves was so bright that she was forced to squint. Some kids were playing in the surf. A couple of lovers strolled by, the

211

foam sliding over their feet. A man in skimpy trunks ran past them, muscles leaping, bronze skin flashing.

He didn't look toward Kim. After he'd run by, she watched his back, the way his buttocks flexed under the tight sheath. She was still watching him when she noticed the young man stretched out on the sand a couple of yards off to her left.

He lay on his belly, arms folded under his face. His head was turned toward her. He wore a strange pair of goggles. They didn't look at all like swimming goggles. They were leather, with small round lenses, the green glass of the lenses so dark that she couldn't see his eyes at all. She felt certain that they were open, though. Open and staring at her.

He'd probably been one of those spying on her from the start.

She frowned at him. 'What're *you* looking at?'

He didn't answer. He didn't move. Playing possum.

No point in getting upset, Kim told herself. He has a right to be here. And there's no law against looking at me.

Not even if you are wearing weird goggles.

Something else seemed wrong about him, though.

Something more than the goggles and the sneaky way he was ogling her.

For one thing, she realized, he was sprawled on the actual sand; he had no towel or blanket under him. He didn't have a shirt or shoes. Instead of a real swimsuit, he wore faded cut-off blue jeans.

He didn't look wet at all, so he hadn't simply come wading out of the water and flopped here to let the sun dry him.

His beltless jeans hung so low that the top of his crease showed. A seat pocket was torn loose at one corner, and Kim could see skin through the hole.

212

The skin there seemed as tanned as the rest of him.

Look who's staring now, Kim thought.

She knew she ought to turn away from him. In those goggles, he just *had* to be a space cadet. She certainly didn't want him to get the impression that she might be interested in him.

All you need is a guy like this deciding to put moves on you.

He's gotta be a nutcase.

But a good-looking one, from what she could see of him. Muscular, slim, with smooth skin tanned a shade darker than the sand and bare all the way down past his hips where his cut-offs hung carelessly low. Or intentionally low. Maybe he wanted her to notice the sleek curve of his back and how it rose to the mounds of his buttocks. Wanted her to think about him being naked under the faded, torn denim.

Kim swung her gaze to his face. It rested on his crossed arms. Those goggles were so damn queer. He might be quite handsome, but who could tell with his eyes out of sight? His hair was cinched in against his head by the leather strap, but neatly trimmed, gleaming like gold, blowing a little in the breeze.

He looked as if he might be a few years younger than Kim. Still a teenager, for sure.

That might explain why he wore the goggles. Teen-aged guys often seemed to take a perverse pride in being strange. They enjoyed calling attention to themselves. Not only that, but they were constantly horny. He might be wearing the goggles just so he could spy on the girls in secret.

Maybe he isn't watching me.

Maybe he really is asleep.

His lips suddenly pursed out. Kissed at her twice.

Kim flinched. She turned away fast, knelt on her

213

blanket and stuffed her blouse and shorts into her beach bag.

Her heart was thumping.

He'd been watching her all along, knew she'd been staring at him, the creep.

Those kissing gestures! Only a jerk would do something like that. They'd been like a crude remark – 'kiss my ass,' or 'suck me off.'

Or maybe he'd meant nothing of the kind. Maybe he'd only wanted to suggest he wouldn't mind kissing her.

Whatever, it was damned embarrassing.

Kim wondered if she ought to pick up her things and move to a different section of beach. She didn't want to do that, though. She'd been here first. At least, she *thought* she'd been here first. She certainly hadn't noticed him when she'd picked this spot, or she wouldn't have put her blanket down so close to him.

No, he'd come along afterwards. He must've snuck over and flopped nearby to watch the strip show.

Maybe while I was spreading the blanket.

This is where I stay, she decided. I'm not about to let him scare me off.

Scare me off?

I'm not scared. Why should I be? He might be a weirdo, but so what? It's not like he can *do* anything to me, not with so many people around.

All he can do is look. So what?

Let him look to his heart's content.

Jerk-off.

Scared of him. Right. Sure.

Kim dug into her beach bag and pulled out a plastic bottle of suntan oil. She moved the bag out of her way. Then she turned around slowly. Though trembling a bit, she felt quite pleased with herself as she taunted him with a good frontal view of her body shifting and twisting inside the bikini.

Turning you on, goggle eyes?

She resisted a sudden temptation to make kisses at him.

That might start something.

So she kept her face toward the water, stretched out her legs, and uncapped the bottle of suntan oil. She squirted a thin stream of warm fluid down the top of each leg to the ankle. The oil gleamed in the sunlight, tickled her as it started to dribble. She set the bottle aside. With open hands, she spread the oil over her shins and knees. Then her thighs. She lingered on her thighs, sliding her hands slowly up and down and between them, slicking her skin all the way to the edges of the blue patch that stretched down from its low cord and hugged her like a narrow, glossy membrane.

Catching all this, Goggles?

Eat your heart out.

Done with her legs, she squirted oil into the palm of her right hand and slicked her belly, fingertips drifting along the cord that slanted down from high on both hips. Her hand drifted over the cord, then came up for more oil. This she spread over her sides and across her ribcage below her bikini top.

She oiled her shoulders and arms next. She grinned to herself as she did it.

Make him wait for the grand finale.

She took off her sunglasses. Eyes shut, she carefully dabbed oil on her face.

Bet I'm driving him nuts.

He's probably *already* nuts, or he wouldn't be wearing those idiotic goggles.

Kim put her sunglasses back on, then filled her hand with oil and began to rub it on her chest. She caressed herself, enjoying the hot slippery feel of her skin and savoring the way she must be tormenting the kid. He had to be watching, had to be wishing this was *his* hand sliding between her breasts and stroking their bare sides.

One hand at a time, she eased her fingers beneath the cords that suspended the garment from her neck. She smoothed oil over the top of each breast. She went in under the clinging fabric and brushed her fingertips over nipples already turgid and jutting.

Bet you never expected a show like this, dipshit.

Right hand still inside her top, oily fingers sliding on her nipple, she turned her head for a glance at her spectator.

He was gone.

Nothing there except the shallow imprint his body had pressed into the sand.

Where the hell'd he go?

Kim slipped her hand out from under the bikini and scanned the beach. She looked from side to side. She swept her gaze across the shoreline and the surf. She even twisted her head around to search the area behind her.

She saw plenty of people, even a few guys wearing cut-offs instead of swimsuits. Nobody was near enough, fortunately, to have enjoyed a ringside seat for her show. But the goggled kid who was supposed to be only a few feet away, who was supposed to be agonizing over her, was nowhere to be seen.

The bastard bailed out on me!

Good, she told herself. I didn't come here to get ogled by some freak.

Damn it! How could he just get up and walk away?

Must be gay. No other explanation. A straight guy would've stayed or come over and put moves on me.

Unless he left just to piss me off.

I'm not pissed off.

I'm glad he's gone. Good riddance. I didn't come here to get pestered by some freaky teenager.

Kim capped the bottle of oil. Her hands were trembling.

Calm down, she told herself. He's gone. Now you can just forget about him and enjoy yourself.

Twisting around, she propped the bottle against her beach bag. Then she lay down. She closed her eyes. She shifted about on her blanket, snuggling against the sand to shape it with the curves of her body.

She took a deep breath that pushed her breasts more tightly into the bikini's smooth, hugging pouches. She liked the feel of that. She liked the feel of the sun's heat and the way the mild breeze brushed over her skin like gentle fingertips.

It's wonderful, she thought. It's perfect, now that the creep is gone.

Almost perfect. She didn't like the way a lump in the sand pressed against her rump. She squirmed until it settled into the groove between her buttocks.

Probably a beer bottle left behind by some damn litterbug.

She thought about getting rid of it. But that would take so much effort: crawling off the blanket, moving it out of the way, digging into the sand, and then she'd have to *touch* the thing. Somebody else's garbage. Probably filthy. It might not even *be* a bottle. Might be an old bone, or something. Yuck. Forget it.

Besides, it didn't really cause any discomfort now. In fact, it felt rather good. She gave it a squeeze with her buttocks.

I ought to roll over and get the most out of it, she thought.

But she had already oiled her front. And she felt too lazy and contented to move. She yawned. She

217

stretched. She snuggled down against the sand and the bump, and soon she fell asleep.

In her dream, the young man in goggles knelt between her legs and slid his hands up her thighs. 'I knew you'd come back,' she told him. 'I knew you wanted me,' he said. She laughed and said, 'Don't flatter yourself.' He smiled. Then he ducked low and licked her. From the feel of his tongue, she realized her bikini bottom was gone. She looked down at herself. The top was missing, too. Gasping, she flung up her hands and covered her breasts. His mouth went away. 'It's all right,' he said. 'Nobody's watching.' She said, 'I'll just bet.' He opened his button and slid the zipper down. 'Would I do this?' he asked, 'if we had an audience?' He let the cut-offs fall to his knees. 'My God,' Kim muttered. 'All for you,' he said. She let her arms fall to her sides. Bending down, he kissed and licked her breasts. He sucked on them. She moaned and writhed. Then she gasped, 'No, wait.' He lifted his head. He smiled down at her and licked his glistening lips. 'What?' he asked. 'I don't even know you.' He answered, 'That's all right. You want me. That's all that matters.' She shook her head. 'I don't care about your name,' she told him. 'But I need to *see* who you are. It's like you're hiding from me behind those stupid goggles.' He smiled again. 'Help yourself.' Easing forward, he lowered himself onto her. As the length of his hot body pressed against her and his tongue slipped between her lips, she reached up and pushed the goggles to his forehead.

He had no eyes.

Empty sockets. Dark, bloody pits.

Kim yelped and pushed him away and flinched awake as she bolted upright. Sweat spilled down her body. She sat there, gasping for breath. A dream. It had just been a dream. A real doozy.

218

A great dream, there for a while. But those *eyes*!

Yeah. What eyes?

'Man,' she murmured. 'What's wrong with me, imagining something like that?'

She leaned back, braced herself up with stiff arms, and rolled her head to get the kinks out of her neck.

And saw him.

He'd returned.

He lay stretched out on the sand a few feet away, but on her right. He'd switched sides. Like before, however, his head rested on his folded arms, turned toward her. Like before, he wore the strange round goggles that hid his eyes behind their dark green lenses.

If he's *got* eyes, Kim thought.

She realized she was grimacing.

'Something wrong?' he asked.

'Yeah. You. What're you doing here?'

'Enjoying the beach.'

'It's a big beach. Why don't you go somewhere else?'

'I like it here. A very beautiful view.'

'Yeah? I thought maybe you were blind, or something.'

He smiled, showing straight white teeth. Then he rolled over and sat up and turned to face her. As he crossed his legs, he brushed sand off his shoulders and chest. 'You were asleep a long time,' he said.

'And I suppose you were watching me.'

'You looked like you were having a nightmare.'

'Why do you wear those stupid goggles?'

'They keep the sand out of my eyes.'

'They make you look like a dork.'

'Sorry.' A corner of his mouth turned up. Then he raised his hands to the sides of his goggles.

Kim's heart gave a lurch. Her stomach seemed to fall. She lost her breath.

'No,' she gasped. 'You don't . . .'

Too late.

He lifted the goggles to his forehead.

And Kim found herself staring at a pair of eyes as blue as the sky, with long silken lashes. They seemed amused, knowing, gentle.

He's gorgeous!

'Is that better?' he asked.

'A lot better,' Kim said. Her voice came out husky, barely making its way through the tightness in her throat.

'My name's Sandy,' he said. Smiling, he shook his head. Some sand came out of his fine, glossy hair, sprinkling his shoulders, falling past his face.

'You're sandy, all right,' Kim said.

'Named after Koufax.'

'Ah. I'm Kim.'

'Pleased to meet you, Kim. But you're going to burn that lovely skin if you don't turn over pretty soon.'

She eased herself down and rolled onto her side. Facing him. Very aware of how her breasts shifted within the flimsy, yielding patches of her bikini.

'If I turn over,' she said, 'my back will burn. Unless you'd like to help me.'

'Help you?'

'With the suntan oil.'

'Ah. I suppose I could do that.'

'Thanks.' She rolled off her side and stretched out. She crossed her arms beneath her face. And watched Sandy gaze at her as she squirmed on the blanket to smooth and shape the sand. She remembered the lump that had been pressing up against her, earlier. She didn't feel it now.

She stopped moving.

Sandy just sat there.

'Well?' she asked. 'Coming over?'

He shook his head. Some more sand fell from his hair. 'I've got a better idea,' he said. 'Why don't you come over here?'

Suddenly playing control games?

Maybe he just wants to watch me stand up and walk, wants to enjoy the bod in motion.

'My blanket's here,' she said.

'That's what I mean. You don't need it. It's in the way. You should be on the sand.'

'I'd get it all over me.'

'Shower afterwards.'

She stared into his wonderful eyes. He's seeing me naked in a shower, she thought. Maybe seeing himself *with* me under the spray. Soaping me.

She pushed herself up. She clutched the slippery bottle of suntan oil and crawled off the blanket. Crawled toward him, head up, watching him, the hot sand sinking under her hands and knees. It was a shame he couldn't see how her breasts swayed, but he must have a nice view of her back, bare except for the two tied cords that held her top on and the third that descended from her hips to the narrow sheath clinging to her buttocks.

She stopped in front of his crossed legs. She pushed herself up. Kneeling, she held out the bottle.

He took it from her.

'Here?' she asked.

'Here's fine.'

She turned aside and lay down flat. The sand felt almost hot enough to scorch her. After a few moments, she got used to the heat. She squirmed, enjoying the way the surface molded against her body.

'Doesn't that feel better than the blanket?'

'It's different.'

'It's like floating,' he said. 'Floating on a warm sea

221

that loves you. Feel how it hugs you? Feel how it holds every curve of you, every hollow?'

'I guess so.' It's nice, she thought, but it's not *that* nice. This guy may be gorgeous, but he's still a little weird. 'Are you going to oil my back for me?'

Smiling, he nodded. As he got to his knees and crawled to her, Kim swept her hair aside to bare the nape of her neck. She untied the cord there. She lowered its ends to the sand, then reached up behind her back and plucked open the bow at her spine.

'I don't want strap marks,' she explained.

'More like strings,' Sandy said.

'Now there aren't any strings in the way.' Kim folded her arms under her face. She stretched and wiggled. It felt very good to be free of the cords, exciting to know that her top was loose, held against her breasts by nothing more than the pressure of the cupping sand. 'I'll have to remember to stay down.'

'If you forget, I doubt that anyone would mind. I know I wouldn't.'

She trembled with delight as Sandy squirted a stream of warm oil across the backs of her shoulders and down her spine. Then his hands were on her, gliding, sliding. They drifted all over her back and sides. They spread the oil. They massaged her. They explored her, even roaming low enough to slick the sides of her breasts. When he did that, she raised herself slightly out of the sand. But he didn't take advantage of it, didn't reach into the space and fill his hand. He simply moved on and Kim, with a sigh, sank down again.

When his hands went away, she lifted her head and looked around. She found Sandy kneeling by her hip. He bent forward and squirted oil down both her legs. His cut-offs hung so low they looked as if they might fall off.

God, he's fantastic, she thought.

222

Then she was lost in the feel of him kneading her calves. She lowered her face against her arm and shut her eyes.

When he's done, she thought, maybe he'll let me oil him.

That would be wonderful. But she would need to tie her top again and get up. She didn't want to do that. She liked being just where she was.

I couldn't get up if I wanted to, she thought.

And moaned as his hands worked their way up her thighs. Slid between them. Slicked her bare skin all the way to her groin, then went up and caressed her hips with oil before swirling over her buttocks. He rubbed them, squeezed them. But stayed away from the little that was covered, as if her bikini were a border he didn't dare cross.

Probably doesn't want to stain it with oil.

Or afraid people might be watching.

I've got to take him home with me, Kim thought. I've got to. Take him home to bed. He can oil me all over, and I'll oil him. It'll stain the sheets, but who cares?

Then he was done.

Kim let out a shaky breath. She opened her eyes, and watched Sandy crawl alongside her. He lay down, crossed his arms, and gazed into her eyes.

'That was great,' she whispered.

'My pleasure,' he said.

'I just wish nobody else was here. And we had the whole beach all to ourselves.'

'I know.'

'Would you like to come over to my apartment?'

He frowned slightly. 'I don't think so.'

You can't mean that, Kim thought. Please. 'There won't be anyone there. Only us.'

'I like it here.'

'We don't have to leave right away. We can stay as long as you want.' She tried to smile. 'I'm not sure I'd be able to move right now, anyway. You've got me so . . . lazy and excited.'

'This is where I belong,' he said.

'Hey, come on.' That sounded a bit whiny. She struggled for control, then tried again. 'Don't you get it? I *want* you. I want us to make love.'

'So do I.'

'Well, then . . .'

Sandy drew the goggles down over his eyes. He straightened his arms overhead, then turned his face downward and pushed it into the sand.

'What're you . . . ?'

He began to shake, his whole body shuddering, vibrating.

Kim raised her face. She gaped at him. 'Sandy? What're you doing?'

He didn't answer. He kept on quaking.

My God! He's having some kind of fit!

'Are you all right? What's wrong?'

Reaching out, she clutched his shoulder. It juddered in her grip. Then sand was pushing up around her fingertips.

My God! He's sinking!

She jerked her hand away.

The sand shivered around his palsied body, seemed to be melting beneath him, sucking him down. His arms were already gone. His face was buried past the ears.

His shoulders vanished competely. Sand spilled in across his lower back, trembled above his legs.

Gotta help him!

Kim almost thrust herself up, then remembered her loose top. She groped for the strings, found them in the sand beside her breasts, strained her arms up behind her back to tie them. Then let them fall again.

Because all that remained of Sandy was the seat of his cut-offs and the back of his head – the leather strap matting down his hair.

The goggles.

He's doing this on purpose.

It's what he does.

It's how he disappeared last time.

He's doing it because of me.

Now he was completely gone, leaving behind an imprint of his outstretched body in the sand.

Holy shit!

Kim looked around. Not far away, people were sunbathing. Others were sitting up, reading, talking. One group was having a picnic. A kid walked by with a bottle of soda.

Nobody was gazing, thunderstruck, at the patch of beach where Sandy had pulled his disappearing stunt.

Nobody had noticed.

Nobody knows but me.

Maybe it didn't happen, at all. A person can't just wiggle down like that and vanish. It's impossible.

But I *saw* it happen. And I'm not dreaming, now.

Reaching up behind her, Kim stroked the small of her back. Her hand came away slick.

I didn't dream him oiling me. I'm not dreaming any of this. He really buried himself. Somehow.

Her throat felt tight and tickly. She kept her mouth shut to hold in the scream or wild laugh that wanted to burst free. From her nose came a high-pitched humm.

It's crazy! Get the hell out of here!

She slapped her hands against the sand, ready to push herself up, then paused, wondering if she should

225

tie her bikini first. No time to lose. Better to risk a little embarrassment than to delay her escape even for a . . . the sand beneath her breasts trembled.

Rubbed her.

My God!

All thoughts of fleeing dissolved as the sand shifted against her breasts and fell away. She felt them hanging free inside hollows. Then hands were cupping them, squeezing them gently. Warm, grainy hands on her bare skin. Kim didn't know what he'd done with her bikini top, but she didn't much care.

It's down there somewhere, she thought.

I can worry about it later.

Trembling, she crossed her arms beneath her face.

This is just too weird, she thought.

He's under me. Touching me. And nobody knows. It's our little secret. Our big secret.

How the hell can he breathe?

It's only been a minute or two, she thought. She'd heard of pearl divers who could stay under water for ever. Ten minutes? Fifteen?

This is incredible. Fabulous.

She writhed and moaned as the hands plied her breasts, stroked and pulled her nipples.

This is why he didn't want me on the blanket, she realized. So he could get to me.

Something hard nudged her groin.

Something like the mouth of a beer bottle buried in the sand.

Oh, Sandy! You devil!

It tore her breath away as it thrust.

Not here. Is he nuts?

I can't untie my bottoms. Somebody'd notice that, for sure. And I don't want sand in me.

Gasping and moaning as Sandy teased her breasts and pushed at the flimsy shield between her legs, she

226

lifted her head. She began to sweep away the sand beneath her face. All she found was more sand.

'Where are you?' she whispered.

And scooped out more. And more. And uncovered his nose. Then his goggles. Then his lips. They were shut tight, a line of sand resting across the crease between them. Kim blew the sand away. She lowered her face into the depression and kissed them. They parted. His tongue pushed into her mouth. She sucked it, moaning.

The sand beneath her body began to shiver and slide.

His hands went away from her breasts, slid down to her hips, fingered the ties, plucked them open.

Don't. Somebody'll see.

But she didn't want to tell him no. Didn't want to pull her mouth away from his. Didn't want to stop what was happening. Because now she could feel all of Sandy. Somehow, he'd done away with the thickness of sand keeping them apart. And with his cut-offs.

Who does he think he is, Houdini?

She chuckled softly into his mouth.

He was long and hot against her oiled skin, smooth except for the rough grains that rubbed her as he shook.

He was shaking like crazy.

Vibrating.

It felt wonderful.

He didn't even stop shaking when he plucked the loose fabric and it slid down between her legs and away.

My ass is bare!

Everyone'll see!

Nobody'll see, she realized. It's all right.

Because sand was rushing in to cover her buttocks. It felt wonderful like warm water flooding down, caressing her bare skin, licking into crevices.

Kissing her shut eyes. Dribbling into her ears.

She realized her face was buried. But she could still breathe. No sand was coming into her nostrils as she sucked air. Couldn't get in between their faces. Not yet. And this shouldn't take long.

As Sandy pushed up at her, she tried to spread her legs wider. The sand held them motionless.

He thrust into her, anyway.

Big and thick and sandy.

Quivering in a frenzy deep inside her while his tongue plunged deeper into her mouth and his lips vibrated against her lips and the tremors of his chest rubbed and shook her breasts and his belly and pelvis and thighs all buffeted her with their mad fluttering.

How does he do this?

Doesn't matter how.

All that mattered was how it felt to be pinned down by the heavy sand, naked against his shuddering body, filled with him, lost in the feel of him.

She gasped into his mouth and quaked.

Sandy jumped in her depths, spurting.

Then he quit the wild shaking. He lay motionless beneath her.

We did it. My God, we actually did it here on the beach right in front of everyone . . . and nobody's the wiser.

His tongue began to slide out of Kim's mouth. She squeezed it between her lips, savoring the thickness of it. When it was gone, she kissed his mouth.

This was the best ever, she thought. I've got to bring him home with me.

She tried to lift her head.

The clutching sand held it firm.

Hey, come on.

'Sandy,' she whispered against his lips. 'Get us out of here.'

His quivering started again.

228

'Thanks,' she whispered.

Ride him up like an elevator.

Uh-oh, she thought. Where's my bikini? I'll be popping up bare-ass.

Then she realized that her beach blanket should be within reach. She could drag it over and cover herself, hide beneath it while she got into her shorts and blouse.

Then she felt sand sliding against her lips. Her next breath sucked dry particles into her nostrils.

Shit!

She blew out air to clear the passages, and held her breath.

Sandy!

Sand, not Sandy, was trembling beneath the length of her body. He was no longer pressed against her. But he was still in her. Hard and vibrating, slowly sliding out.

No!

She willed herself to reach down and grab hold before he was gone entirely. But the sand refused to let her arms move.

She clenched muscles around the retreating shaft. Hugged it, but couldn't stop it.

It went away.

Please! My God!

Don't get crazy, she thought. He'll be back. He's just fooling around, trying to throw a scare into me. Playing some kind of masculine control game. Wants to show me who's boss.

He can't just leave me here!

She tensed her muscles, made them shiver.

Two can play this game. If he can vibrate through the sand, so can I.

But the sand only squeezed her. Didn't slide away at all.

Her lungs began to burn.

She went limp.

He'll be back. He won't let me . . .

The sand began to shimmy beneath her trapped body.

I knew it! Thank God!

A pocket opened beneath her right breast.

A tongue slid against her nipple.

Damn it, Sandy! This is no time to fool around! I'm suffocating here!

She felt his lips, the edges of his teeth, his swirling tongue as he sucked her breast into his mouth.

You bastard! Get me out of here!

When his teeth snapped shut, Kim screamed.

When the scream was done and she gasped for air, sand filled her mouth.

Choking, on fire with agony, she struggled to shove and kick and buck, to get away from his teeth, to get free of the sand.

It clutched her, wouldn't let her move.

Held her for Sandy while he ate.

Phil the Vampire

'It's my husband,' she said.

'I see.'

'I don't think so.'

'Tell me about it, then.'

'He's . . . seeing other women.'

I nodded. It was what I'd figured.

The gal's name was Traci Darnell. She looked too young, too sweet, too terrific to have a husband stepping out on her. But all that doesn't matter if you're hooked with the wrong kind of guy. Some fellows don't care how good they've got it at home.

I'd seen it plenty of times before.

It never made much sense. It always made me a little sad, and more than a little disgusted.

'I'm sorry,' I told Traci.

'Well.' Her shoulders gave a quick, nervous hop. The rest of her didn't move at all, just sat rigid in the chair across from my desk, leaning forward slightly, hands folded on her lap. 'It's not as if . . . I mean, I knew what I was getting into.'

'What do you mean?'

'I knew there would be other women. A lot of them. I knew that going in. But . . .' She pinched her lower lip between her teeth. Her shoulders hopped again. 'I thought I could handle it. I thought it wouldn't matter. But it does.' Her eyes met mine. They were blue, intelligent, the sort of eyes that should gleam with fun. But they were grim. They made me want to hurt the guy responsible. 'I love him,' she said. 'I love him so much. It just . . . rips me apart. I can't stand it any more.' Her eyes brimmed.

'Are you sure he's seeing other women?' I asked.

She sniffed. 'Oh, he's never made any secret of it.'

'He admits it?'

'Admits? He doesn't *admit* anything, he *shares his experiences* with me. He tells me every detail of every conquest. Her name, what she looked like, what she was wearing – or not wearing – exactly where he had her. He tells me everything that was said. What she did, what he did. The feel of her, the smell of her, the taste.'

Leaning forward, I shoved a box of tissues closer to the edge of my desk. Traci plucked one out and blew her nose.

'Why did he tell you those things?' I asked. 'To rub it in? To make you squirm?'

'Oh, no. It wasn't anything like that. It was like I said, his way of sharing. He wanted me to know what was going on in his life, that's all. It was never meant to hurt me. He thought it would bring us closer.'

'Bring you *closer*? Telling you about the women he's . . .' I hesitated, reluctant to use any graphic terms in front of a gal who seemed so innocent and vulnerable.

'Sucked?' she suggested.

For a second there, I wondered if Traci had a lisp. 'Did you say "sucked"?' I asked.

'Sucked.'

'Sucked or fucked?'

Her face blushed scarlet. 'Ssssucked.'

'Oh. Sorry.' I felt my own face get hot. 'He told you about *sucking* these other women?'

232

'That's right. And he . . . he certainly didn't do that *other* thing.'

I couldn't see one whole hell of a lot of difference, myself. It seemed to me that Traci was splitting hairs.

Indignant, she said, 'He's never been unfaithful. He's not a lech, he's a vampire.'

I didn't miss a beat. 'Ah,' I said. 'I see.'

'Do you?' She looked hopeful.

'Sure. He's a vampire. He isn't having affairs with any of these women, he's just sucking their blood.'

'You really *do* understand?'

'Sure. *Dracula*, *Salem's Lot*, Lugosi and Christopher Lee, Barnabus Collins – you'd have to be culturally illiterate not to know a thing or two about vampires. And your husband's a vampire. What's his name, by the way?'

'Phillip.'

'Phil the vampire.'

I wished I hadn't said that. Traci looked betrayed.

'You think this is all a great big joke.'

'No. I really don't. Whatever's going on, it's obvious that you're . . .'

'I *told* you what's going on.'

'Well, not exactly.'

'Every night, he leaves me alone and goes off stalking victims. He drinks their blood. Then he comes home and *tells* me all about it. I hate it that he's seeing these other women . . . that he *needs* them. It makes me feel so . . . inadequate. You know, that *I'm* not enough for him.'

'No woman would be enough for his kind,' I said.

'Is that another wisecrack? Because if it is, I'm going to waltz right out that door and . . .'

'I was being entirely serious,' I explained. 'As a vampire, he couldn't possibly subsist on your blood alone. You'd be depleted in no time flat. You'd be

233

dead. Phil *has* to play the field. He would kill you otherwise. His roaming, actually, might be viewed as an act of love. Love for you.'

'I know that.' She looked ready to start weeping again. 'But that doesn't make it any easier . . . to live with.'

'You're jealous of these women he sucks?'

'Of course I am.'

'Does he ever suck you?'

'Sometimes.' She dipped her fingers under the collar of her blouse and pulled it aside. Her top button came undone, but she didn't seem to notice. The side of her neck had a pair of wounds just where you'd expect to find them in a Dracula movie. Healed, though. Scar tissue that looked like small, pink craters.

Real or make-up? I wondered.

Only one way to find out. I knocked my chair back on its rollers, stepped around my desk, and crouched in front of Traci. Close up, the scars looked pretty authentic.

'Do they hurt?' I asked.

'No. They never did hurt. Not even when he had his teeth in me.'

'Getting bit like that didn't hurt?'

'Oh, no.' With a dreamy look on her face, she fingered the tiny remains of the punctures. 'It felt . . . incredible.'

I raised my index finger. 'Do you mind?'

Shaking her head, she moved her hand out of the way. I gently probed both the scars. They felt real, all right. 'Phil actually made these with his teeth? He actually sucked blood out of your neck?'

'Yes.'

While Traci straightened her collar, I stood up and sat on the front edge of my desk. She didn't fasten the button that had come undone.

234

'And you're here because you don't like him doing it to other women?'

'That's right.'

'Has Phil killed any of these women?'

'No. Oh, no, I'm sure he hasn't. He's not at all like – you know, Dracula. He's a kind, gentle man. He respects life.'

'Wouldn't harm a fly, huh?'

'Oh, he sometimes eats them. But he doesn't have a malicious bone in his body. He wouldn't kill a *person*. He's very careful never to harm anyone.'

'Is he taking their blood by force?'

She looked confused. 'Well, he's sucking it out.'

'But with their permission? Are they willing partners?'

'Oh, of course. Who wouldn't be? Phil's . . . a hunk, you know? And smart and witty. I think most women find him irresistible. But he also has his powers.'

'Powers?'

'What I mean is, he can pretty much zap the mind of anyone he meets. He has this hypnotic thing he can do. Puts them under.' Traci snapped her fingers. 'Just like that, they're zombies. Not *literally* zombies. You know what I mean.'

'He can put them into a trance, and they'll comply with whatever he wants.'

'Right. But also, the main thing is they can't remember anything afterwards.'

'And Phil uses this power on his victims?'

'I don't know if I'd call them victims.'

'Whatever. The women he sucks. He zaps them?'

'All the time. Not me, though.'

'Why's that?'

Her look suggested it was a dumb question. 'Because I'm his wife, of course.'

'Ah. All right. But here's the thing. If your husband

235

is putting these women under – by hypnosis or whatever – he's compromising their ability to consent. In other words, he does not legally have their permission. If he was having sex with them . . .'

'He's not.'

'But if he *was* having sex with them, it would be rape. So I'm pretty sure he's violating some sort of law by biting them and taking their blood without permission. That would make it a police matter. I'm just a private investigator, and don't have the authority to—'

'I don't want Phil *arrested*!' Traci blurted, shaking her head. 'That's not why I came here. I don't want anything like that.'

'What exactly *do* you want?'

'I want him to stop. I want him all to myself. I want him to quit using all those others!'

The way she looked made me want to take her into my arms. To comfort her. To make her hurts go away. But I knew better. My self-control isn't always terrific when it comes to gals, especially the pretty, vulnerable ones. So I kept to my perch.

She gazed up at me with shiny, imploring eyes. 'Will you help me?' she asked.

'I'd like very much to help you,' I said. 'But maybe what you need is a shrink or . . .'

'A shrink? Are you saying I'm crazy?'

'Nothing of the sort. You obviously didn't put those bite marks on your own neck.' A moment after I'd said that, I wondered how she *might've* gone about putting them there.

Self-inflicted wounds are a fairly common trick. Perps think them a very clever way to deceive cops, lawyers, doctors, insurance companies, and even PIs like me.

Traci might have made the punctures herself. Physical evidence to back up her weird tale. If she'd made them, though, she'd done some major advance planning. From the appearance of the scars, the injuries must've been inflicted at least a month ago.

Either she was a major-league schemer, or she was telling the truth – the truth as she saw it, anyway.

'The thing is,' I explained, 'a therapist might be better equipped to help you confront your problem.'

She studied me with narrowed eyes. 'My problem?'

'I want to help you, Traci. I honestly do. You wouldn't believe the creeps and losers and slimes that I have to deal with all the time – mostly attorneys. My clients. So I tell you, it really brightened my afternoon when you showed up. You seem to be a very nice young lady. Easy on the eyes, to boot,' I added.

She gave me a smirk for that one. And blushed as she smirked. And kind of rolled her eyes toward the ceiling in a way that said, *Boy, what a line*.

'I'll do what I can for you, Traci. But we won't do each other any good unless we're honest about the situation. I intend to be honest with you. It might not be pleasant, but it's how I work. Okay?'

'Okay.'

'Your problem. You come in here and tell me your husband's a vampire. Now, we all know about vampires. The living dead. They sleep in coffins during the day, prowl at night, suck the blood out of people. They've got magical powers. They can control people's minds, turn themselves into bats, wolves, fog, pretty much anything that suits their fancy. They're immortal – or as good as. Live hundreds of years, who knows? They're afraid of the cross, find garlic disagreeable. Their reflections don't show up in mirrors. They can't cross moving water. They can't be killed by ordinary means, you've gotta nail them with a wooden shaft. Or trick them into the sunlight. Probably other ways, but I'm no expert. I just know what every red-blooded American guy knows on the subject. Which includes that such things just don't exist.'

'That's what you think.'

'It's what I know, Traci. It's what everyone knows. I'm not saying there aren't weirdos who *think* they're vampires and maybe even act accordingly. But the actual supernatural-Dracula-immortal-batman-vampire is nothing but fiction. You just aren't gonna meet one, not in this life. That means Phil isn't one. That's for starters.'

'So, you are saying I'm crazy.'

'I told you. I'm not a shrink. I'm just a gumshoe, the poor man's Spade. What I'm doing here with you is trying to apply some tricks of my trade, and the best tricks I've got are my instincts and common sense.'

'So what do they tell you?'

'First, I don't think you're crazy. Second, I'm pretty sure you aren't trying to put one over on me. So I'm forced to conclude that Phil has convinced you he's a vampire.'

'He *is* a vampire.'

'He bit your neck and sucked your blood.'

She nodded. 'Many times.'

'He goes off by himself every night and comes back with stories of his conquests. Of women he entranced and sucked.'

'Yes.'

'And you believe him.' I gave one of my bushy eyebrows a meaningful hoist. 'Have you ever followed him during one of his nightly prowls?'

She frowned. 'You're saying it might all be a lie?'

'Do you have any proof that it isn't?'

'He sometimes comes home with blood on his clothes.'

'A *lot* of blood, or . . .'

238

'No, just a few little spots or smudges.'

I fished my Swiss Army knife out of my pants pocket, opened the main blade, and nicked the back of my hand. A dot of blood bloomed out. I blotted it on the front of my white shirt. 'Now I'm a vampire, too,' I said.

And Traci smiled. It was the first time I'd seen her smile. It looked great. 'You've ruined your shirt.'

'Hire me, and I can afford a new one.'

'Hire you?'

'That's why you came in here, right?'

'Well. Yes. I guess so.'

'We were exploring the nature of your problem, right? Your husband has convinced you he's a vampire. As a vampire, he needs to drink human blood. So he goes out and sucks women, and you're jealous. You want it stopped. You want him to devote all his attention on you, not spread it around among strangers.'

'That's pretty much it, I guess.'

'That's your problem. But here's the question: what's Phil *really* up to? You can bet it's not sucking necks.'

'You're saying . . . it might all be like a cover while he's doing something he doesn't want me to know about?'

'I say you can bet on it. He might just be boozing with his buddies, something as innocent as that. Or maybe he's into some kind of criminal activity. Could be anything. But I've got to warn you, the most likely thing is that he's seeing another woman.'

'That's what I *told* you. He's seeing another woman every night.'

'But not to suck blood. To have sex.'

'No.'

'I realize it's a painful—'

'It's not painful because I know he doesn't mess

239

around with anyone.' Though she spoke calmly, her face was bright red. 'He *tells* me what he does to those women. Everything. Every small, intimate detail. And he . . . we . . . make out while he talks. We, you know, get naked. And then we fool around while he tells me all about the woman he'd been with that night, and when it comes to the part where he sinks his teeth into her, that's when he . . . sinks his, uh . . . that's when he enters me.'

She wasn't so much red, really, as pink. Her face, her ears, her throat, the smooth skin that showed between the edges of her blouse where the button was undone.

I had a bulge in my lap. I folded my hands down there to hide it.

Dry-mouthed, I said, 'So, he uses his stories to excite you. As a form of foreplay?'

'Something like that.'

'And the story always finishes with . . . intercourse?'

'Not always.' She gazed down at her own folded hands. 'Sometimes he . . . we . . . use our mouths. You know.'

'Oh.'

She raised her eyes. 'Anyway, so I guess you can see how come I know he's not having any affairs.'

'It may very well be that he's not. I hope he isn't, but obviously he's up to something. Something he means to keep secret from you, so he fabricated the vampire story.'

'I don't think it's a fabrication.'

'Does Phil have a job?'

'He doesn't need one. He's very rich.'

'What does he do during the day?'

'He sleeps. In his coffin. In the basement.'

That shouldn't have surprised me, but it did. Obviously, Phil was carrying his act to some rather major extremes.

'Have you ever seen him go outside in the sunlight?'

Traci shook her head. 'He never leaves his coffin from dawn till after sunset.'

'As far as you know.'

'Well, I don't stand guard, if that's what you mean.'

'What do *you* do during the day?'

'Sleep, do the shopping.' She shrugged. 'Different chores.'

'Do you look in on him often?'

'At first I did. I couldn't . . . you know, believe he'd stay down there so long. But he always did. It was a waste of time, checking on him. So I don't do it much any more.'

'So you can't say for sure whether he stays in the coffin.'

'Not absolutely for sure,' she admitted. 'But pretty sure. What's the big deal?'

'No big deal. Just curious. Have you ever seen Phil turn into a bat or anything?'

'He knows I can't stand bats.'

'Have you ever seen him change into . . . ?'

'He changed into a dog once. A big black lab.'

Right, I thought. But I kept the opinion to myself and asked, 'He changed into it before your eyes?'

'Look, if you don't want to believe any of this . . .'

'I just want to get at the truth, that's all. If you actually watched Phil turn himself into a dog, I guess I'd have to believe he's got supernatural powers.'

'You wouldn't have to believe any such thing. You'd figure I was either lying or hallucinating, or that Phil had fooled me with some kind of magic trick.'

'Is Phil a magician?'

'He's a vampire.'

'Did you watch him turn into the dog?'

'No.'

241

'Then what makes you think . . . ?'

'The dog was Phil.' She'd turned pink again. 'I know it was him.'

'How do you know?'

'Never mind. Can we change the subject?'

'All right. Let's change it to mirrors. Does Phil show up in mirrors?'

'Yes.'

I managed not to blurt, *Ah-ha!* But I couldn't help smiling. 'You've seen his reflection in mirrors.'

'Yes.'

'Well, doesn't that suggest a hole in his vampire story?'

'I asked him about it.'

'And?'

'He told me that mirrors aren't the same as they were in the old days. A lot of them used to be backed with silver, but that's pretty rare now. He said he wouldn't show up in a mirror that has a real silver backing. I don't have one like that, so I don't know.'

'Convenient for Phil.'

She frowned. 'You know, I've never felt any great need to *prove* he's a vampire. I know what he is. So I haven't gone around *testing* him.'

'If he's not a vampire, Traci, he has no excuse to go roaming at night.'

'I know that. I know that better than anyone.'

'If he's not a vampire, then he's not sucking those women you're so jealous of.'

'I know. But he *is* one.'

I let out a sigh. 'Then how do you expect me to stop him from seeing those other gals? He *needs* blood, right? If he doesn't take it from strangers, where's he supposed to get it? He can't rely only on you. It'd kill you. Is that what you want?'

'No.'

'What *do* you want?'

Traci bent down and reached for her handbag. She had placed it on the floor beside her chair immediately after sitting down. It was a large leather bag with a shoulder strap. As she took hold of the bag, I glanced down the front of her blouse. She wore a pale blue bra that was too skimpy to cover much. What it did cover, it was too transparent to hide. What I could see was her entire right breast.

My view went away when Traci sat up, lifting the handbag onto her lap. She slipped her hand inside the top and came out with a wooden stake.

It looked like a foot-long section of broom handle that had been whittled with a knife until it tapered down to a point.

'You're kidding me,' I said.

She stared into my eyes.

'You want me to kill Phil?'

'It's the only way to stop him.'

'Terrific,' I muttered.

She handed the stake to me. I looked it over, thumbed its point. The point was very sharp.

'You said you wanted to help,' she reminded me.

'You've got the wrong guy.'

'I don't think so.'

'I don't do murder.'

'It wouldn't be murder.'

'No, sure, of course not. He's a vampire. Right.'

'It's the truth.'

'Yeah, and I'm Tinkerbell.'

'You've *got* to do this for me. Please. I'll pay you whatever . . . How much do you want? Five thousand? Ten?'

'I don't get it. Why do you want him dead? I thought you loved him?'

'I do.'

'You're just so jealous of these other gals . . . ?'

'Yes!' Her eyes flashed. 'Is that so hard to understand? Every night – every night he leaves me alone and goes to someone else. I can't stand it!'

'But he always comes home to you,' I said. 'Those others are nothing to him except . . . nourishment? It's you he loves. It's you he *makes* love to. And it sounds pretty damn passionate, if you ask me.'

Lowering her head, she murmured, 'It is. But . . . *they're* the ones he sucks.'

'You'd *rather* be sucked?'

'It's so much more . . . more everything. Than sex. There's no comparison. It's a kind of rapture that you . . . you just can't imagine.'

'Does Phil know how you feel about this?'

'Of course he does. But he won't give in. He says that he likes me the way I am, that if he sucks me too often, I'll lose my spark. My spark. That's a laugh.'

'It sounds as if he cares a lot about you.'

'Well, he does. But not enough to stay home and bite *my* neck. That's all I want.'

'And since he won't do it, you want me to kill him? That doesn't make any sense at all.'

Her eyes darkened. 'If I can't have him, nobody else will. You know what I mean? I'm sick to death of it.'

All of a sudden, I believed her.

I didn't believe the part about Phil being a vampire. I knew she believed it, though, and I knew she wasn't kidding that she wanted him dead.

If I can't have him, nobody else will.

The magic words.

Graveyards are full of people who died because someone loved them – loved them too much, would rather see them dead than lose them to another person.

'I'm not a killer,' I explained again.

244

'It's not as if you'd be killing a man.'

'He *is* a man. You may think he's a vampire, but he's flesh and blood. If I took your money and whammed that stake through his heart, it'd be murder. In this state, it'd be first-degree murder with special circumstances. That'd make it a capital crime. Not me, lady.'

'How much?' she asked.

'Uncle Sam doesn't print enough.'

'What if I can prove to you that Phil's a vampire?'

'Ain't gonna happen.'

'But just suppose. How would you feel about killing a real . . . what did you call it? A real, supernatural-Dracula-immortal-batman-vampire? There's no law against *that*, is there?'

'Of course not. But . . .'

'*Would* you be willing to kill an actual vampire? For ten thousand dollars? And for me?'

I didn't miss a beat. What was to think about?

'Sure I'd do it,' I told Traci. 'But it won't happen. There's no way, not a chance in hell, you could ever prove to me that Phil's a vampire.'

For the second time that afternoon, Traci smiled. 'Want to bet?' she asked.

She glanced past me at the office window, then checked her wristwatch. 'Sunset isn't till six-twenty-five. That gives us almost an hour and a half.'

I suddenly got an ucky feeling in my gut. 'You want to do this now? Today?'

She nodded. 'Before Phil wakes up.'

Traci drove. I rode with her in the passenger seat of her Porsche. Normally, I would've driven my own car. There wasn't much normal about this trip, though. No telling what I might be getting in to. If it got messy, I didn't want some neighbor or passerby giving the cops a description of my vehicle.

Besides, riding with Traci gave me more time to enjoy her. She didn't talk much. She smelled good, and had a fine profile. Her black leather skirt was very short, her legs long and smooth.

I thought a lot about how Phil told his stories every night while they worked on each other. How he timed things. *When it comes to the part where he sinks his teeth into her, that's when he sinks his . . .* That's when he put it to her.

Lucky stiff.

The whole vampire thing seemed to be a huge turn-on for both of them.

Assuming, of course, that Traci'd been telling me the truth.

I didn't like to think that she'd been lying about any of it. Lying would mean I'd signed on for a whole different ballgame. Maybe not even a ballgame, at all.

There wasn't much traffic, so we made good time. We left the city behind. Traci sped us through the woods on narrow roads shrouded with shadows.

It took us nearly an hour to reach the house.

A nicely kept two-story colonial. Normal looking. Nothing creepy about it, if you don't count finding it all by itself at the end of a half-mile of unpaved road.

'Where does Phil find all these gals he sucks?' I asked as Traci stopped the car.

'In the city, mostly.'

'A commuter vampire.'

'We'd better hurry.'

As I followed her toward the front door, I checked my wristwatch. Five-fifty. If Traci was right about the sunset, Phil would be rousing himself in thirty-five minutes.

Not much time.

Not much, right. I felt like a dope for letting myself worry about it. Who cares when the sun goes down?

246

It would only matter if Phil was a vampire, and I knew better.

I had better things to worry about.

What's really going on? for instance.

Traci entered the house first. I stepped in behind her. Even though the sun hadn't gone down yet, the house was pretty dark and gloomy inside. She didn't turn on any lights. Not till we stood at the top of the basement stairs. The basement was very dark. She flipped a switch. Lights came on. They made it a little better, but not much.

'He's down there?' I whispered.

Traci nodded. She removed the stake from her handbag and offered it to me.

I shook my head. I reached under my jacket and unlimbered my .45. It was a big heavy Colt, army model. Out of fashion, I know. These days, it's all 9 mm Berettas and such. But the Colt auto was good enough for my old man in the Pacific. You remember the Pacific? That's when the Japs were too busy killing us to buy the country out from under our sorry butts.

I jacked a round into the chamber.

'That won't do you any good against Phil,' Traci warned.

'Let's go,' I said.

No reason to waste time explaining that vampires were the least of my worries.

For all I knew, this whole bit might've been a trap they'd laid for *me*. Maybe Phil was a guy I'd pissed off, one time or another. Maybe Traci was his cute little helper.

As Yogi Bera might've said, *You never know till you know*.

Traci kept hold of the stake, and started down. I let her get a few stairs below me, then followed. The stairway was wood. It creaked and moaned. It had open

247

spaces between the treads, spaces that somebody could reach through and grab your ankle. I tried to brace myself for something like that.

The basement air was cool. It had the normal basement smell of dank concrete.

The walls and floor were concrete.

Phil's coffin was on the floor just beyond the foot of the stairs, just beneath a glaring, bare lightbulb.

He was inside. Stretched out on a lining that looked like red satin. Eyes shut. Hands folded on his belly. Dressed to the hilt in a vampire garb that looked like it might've been filched from the Universal Studios wardrobe department.

He looked a lot younger than Lugosi'd been back in those days. He had sort of a clean-cut, boyish appearance. Long, blond hair. He might've looked like a Santa Monica surfer if he'd had a good tan. But his face was pale, pasty. And his lips were bright red.

I stopped beside Traci. We both stood over the coffin, staring down at Phil.

'Now do you believe me?' she asked. She spoke in a normal tone, and her voice resounded through the basement, damn near echoed.

'Shhh.'

'It's all right,' she said. 'We won't disturb him. He's totally out of it till the sun goes down.' She checked her watch. 'That's almost half an hour from now.'

'Sure,' I said.

Five minutes ago, the guy probably had his face pressed to the living-room window. Saw us coming and hightailed for the basement, his black cloak flapping.

If that's how it had gone, though, he hadn't winded himself.

From where I stood, I couldn't tell whether he was breathing at all.

248

'Will you do it now?' Traci asked. She held the stake out for me. Again.

'No such thing as vampires,' I said.

I gave the side of the coffin a good, rough kick. It gave the box a jolt. It shook Phil. But it didn't wake him up.

'Just take it.' Traci pressed the stake into my hand. Then she hurried across the basement, heels clacking, rump flexing nicely against the seat of her skirt. She snatched something off a workbench near the wall. When she turned around, I saw it was a claw hammer. She gave it a little shake. 'You'll need this.'

'Not likely.'

She stopped in front of me. She held out the hammer. 'Please. Take it.'

'My hands are full,' I muttered.

'The gun won't do you any good, anyway. Here.'

'No thanks.'

'You *said* you'd do it.'

'Yeah. And I will. If you can prove he's a vampire.'

'Just look at him.'

'That's no proof. That's a guy in a coffin and an outfit.'

'I mean *look* at him. He's not alive.'

He's not alive.

Holy shit!

I suddenly knew the score.

I jammed the muzzle of my .45 into Traci's gut. Her mouth sprang open. 'Lose the hammer, honey,' I said.

She dropped it. The steel head struck the concrete with a clank.

'Put your hands on top of your head and interlace your fingers.'

She blinked at me. 'What's—'

249

'Do it.'

She did it.

'Stay put.'

'What's *wrong*?' she blurted. 'Why are you *doing* this?'

I didn't answer. I dropped the stake, shifted the Colt to my left hand, and crouched beside the coffin. Keeping the pistol aimed at Traci, I reached into the coffin with my right hand and found Phil's neck.

Its skin felt cold.

I fingered around, searching for the pulse. From the temperature of the skin, though, I knew I wouldn't find one. And I didn't.

'He's dead, all right,' I said.

'That's what I *told* you. He's not a man, he's a vampire.'

'He's dead.'

'He's *un*dead.'

'Right. Where'd you get the idea I'm an idiot, lady?'

'What are you *talking* about.'

'This.' I stood up and stepped toward her. 'Keep your hands on your head and turn around.'

She turned around.

I stepped in close behind her. I started patting her down. 'You murdered him. You put together this vampire story, got him into the outfit and coffin, checked your phone book for a likely—'

'You're crazy!'

'Not crazy enough to fall for your game.' She was clean. I holstered my piece, brought her arms down behind her back, and cuffed them.

I go plenty of places without my Colt. I never leave home without my handcuffs.

They come in useful when I need to keep someone in custody. And they're a turn-on for a lot of my lady friends.

250

Traci fell into the former category.

Too bad. I'd liked her. I'd wanted her. Beautiful, sexy, innocent and vulnerable.

Cancel those last two.

Still beautiful and sexy, but about as innocent and vulnerable as a sidewinder.

A sidewinder. Rattlesnake or missile, take your pick.

After she was cuffed, I let go of her. She turned around and gazed at me with wide, stunned eyes.

'You had me going,' I said. 'Thing is, I'm an open-minded sort of guy. You tell me far-out stuff, I'll listen to reason. You had me about eighty percent convinced Phil might really *be* a vampire. But you fell a little short. Short to the tune of a murder rap.'

Traci shook her head.

'If you'd just been a little more convincing, I might've given Phil the stake treatment and taken you off the hook.'

'It's not too late,' she said. 'There's ten thousand in my handbag. Cash. Just kill him and—'

'And take the fall for you. Right. 'Fraid not.'

'I've seen how you look at me.'

'You're a good-looking woman.'

'I'll be yours.'

'Nope. I'll be in prison. Either that, or dead. More than likely dead. Otherwise, I might explain your little vampire fairy tale, and the cops might buy it. You planned to kill me, didn't you? I guess you'd claim you caught me in the act of staking your hubby . . . How were you going to explain his getup?'

'Please!' She started to weep.

'Forget it. I'm no one's patsy.'

Cuffed and all, she made a break for the stairs. I grabbed for her but missed, so she got a short lead. I raced after her. She was partway up the stairs before

251

I got hold of her. Just reached up, caught the hem of her skirt and gave it a tug.

I meant to yank it down around her ankles, hobble her, trip her up.

But the skirt didn't pull down. When I gave it that tug, I plucked Traci backward off the stairs and she came falling at me. I had time to dodge her. But I stayed my ground. It was either catch her, or let her crash to the concrete floor. I couldn't allow her to crash, not with her arms cuffed behind her back. Even a gal who'd tried to frame me for murder deserved better than that. So I braced myself and spread my arms.

I almost stayed on my feet.

But not quite.

Her weight hit me. I grabbed her, stumbled back, and fell. She pounded down on top of me. The cuffs got me in the nuts. The back of her head clopped my chin, and the impact of that bashed my head against the concrete.

I went out.

When I came to, Traci wasn't on top of me any more. But I spotted her easily enough. Opened my eyes, and there she was. Didn't even need to raise my head off the floor.

She was hanging from a ceiling girder. Dangling by her tied ankles. She was naked. Her skin was the color of a gloomy, overcast morning. Except where it was smudged with red handprints and lip marks, and where it trickled blood from punctures.

The punctures were bite marks like those she'd shown me on her neck. But these were fresh. Open, raw. And they were all over her, as if her attacker had been a connoisseur sampling tastes from her different regions – her thighs, her groin, her navel, her breasts, her face and the undersides of her drooping arms.

She still wore my cuffs. They were no longer connected, though. With the links between them broken, they encircled Traci's wrists like quirky silver bracelets.

I had reasons of my own for feeling miserable. But the way Traci looked made me feel a lot worse. She'd been broken. Used and trashed. And I was to blame.

I'd fucked up.

And she'd paid for it.

Without moving, I could feel the weight of the Colt in my shoulder holster. I snatched it out, tossed myself sideways, and rolled fast, ready to blast trouble.

What I saw while I rolled was Phil.

I came up to a squat, facing him, taking aim.

He was sitting on the basement stairs, watching me. Second stair from the bottom, feet on the concrete floor, elbows resting on his knees, hands folded. He didn't have his outfit on. He had nothing on, at all. Except a lot of Traci's blood.

Sighing, he shook his head. 'Women,' he muttered. 'You know what I mean?'

I put two slugs in his chest and one in his forehead.

They went through him like he was jelly. The holes flowed shut, and he was good as new before the bullets had time to quit ricocheting around the basement.

'Oh, shit,' I muttered.

He acted like it hadn't happened. 'You know what I mean?' he asked again.

I just gaped at him.

'You know?' he said. 'I mean, what'd I ever do to Traci? I loved her. I treated her great. And what does she do? She brings you over to put a hit on me. Jesus H. Christ on a rubber crutch.'

'She was jealous,' I said.

'Jealous? Shit. I screwed her head off, man. Every single night . . .'

253

'She didn't want that,' I explained. 'She wanted you to suck her.'

'Figures. They never listen. I told her over and over again, "Traci," I said, "I'd *love* to suck you every night. You *know* that. But it'd *kill* you." That's what I told her. But does she listen? Shit.'

'Looks like she finally got her wish.'

Phil gave me a weary smirk. 'Well, she died happy.'

'Will she become a vampire now?'

Phil huffed. 'No way. I'm leaving her dead, man. She tried to have me snuffed. Good riddance.' He shook his head again. He backhanded some blood off his lips. 'Broads,' he muttered. 'You can't live with 'em, you can't live without 'em.'

'Know what you mean,' I said.

'What's your name?' he asked.

'Matthews. Cliff Matthews.'

'Go on home, Cliff. I got no beef with you.'

Paying Joe Back

Folks say everything changes, but that's not so. I've lived in Windville all my life, and Joe's Bar & Grill looks just the same to me as always.

It has the same heavy steel grill, the same counter, the same swivel stools. Those long tables sticking out of the walls aren't much different than they were thirty years back, when Joe first opened – just older and more beaten up. The booth cushions got new upholstery seven years ago, but Joe had them fixed up in the same red vinyl stuff as before, so you can't hardly tell the difference.

Only one thing has changed about Joe's place. That's the people. Some of the old-timers keep dropping by, regular as clockwork. But time has changed them considerably. Lester Keyhoe, for instance, fell to pieces after his wife kicked over. And old Gimpy Sedge lost his conductor job, so he just watches the train pull in and leave without him, then comes by here to tie one on with Lester.

Joe's gone, too. Not *gone*, just retired. I've kept the place going for the past three years, since I turned twenty-one. When Joe isn't shooting deer in the mountains, he comes in for coffee and a cinnamon bun every morning. He likes to keep an eye on things.

I sure wish he'd been after deer the morning Elsie Thompson blew in.

The place was empty except for me and Lester

Keyhoe, who was sitting down the bar where he always sits, getting a start on the day's drinking.

I was toweling down the counter when the car pulled up. I could see it plain through the window. It was an old Ford that looked like somebody'd driven it a dozen times back and forth through Hell. It sputtered and whinnied for a minute after the ignition key was turned off.

I stopped toweling and just stared. The old gal who jumped out of the Ford was a real sight – short and round, dressed in khakis, with gray hair cut like Buster Brown, and wearing big wire-rimmed glasses. She chewed on some gum like she wanted to kill it. A floppy wicker handbag hung from her arm. I said, 'Get a load of this,' to Lester, but he didn't even look up.

The screen door opened and she thumped toward the counter in her dusty boots. She hopped onto the stool in front of me. Her jaw went up and down a few times. One time when it was open, the word 'coffee' came out.

'Yes, ma'am,' I said, and turned away to get it.

'Does this establishment belong to Joseph James Lowry from Chicago?' she asked.

'Sure does,' I said, looking at her.

Behind the glasses, her round eyes opened and shut in time with her chewing mouth. She gave me a huge grin. 'That's mighty good news, young man. I've been driving through every one-horse town west of Chicago looking for this place, looking for Joe Lowry and his damned tavern. There's a place called Joe's in every single one of them. But I knew I'd find Joe Lowry's place sooner or later. Know why? Because I've got willpower, that's why. When do you expect him in?'

'Well . . . what did you want to see him about?'

'He *is* coming in?'

I nodded.

'Good. I expected as much. I'm only surprised not to find him behind the counter.'

'You know him, huh?'

'Oh, yes. My, yes.' Her eyes turned sad for a second. 'We used to know each other very well, back in Chicago.'

'How about if I give him a ring, tell him you're here?'

'That won't be necessary.' Snapping her gum and grinning, she opened the handbag on her lap and pulled out a revolver. Not a peashooter, either – one of those long-barreled .38s. 'I'll surprise him,' she said. Her stubby little thumb pulled back the hammer and she aimed the thing at me. 'We'll surprise him together.'

I didn't feel much like talking, but managed to nod my head.

'What time will Joe be in?' she asked.

'Pretty soon.' I took a deep breath and asked, 'You aren't planning to shoot him, are you?'

She pretended like she didn't hear me, and asked, 'How soon?'

'Well . . .' Far away, the 10:05 from Parkerville let loose its whistle. 'Well, pretty soon, I guess.'

'I'll wait for him. Who's that slob over there?'

'That's Lester.'

'Lester!' she called.

He turned his head and looked at her. She waved the gun at him, grinning and chewing, but his face didn't change. It looked the same as always, long and droopy like a bloodhound's, but more gloomy.

'Lester,' she said, 'you just stay right on that stool. If you get up for any reason, I'll shoot you dead.'

His head nodded, then turned frontwards again and tipped down at his half-empty glass.

'What's your name?' she asked me.

'Wes.'

'Wes, keep Lester's glass full. And don't do anything to make me shoot you. If some more customers come in, just serve them like everything is normal. This revolver has six loads, and I can take down a man with each. I don't want to. I only want Joe Lowry. But if you drive me to it, I'll make this place wall-to-wall corpses. Understand?'

'Sure, I understand.' I filled Lester's glass, then came back to the woman. 'Can I ask you something?'

'Fire away.'

'Why do you want to kill Joe?'

She stopped chewing and squinted at me. 'He ruined my life. That's enough reason to kill a man, I think. Don't you?'

'Nothing's a good enough reason to kill Joe.'

'Think so?'

'What'd he do to you?'

'He ran off with Martha Dipsworth.'

'Martha? That's his wife – was.'

'Dead?'

I nodded.

'Good.' Her jaw chomped, and she beamed. 'That makes me glad. Joe made a mistake, not marrying me – I'm still alive and kicking. We'd be happily married to this day if he'd had the sense to stick with me. But he never did have much sense. Do you know what his great ambition was? To go out west and open up a tavern. Martha thought that was a *glor*ious idea. I said, "Well, *you* marry him, then. Go out west and waste your lives in the boondocks. If Joe's such a romantic fool as to throw his life away like that, I don't want him. There's plenty of fish in the sea." That's what I said. More than thirty years ago.'

'If you said that . . .' I stopped. You don't catch me arguing with an armed woman.

'What?'

'Nothing.'

She shifted her chewing gum over to one corner of her mouth and drank some coffee. 'What were you going to say?'

'Just . . . well, if you said they could get married, it doesn't seem very fair of you to blame them when they went ahead and did it.'

She put down the cup and glanced over at Lester. He still sat there, but he was staring at the gun. 'When I said that about the sea being full of fish, I figured it'd only be a matter of time before I'd land a good one. Well, it didn't work out that way.'

She chewed a few times, gazing up at me with a funny distance in her eyes as if she was looking back at all the years. 'I kept on waiting. I was just sure the right man was around the next corner – around the next year. It finally dawned on me, Wes, that there wasn't ever going to be another man. Joe was it, and I'd lost him. That's when I decided to gun him down.'

'That's . . .'

'What?'

'Crazy.'

'It's justice.'

'Maybe the two of you could get together. He's unattached since Martha died. Maybe . . .'

'Nope. Too late for that. Too late for babies, too late for—'

All at once, Lester flung himself away from the bar and made a foolish run for the door. The old gal swiveled on her stool, tracked him for a split second, then squeezed off a shot. The bullet took off Lester's earlobe. With a yelp, he swung around and ran back to his stool, cupping a hand over what was left of his ear.

'You'd better pray nobody heard that shot,' she said to both of us.

259

I figured nobody would. We were at the tail end of town, so the closest building was a gas station half a block away. The cars passing by on the highway kicked up plenty of noise. And around here, with all the hunting that goes on, nobody pays much attention to a single gunshot unless it's right under his nose.

But I was nervous, anyway. For five minutes, we all waited without saying a word. The only sound was her gum snapping.

She finally grinned and squinted as if she'd just won a raffle. 'We're in luck.'

'Joe's not,' I said. 'Neither's Lester.'

Lester said nothing. He was pinching his notched ear with one hand and draining his glass with the other.

'They shouldn't have run,' the woman said. 'That was their mistake – they ran. You aren't going to run, are you?'

'No, ma'am.'

'Because if you do, I'll shoot you for sure. I'll shoot anyone today. Anyone. This is my day, Wes – the day Elsie Thompson pays Joe back.'

'I won't run, ma'am. But I won't let you shoot Joe. I'll stop you one way or another.' I went over to fill Lester's glass.

'You can't stop me. No one can stop me. Nothing can. Do you know why? Because I've got willpower, that's why.'

Grinning mysteriously, she chomped three times on her gum and said, 'Today I'm going to die. That gives me all the power in the world. Understand? As soon as I gun down Joe, I'll drive out of this burg. I'll get that old Ford up to seventy, eighty, then I'll pick out the biggest tree . . .'

I made a sick laugh, and came back to her.

'Think I'm fooling?' she asked.

'No, ma'am. It's just kind of funny, you talking like

260

that about crashing into a tree. Not funny ha-ha, funny weird. You know?'

'No.'

'That's 'cause you don't know about Joe. He crashed into a tree – an aspen, just off Route 5. That was about three years back. Martha was with him. She got killed, of course. Joe was in real bad shape, and Doc Mills didn't give him much chance. But he pulled through. His face got so broken up he didn't look quite right, and he lost the use of an eye. His left eye, not his aiming eye. He wears a patch over it, you know. And sometimes when he gets feeling high, he flaps it up and gives us all a peek underneath.'

'You can stop that.'

'He lost a leg, too.'

'I don't want to hear about it.'

'Yes, ma'am. I'm sorry. It's just that . . . well, everyone that crashes into a tree doesn't die.'

'I will.'

'You can't be sure. Maybe you'll just end up like Joe, hobbling around half blind on a fake leg, with your face so scarred up that your best friends won't recognize you.'

'Shut up, Wes.'

She stuck the pistol into my face, so I slowed down and said quietly, 'I just mean, if you want to make sure you die, there's a concrete bridge abutment about a mile up the road.'

'Warm up my coffee and keep your mouth shut.'

I turned around to pick up the pot. That's when I heard the footsteps outside. Boots against the wood planks out front, coming closer. I faced Elsie. She grinned at me. Her jaw worked faster on the gum. Her eyes squinted behind her glasses as the unsteady clumping got louder.

Through the window I saw his mussy gray hair, his

scarred face with the patch on his left eye. He saw me looking, smiled, and waved.

I glanced at Lester, who was holding a paper napkin to his ear and the glass to his mouth.

Elsie pushed the pistol close to my chest. 'Don't move,' she whispered.

The screen door swung open.

Elsie spun her stool.

'Duck, Joe!' I cried out.

He didn't duck. He just stood there looking perplexed as Elsie leaped off the stool, crouched, and fired. The first two bullets smacked him square in the chest. The next hit his throat. Then one tore into his shoulder, turning him around so the last shot took him in the small of the back.

All this happened in a couple of seconds as I dived at Elsie. I was in mid-air when she wheeled on me and smacked me in the face with the barrel. I went down.

While I was trying to get up, she jumped over the body and ran out. I reached the door in time to see her car whip backwards. It hit the road with screeching tires, then laid rubber and was gone.

I went back inside.

Lester was still sitting at the bar. His stool was turned around, and he was staring at the body. I sat down at one of the booths, lit a cigarette, and kept Lester company staring.

We spent a long time like that. After a while, I heard the sheriff's siren. Then an ambulance's. The cars screamed by and faded up the road in the direction of the bridge abutment.

'Guess that's Elsie,' I said.

Lester just kept staring.

Then the screen door swung open.

'My God!' The big man looked at me, then at Lester, and knelt down over the body. He turned it

262

over. 'Gimpy,' he muttered. 'Poor old Gimpy.' He patted the dead conductor on the back, and stood up. His eyes questioned me.

I shook my head. 'Some crazy woman,' I muttered. 'She came in here dead set to kill you, Dad.'

The Fur Coat

Janet wore her white ermine coat to the theater that night. The play was *Cats*. She went alone.

The evening was meant to signal a new beginning for her. She hadn't treated herself to a play since Harold's death. He had adored the stage. They'd seen *Cats* together many times during their eight years of marriage. He'd been dead, now, for more than two years. Janet knew that she had to quit mourning, quit feeling sorry for herself, and get on with her life.

She attended *Cats* as a final tribute to Harold.

She wore the ermine coat as a tribute to him, too.

It was a lovely coat, its fur as white as a drift of fresh snow and soft as down. A gift from Harold. She'd yelped with delight the morning she found it under the Christmas tree. Because they had no children and were celebrating the holiday alone, she had immediately thrown off her robe and nightgown. She'd caressed her naked body with the luscious fur coat, then slipped her arms into its sleeves and twirled around for Harold. In his arms, she thanked him for the coat. She kissed him. She hugged him. She stripped him. She urged him to the floor. There, kneeling over him in nothing but her wonderful new coat, she had stroked him, kissed him all over, licked and sucked him, and finally eased down onto him.

Afterward, he'd said, 'My God. Wish I'd bought you this coat years ago.'

'You couldn't have afforded it.'

'So what? Debt, where is thy sting?'

During the next few months, she'd worn the coat every time Harold took her out to dinner or the theater. A few times, when their evening activities were such that she wouldn't need to remove her coat, she'd worn only a garter belt and stockings underneath it – which drove Harold crazy.

The coat never failed to make Janet feel special. Partly because Harold had blown a small fortune on it, she supposed. Partly because it looked so pure and beautiful, felt so soft and smooth against her skin. But mostly, she thought, because of how it had changed their marriage. The coat not only inspired its share of raw lust, but also tenderness, laughter, a fresh assortment of surprises and adventures.

Her first night alone in the house after Harold's accident, she took the coat to bed with her. She wept into its silken fur and fell asleep hugging it.

Soon, however, the coat ceased to give her comfort, became only a reminder of her loss. She couldn't stand to look at it, much less touch it, wear it.

And so she had put it in storage.

Left it there.

For over two years.

Until the day she was brushing her rich brown hair in front of the medicine cabinet mirror and spotted the silver thread.

Her first gray hair.

But I'm only thirty-six! Thirty-six isn't old!

Old enough to start going gray.

It was then that she decided to get on with her life. She phoned the Barkley Theater and made a single reservation for the Saturday night performance of *Cats*. Then she took her ermine coat out of storage.

At Bullocks, she bought an elegant black evening gown for the occasion.

On the day of the performance, she went to the beauty shop. She'd considered having her hair dyed. But she liked her natural color. Besides, the idea of masking the gray hair seemed cowardly. Better to accept it, to face the knowledge that her life was moving on, and make the most of each day ahead.

She had her hair trimmed very short. It made her look spritely. And quite a bit younger.

That evening, ready to leave, she stood in front of the full-length hall mirror for a while and gazed at herself.

The sleek, low-cut gown was brand new. The ermine coat *looked* brand new. And Janet *felt* brand new.

If only Harold could see me now, she thought.

Her eyes filled with tears.

She had to redo her mascara before leaving the house.

The drive into Hollywood took half an hour. Rather than hunt for street parking, she left her Mercedes in a brightly lighted pay lot four blocks from the theater.

The autumn wind had a chill to it. Janet was snug in her fur coat.

She picked up her ticket at the box office. In the warmth of the Barkley's lobby, she removed her coat and draped it over one arm. In her seat, she folded it and set it on her lap. She stroked it during the play. It was almost like having a cat on her lap. But no cat ever had such lovely, smooth fur.

She went nowhere during intermission. Instead, she stood in front of her seat and looked about. She saw no familiar faces, of course. But she noticed several women in furs. More in stoles than in coats, it seemed. Most of the women who wore furs were considerably older than Janet. Most, in fact, were very old.

Was she the only person under sixty, in the entire theater, who'd worn a fur to the play?

Sure looked that way.

Had it always been like that?

Janet didn't think so.

Could things have changed so much in such a short period of time? In less than three years?

Maybe it's because of those animal-rights fanatics, she thought. Had they turned an entire generation away from wearing furs? Sure looked that way. *Something* had happened.

Unless it's the bad economy, and most people simply can't afford the luxury . . .

The lights dimmed.

Janet sat down.

At the end of the play, she wept and clapped. Then she wiped her eyes, pressed the coat to her belly and sidestepped to the aisle.

On her way to the lobby, she was aware of feeling proud.

She had taken such a large step, coming here tonight. She'd actually dressed up and come to the play all by herself. And she'd enjoyed the performance. In a way. If only Harold had been with her . . .

I'm on my own, she reminded herself. *And I got along just fine.*

Things would be easier from now on.

She would try a new play next week. Maybe, sooner or later, she would actually gather enough courage to dine alone in a fine restaurant.

Eventually, she might even meet a man as wonderful as Harold.

Fall in love.

God, wouldn't that be something!

Sighing, she slipped her arms into the sleeves of her coat. The lobby was hot, so she didn't fasten

267

the buttons. Stuck in the mob waiting to exit, she wished she had left the coat off entirely. People pressed against her. The air seemed hot, heavy, suffocating.

Until finally she made her way through the door.

The chilly autumn night felt great.

She breathed deeply. The air beneath the theater marquee was fragrant with scents of myriad perfumes, with men's musky after-shave colognes, with liquor aromas, with smoke from cigarettes and cigars. Whether exotic or comforting or disgusting, the odors excited Janet. They were old, familiar friends. She filled her lungs and smiled.

This is so wonderful, she thought. *I'm really out in the world again.*

Look at me, Harold. I didn't wither up and die. I wanted to, but I didn't. I survived.

The crowd loosened as people headed off in different directions. Janet paused to recall where she had parked her car.

The parking lot. That way.

She turned to the right.

And took only three strides before a voice shouted, 'Murderer!'

Janet was twisting around when a woman cried out, 'No!'

She spotted her at the curb. Old, frail, silver-haired, wrapped in a mink stole, flinging up her arms as she was rushed by a pair of young women.

The two women looked vicious.

'Murderer!' the skinny one shouted into the old woman's face.

'Evil bitch!' shouted her partner, a tubby woman with stringy brown hair. 'Those minks died for your sins!'

Both women dug into their handbags. Janet's heart

268

thumped. She thought they were going for guns. But they came up with cans of spray paint.

'No, please!' the old woman whined.

Red paint sprayed her hands as she scuttled backward, trying to get away. Some got past her hands, misted her hair and forehead and glasses.

At least twenty people seemed to be frozen beneath the theater marquee, watching the attack.

Why was nobody trying to help?

Because the assailants were women? Or were all the spectators on their side, hating the old lady for wearing fur?

The old lady, sandwiched between the pair, whimpered and hugged her head as they sprayed her. Her hair dripped red paint. The fur of her stole was matted down, scarlet.

'Leave her alone, goddamn you!' Janet shouted.

The heads of both assailants snapped toward her. The chubby one squinted through glasses that were speckled with red paint. Round lenses in wire frames. Granny glasses.

'She didn't do anything to you!' Janet yelled. 'Look what you've done to her! What's the matter with you?'

The one in the granny glasses grinned.

The skinny one raised her spray can high overhead. 'Listen up, all you rich capitalist fucks! We're ADF. Hitters for the Animal Defense Front. What you've seen here is a lesson. It's what we do to assholes we catch wearing dead animals.

'You've been fucking Mother Earth long enough! Butchering her forests, poisoning her air and water, slaughtering her innocent creatures. *Murdering* her creatures! Bashing their heads! Slashing their throats. *Experimenting* on them! Eating their flesh! Clothing yourselves in their skins! No more! No more!'

269

'No more!' the chubby one joined in.

'ADF forever!'

'ADF forever!'

'Get *her*!' The skinny one hurled the old lady aside and rushed toward Janet.

The other grinned.

Janet whirled away.

The tight skirt of her evening gown bound her legs, but not for long. With her third stride, her knee punched through its front. A kick finished the job. The skirt split open from hem to waist, freeing her to run.

People nearby dodged clear, some yelping with alarm, others watching as if amused, none trying to help.

Janet glanced over her shoulder. Her pursuers were side by side, no more than fifteen feet back.

What sort of range did the spray cans have?

I'll die if they ruin my coat!

But she knew that she couldn't outrun them – not in her heels.

The shoes, like the gown, could be replaced.

Without slowing, she kicked off her right shoe. The left gave her some trouble, but after a few strides she managed to fling it clear. Shoes gone, her feet felt light and quick.

She dashed along the sidewalk, silent except for her huffing breath and the slap of her feet and the whispery sounds that her pantyhose made as she whipped one leg after the other out through the split front of her skirt.

The girls behind her made a lot more noise. One seemed to be wheezing. One wore footwear, probably sandals, that smacked the concrete with harsh claps. One jingled with Christmas bells. From their spray cans came rattling sounds, as if each contained nothing more than a ball-bearing.

The sounds of the pair didn't seem to be getting any closer. But not fading, either.

So far, Janet was keeping her lead.

Just ahead, her way was blocked by a knot of people standing at the corner. Waiting to cross the street.

'Help!'

Some looked around at her.

'What's the trouble?' asked a young man in a sweater. He looked innocent, collegiate.

'They're after me!' Janet cried out.

'What for?'

'Animal Defense Front!' shouted one of the gals. 'Keep out of it!'

'Huh?' He wrinkled his nose.

And it was already too late. Janet had no time to stop and explain. Give the attackers two or three seconds, and her coat would be dripping crimson paint.

Just short of the group, she cut to the right.

'What's going on?' the kid called after her.

She didn't bother to answer. She poured on speed.

The sidewalk in front of her was deserted. Just as well, she thought. Nobody was likely to help her, anyway – not without an explanation. No explanation was possible. They'd be on her too quick.

If only someone would take out the two bitches on general principles!

Isn't it obvious who's the victim here?

Apparently not.

Or people just don't care.

It'd all be different if guys were chasing me.

Men would be climbing all over each other to save me.

But these're gals after me. So I'm fucked.

Wonderful.

Her pursuers sounded farther away than before.

Thinking that she was beginning to outdistance them, Janet risked a look back.

And gasped.

The skinny one was closer than ever before. No more than seven or eight feet separated her from Janet.

The heavy one was much farther back. She was the noisy one. The one with a wheeze. The one who wore sandals and sleighbells. The one who now carried both clinking canisters of paint.

Her friend in the lead was sprinting almost silent. Long blonde hair streaming. Lips peeled away from teeth that looked very white in the streetlights. No earrings or necklace or bracelets or rings. No bra. No shoes or socks. Dressed in a white T-shirt, old cut-off jeans and apparently nothing else. Stripped for action, for silent running.

'Leave me alone!' Janet blurted.

'Butcher!'

'I'm *not*!'

'Gimme the coat!'

'No! Go away!'

'Yeah! After I've . . . ripped that fur . . . off your fucking back!'

Janet twisted sideways and hurled her clutch bag. Like the coat, it had been a gift from Harold. But she had nothing else to throw.

Inside the black satin bag were several odds and ends: some cash, tissues, a tampon, her parking lot ticket, the stub of her theater ticket, the folded playbill, and her driver's license. Also her key case, her compact and opera glasses – which gave the bag some weight.

Her pursuer saw the airborn bag. She flung up an arm to block it, but missed. She tried to jerk her head out of the way. The bag caught her in the right temple. Her face scrunched. She turned and tripped herself, hit the sidewalk shoulder first, and skidded.

Janet rushed back to her. She snatched up her purse.

'I warned you to leave me alone!' she said as the gal, moaning, tried to push herself up.

'Hey!' yelled the chubby one. 'What'd you do to her! Leave her alone!'

'You leave *me* alone!' Janet snapped, backing away. While the big one chugged toward her, the other got to her knees. The fall had torn down the sleeve of her T-shirt. Teeth clenched, she took a quick look at her dark, scuffed shoulder.

'Are you hurt?' her friend asked, staggering to a halt.

'Get her!'

'No!' Janet yelled. 'Quit it! She's already gotten hurt.'

'Damn it, Glory, *spray the fuckin' coat!*'

Glory lurched past her, bells jingling.

'No,' Janet said. 'Come on. Please.'

Glory kept coming, so she flung herself around. As she broke into a run, the cans hissed. She glanced back. Glory, firing with both barrels, was hidden from the chest up behind clouds of red mist. The paint didn't seem to shoot far enough to hit Janet.

But if Glory got much closer . . .

Janet rammed the clutch bag to her mouth. She bit it. The bag flopped, whapping her beneath the chin as she dashed along the sidewalk and struggled out of her coat. She brought the coat in front of her. Mashed it into a thick bundle. Clamped it to her chest with her left arm. Took the bag from her mouth with her right hand. And kept on running, hugging the coat.

They won't get you now, she thought.

The corner ahead looked deserted. Approaching it, she glanced both ways.

The parking lot.

If I can get to the parking lot . . .

Where the hell is it?

She had no idea.

But the traffic light was green for her and the intersection looked clear, so she leaped off the curb and raced into the street.

A horn blast stunned her.

She snapped her head to the left.

A cab running the red light sped straight at her. It swerved. She lurched to a stop, teetered backward. It rushed by, fanning her with a warm breeze.

Stunned by the near miss, Janet hardly noticed the sounds of smacking sandals and tinkling bells. The *sssssssss* took her by surprise.

She sprang forward.

But not fast enough.

Her evening gown was backless, so the cool paint plastered her bare skin from the nape of her neck and downward almost to her waist before she put on enough speed to leave Glory behind.

That would've been it for the coat, she thought.

Thank God! Got it off just in time.

At the other side of the street, she bounded over the curb. Then looked over her shoulder.

Glory, still pursuing her with a canister in each hand, had stopped spraying. Her hair was matted, her face slick with red paint. Janet wondered how she could possibly see through her glasses. The gal had obviously been racing into her own spray, soaking herself. Her sleeveless sweatshirt looked sodden. It was mostly red, only a hint of its original gray still visible low on the belly. Her plaid Bermuda shorts and heavy legs had caught some spatters. Janet noticed that the jingling came from a leather collar of bells around her left ankle.

Leather?

274

And what about those sandals?

Leather?

Maybe not. Maybe fake.

Or maybe the bitch is a hypocrite.

Fake?

Janet yelled over her shoulder, 'My fur isn't real! It's simulated! You've got no reason to . . .'

Her voice went dead as the skinny one – the fast one – raced up behind Glory, overtook her and left her behind, charging toward Janet with shocking speed.

Janet bolted.

With the coat in her arms, she'd been able to stay ahead of Glory. But this one was so much quicker. Janet couldn't hope to outrun her – not without her arms free to pump.

Just a matter of time.

Janet began to weep.

I don't want them to ruin my coat! Please! Why do they want to do this?

She heard the girl's bare feet slapping the sidewalk, heard the girl's quick, sharp breaths.

'Please!' she yelled.

The word was still on its way out when a tackle took her down. Her arms, wrapped around the coat, were first to strike the concrete. Then her knees. The coat cushioned her like a big pillow, saving her face and chest as she slammed the sidewalk.

The girl scurried up her body, squirming, sliding on Janet's painted skin, embracing her, reaching for the coat. Janet tried to elbow the hands away.

'All *right!*' Glory called, rushing closer.

Just as Glory halted, sandals and bells going silent, a sudden writhing tug by the other flipped Janet over. She found herself on top, the girl pinned beneath her back, Glory looming above her.

'Nail the bitch!'

275

Grinning, Glory squatted, stretched her arms toward Janet, and sprayed. Both canisters spat red paint.

Janet felt the spray on her arms.

On her arms, wrapped around the ermine coat.

And she knew that the coat was finished.

'You getting her?' asked the girl underneath Janet.

'You bet.'

'Got the coat good?'

'Yep.'

'Nail her in the face.'

Janet let go of the fur. She squeezed her eyes shut, closed her mouth, and flung up her arms to protect her face. An instant later, the spray hissed at her.

While it showered her, she felt the coat being snatched off her chest.

She felt hands rip open the bodice of her gown. They plucked and tore, savaging her gown and undergarments.

'Nail her!'

The spray slathered her breasts, worked its way down her belly, burnt between her legs.

'Okay,' Glory said.

The spraying stopped.

With a shove from below, Janet was sent rolling off the girl. She tumbled over the curb, dropped, and landed face-down in leaves and debris at the edge of the street. She lay there motionless. She didn't dare to breathe.

She heard quiet sounds of fabric being torn.

She knew they were ripping her coat to shreds.

Soon, the pieces of it fell softly onto her bare back and rump and legs.

'You think this was bad?' asked the nameless one.

Janet didn't answer.

'This wasn't bad. This was nothing. Imagine how the ermines felt.'

276

'Ermines have feelings, too,' Glory added.

'You had no right to slaughter them for your vanity,' said the other.

She stepped on Janet's back, stepped down to the street beside her, knelt, grabbed Janet's painted hair and lifted her face off the pavement. 'They were poor, innocent creatures. They only wanted to live, just like the rest of us. They didn't want to be made into a coat for a rich bitch like you.'

'You had no right,' said Glory.

The other one jerked Janet's hair down quick and hard. Janet's face crashed against the pavement. Her nose burst. Three teeth crumbled.

'Animals have feelings, too.'

'Do you think they *enjoy* being skinned?' Glory asked.

'How do you think *you'd* like it, bitch?'

Janet began to struggle, but the girl bounced her face off the street again.

She was unconscious when they dragged her into the alley.

She woke up screaming when they started in with the razor blades.

Blarney

'What's that?'

Deke looked to the right, where Val was pointing. Half a mile up the coast, on a rocky point high above the surf, stood the gray stone walls of a castle ruin. 'A castle, I guess,' he said.

'In California?'

'Probably some nut put it up. Some guy didn't know what to do with his money.'

She tugged his arm. 'Can we go over to it?'

'Leave off my arm.'

She let go. 'Can we?'

'We'll see,' Deke said. He slipped a .32 automatic out of his belt.

'Hey, what are you doing?'

'Kissing it goodbye.'

'You're not throwing it away!'

'Oh yes I am.'

'Deke!'

He generally didn't dislike Val. After all, she wasn't bad looking for a gal her age. Her hair was dyed a gaudy reddish-brown. Her face had a few sags, same as her body, but what can you expect? Gals start downhill at eighteen, and Val was pushing fifty. No, he didn't dislike her looks much. Her big trouble was she didn't have much common sense. 'I have to ditch it,' he told her.

'Maybe we'll need it.'

'We can always get a new one. They catch us with this baby, they can tie it into the shooting of that idiot clerk, and it's *adios* for both of us.'

Val's wide eyes looked shocked. '*I* didn't shoot him!'

'Doesn't matter, stupid. You were there. You were in on it. That's the same as if you dropped the hammer.'

'It is?' She looked desolate, and ten years older.

Deke grinned. 'It's okay. Don't let it worry you. I'll just deep-six this baby . . .' With all his strength, he hurled the automatic. It flipped and spun, its blue-steel dark against the overcast sky, dropping like a shot raven. In the tumult of the surf far below, he couldn't see it splash.

'Now we're off the hook. No hard evidence, no witnesses . . .'

'*I'll* never speak a word,' said Val.

'Oh boy,' he muttered. In the two months he'd known her, he never quite trusted her. Now she comes up with a remark like that. If she thought about squealing enough to deny she would ever do it . . .

'What's wrong?' she asked.

'Nothing,' Deke said.

He'd been too quick to throw away the gun.

He looked again at the distant stone fortress. That tower on the ocean side looked like a great place for an accident. 'Still want to visit the castle?' he asked.

Val beamed.

They hurried back to the car.

Walking the barren ledge, Deke took a long look at the castle. It stood on an outcropping of rock, cut off entirely from the bluff. A rickety footbridge, about thirty feet long, reached over to it.

He could heave Val off the bridge easy enough. But

279

what if it gave out under the weight of two people and he took the dive with her?

The castle itself seemed to be nothing more than four stone walls with the big tower on the southwest corner. Forget the footbridge. The tower was the place to do it.

'Isn't it lovely!' Val blurted. 'It's so . . . I don't know . . . *majestic*! You'd think it would be in the guide books.'

'Maybe it is.'

'Oh, it's not. I've read them all. I know California like my own face, and I've never heard of a castle like this. There's the Hearst Castle, of course, but it's so different. I've been there twice, you know. Once with my second husband, and . . . Where's the ticket booth, do you think?'

'I don't think there is one.'

'Oh, there *has* to be.'

'Maybe inside,' Deke said. He was sure there would be no ticket booth. The place looked deserted and forlorn. He didn't feel like explaining, though. Val would see for herself, soon enough.

They reached the footbridge. Far below it, the surf beat and churned.

'So far down!'

'I'll go first,' Deke said. 'You stay put till I'm across.'

Val nodded.

Deke hurried across the swaying bridge, and sighed with relief when he reached the far end. He was trembling. As he tried to calm down, Val appeared beside him.

'Oh look!' she said, and pointed at a sign above the castle gate. '"Herlihy's Castle",' she read. '"May age ne'r wither thy brow."'

'Cute,' Deke said.

They stepped beneath the arch of the gateway. Except for a dozen seagulls taking shelter from the wind, the courtyard was deserted. 'Guess we don't have to buy tickets, after all.'

Val pushed her hands into her coat pockets. 'I don't like this place, Deke. It makes me jumpy.'

'A minute ago you said it's majestic.'

'Yeah, but . . .'

'Yeah but, yeah but,' Deke mimicked.

'It shouldn't be here, you know what I mean?'

'No, I don't.'

'I mean, a castle in California?'

Ignoring her, he started walking across the courtyard. Seagulls in his way took flight, circled, and landed again.

Val hurried to catch up. She gripped his elbow, but he kept walking. 'I've got this crazy weird feeling, Deke. Like we're in a nightmare. We oughta get out of here. Something bad's gonna happen, I can feel it in my bones.'

'That's arthritis.'

'Very funny. Please, let's go back to the car.'

'You're the one who wanted to see this place. "Can we go see it? Can we, can we?" Well, now we're here. And I don't leave till I've been up that tower. You stay here and wait, if you want, but I'm going up.' Jerking his arm free, he stepped toward the dark entryway.

'Don't leave me here.'

'Stay or come, it's up to you.'

'Deke, please! We shouldn't be here. I can feel it.'

'Sure. See you later. Probably won't take me half an hour.'

He entered the opening and began to climb the spiral stairs. His shoes made loud scuffing sounds on the concrete. He realized, by the third stair, that there was no handrail.

281

'Wait!' Val cried. 'Don't leave me!'

'Then put a move on.' He waited until she reached the step below him. 'Stay close,' he said, and continued to climb.

The stairs were shaped like wedges, a foot wide near the outer wall and tapering down to nothing at Deke's right. He stayed close to the wall. He kept his left hand against its cool, damp stone.

After one full turn of the stairs, the light from below was lost. The stairway was dark except for a thin band of light from a window slit.

'Deke, let's go back.'

'Forget it.'

'I feel like I'm gonna fall.'

You must be psychic, he thought, and grinned. 'Just keep a hand on the wall,' he advised. As he spoke, his right foot found only enough stair for his toes, and slipped off. His knee slammed the concrete. 'Damn!' he snapped.

'I *told* you—'

'Shut up.'

They kept climbing with only the light from the window slits to show the way. Once, the light vanished so completely that Deke could see nothing. Disoriented and dizzy, he stopped climbing. He flinched as Val touched his back.

'It's getting to you, isn't it?' she asked.

'Nothing's getting to me but the darkness. I'll be okay in a minute.'

'Let's go down, Deke.'

'We're almost to the top.'

'How do you know?'

'Don't worry, I know.'

As he started to climb again, his legs felt shaky.

'How're we gonna get down?' Val asked.

'Walk,' he said.

'It'll be dark outside. We won't be able to see a thing.'

'So we spend the night.'

'I don't want to go any higher. Not now. It's all too creepy.'

'Suit yourself.'

He suddenly saw light above him. 'Ha! We made it!' He hurried up the final stairs and stepped through the doorway. Directly in front of him, back to the tower wall, sat a man.

'Is it come to kiss the stone, you are?' he asked in a lilting accent Deke took for Irish. He wore an old gray jacket, and baggy trousers with leather knee patches. He had a sly look on his face.

'What stone?'

Val stepped up beside Deke. She smiled when she saw the stranger.

'Why, the Herlihy Stone. Have you not heard of it, then?'

Deke shook his head.

The man stood up, using a blackthorn walking stick. A young, powerfully built man, he didn't appear to need the stick. 'You know of the Blarney Stone, no doubt?' he asked. 'It's a bit of marble you find on a castle wall near Cork, in Ireland.'

'If you kiss it,' said Val, 'it's good luck.'

'A common bit of misinformation that's on your tongue, ma'am. It's not good luck you'll be getting from the Blarney Stone, but the gift of eloquence. Your tongue'll walk circles 'round all who listen, and they'll not understand a word of it. That's the gift of the Blarney Stone. Now you take the Herlihy Stone, it's a different story altogether. One kiss of it, and you'll stay forever young.'

'I've never heard of the Herlihy Stone,' Val said.

'It's not many as have. We don't let it get around,

283

you see. It's a hundred years the Herlihys have kept this castle keep, and we've all been modest men. We like our quiet and solitude. We like a bit of desolation, for it's calming to the soul. Crowds are the curse of God, after all, and it's surely crowds we'd be getting if the gift of our Stone got around. A few wanderers, now and again, put money enough in our pockets. We are not greedy men.'

'What does it cost to kiss this stone of yours?' Deke asked, trying to keep the anger and frustration out of his voice. All that work, all that climbing, for this! He should've known the castle wouldn't be deserted.

'Would two-fifty a head be too dear?' the man wanted to know.

'Two dollars and fifty cents?' Val asked.

'That's all it would cost, and you'd have a kiss of the Herlihy Stone and never lose your youth.'

Val smiled. 'I wish I'd come here thirty years ago.'

'I shouldn't worry. It's still a lovely woman you are.'

She gave Deke a superior, accusing smile, as if he'd been too ignorant to notice the qualities so obvious to this stranger.

'Go ahead and kiss the damned thing,' Deke said. 'What've you got to lose?'

'Before you decide, have a look at the stone itself.' The man pointed his stick at a gap between the stone walkway and the parapet. 'Step up and have a look.'

Deke and Val moved closer.

'My God!' Val said.

Kneeling beside the gap, the man reached down with his cane and tapped the wall. 'There's your Herlihy Stone, the bit of marble down there.'

Two hundred feet below the bit of marble, waves

crashed and exploded against the rocks of the prom-
ontory.

'It's not so dangerous as it might appear,' the man
said. 'You must sit on the edge of the walk here and
lean back, same as if you were giving the Blarney
Stone a kiss. I'll be holding your legs, of course.'

'How many have you lost?' Deke asked, and grinned.

The man grinned back. 'Hardly enough to mention.'

'Well,' Val said, 'I don't think I'm up to it. I really
don't.'

'A good many folk feel that way, at first. I must tell
you with all me heart, however, a kiss of the Herlihy
Stone will keep you young, indeed. How would you
guess my age?'

'Thirty?' Val tried.

'And you, sir?' he asked Deke.

'Thirty-five?'

'It's eighty-three I'll be come October.'

Deke laughed.

'Fifty years it's been since I kissed the Herlihy
Stone.'

'Sure,' Deke said.

'Is it a liar you're after calling me?'

Deke considered the man's size, and the walking
stick. 'No. Not me. Go ahead and kiss the stone, Val.
Look what it did for him.'

She shook her head.

'I'll be holding your legs good and tight, ma'am.
Me hands have not failed me yet.'

'Well . . .'

Deke could see that, in spite of her hesitation, she
wanted to go ahead with it. Did she really believe that
garbage about eternal youth? She couldn't be that stupid. More likely, she was looking forward to the feel of
those big, powerful hands pressing down on her legs.

285

'Okay,' she said. 'I'm game. Deke?'

Maybe he could figure a way to lose her through the hole. Grinning, he took out his billfold. He handed the man three dollars.

'It'll be five dollars for you and the lady both.'

'Right. You owe me fifty cents.'

'Are you not going to kiss the Stone yourself, then?'

'You kidding?'

'Deke, you've got to.'

'I haven't *got* to. You go ahead and have your fun, you two. I'll watch.'

'Deke, please! Don't you want to stay young?'

'Do you believe that bunk?' Deke pointed toward the small slab of marble. 'He ought to call it the Hooey Stone.'

'Well, I'm doing it anyway.'

'Be my guest. I'm not trying to stop you.'

'Okay then,' Val said.

The man reached into a pocket and took out a pair of quarters. 'Your change, sir.'

Deke put them away. He zipped his coat against the cold wind.

The man tapped his stick on a stone platform beside the gap. 'If you've any valuables in your pockets, ma'am, set them here or they'll be in for a great long fall.'

Val put her purse on the platform. She took gloves from her coat pockets. Last, she removed her glasses. The man held her arm as she sat down on the walkway, her back to the battlements.

Deke grinned. 'Say, do you want *me* to hold your legs?'

'No,' Val said. 'That's okay.'

'Come on. Why not?'

'I couldn't allow it,' the man intervened. 'It's *I* must do the holding.'

286

'I don't see why.'

'It's the rules, sir.'

'Whose rules?'

'If you wish the lady to kiss the stone, it's I must hold her. I'll not be arguing about it.'

Deke shrugged. 'Do it your way,' he said.

As the man knelt beside Val, Deke glanced at the blackthorn stick. Its knobby handle looked lethal. A good bash at the right instant, he could wipe them both out. Unfortunately, the stick was propped against the parapet within the man's reach.

'Ready?'

Val nodded.

The man gripped her thighs. 'Now gently lie backwards. Aye. Don't be afraid.'

Deke watched Val's head lower into the gap. He glanced at the blackthorn stick.

What if he couldn't nail the guy fast enough? He'd stand little chance against a strong, young man like that.

Val was bent backward like a bow, her shoulders and head completely out of sight.

Now or never!

Never, Deke decided. Not up here. Not with this fellow to deal with. He'd wait for a better chance. Maybe the dark stairs on the way down. Or the footbridge.

'Have you kissed the Herlihy Stone?' the man called down.

'Yes,' came Val's strained voice.

He flipped her legs upward and let go. Deke watched, astonished, as Val's feet vanished through the gap.

She screamed for a long time.

The man picked up his blackthorn stick and got to his feet.

Deke backed away. 'What're you doing?' he demanded. 'You dropped her on purpose!'

'I surely did, and there's no denying it. Now it's your turn, sir, to kiss the Stone.' He raised the stick to his shoulder and stepped toward Deke.

'No! Stay back!'

The stick cut through the air and pounded Deke's shoulder. His arm went numb. The next blow glanced off his head. Dazed, he dropped to his knees.

'It's down you go,' said the man, dragging him to the gap.

His back bent painfully as he was lowered headfirst. He saw the smooth marble inches from his face.

'Have you kissed it yet?'

'No!'

'Doesn't matter, actually.'

'Let me up!'

'I can't do that. It's me job. It's the family line, so to speak, conferring the gift of the Herlihy Stone.' As he let go of Deke's legs, he called, 'You'll not grow old now, my friend, not at all!'

Dracuson's Driver

The graveyard shift at the Wanderer's Rest Motel suited Pete fine. It went from midnight to 8:00 a.m. Between those hours, there wasn't much to do: answer the phone, though it rarely rang; once in a great while register a guest arriving unusually late. The job consisted mostly of simply being there to keep an eye on things.

Pete liked keeping his eye on things.

In particular, the younger and more attractive of the motel's female guests.

Few of them ever visited the motel office during the long, late hours of Pete's shift. But he made up for their absence by visiting them.

All the ground level rooms had rear windows. None of the rear windows had curtains that worked quite properly – Pete had seen to that. The curtain gaps gave him many wonderful sights. As did the bathroom windows. Because the bathrooms had no ventilation fans, and because the rear of the motel was sheltered by a steep rocky slope, the windows were often left open. As a result, Pete had spied many sweet things stripping for showers, stepping into and out of the stalls, afterward rubbing gleamy slick skin with thread-bare towels.

'Yo, Boydy-babes,' Pete said as he entered the motel office to relieve Boyd Marmon. 'How's it swinging?'

Boyd abandoned the rear of the registration counter

fast enough to avoid a friendly smack on the shoulder or back.

Alone, Pete inspected the registration cards. All but three of the downstairs rooms were supposedly taken for the night. So he waited until 12:30, then did what he called a 'window run.' And another at 1:00 a.m. Still others at 1:15, 1:30, 1:45 and 2:00.

For all his efforts, Pete viewed two dumpy women, one cute teenaged girl who'd already changed into her Garfield nightshirt and would probably not be removing it in the near future, and a gal who sat in an armchair, her back to the window. Though this one had lush blonde hair and bare shoulders, she would not stir from her chair. She looked wonderful from behind. Was she beautiful? What was she wearing that left her shoulders bare? Something strapless? Maybe a towel? Or nothing at all?

She was the main reason Pete kept making window runs that night. After first spotting her during the one o'clock trip, he pretty much ignored the other windows and spent his few minutes gazing in at her, aching, *willing* her to get out of the chair and turn around. But she never did. Not while he was watching. And when he made his two o'clock run, her window was dark.

He peered in, anyway, but saw nothing.

She must've already gone to bed.

He'd missed her.

He thought, *Shit!*

He thought, *No damn fair!*

On his way back to the office, he nearly tripped over a black cat that had been hanging around the motel lately. He tried to give it a punt. It scooted, however, so his shoe only nicked its rump. He threw a rock at it, but missed.

At the office, he kicked open the glass door. He kicked the front of the registration counter.

If you had any guts, he thought, you'd kick open that babe's door and *take* her.

She might even like it. A sweet, balmy night like this, she's *got* to be horny.

'Course, the card says she's in there with her husband.

So what? Break his head open, and *then* nail her.

It perked up Pete to imagine such things.

He sat behind the counter and dwelled on his fantasies. What she would look like naked. How she would feel. What he would do to her. What he would force her to do to him.

Pete had only been with one naked girl. Beth Wiggins. Last June in his dad's car after the Senior Ball. She was the worst-looking girl in school – therefore the only girl he could work up enough guts to invite.

She'd been as eager as a puppy dying for affection.

In the car after the dance, she'd been all over him.

She had onion breath and boobs like uncooked bread loaves and a jumbo gut and an ass a mile wide. She'd wanted it bad. Pete had always thought *he* wanted it bad. Confronted with a lusting and unattired Beth, however, he found out that all he wanted was to get away. He didn't even get hard when she sucked on him. So then she'd started to cry.

So then he'd smacked her.

When he smacked her, he *did* start getting hard. So he did it again, and got harder. But she squealed and slugged him in the nose, and that put a stop to everything. They both got dressed and she sobbed all the way back to her house.

Never again, he'd vowed that night.

No more pigs.

Unfortunately, he was terrified by the idea of speaking to – much less asking out – any female he found the least bit attractive.

He could *look* at them, though.

Spy on them through windows.

Dream about sneaking into their rooms, subduing them, stripping them, forcing them to comply with his every wish.

Hardly a night went by that he didn't pursue such thoughts about one or another of the motel guests.

He would *love* to make the dreams come true.

If only he were invisible . . .

Or if he could figure out a way to hypnotize or drug one of them without her ever suspecting . . .

A way to have his fun with a gal and get away with it, that's what he wanted. And he savoured the problem, toyed with it, considered possible solutions. He knew there *was* no solution. No way, ever, to act out his fantasies and be totally, absolutely, utterly one hundred per cent certain of not being so much as suspected.

Still, it was fun to think about.

Pete spent a lot of time, during the long silent hours after quitting his window runs for the night, imagining what he might do to the bare-shouldered woman. And then he spent even longer toying with various plans he might employ for getting away with it.

At times, all of it seemed very real.

He could see her, smell her, taste her, hear her rough breathing and gasps and squeals. Shrieks of ecstasy and pain sounded so much alike.

If he drugged her, of course, she would feel neither.

Maybe bash her on the head. Tie her to the bedframe. Wait till she comes to before starting in on her. Yes.

Shiny with sweat. Striped with bright red ribbons of blood.

Writing, squirming, screaming . . .

Pete was startled from his reveries, just after 4:00 a.m., when a hearse glided to a stop beneath the motel's portico. It looked like the real thing – long and black and shiny, its rear side windows draped with curtains.

The moment he saw it, icy prickles raced up Pete's spine, stiffened the nape of his neck, made his scalp crawl.

'Oh shit,' he muttered.

A hearse!

Why's a *hearse* stopping here?

For just a second, he considered a quick drop behind the counter. He could pretend not to be here.

But maybe the driver had already spotted him.

Anyway, he told himself, that'd be chicken.

Nothing to be scared of.

Instead of trying to hide, Pete lowered his head and gazed at the stack of registration cards. He heard a car door thump shut.

A hearse had never stopped here before.

Pete had never *heard* of a hearse stopping at a motel.

Weird. Awful fucking weird.

The bells above the office door jingled.

Sweat trickled down Pete's sides. He drilled his eyes into the stack of cards, terrified of looking up.

Footsteps approached.

Make him go away! Please! I don't like this!

'Hi.'

The sound of the voice shocked him. It sounded cheerful. Cheerful and young and female.

He raised his eyes.

The girl on the other side of the counter wore a black uniform: a black, visored cap tilted up in a jaunty way

293

atop a head of very short, pale blonde hair; a black tunic with two rows of brass buttons down its front; black slacks that hugged her legs; gleaming black leather boots as high as her knees.

The uniform might've looked grim and severe on someone else. On this smiling, slender girl, it looked like a lark. She was a pixie playing dress-up.

Gazing at her, Pete felt as if his heart might quit.

He'd never seen anyone so . . . so fine.

He felt stunned nearly senseless by the curve of bangs that hid her entire right eyebrow, by her huge blue eyes, by the smooth warm cream of her skin and the delicate curves of her cheekbones, nose, lips and chin, by the long smooth glide of her neck.

'Are you quite all right?' she asked.

'Me? Sure. Fine.' He bobbed his head. 'You . . . You just reminded me of someone, that's all. Would you like a room?'

'That I would. It's been a mighty long night.' She raised her index finger. 'A single should do nicely. My companion won't be requiring a bed.'

'Your companion?'

She swung a thumb over her shoulder. 'My stiff friend out in the bone-mobile.'

'*What?* You've got a . . . a dead person in there?'

'Don't fret. I won't allow him out of his coffin.'

Pete stared out at the hearse. 'My God,' he muttered. 'There's really a dead guy . . . ?'

'Oh, yes, quite. Does that present a problem?'

'I don't know.'

'He needn't be registered, you know.' She gave Pete a quick, gamine grin.

'I guess it'll be all right,' he said.

'Super.'

'How long would you be staying with us?'

'Ah, the rub.' She sighed. 'You see, the thing of it is, I've been at the wheel since sunrise.'

'Sunrise *yesterday*?'

'If I stay up a few more hours, it'll be an even twenty-four. In other words, I'm wasted. So what I should like to do is climb into bed and sleep through the day.'

'Mmmm.'

'Not the way things are usually done, eh?'

'You're right about that. Check-out time is noon.'

She shrugged. 'I'll really need to stay on until evening. Perhaps as late as nine o'clock.'

'That is sort of a problem.'

'I know. I've been around this particular bend a few times before. Next, you'll be explaining that you've no choice but to charge me for two days occupancy.'

I can't lose her.

'No. That wouldn't be fair. I tell you what, I'll fix things so you only need to pay for one night.'

'You can do that?'

'Sure. My parents own the place.' It was a lie, but the girl had no way of knowing any better. 'I'll give you a nice ground-floor room at the end of the wing. If you'll just fill this out?' He peeled a registration card off the stack, slid it across the counter to her, and snapped a pen down on top of it.

Pete was good at reading upside-down.

The girl's name was Tess Hunter.

She was with the Greenfields Mortuary of Clayton, New York.

'You're a long way from home,' Pete said.

'So's he.' She gestured again with her thumb. 'The poor bloke burnt himself up in a yacht fire on the St Lawrence. His family intends to finish what the fire started, and spread his ashes on their beach property in Malibu.'

Pete found his nose wrinkling. 'He *burnt up*?'

'Not quite. Charred on the outside, though I should imagine he's still rather rare on the inside.'

She pushed the card toward Pete.

'And how will you be paying?'

'Cash.'

He charged her for one night in the room. After receiving the payment, he gave her the key to room ten. 'There's an ice machine right next to the office here, and . . .'

She shook her head. 'Won't be needing it. It's just a quick shower for me, if I can stay awake long enough, and then to bed.'

A shower!

'Could I give you a hand with your luggage?' Pete asked. He knew his face was red.

'Does the offer include a hand with the coffin?'

'Huh?'

'Oh, I'm afraid I can't leave poor Mr Dracuson in the hearse. Somebody might make off with him, you know.'

'I'm sure nobody would . . .'

'It's quite a responsibility, chauffeuring the dead.'

'But . . .'

'I'd be sacked for sure if I should lose him.'

'Where do you want to put him?' Pete asked.

'In my room, of course.'

'In your *room*?'

'You haven't a rule against it, I hope.'

'Not that I know of. But . . . do you *do* that? Keep the dead guys with you in your *room*?'

'Oh, sure. Doesn't bother me a whit, actually. 'Cept for those that snore.'

Pete surprised himself by laughing.

'What's your name?' Tess asked.

'Pete.'

'So, Pete, you'll lend me a hand with the box?'

He gave her a nod, then hurried around the end of the registration counter. He opened the office door for Tess. She stepped quickly to the hearse and opened its passenger door for Pete.

She wants me to ride with her!

The thought of sitting beside Tess in a car made Pete's heart pound fast. To be so close to her! In the darkness!

Not in a hearse, though.

No way.

'Thanks anyway,' he told her.

'Pop in. I'll give you a ride to the room.'

'That's okay. I'll walk.'

'The hearse puts you off, does it?'

Already on his way, he looked back at Tess and said, 'No, no. Just that there's no point. The room's just over there.'

'You may not get another chance, you know, to ride in the front of one.'

'That's okay.'

She entered the passenger side, herself, swung the door shut behind her, and slid across the seat. She was no sooner stationed behind the wheel than the engine *voomed* to life. The headlights came on.

Pete was already halfway across the parking lot by the time the hearse began rolling forward. It turned slowly, beams creeping over the blacktop until they found him. Framed in their brightness, he followed his long shadow to the parking space in front of room ten.

He faced the car, squinting until its headlights died. The engine went silent. The door swung open and Tess climbed out. She walked toward him briskly, swinging an overnight case at her side.

'Let me get the door for you,' he said.

'Thanks.' She handed the key to him.

He unlocked the door, reached into the room and flicked a switch. The chandelier came on. Though it was suspended above the front table, its six small bulbs brightened all but the farthest end of the room. Beyond the shadows there, Pete glimpsed the window. *His* window.

The sight of it sucked his breath out.

Oh, to be standing on the other side of it! Staring in at Tess!

This'll be the best ever!

The very best!

And she mentioned a shower!

In just a few more minutes . . .

Tess stepped past him, tossed her bag onto a bed and swung around, grinning. 'Spiffy room,' she said.

Pete nodded. 'Is that all the luggage you have?' he asked.

'It's all I need.'

He backed out of the doorway as she approached. Then he followed her. The seat of her trousers looked very tight. It hugged her rump, flexed and shifted with every step she took.

At the rear of the hearse, he kept his eyes on Tess, savoring her looks, thrilling himself with the knowledge that he would soon be spying on her, and also avoiding the sights that he preferred not to see.

He watched Tess, not the hearse, as she swung open its rear door. He watched Tess, not the coffin, as she pulled at it and dragged it toward her.

'Poor Mr Dracuson isn't very heavy,' she said. 'But if you'd like to take hold of the front . . . ?'

Pete realized she was standing motionless, waiting for his help, an end of the coffin braced against her chest, the other end resting at the edge of the hearse.

He hurried to the front, found handles on both sides of the dark wood box, and swung it clear.

298

The coffin wasn't nearly as heavy as Pete had expected. In spite of Tess's comment about the weight, he'd thought it would be a lot tougher to carry. He supposed that large amounts of Dracuson must've been left behind in the boat or river. Ashes.

Tess maneuvered herself close to the rear of the hearse. She shut the door with her rump. 'Okay,' she said.

'You got it?'

'I'm fine. How about you?'

'No sweat,' Pete said.

As he lugged the coffin backward, he imagined dropping it. He pictured it smashing down, the lid dropping away, a charred black husk tumbling out. A withered thing, faceless, hunched like a fetus. Black dust rising off its skin shell. Flakes falling. Pieces – a nose, a finger – silently breaking off.

But it didn't happen.

Together, they carried the coffin into the room.

Just inside the doorway, Tess said, 'Right here's fine.'

They lowered it to the floor.

'Have you ever seen him?' Pete asked.

'Oh, yes. I helped put him in, you know.'

'How does he look?'

'Bloody awful.' She tapped the box with the toe of her boot. 'I'd open it up and show you, but the smell might be rather off-putting.'

He tried to laugh. 'I wouldn't want to see him. Thanks anyway.'

'Well, thank you for the help. He's a bit tough to manage by myself.'

Pete returned the room key to her.

She put it on the table, then pulled the wallet out of her back pocket. Pete held up his hands.

'No. It was my pleasure.'

'A pleasure, was it? Lugging a stiff?'

'Well . . .' He shrugged. 'You know.'

As he stepped past the coffin, Tess returned the wallet to her pocket. She moved out of his way, but extended her hand. 'Thank you again,' she said.

'You're welcome.' He shook her hand.

It sent heat rushing up his arm, heat that spread and filled his entire body.

The heat stayed, even after her hand went away.

Pete swallowed. His voice trembled slightly as he said, 'If you need anything, I'll be right in the office.'

'Have a good night, now,' Tess said.

He stepped outside, and she shut the door.

He headed straight for the office. Walking fast. It would've been much quicker just to hurry around the corner of Tess's room, but he wanted to *appear* to be returning to the office. Just in case.

He entered the office, glanced about. Saw it was deserted. Heard no phone ringing. Then turned around and left. He rushed around to the rear.

No light spilled into the darkness from *any* of the windows.

Not even from Tess's at the far end of the building.

This can't be!

If I get cheated out of this . . . !

It's okay, he thought, that the bathroom light isn't on. Only means she hasn't started her shower. Good. I haven't missed anything yet.

But the window at the back of her *room* looked dark.

That light *has* to be on, he told himself. I just can't see it from here.

After all, the gap between the edges of the curtains was only a couple of inches wide. It wouldn't allow more than a narrow strip of light to shine out.

Maybe she pinned the gap shut, or something.

300

Pete crept toward Tess's windows.

Not even so much as a flicker of televison light showed within any room along the way.

He stopped at Tess's bathroom window. Frosted glass, gray in the darkness. One side open all the way.

Fantastic, Pete thought. Incredible.

When she takes that shower . . .

If she takes it.

He rushed in a crouch to the main rear window and peered in.

Peered into a black void.

She just got here! I was only gone a minute! What the hell's going on!

Calm down, he told himself. You didn't miss anything. She hasn't had time to change for bed, much less take a shower. She probably just left the room for some reason.

What if she's on her way to the office?

She needs something. No towel in her room? Something like that. Phoned the office. Now she's looking for me.

Shit! What if she finds me?

As fast as he could move without making too much noise, Pete made his way to the end of the building and alongside the windowless far wall. At the front corner, he leaned forward.

The hearse was parked in front of the room, just where Tess had left it.

The lighted walkway leading to the office looked deserted. Except for the cars lined up in front of the ground-level rooms, the parking lot was empty. Even the road beyond the parking lot seemed abandoned and desolate.

Pete studied the windshield of the hearse. When he opened the driver's door, a courtesy light came on.

301

Tess was not in the hearse.

He went to the motel office. Tess was not there, either.

She's gotta still be in her room, he thought. Maybe she just turned off the light, flopped on one of the beds and zonked out.

Too worn out for that shower she wanted.

So tired she probably fell asleep in her clothes.

Wasted.

What if she's so wasted she can't wake up?

Nobody will ever know, Pete told himself as he slipped his spare key into the lock of room ten.

He wished he had gotten started earlier.

It had taken him a while, though, to work up the nerve. By the time he'd left the office, light had already begun to creep across the sky from the east.

He'd nearly lost his nerve.

But all the windows along the front of the motel were still dark.

Even if somebody does see me, he thought, it won't matter. I'm the night manager. I have every right to go into a room. Besides, none of the guests had signed up for more than one night. All of them would be gone by noon.

It'll work out fine.

If Tess doesn't wake up.

She won't.

As long as I'm very quiet . . . and don't shine the flashlight on her face.

Anyhow, Pete knew that he might not be able to get into her room, at all. Most guests, before retiring, fastened the safety bolt. If Tess had done that, the game was over. Pete sure couldn't risk breaking in. It was silently with the key, or nothing.

302

If she was dead tired, though, maybe she'd neglected to fasten the latch.

Maybe.

Pete turned the key, twisted the knob, and pushed. The door swung inward.

Oh my God! Fantastic!

The door hinges squeaked a bit. Pete cringed, but he didn't quit. He inched the door open wider and wider, then slipped inside the room and eased the door shut behind him.

The room was not totally dark. Strips of dim gray showed between the curtains of the big front window, the small rear window. The vague hints of light were useless, however. Pete could see no details of the room's interior. Not the furniture, not the coffin, not Tess.

He heard nothing except his own quick heartbeat.

Then the quiet rub of his hand against cloth as he slipped the key into the front pocket of his jeans, another rub as he drew his hand out.

He switched the heavy, steel-cased flashlight to his right hand. He curled the fingers of his left hand over its lens. Turning the light toward his face, he thumbed the switch. His fingers went rosy, so nearly transparent that he could see their shadowy bone-shapes.

Though the darkness had prevented him from seeing either bed, he knew exactly where each had to be. He aimed his flashlight, spread his middle fingers slightly, and watched a bright ribbon stretch down to the surface of the nearer bed.

No feet or legs. Not so much as a bulge in the covers.

He swept the light sideways.

The bed was neatly made, empty except for Tess's overnight bag. The top of the bag was spread open a bit. She must've been into it.

Pete lit the other bed, and gasped.

For just an instant, he thought Tess was sprawled out, dismembered, decapitated. Then he realized he was looking at her strewed clothes. Cap, tunic and trousers black against the smooth pale bedspread. Tall boots standing upright on the floor beside the bed.

But no blouse. No bra or panties or even socks.

Had she been going around with nothing on, at all, beneath her black costume?

Pete heard his heartbeat quicken its pace. His mouth felt dry. He was suddenly short of breath. As he panted for air, he felt himself getting stiff and hard.

She must've done it in the dark, he thought.

Turned out the light right away, even before starting to undress.

Did she suspect something?

Is she naked now?

Maybe just in her bra and panties.

Flimsy little things . . .

Black like the rest of . . .

Where the hell is she!

Hiding? Maybe she heard me unlocking the door.

Oh, my God.

If she's awake and knows I'm here, Pete thought, it means major trouble. Huge trouble. Disaster.

Getting fired, he realized, might be the least of his troubles.

Could he end up in jail?

I just wanted to look at her!

He dropped his hand from the front of the flashlight, and the full bright beam shot forward. He shined it on the coffin just beyond his feet. Sidestepped around the coffin. Knelt between the beds and lifted the hanging covers to make sure she wasn't hiding under either bed. Got to his feet and checked the space on the other side of the far bed. Turned in a full circle to light every corner of the room. Then entered the bathroom.

No tub, just a shower stall.

He swept aside the plastic curtain and shined his light in, ready and hoping to find Tess cowering naked on the tile floor.

She wasn't there.

Where is she?

She hasn't left. The hearse is still here. Her clothes are still here.

Outside the bathroom, Pete played his light over the scattered clothes.

She was the best, the finest. He had never in his life seen such a girl. All the others were . . . crud . . . compared to Tess.

This isn't fair! Where are you?

In despair, Pete sank down onto the corner of the bed.

I'll wait for her, he thought. She's got to show up.

What if she had spare clothes in that bag, changed into them, and walked away? Fed up, maybe, with chauffeuring stiffs.

Maybe that's it.

If that's it, she'll never come back.

No. No, she talked about responsibilities. She wouldn't even leave the coffin outside in the hearse, so she certainly wouldn't abandon the thing.

She acted as if it was her *duty* to transport this Dracuson fellow's . . .

Dracuson?

Pete shined his light on the coffin.

Could that really be the stiff's name – Dracuson? Maybe Tess was kidding. Thought it would be fun to tag the poor jerk with a name that sounds like Dracula.

Like I'm sure there's a vampire in there.

305

Like Tess is some sort of chauffeur for a fuckin'
vampire, rides him around all night, maybe pulls off
the road sometimes to let him fly off and suck people,
and then they hole up all day long in some crummy
motel. So Drac can rest up in his coffin till dark, and
Tess can get her beauty sleep.

Stupid, Pete thought.

Crazy.

No such thing as vampires.

If there *is* such a thing, though, everything would
make sense. Everything except Tess's disappearance.

Hell, Pete thought, that's an easy one.

She isn't just Dracuson's chauffeur. She's his lover,
too. She's right there inside the coffin with him.

Yeah, right. Every day and twice on Sundays.

Pete knew that the notion was stupid, crazy, ridiculous. But he suddenly *had* to look inside the coffin.

He stood up. His legs shook as he sidestepped past
the coffin. He felt as if his stomach was shivering.

She isn't going to be in there, he told himself.

If you open it up, all you'll find is crispy black Mr
Dracuson.

Yeah? Then where is Tess?

Pete crouched at the foot of the coffin. He shined
his light on the lid. The wood looked like mahogany,
reddish brown and glossy.

He listened.

No heavy breathing came from the box. No thrash-
ing sounds, no thumps.

If she's in there, he thought, she isn't humping any
vampire. She's lying quiet and still.

Maybe she heard me, knows I'm here. What if she
tries to nail me when I open the thing?

He thought, *Ha*.

He almost laughed out loud.

If Tess was inside with her vampire lover, which

306

seemed highly unlikely, she would be face-down on top of him. She could hardly spring upon Pete from that position.

He gripped the flashlight in his right hand.

He hooked the fingertips of his left hand under the edge of the coffin lid.

Throw it off quick. Don't give her a chance to roll over.

But he imagined the noise of the heavy lid thumping the floor.

No way.

What I need here, he thought, is silence and stealth.

Instead of casting the lid to the floor, he eased it upward a few inches. He ducked his head. He shined his light inside.

And glimpsed pajama legs of pale blue fabric as shiny as silk.

A hot jolt raced through him.

He raised the lid higher, crept his light up the body.

There was only one.

It lay on its back, cushioned by the white satin of the coffin's lining.

A slim body garbed in loose, clinging pajamas that took on the curves they covered. The shirt overhung the waist of the pants. It had four big white buttons. It rose smoothly over the mounds of her breasts and jutted with the thrust of her nipples. It was spread open above the top button, showing a wedge of bare chest, the hollow of her throat.

Pete saw the underside of her chin. Though his angle was all wrong to see the face, he knew this was Tess.

Who else *could* it be?

So where's Dracuson?

Who the hell knows?

307

Who the hell cares?

It only mattered that he had found Tess and she still seemed to be asleep.

Pete set down the flashlight to free his right hand. Then he worked his way to the side of the coffin. Slowly, carefully, he lifted off the lid. He swung around and lowered it onto the bed.

Kneeling, he picked up his flashlight. He held it low as he changed it from his left hand to his right.

Don't shine it in her eyes, he warned himself. That'd wake her up for sure.

Why the hell is she sleeping in the coffin? Two perfectly good queen-size beds.

Must be nuts.

Seriously weird.

But, oh man! So what?

He raised the flashlight. He shined it on her chest, holding it close enough to her body so that the bright disk would stay tight and away from her face.

He gazed at her breasts.

He wanted to touch them.

He wanted to slip the big white buttons out of their holes and spread open the pajama shirt and see her breasts naked and touch them, caress them, squeeze them, try them with his mouth.

This is it. My big chance. She's zonked, dead to the world.

But she'll wake up if I try to undo any buttons. She'll wake up for sure if I touch her.

Wake up screaming.

Unless . . .

He shined his light on her face, saw her open eyes, gasped as his heart lurched, then leaned and swung, hammering her forehead with the flashlight. The first blow shattered the lens and killed the bulb. After that, he swung and pounded in darkness.

When his arm wore out, he dropped the flashlight.

He got to his feet, staggered to the wall, and flicked the switch. The chandelier came on.

He looked down at Tess.

Her face was a bloody ruin.

But the rest of her was unharmed.

Pete took a pillow off one of the beds. He covered Tess's face with it, thinking only to hide the ugly damage, but then pressing the pillow down hard just to make sure she wouldn't wake up and cause trouble.

He held the pillow down tight against her face for a very long time.

Leaving the pillow on her face, he unfastened the big white buttons of her pajama shirt. The shirt was spattered with blood. He opened it wide. Some of the blood had soaked through, staining her skin pink.

'Oh, Tess,' he whispered. 'Oh, Tess.'

Her breasts were wonderful. More than wonderful. He lingered over them, gentle and rough, savoring their weight and texture and taste.

Later, he plucked apart the snap at the waist of her pajama pants, drew the pants down her legs and tossed them onto the bed. He raised her legs, spread them, and hooked her knees over the edges of the coffin.

He stripped and climbed in.

He kissed her and caressed her, squeezed her, licked her, nipped her, probed her, and it was the best, better than anything, worth everything, worth killing her for especially when he thrust into her slick heat.

It was what he had always wanted to do, and better than he'd ever dreamed.

The cleanup went off without a hitch.

Though the sun was bright above the cornfields to the east by the time he dragged the coffin out of room

309

ten, nobody seemed to be wandering about. Pete was pretty sure that nobody saw him.

He got the coffin into the rear of the hearse.

He drove the hearse for a while, then turned up a dirt road and parked it inside a shabby, abandoned barn.

He left the coffin in the hearse, Tess in the coffin with her various garments and overnight case. But not with the pillow, because he was afraid it could be traced back to the motel.

He spent a few minutes wiping away his fingerprints with a rag. Then he hiked back to the motel.

The hike of two miles took him half an hour.

He made one more visit to room ten for the pillow and his broken flashlight. He concealed them in the trunk of his car.

At the office, he returned both room keys to their proper nook and destroyed the registration card. He kept the cash payment for himself.

So far as anyone except Pete would ever know, Tess Hunter had never checked into the Wanderer's Rest Motel.

At 8:00 a.m. that morning, Pete was relieved by Claire Simmons. He ate breakfast at Joe's Pancake Emporium. Then he drove out to the barn where he had left the hearse.

He spent the hot, summer morning with Tess. And much of the afternoon.

Late in the afternoon, tired to the bone, he drove home to the one-room house that he rented on the far side of town. He set his alarm clock for 11:00 p.m., stripped and climbed into bed.

He closed his eyes and smiled.

Life could be so great when you just had the guts to take what you wanted.

Wow!

He wondered how long Tess would keep.

Pretty hot in that old barn, but . . .

The alarm didn't wake Pete. He was stirred from his slumber, instead, by light shining in his eyes.

He blinked at the glare of the lamp beside his bed.

He squinted at his clock. Only 10:03.

What the hell . . . ?

'You slimy creep.'

He knew the voice.

Young and female, with a lilt that sounded a bit English.

Pete bolted upright.

Tess, naked, stood beyond the end of his bed, fists planted on her hips, legs apart. She was shaking her head at him. Her face was clean. Unswollen, unbroken. As if Pete had never battered her to a mess with the flashlight.

Her short, pixie hair was matted down and dark. Wet. Her skin had a rosy hue. She looked as if she had just stepped out of a shower.

But Pete didn't find himself thrilled by the sight of her.

He didn't get stiff and hard. On the contrary, he shriveled.

He peed.

He began to whimper.

'I only wanted a bit of a rest, you know,' Tess said.

'Ya . . . you're *dead*!'

A corner of her mouth tilted upward. 'Not quite, actually – in spite of your moronic efforts, you sniveling pervert. If you'd had half a brain, you would've put a stake through my heart. My God, you *had* to know what I was.'

She stepped up onto the bed.

311

'Don't . . . Don't hurt me. Please.'

'Oh, I fully intend to hurt you. I'll hurt you quite a lot, word of honor. Cross my heart.' She flicked a fingernail against the creamy skin between her breasts, drawing a quick invisible X. 'You'll hurt beyond your wildest dreams.'

Baring her teeth, Tess bellowed and threw herself down on Pete.

And kept her word.

Roadside Pickup

When the piano stopped, the voice came back. It was soft and friendly, like the music, and kept Colleen's thoughts from dwelling on the empty road. 'That was Michel Legrand,' it said, almost whispering, 'and this is Jerry Bonner bringing you music and talk from midnight till dawn here on easy-listening KS . . .' She rolled the knob of her car radio and the voice clicked off.

It wouldn't be smart to keep listening. Not smart at all, since there was no telling how long she might be sitting here. Maybe all night. You can't play a radio all night without running down the battery. Or can you? She would have to ask that mechanic tomorrow. Jason. He was so good at explaining things.

She sighed with weariness and pressed her fingertips against her eyelids. If only someone would come along, and stop, and offer to help her.

The way Maggie was helped?

She felt her skin tighten.

No! Not like Maggie!

As Colleen rubbed her bare arms, she started to remember it again . . . the telephone that rang in her dream until it woke her to the real ringing, the roughness of the bedroom rug under her feet, the cool slick linoleum in the kitchen. And all the time the sickening lump of fear in her belly because the phone just doesn't ring at 3:00 a.m. unless . . .

313

'Cut it out,' she muttered. 'Snap out of it, okay? Think about something pleasant for a change.'

Sure, something pleasant.

Otherwise she would start remembering the cop's voice on the phone and the drive to the morgue and the way her sister had looked lying there . . .

'Shine on, shine on, harvest moon,' she started to sing. She kept on singing it. Then she began, 'Sentimental Journey.'

When they were kids, they used to sing those songs on long trips. Mother and Father would be sitting up front, she and Maggie in the back, four shadows holding off the lonely night with sweet, half-remembered lyrics.

Maggie always had lots of trouble remembering the words. Whenever she got stuck, she would listen to the others and sing out the right words a moment later, like a cheery echo.

The night her car broke down, nobody was there to sing her the right words.

Colleen caught her breath. A light! A speck of light no bigger than one of the stars high above the cornfields moved in her side mirror. A car was coming.

Would this one stop? Three, so far, had whooshed by without even slowing down. Three in almost as many hours.

Maybe one of them had stopped, somewhere farther on, and phoned the state troopers.

The headlights of the approaching car were set low and close together. Not like a patrol car, more like a sports car.

She flashed her lights on and off, on and off.

'Stop,' she whispered. 'Please stop.'

As the car bore down, Colleen squinted at the glaring slab of her mirror. It hurt to look, but she didn't take her eyes away, not even when the headlights exploded across the mirror in a final brilliant flash.

After the painful brightness, the soft glow of the tail lights felt soothing to her eyes.

When the brake lights flashed, something clutched the inside of Colleen's stomach. She hunched over to ease the pain and saw the cold, white backup lights come on.

Her hand trembled as she rolled up her window. She glanced across her shoulder. The lock button was down. Swinging her eyes to the passenger door, she saw that it too was locked.

The car stopped inches from her bumper.

Colleen filled her lungs with air and let it out slowly.

A sports car, all right – small and shiny, with the canvas top of a convertible.

The driver's door swung open.

Colleen's breath made raspy, heartbeat sounds in her throat. Her mouth was parched. Did Maggie feel this way the night she died? She must have. This way, only a lot worse.

A tall, slim man stepped out. He looked to be in his late twenties, close to Colleen's age. His hair was fashionably long, his checkered shirt was open at the throat, his trousers flared at the cuffs.

She couldn't see his lean, dark face until he bent down and smiled in at her. She nervously returned the smile. Then the stranger raised his hand into view and made a circular cranking motion.

Colleen nodded. She lowered her window half an inch.

'What's the trouble?' he asked, speaking directly into the slit. His breath, so close to her, smelled sweet and heavy with liquor.

'It's . . . I'm not sure.'

315

'Something the matter with your car? Your car break down?'

His breath filled her nostrils. She gripped the window crank and told herself to roll it up – roll it up *now* because he's been drinking . . . and she saw the dead battered face of her sister.

'You all right?' the man asked.

She rubbed her face. 'I'm feeling kind of woozy, I guess.'

'You ought to roll down your window, get some fresh air.'

'No, thanks.'

'The fresh air'll do you good.'

'I'm all right.'

'If you say so. What's wrong with your car?'

'It overheated.'

'What?'

'Overheated,' she said into the window's gap. 'I was driving along and a red light on the dashboard came on, and then the engine started to make some kind of awful whiny noise, so I pulled over.'

'I'd better have a look.'

He walked to the front of the car and touched the hood the way a person touches something that might be hot. Then he slipped his hands under the hood's lip. He couldn't get it open. Finally, he crouched, found the latch, and opened it.

He spent only a few moments under the hood before returning to Colleen's window. 'You've got a problem,' he said.

'What's wrong?'

'What? I can hardly hear you. If you'd just roll down your window a bit more . . .'

'Roll it down?'

'Sure.'

'No, I don't think so.'

316

'Hey, I don't bite,' he said, grinning and shaking his head.

Colleen smiled back at him. 'Are you sure?'

'I only bite when there's a full moon. It's just a half-moon tonight.'

'A gibbous,' she corrected.

The man laughed and said, 'Either way.'

Colleen opened the window and breathed deeply. The breeze tasted wet with the freshness of the cornfields. A train, far away, was making a snickity sound. Somewhere a rooster heralded dawn three hours early.

It's a beautiful night, she thought. For a moment, she wondered if the stranger was also thinking about the peaceful sounds and smells. She looked at him. 'What's wrong with my car?'

'Fan belt.'

'Fan belt? What does that mean?'

He moved his face down closer to hers. 'It means, young lady, that it's a good thing you stopped.'

'Why's that?' she asked, and turned away fom his liquored breath.

'If you go far without a fan belt, you burn up your engine. *Kaput*, kiss your motor goodbye.'

'That serious?'

'That serious.'

'What could've happened to the belt?'

'It probably just broke. They do that sometimes. Me, I change mine every two years just to be on the safe side.'

'I wish *I* had.'

'I'm glad you didn't,' he said, and grinned a charming, boyish grin that frightened Colleen. 'It isn't every night,' he continued, 'that I'm lucky enough to run into a damsel in distress. Especially one as pretty as you.'

She rubbed her perspiring hands on her skirt. 'Can you . . . can you fix it?'

317

'Your car? Not a chance. Not unless you've got a new fan belt in your pocket.'

'What'll I do?'

'You'll let me give you a lift to the nearest service station. Or somewhere else, if you'd prefer. Where would you like to go?'

'Well, I don't think I should . . .'

'You can't stay here.'

'Well . . .'

'It would be foolish to stay here – a woman as pretty as you. I don't want to alarm you, but there've been a number of attacks on this stretch of road.'

'I know,' she said.

'Not to mention half a dozen murders. Men and women both.'

'You've alarmed me.' She smiled nervously. 'I'll come with you.'

'That's what I like to hear.' He reached into the car, unlocked the door, and opened it for her. She climbed out. When he shut the door, it made a dull thump that sounded very final.

'Do you live far from here?' he asked, taking Colleen's elbow with cold, firm fingers and leading her toward his car.

'Thirty miles, maybe.'

'So close? Why don't you let me take you home?'

'That would be very nice. But I hate to put you to the trouble. If we can find a gas station . . .'

'No trouble. Thirty miles is nothing.' He stopped walking. His fingers tightened around her arm. 'I guess I'd be willing to drive a woman like you just about anywhere.'

She saw the way he smiled and knew it was happening.

'Let go of me,' she said, trying to sound calm.

But he didn't let go. He jerked her arm.

318

'Please!'

He mashed his mouth against hers.

Colleen closed her eyes. She started to remember it again – the telephone that rang her awake, the long walk to the kitchen, the rough apologetic voice of the cop.

I'm afraid that somebody assaulted your sister.

Is she . . . ?

She's gone.

Gone. A funny way for a cop to put it.

She bit the stranger's lip. Her forehead snapped against his nose. She jabbed her knuckles into his throat and felt his trachea collapse. Then she ran back to her car.

By the time Colleen returned to the man, he was lying motionless on the road. Kneeling beside him, she lifted his hand and searched for a pulse. There was none.

She dropped the hand, stood up, and took a deep, deep breath. The breeze off the cornfields smelled so fresh and sweet. So peaceful. Yet there was something a little sad about the aroma, as if the cornfields, too, missed Maggie.

Colleen stifled a sob. She glanced at the luminous face of her wristwatch. Then she bent under the hood with her wrench and fan belt, and got to work.

It took her less than six minutes to complete the job.

Not bad.

Faster than ever before.

Wishbone

'Some honeymoon,' Diane muttered, stepping to the side of the trail. She squatted until a boulder took the weight of her backpack.

Scott, farther up the trail, stopped and turned around. 'What's the matter now?'

'What isn't?'

He came toward her, shaking his head. Diane knew that his pack was even heavier than hers, but he seemed just as energetic as when they had started out this morning.

She took off her hat and sunglasses. Squinting against the brightness, she unknotted her neckerchief and used it to mop her sweaty face.

'We'd better keep moving,' Scott said. 'We've only got a couple more hours before sunset.'

'Why don't we just camp here?'

'You're kidding.'

'I mean it. I'm wiped out.'

'There's no water here, for one thing.'

'Well, I'm not moving another inch.'

'For godsake . . .'

'We've got plenty of water for one night.'

'There's supposed to be a lake just on the other side of the pass.'

'Well, fine. *You* go to the lake. I'm staying.'

'Diannnnne.'

'I mean it. My blisters have blisters. Every bone

320

in my body aches. Besides that, I've got a head-ache.'

'But this place really sucks.'

'*I* wanted to stop by that stream, remember? But no. "Oh, we can make it over the pass,"' she mimicked him. '"No sweat, sweetheart." You want to see sweat?' She raised her red bandanna toward Scott, balled it up with one hand, and squeezed. Sweat spilled out, fell between her boots and made dark spots on the trail dust.

'Just think how nice the lake'll be,' Scott said. 'These are glacial lakes up here. Ice cold. You can take a dip while I set up camp.'

'I'm not budging.'

'All right. Suit yourself.' He turned away and started hiking up the trail. His boots scuffed up pale puffs behind him. The gear on his backpack and belt creaked and clanked.

He isn't really going to leave me here, Diane told herself.

The bandanna felt a little chilly when she tied it around her hot neck. She slipped out of her pack straps, made sure the bundle was steady on the boulder, and stood up. Her feet felt cramped and burning. But she enjoyed the feel of standing without the awful weight of the pack. The breeze cooled the sweat on her back.

Scott was still walking away.

'I know you're just bluffing!' she called.

He acted as if he didn't hear her.

He passed a bend in the trail and disappeared behind a cluster of blocky granite.

He's just going to stop there and wait for me, Diane thought. It'll be a long wait.

Groaning, she rubbed her sore neck. She peeled the sodden shirt away from her back and fluttered

321

it. Shoving a hand down the seat of her jeans, she plucked her wet panties out from between her buttocks.

'Scott?' she called.

He didn't answer.

'Stop playing games, okay? Come on back here.'

She heard only the wind.

What if he didn't stop?

Diane felt a squirmy coldness in her bowels.

He wouldn't leave me here. He just wouldn't.

She left her pack on the boulder, and strode up the trail.

Scott wasn't behind the outcropping. The trail ahead slanted upward, bordered by blocks and slabs of rock. About a hundred feet ahead, it bent out of sight.

She saw Scott nowhere.

Either he'd hidden, or he'd kept on going.

'You shit!' Diane yelled.

Then she hurried back to the place where she'd left her pack. She put on her hat and sunglasses. She slipped her arms through the straps, leaned forward, and felt like weeping as the weight came down on her shoulders like the hands of a giant trying to shove her into the ground.

She began trudging up the trail.

How could he go off and leave me? I'm his wife.

Shouldn't have married him, she thought. She'd known he could act like a real bastard. But that side of him had always been directed at other people, not at her.

If I'd known he might treat *me* like this . . .

What if I can't find him?

She found him nearly two hours later atop a high boulder beside the trail, perched up there in the last rays of sunlight, a corncob pipe in his teeth and a

322

flask of rum resting on his knee. He smiled down at her. 'What took you so long, sweetheart?'

Diane gave him the finger. Staggering past the boulder, she saw their campsite surrounded by a stand of trees. The tent was already up. Pale smoke curled and drifted above a campfire. Beyond the encampment was the lake, dark blue in the shadow cast by the bleak wall of granite along its far side.

She almost made it to the tent, then yanked the straps from her shoulders and let her pack drop. She sank down in front of it. Struggling for breath, she unlaced her boots and tugged at them. Her feet made sucking sounds when they came out. Her white cotton socks were filthy and drenched. They were dappled at the heels and toes with rusty bloodstains. She peeled them off. She slumped back against her pack, gasping and trembling.

Scott loomed over her.

'I knew you could make it,' he said.

'Go to hell.'

'I tell you what. Why don't you just relax. Camp's already up, and I'll take care of tonight's supper.'

He walked away.

Diane remained where she was, her back braced up by the pack, her rump on the ground, her legs stretched out. Soon, her breathing was almost normal. But the wind was stronger now, and colder. Though the sky remained pale blue, the sun was below the ridge and gave her no heat. Something on the ground was digging into her left buttock. Her skin felt itchy because of the damp clothes.

She felt miserable, but she couldn't force herself to move.

She wished she had the strength to get up and change her clothes. Put on something warm and dry. She wished she had socks on. Warm, dry socks.

I'll never be able to move again, she thought.

They'll find me up here someday, frozen like that leopard on the western summit of Kilimanjaro. And they'll wonder what I was doing up here.

Killed by an asshole.

Who strolled by, just then, and took the corncob out of his mouth long enough to say, 'You shouldn't just lie there. You'll get hypothermia, or something.'

'Thanks for the warning,' she muttered.

'Want me to get you something?'

'Yeah. An annulment.'

He chuckled. 'I think I'll do a little exploring around the lake before I start cooking. You want to come along?'

'Gee, I don't imagine so.'

He wandered off.

Diane was glad to be rid of him. After a few minutes, she managed to sit up. She crawled to the other side of her pack. Kneeling there, she opened it. She tossed her rolled sleeping bag toward the tent, took out her coat and spread it on the ground. Soon, she managed to dig out a fresh pair of socks, sweatpants and a hooded sweatshirt.

She pulled the socks over her tender, wounded feet. Then she stood on the coat. She looked all around. No sign of Scott. Shivering, she stripped off her cold, damp clothes. She stooped, picked up her sweatpants, lowered one foot into the waist hole, lifted her foot off the ground as she sought the opening at the ankle of the pants, and lost her balance. She stumbled backward, fighting to stay up.

She landed on her back, feet in the air.

The ground felt moist and cold. Twigs and rocks dug into her bare skin.

'Great,' she muttered through her tight throat. 'Just great.'

Then she saw someone high in the branches of a nearby tree, staring down at her.

Not *someone*, exactly.

Not *staring*, exactly.

The skeleton of someone. It had a skull with empty sockets.

It seemed to be sitting up there, the gray bones of its legs straddling a limb, its back resting against the trunk, its skull tipped downward as if watching her.

Diane felt icy fingers squeezing her insides.

She thrust both feet through the sweatpants and scurried up. She brushed damp debris off her buttocks, then tugged the pants around her waist.

'Scott!' she yelled. 'Scott, get back here!'

She heard only the wind.

It's just a skeleton, she told herself. Nothing to be afraid of.

Shivering, she swung the sweatshirt behind her back. She held it by the sleeves and swept it from side to side a few times. Then she put it on. She brushed some dirt and bits of leaves and twigs off the front. She pulled up the hood. She hugged herself, clutching her breasts through the soft fabric.

Shoulders hunched, legs tight together, she stood there trembling and gazed at the skeleton.

It really did seem to be staring down at her.

Just a heap of bones, she told herself. It isn't watching me. It's dead. It's got no eyes, no brain. Nothing but bones. It's no more alive than a rock.

It doesn't even know I exist.

We've gotta get out of here.

Kneeling on her coat, Diane searched her backpack until she found her sneakers. She put them on fast, got up wincing, snatched up her coat and hobbled toward the lake.

She stepped out onto a flat shelf of rock that jutted

into the water. From there, she spotted Scott roaming among the jumbled granite beyond the lake's northern tip. She shouted his name. He turned his head and waved, then gestured for her to join him.

'Come here!' she yelled. 'Quick!'

With a shrug, he started to come back.

'What's the matter now?' he asked, obviously annoyed that Diane had interrupted his exploration.

'We've got a visitor,' she said.

Scott raised his eyebrows, looked toward the campsite, and shook his head. 'What're you talking about?'

She pointed toward the high branches of the tree.

'I don't see anything.'

All that Diane could see was one bony foot. The rest of the skeleton was hidden behind limbs and leaves.

'What is it, an owl or something?'

'You'll see.' She led the way, and stopped beside her pack where she'd changed her clothes. From there, the entire skeleton was in plain sight. She pointed up at it. 'That's no owl,' she said.

She watched Scott. When he saw the thing, his eyes opened wide and his jaw dropped. After a few moments, he rearranged his face into a smile. He met Diane's eyes. 'Big deal,' he said. 'A skeleton.'

'*I'll* say it's a big deal. I'm not spending the night here. No way. Not a chance.'

Scott smirked at her.

'I mean it.'

'Don't be ridiculous.'

'It's a *dead* person, for Christsake!'

'So? It won't hurt anything.'

'Damn it, Scott.'

His smirk twisted into a scowl. 'You've been dragging your ass all day, belly-aching about how fucking *tired* you are, and now that we're finally here and the camp's all set up, you wanta get every-thing *alllll* packed up again and go looking for some-place *else*, just 'cause of some crummy skeleton? Right. Sure thing. Every day and twice on Sunday. Has it ever occurred to you that maybe *I'm* tired, too? I spent a fucking *hour* putting up the tent all by myself and fixing the place up for you while you're taking your sweet time back on the trail some-where and now you wanta just keep going? Well, fuck that!'

'Fuck *you*!' she yelled.

'Fuck *me*?' He slapped her, smacking her face sideways.

Diane twisted away from him, held her cheeks and hunched over, crying.

'You don't like Ol' Bony up there, go and hide in the fucking tent. Go on, get.' He swatted the back of her head.

Whirling around, Diane smashed her fist into Scott's jaw. For a moment, he looked stunned. Then he chuckled.

Diane grabbed her sleeping bag and rushed for the tent.

She was snug inside the down-filled mummy bag when she heard the rustle of the tent flap.

'You'll come out to eat, won't you?' Scott asked. He sounded calm and caring.

Diane raised her face off her crossed arms. She looked over her shoulder. Scott was crawling over the floor of the tent. The tent was dark inside. Behind Scott, she saw the glow of the campfire, the gloomy hues of dusk.

'What can I say?' he said. 'I'm sorry. I don't know what got into me. I can't believe I really hit you.'

'Twice,' she murmured, and sniffed.

Reaching out, he gently stroked her hair.

'Are you okay?' he asked.

'What do you think?'

'I told you I'm sorry.'

'That's a big help.'

'Don't be that way, honey. I love you. I just lost my head. Come on. Why don't you get up and come out by the campfire? You'll feel much better once you've got some good hot food inside you.'

'All right.'

'That's my girl.' He patted her back.

After he was gone, Diane struggled free of her mummy bag. She put on her coat and sneakers, then crawled from the tent and stood up. She peered into the tree. The skeleton, way up there, looked as if its gray bones were melting into the darkness.

'You oughta stop worrying about that thing,' Scott told her.

'Sure.' She moved in close to the fire and sat down on a rock. The surface was rough, but fairly flat. Cold seeped through the seat of her sweatpants.

Scott, bending over the fire, ladled stew out of the pot. He filled a tin plate, added a fork, and brought it to her.

'I just wonder what Ol' Bony's doing up there,' he said.

'Watching us,' Diane muttered.

Scott laughed.

She set the plate on her thighs. It felt nice and hot. Steam rose off the stew.

'I mean, I find it intriguing. What's he doing up there, you know? Who was he? How'd he get there?' Scott filled a plate for himself and stood at the other side of the fire as he started to eat. 'Maybe he fell out of an airplane. You know? Could've been a mid-air

328

collision. Or maybe he parachuted. Hey, maybe he's D.B. Cooper.'

'Cooper didn't even jump in this state,' Diane pointed out. 'Besides, where's the parachute?' She took a bite of the stew meat. It was stringy and tough, but hot. It tasted good. 'For that matter, where are his clothes?'

'Probably the same place as his skin and eyes.'

'Oh, very clever.'

Scott laughed, and ate some more. 'I've got it!' He pointed his fork toward the skeleton. 'Jimmy Hoffa. No, I've got it! Judge Crater!'

Diane smiled.

'All right! She's perking up!'

'That's just because God's gonna strike you dead, any second now, for being such a wise-ass.'

'You'd find that amusing, would you?'

'It'd serve you right for making fun of dead people.'

'Ol' Bony doesn't mind.' Scott turned toward the tree and tipped his head back. 'Yo! Up there! Wishbone! Yeah, you!'

'Don't,' Diane said. 'Come on.'

Laughing, ignoring her, Scott cupped a hand to the side of his mouth and called, 'You got any problem up there with what I been saying? Are you . . . taking offense at my remarks?'

'Would you shut up!' Diane snapped.

He looked at her. Grinning, he said, 'What's the matter, afraid he might answer?'

'It's just not right. Okay? That was a person once.'

'Whoop-dee-doo.'

'God, why don't you grow up.'

'Oooo, the little woman's getting testy. Again.'

She hunched low over her stew and forked some into her mouth.

'Yo, up there! Now look what you've done! You've got my bride all upset! How dare you!'

Diane kept her head down and kept on eating.

What's *wrong* with him? Maybe it's marriage. Now that he's got me, he thinks he can start dumping all over me. Now he can treat me like shit, the way he treats everyone else.

Maybe it's just being in the mountains. Maybe roughing it brings out all this nasty macho shit.

'You're really fucking up our honeymoon, Bonebrain!'

Diane raised her head.

Crouching, Scott set down his plate. He picked up a stone, and cocked back his arm to hurl it at the skeleton.

'No!'

He threw it.

The pale chuck of rock flew high and vanished into the darkness. For a moment, Diane heard only the crackle and pop of the campfire, the distant howl of the wind. Then came a faint thud as if the rock had struck the tree. Or the skeleton.

'Did I getcha?' Scott yelled. 'Huh? Want me to try again?' He squatted and searched the ground for another rock.

Diane flung her plate down. She leaped to her feet. 'Damn it, don't you dare!'

'Oh, dry up.' He found a rock. He stood up. He tossed it underhand, caught it, and grinned at Diane.

Oh shit, she thought. *This one's for me.*

But she never found out for sure.

Out of the corner of her eye, she saw something sailing down from the tree. She jerked her head that way and squinted.

A big, pale rock was curving down through the darkness at Scott.

Not a *rock*, exactly.

A skull.

Just as Scott turned toward the tree, the skull crashed

330

against his forehead. It didn't shatter. It didn't bounce off. Its teeth clamped, biting into his scalp and eyebrow. It stayed there, hanging on as Scott staggered backward and dropped his rock and fell to the ground beside the fire.

Diane stood frozen, staring and dazed.

That didn't happen, she told herself. Impossible.

This isn't happening, either, she told herself when she looked toward the tree and saw the headless skeleton on its way down.

It seemed very agile for a pile of bones.

It shinnied down the trunk to the bottom branch, some ten or twelve feet above the ground. It sat on the branch. Then it pushed itself off, dropped, and landed standing up.

It seemed to have a bounce in its step as it walked toward Scott.

Bending over him, it grabbed its skull with both hands and tugged. Its teeth ripped free of Scott's face.

He groaned.

Through the disbelief that fogged her mind, Diane realized he was still alive. He'd been knocked unconscious by the skull. Now, he was coming to. His face was bleeding horribly.

The skeleton, holding the skull in one hand, seemed to examine it for a moment. Then a fingertip of bone flicked a scrap of Scott's flesh off one of its upper teeth. With that accomplished, it raised the head and planted it atop its spinal column.

Scott, eyes still shut, squirmed a little bit.

The skeleton placed a foot on his chest. It rubbed its hands together.

Then its head slowly swiveled until its eyeless sockets seemed to fix on Diane. It raised an arm and waved.

Waving goodbye? Wants me to leave?

This can't be happening, Diane thought.

But just in case it is . . .

She staggered backward a few steps, then swung around and ran.

Diane didn't sleep.

She spent that night huddled in a crevice, hiding from the skeleton and the wind, shivering, wondering what had happened.

When dawn came, she climbed onto a boulder. From there, she could see the northern end of the lake at the bottom of the slope. But not the campsite. Outcroppings along the shore hid that from her view. She was glad.

Soon, the sun appeared above the eastern ridge. Its rays slanted down across the valley, warming her. She took off her coat and sat on it for a while, savoring the feel of the heat.

She didn't want to return to the camp. But she knew it had to be done.

And so, with shaky legs and a sick lump of dread in her stomach, she made her way down the slope and along the lakeshore.

The campsite was just as she had left it.

But the fire was dead. And Scott no longer lay sprawled on the ground beside it.

His clothes were there. Shredded and bloody.

Diane gritted her teeth to stop them from chattering. She wrapped her arms tightly across her chest. She turned toward the tree and raised her eyes.

Scott was straddling a high limb. The skeleton, braced between his body and the tree trunk, appeared to be sitting on his lap. His face rested against its skull, his lips mashed to its teeth. His bare legs dangled. Diane could see one arm of bone wrapped around his back, one fleshless leg against his side like the thigh of an eager lover squeezing him.

Some honeymoon, she thought.

She started to giggle.

First Date

Shannon latched her seatbelt, then turned to Jeff as he started the car. 'Can we go someplace?' she asked. 'I don't really want to go home yet. Okay? It's still early, and . . . I mean, I'd like to spend more time with you.'

'Hey, fine,' Jeff said, suddenly feeling shaky. 'Great. I was thinking the same thing.' He gave her a smile, then looked over his shoulder and started to back out of the parking space.

Oh God, he thought. Is it really possible that she *likes* me?

She must. She came to the movie with me. Now she wants to *go someplace*.

Unbelievable.

Swinging forward onto the road, he asked, 'What time do you have to be home?'

'Not till midnight.'

'So we've got a couple of hours.'

'Looks that way,' she said. 'Is it all right if I roll down my window?'

'Sure, go ahead.'

As Shannon lowered her window, Jeff shut off the air conditioner and opened his own window.

'It's such a lovely, warm night,' she said.

'A night made for roving,' Jeff said.

He glanced at Shannon and saw her smile in the dim glow cast by the streetlights.

God, she's so beautiful, he thought. And she's with *me*. She's sitting right there, Shannon Ashley, *smiling* at me. And she wants to *go* someplace.

He suddenly wished he'd had the guts to hold her hand during the movie.

Maybe she would've liked it, after all.

But he'd been too afraid to try.

I should've just done it!

Why not now? he asked himself.

NO!

'Are you hungry?' he asked. 'We could go some-place . . . Pizza Hut or Jack in the—'

'I'm stuffed. Really.' She suddenly frowned. 'But if *you're* hungry . . .'

'No, no, I just thought *you* might be.'

'I'm fine.'

'So, where would you *like* to go?' he asked.

'Someplace . . . *different*.'

'Ah,' Jeff said.

'Ah,' Shannon echoed.

They looked at each other. Shannon was all blurs and shadows, dim angles and patches of darkness. She seemed to be smiling. Her teeth were as white as her blouse. Jeff found his gaze sliding down the front of her blouse, lingering on the rises formed by her breasts.

'Maybe you should keep your eyes on the road,' she said.

Jeff looked forward fast, blushing. 'Sorry,' he muttered.

'I just don't want to end up in the hospital.'

'It'd be *different*.'

'I hate hospitals,' Shannon said. 'The *morgue*, on the other hand . . .'

'Morgues are cool.'

'Ever been to one?' Shannon asked.

'No.'

'Me neither.'

'No time like the present.'

'No way!' Shannon gave his upper arm a gentle punch.

It felt *wonderful*.

He was tempted to give her a nice, soft punch in return – a way to touch her – but he didn't dare.

'What was that for?' he asked.

'Being an idiot.'

'Ah.'

'I mean, it'd be crazy. Even if we could *find* a morgue and get in, we'd probably end up being arrested.'

'Jail would be different.'

'*I've got it!*'

'What?'

'That old graveyard! The one out there by the church!'

'What church?'

'You know. Out on County Line Road.'

'Oh!'

'You know?'

'Jesus. You don't want to go *there*.'

'Sure. Why not? I mean, wouldn't that be just *perfect*?'

The idea of it made Jeff feel shivery inside. 'I don't know,' he muttered.

'Scared?' Shannon asked.

'Who, me?'

'How about it?'

It seemed like a bad idea. An old cemetery behind a long-abandoned church in the middle of nowhere seemed like a *very* bad place to go, especially late at night.

But Jeff didn't want to look like a coward.

And, somehow, the idea of being in such a horrible

place with Shannon made him tremble with excitement as much as dread.

'I'm game,' he said. 'If you're sure that's where you want to go . . .'

'I'm sure.'

'Okay. We'll go. It's this way, isn't it?'

'Yeah, just keep heading out of town. I'll tell you where to turn.'

'Have you been there before?' Jeff asked.

'Just driving by. I've never even gotten close enough to take a good look. But I've always thought it'd be a neat place to stop. I mean, it looks so *creepy*. I just *love* creepy stuff.'

'Me, too.'

'I know. That's how come it's so perfect, you and me going there tonight.' She reached over and put a hand on his thigh.

Jeff struggled not to moan.

Her hand felt warm through his jeans.

'We're so much alike,' she said. 'I kept waiting and waiting for you to ask me out. I *knew* we'd be perfect together. We're two of a kind.'

'What kind is that?' he asked, blushing so fiercely that he thought he might melt.

'Dark.'

'Yeah?'

'Lured by the mysteries of the night, the gallows, and the grave. I knew it from the moment I first saw you.'

'That's why you asked me out tonight?' he asked.

'We just *had* to see *Eyes of the Vampire* together. I didn't want to go alone, and everyone else I know . . . they would've *mocked* it. I *had* to see it with you. *Share* it with you.'

'*Near Dark* was better.'

'Ten times better.' Her hand moved slightly higher,

337

and her curled fingers rubbed the side of his thigh. 'I wish we'd known each other then.'

'You and me both,' Jeff managed to say, squirming a little. Her hand remained where it was, barely moving, but caressing him.

Doesn't she know what she's doing? Jeff wondered.

She's so *close*.

'Here comes County Line Road,' Shannon said. 'You'll want to hang a left at the stop sign.'

After he made the turn, she said, 'This is going to be so exciting. I've never been to *any* graveyard at night. Have you?'

'No.'

'So it'll be the first time for both of us.'

'Guess so.'

'And a full moon.'

'Maybe we'll run into a werewolf,' Jeff said.

'I'm not real big on werewolves.'

He turned his head and smiled at her. 'You're a vampire person.'

'You bet,' she said, and squeezed his thigh. 'Wouldn't you just love to run into a vampire?' she asked.

'I think there's a pretty slim chance of that.'

'But if you *could* . . . you know?'

'I guess it'd be pretty cool.'

'What would you do?'

'Run like hell.'

She laughed and slapped his thigh and took her hand away. Where her hand had been, the leg of his jeans felt warm and slightly moist.

'What would *you* do?' he asked. 'Interview him?'

'You think he'd let me?'

'If you ask nicely.'

'I think he'd probably be a lot more interested in biting my neck.'

338

'More than likely,' Jeff said.

'Or she.'

'Good point. I'd *much* prefer a female, myself.'

'Not me. If a vampire's going to chomp on my neck, I want it to be a *guy*.'

'So then, I guess *ideally* we'll need to get attacked by *two* vampires – a guy for you and a gal for me.'

'And they've got to be *heterosexual* vampires,' Shannon added.

'Do they come both ways?'

'Do they come at all?'

Blushing, Jeff shook his head. 'I guess it all depends on who you read,' he said.

'What about *real* vampires?' she asked.

'What do you mean by real?'

'The kind that are really *out* there.'

Jeff smiled at her. 'I hate to break it to you, Shannon, but there ain't no such animal.'

'Think not?'

He chuckled softly. 'Hope not,' he said. 'Oh, I know there are nutcakes who like to *think* they're vampires . . . But I have some serious reservations about the existence of the genuine article. The "undead" variety? You know, going on for centuries, turning into bats and mist and stuff, scared of crosses . . . the whole nine yards.'

Shannon didn't say anything.

He looked over at her. On this stretch of road, there were no streetlights. She seemed to be made of black and a few shades of gray.

'What if I told you *I'm* one?' she asked.

Jeff suddenly felt a squirmy chill inside. 'You're not,' he said.

'Are you sure?'

'Pretty sure.'

Her hand returned to his thigh. Her fingernails dug in. He groaned and squirmed.

'*How* sure?' she asked.

'I'm sure I've seen you in daylight. And I've seen you in mirrors a couple of times. I've *definitely* seen you eat real food. Who's ever heard of vampires eating popcorn and Milk Duds?'

'Hmm. Good points. You must be right. I must *not* be a vampire.'

He said, 'You're not.'

'Apparently not.'

'Hey, come on. You're making me nervous.'

'You'd better slow down,' she said. 'The turn-off's just around the next bend.'

He took his foot off the gas pedal. 'Are you really sure you want to do this?' he asked. 'Go to a cemetery at this hour?'

'I spooked you, didn't I?'

'I *know* you're not a vampire.'

'If you say so.'

'There *isn't* any such thing.'

'Of course there isn't.'

'And even if they *do* exist, which I doubt, *you* can't possibly be one. Hell, you've got a *suntan*.'

'But is my suntan *real*?'

'Come on, cut it out.'

'Here it is.'

Jeff stepped on the brakes and swung onto the side road. The old strip of asphalt looked gray in the moonlight. Nothing remained of its center line, if there had ever been one. The surface was potted and cracked. Weeds grew in the fissures. Though Jeff drove slowly, the car shook and bounced.

'Kill the headlights,' Shannon said.

'I thought you didn't want to end up in the hospital.'

340

'There's plenty of moonlight.'

He shut off the headlights. 'Jesus,' he muttered, and slowed almost to a stop.

'It's all right. There's not much to hit, anyway.'

'Hope not.' He could see almost nothing in front of his car. 'This is weird.'

'I think it's neat,' Shannon said, her voice hushed.

'Well . . . it *is*, sort of.'

'It's like we're invisible.' She was a dim silhouette in the passenger seat, her features shrouded by darkness.

Jeff grinned at her and said, 'Maybe we can sneak up on the vampires.'

'Nah. They'll hear us coming.'

'We could park here and walk in.'

'What if we need to make a quick getaway?' Shannon asked.

'I thought you *wanted* to run into some vampires.'

'Vampires, yes; perverts and murderers, no.'

'Ah. Okay.'

'Let's park right up close to the graveyard,' Shannon suggested.

Jeff realized that he could now *see* it.

With his headlights off, the night had been infiltrated by moonlight.

The moonlight seemed to wash everything with a dim, pale mist: the cracked and pitted road ahead; the weeds growing through the asphalt; the thickets and scattered trees on both sides of the road; the old wooden church with its boarded windows and broken steeple; the desolate, flat, weed-cluttered landscape of the parking lot in front of the church; and the graveyard off to the right.

As he drove onto the parking lot, Jeff said, 'At least we're the only car.'

'So far, so good,' Shannon said.

He steered toward the cemetery: a field of tomb-stones, burial vaults and statues, stunted trees, thickets, and long, dry grass.

'I don't see anybody,' Shannon said.

'Me neither.'

'This is *so* cool.'

'Yeah.' Jeff's voice sounded steady, though he felt as if his entire body was being shaken by quick, tight tremors. 'I'll turn us around,' he said.

'Good idea.'

He made a U-turn, then backed up, swinging the wheel until the front of his car pointed to the entry road. Then he looked at Shannon. 'Now I suppose we have to get out.'

'Of course.'

'Fun and games.'

She reached over and rubbed his shoulder. 'It'll be great,' she said.

They unfastened their seatbelts. When Jeff opened his door, the overhead light came on. He muttered, 'Shit!' and scampered out.

Shannon hurried out the passenger side.

They both shut their doors quickly, silently. The light in the car went dark.

Standing by his door, Jeff watched Shannon stride around the front of the car. In the moonlight, her white blouse and white jeans looked as bright as a field of snow. Her blonde hair, face and hands were much darker, and hard to see.

'So much for the element of surprise,' she said. She was smiling. Her teeth were white.

'I forgot all about the interior light.'

'Well, nobody's here anyway.'

'Maybe.'

Side by side, they faced the cemetery.

Jeff saw many figures that might be people. Some

342

were apparently statues, while others were formed by combinations of bushes, crosses, shadows . . .

'I don't see anyone,' Shannon said. 'Do you?'

'No. But there must be a thousand places to hide.'

'You aren't going to chicken out on me, are you?' As she asked, she moved slightly sideways.

Their arms touched.

'Not me,' Jeff said. Then he added, 'You wouldn't happen to have a gun?'

'No, but I've got this.' Her arm went away from his. As she turned to face him, she shoved a hand into a front pocket of her white jeans. She pulled out a folding knife. Using both hands, she pried open its blade. 'See?' The three-inch blade glinted like silver.

'Hey, cool.'

'I'm a dangerous woman.'

'So I see. You wouldn't happen to have a cross or two?'

She shook her head. 'I used to wear a cross all the time. You know, on a gold necklace? Never took it off. Not even in the shower. I figured the minute I took it off, I'd get nailed by a vampire. But then, a couple of years ago, I sort of started to think I might *like* it.'

'Getting nailed by a vampire?'

'Yeah. You know? I *wanted* it to happen, so I ditched the cross.'

'You really *are* a believer.'

'A hoper.'

'But no luck, so far?'

'Maybe tonight,' she said. 'Let's take a look around.'

'Okay.'

Shannon folded her knife shut. Instead of returning it to her pocket, she held it in her right hand.

They walked toward the cemetery.

'If there's trouble,' Jeff whispered, 'make a run for the car. The keys are in the ignition . . . in case I don't make it.'

'If there's trouble,' Shannon said, 'I'll stick with you. Like I told you, I'm a dangerous woman.' She took Jeff's hand in hers.

This was the first time they'd ever held hands.

The feel of it sapped his strength, quickened his heartbeat, numbed his mind.

It's no big deal, he told himself. It's just her hand. Calm down.

Just her hand.

He gave it a gentle squeeze. She squeezed back, and turned her head and smiled at him.

'My heart's pounding like crazy,' she whispered.

'Mine, too.'

'This is *so* creepy.'

'Me?' he asked.

'Not you, *this*. The *bone orchard*.'

'Oh. Yeah.' He saw that they were standing among the graves. It came as no great surprise. After all, this was where they'd been heading when Shannon took his hand. But he had no memory of actually *entering* the cemetery.

Must've been on automatic pilot, he told himself.

He looked over his shoulder. They hadn't gone far. The rear of his car was probably no more than twenty feet away. But they'd already waded through the tall grass past several tombstones.

Shannon whispered, 'This is better than any old movie, isn't it?'

'You can say that again.'

'This is *real*. We're actually sneaking around in a *graveyard*.'

Pulling him by the hand, she led the way. They walked slowly, trudging through the dry grass, ducking

344

under low branches, stepping around stone monuments, sometimes pausing to stare at human figures – and to make sure they were seeing statues, not people.

They wandered deeper and deeper into the cemetery. Soon, the car was out of sight.

They kept walking.

And found themselves in a moonlit clearing surrounded by burial vaults. The pale, stone buildings, all the same size and evenly spaced, looked as if they'd been carefully positioned to form a large circle. In the center of the circle, perhaps forty feet away from the chambers that surrounded it, was something that looked like a large block of stone.

'What is this?' Jeff asked.

'Who knows? I didn't even know it was here. You can't see it from the road.' Shannon turned her head slowly. At first, Jeff thought she was admiring the vaults. Then he realized she was counting them. 'Thirteen,' she said. 'Creepy.'

'You like creepy, right?'

'Love it,' Shannon whispered. 'Come on, let's see what this thing is.'

Still holding hands, they walked toward the strange, blocky object at the hub of the thirteen vaults. It was about the height of Jeff's shoulders, flat on top, apparently round in shape and ten or twelve feet in diameter.

'What do you think it is?' Shannon asked.

'I don't think it's a fountain. Looks like nothing . . . a platform, a stage?'

'An altar?' Shannon suggested, and squeezed his hand.

'Could be.'

They stopped a few paces away from it.

'This must be where they perform their human sacrifices,' Shannon said.

'More than likely.'

She bumped against Jeff's side. He bumped back.

'There're thirteen vampires, and they all come out to watch,' she said. 'The king of the vampires actually does the killing.'

'They've got a king? What's his name?'

'Pete.'

Jeff burst out laughing.

'It's blasphemy to laugh at King Pete.'

'Oh. Okay. Sorry.'

'So then, after King Pete opens the throat of the victim . . . and drinks his fill . . . he leaves her there for the others. They swarm in and scamper up and have at her. They're ravenous. They plant their mouths everywhere on her. Thirteen mouths, all of them *sucking* on her.'

'Wow,' Jeff said. He felt shaky and a little breathless.

'She's naked, of course.'

'Of course.'

'Come on.' Shannon let go of his hand. She stuffed the knife into her pocket, then stepped forward, placed her hands on the stone, leaped and thrust herself up. She swung a knee over the edge. Jeff thought maybe he should help her. But she might take it wrong, so he kept his arms at his sides.

She crawled forward. When she was safely away from the edge, she got to her feet. She turned around. 'Hey, this is great. Come on up.'

'Okay.' Jeff placed his hands on top of the stone, then just stood there and gazed at Shannon.

She looked wonderful standing up there in the moonlight, feet parted, hands on hips.

'You know what I think this might've been?' he asked.

'You mean *really*?'

'Yeah. A pedestal for some sort of statue.'

'What makes you think so?'

'Seeing you up there.'

'Yeah?' She suddenly raised her right leg, planted an elbow on its knee, and rested her chin on her fist.

'Exactly.'

'So where'd the statue go?' she asked.

'They must've gotten rid of it.'

'Maybe because it represented hideous, unspeakable evil. The thirteen worshipped it.' She turned around slowly, arms raised. 'Thirteen vampires. They built their tombs around the statue of their king. But the villagers grew wise to this foul sect of blood-sucking fiends and attacked in the night. They slew them all, then tore down the statue and destroyed it.'

Jeff grinned. 'That's probably just what happened.'

'But they couldn't destroy the *evil*.'

'Which is with us always.'

'Right.'

He boosted himself up, scurried over the edge, and got to his feet. 'I think it must've been a statue of King Pete.'

'Hail to King Pete!' Shannon called out.

Jeff cringed.

'The blood is the life!'

'Shhh!'

'What's wrong?'

'You don't have to yell.'

'Scared?'

'Want to get us kicked out?'

'By who?' Shannon asked.

Jeff shrugged. 'I don't know, but . . .'

'I think you're afraid I'll bring out the vampires,' she said.

'They were slain by the villagers, remember?'

'That was just a story. Don't you know a story when

347

you hear one? Come here.' Standing in the center of the pedestal, Shannon gestured for Jeff to approach.

When he stopped in front of her, she put her hands on his hips. 'If there *are* any vampires around here . . . real ones . . . they must've heard me. Don't you think so?'

He swallowed hard. 'You were loud enough to wake the undead,' he assured her.

'So they know we're here.'

'I guess so.'

'They'll be coming for us.'

'Any moment.'

'They'll come and suck our necks,' she whispered. Easing forward, she slid her arms around Jeff and pressed herself against him. Stunned, confused, he wrapped his arms around her. He had never held a girl this way before. He could feel the warmth of her thighs. He could feel the rise and fall of her chest. And the push of her breasts. And the tickle of her breath on the side of his neck. Her hair, soft against his cheek, carried a mild scent so fresh and clean that it made him ache.

He moved his hands up and down her back. Through the cloth of her blouse, he felt smooth slopes and curves and no straps.

She kissed the side of his neck.

It gave him a sudden rush of goosebumps and made him squirm.

'That's where they'll get us,' Shannon whispered. And licked him there.

He shuddered. 'Gives me goose pimples,' he said.

'Do it to me, okay?'

Shannon released him, so he loosened his hold on her. She took a small step backward. Head down, she unfastened a button of her blouse. Then another. Then she slipped the left side of her blouse off her shoulder.

It fell and hung against her upper arm. With a fling of her hand, she swept her hair out of the way.

She was bare skin from her ear down the side of her neck, bare skin along her shoulder and down her arm halfway to the elbow.

And bare down her front to where a button held the blouse together.

Her left breast was only half covered, the nipple just out of sight, shrouded by white cloth.

If that button goes . . .

Shannon curled a hand around the back of his head. Fingers in his hair, she drew his head down to the curve at the base of her neck. He kissed her gently there. Her skin felt smooth and warm.

'Harder,' she whispered.

He opened his mouth, pushed with it, slid his tongue back and forth.

She moaned and squirmed.

While her left hand clutched Jeff's head, her right hand rubbed up and down his side from his hip to his armpit. His own left hand, he realized, was gripping her shoulder as if to hold her in place. His right was locked on her upper arm – but not where it was bare.

He moved it higher.

Up to where her skin was.

Shannon didn't protest.

So he caressed the smooth, naked skin of her arm and shoulder while he licked and sucked her neck.

Shannon writhed and trembled.

Jeff thought about the half-bare breast only a few inches below his hand.

But he stayed away from it.

'Bite,' she gasped.

He pressed the edges of his teeth against her skin. It felt firm and springy. He squeezed a little harder.

'Make me bleed,' she gasped. 'Break my skin and suck my blood.'

'I don't—'

'No! Wait!' She suddenly jerked his head back by the hair. Gazing into his eyes, she shook her head and muttered, 'Wait,' again. Then, 'No good. Stupid.' She released Jeff's hair and dropped her hands away from him.

In the moonlight, Jeff saw a silvery slick of spittle on the left side of her neck.

'You all right?' he asked.

'Yeah.'

'Did I hurt you?'

'It was great,' she said. 'We've just gotta take our clothes off.'

'*What?*'

She unfastened the next button of her blouse. The left side fell and hung below her breast.

Jeff gazed at her bare breast, stunned. He'd never seen a real one before. He felt as if his breath was being sucked out. His heart thudded. His penis, growing stiff, shoved at the front of his pants.

Finished with her buttons, Shannon pulled her blouse off.

Jeff gaped at her.

She was naked above her white jeans.

'Get yours off, too,' she said, and tossed her blouse toward the edge of the pedestal.

'I . . . what's going on?'

'We don't wanta get blood on our clothes.'

'Huh?'

Balancing on one leg, she brought up the other and pulled her sneaker off.

'What blood?' Jeff asked.

'*Our* blood.' She tossed the sneaker aside. It landed near her blouse, but bounced and fell off the edge of

350

the pedestal. 'Don't just stand there.' She tugged off her sock and gave it a fling.

Jeff began to unbutton his shirt. 'What's going on?' he asked.

'We're gonna *do* it.' She worked on her other sneaker and sock.

'Do what?'

'You see any vampires around here?' Shannon asked, and opened the button at the waist of her jeans.

'No.'

'Me neither.' She pulled the zipper down. 'I don't think they're coming.'

'Probably not.'

'Never a vampire around when you need one.' With that, she bent over, sliding her jeans down. She stepped out of them. Then she dropped to a crouch. Holding the jeans up between her knees, she dug into a pocket. 'We'll have to do this ourselves,' she said, and took out her knife. 'Come on, take your clothes off.'

'What's the knife for?' Jeff asked, and tossed his shirt out of the way.

'All the better to cut ourselves with.'

Shannon stood up. Turning aside, she threw her jeans. They tumbled and flapped. In midair, her panties drifted free and fell toward her blouse. Her jeans disappeared over the edge of the pedestal. 'Pooey,' she said. Then she turned toward Jeff.

Pale moonlight dusted her hair, her face, her shoulders and breasts. Each breast cast a shadow below it.

So many shadows.

So many hidden hollows.

But her belly was brushed with light. So were her hips. And a tongue of moonlight found its way to a wispy tuft of hair between her legs.

Groaning, Jeff looked away from her.

351

'I'll help,' Shannon said. She stepped up to him. 'Here, you hold the knife.'

She gave it to him. Then she unfastened his jeans. She crouched and tugged. His briefs went down with the jeans and his erection leaped at her face. 'Holy mackerel!' she gasped.

'Sorry.'

'Just, uh . . . keep it to yourself, okay?'

He swallowed hard. 'Sure.'

She finished pulling his pants down, then stood up and said, 'I mean, we're not here to . . . you know, screw around.'

'Maybe we should've kept our clothes on.'

'And get them all bloody? My parents'll probably be up and waiting when I get home. They'll go apeshit if I walk in drenched with blood. Sit down. We have to get these off you.'

Jeff eased himself down. The cool, stone surface of the pedestal felt rough and grainy against his buttocks. Leaning back, he stretched out his legs and braced himself with his arms.

Shannon squatted in front of him. She removed his shoes and socks, his jeans and shorts. Then she picked them up, twisted around and snatched up his shirt. Holding them all, she stood and walked toward the edge of the pedestal.

Her hips swept slightly from side to side. Her buttocks looked creamy in the moonlight. Jeff watched how they moved with each step. And he stared at the shadowed cleft between them.

Instead of avoiding her clothes and sneaker scattered in front of her, Shannon swept them together with her feet. Then swept them off the edge of the ped-estal.

'What're you doing?' Jeff asked.

'Clearing the deck.' She opened her arms. Jeff's

352

clothes and shoes fell over the side. She turned around. 'They'll be fine down there.'

'Fine,' he said.

'This way, there's no chance they'll get bloody.' She came toward him.

Look at her, look at her, look at her. My God!

Jeff was dry-mouthed, trembling, hard – and a little embarrassed about the way that his penis was sticking straight up out of his lap.

Shannon stopped at his feet. 'Maybe we should do it standing up,' she said.

Jeff licked his lips and said, 'Fine with me.'

He got to his feet.

It felt very strange to be standing up, this high above the ground, with no clothes on. In the middle of the night. In front of beautiful, naked Shannon. In a graveyard. Surrounded by thirteen burial vaults.

He turned around slowly, looking at the moonlit chambers, at the shadows between them, and at the pale, grassy clearing.

With a glance at Shannon, he saw that she was looking, too.

'Oh, my God!' she suddenly blurted. 'Who's that?'

Jeff's heart slammed. He whirled around. 'Where?'

'Gotcha!'

'Jeez!' He turned to her. 'Real nice.'

Laughing softly, she stepped over to him and put her hands on his hips. 'Did I scare you?'

'Yeah. A little.'

'I didn't really see anyone,' she said.

'I know.'

'But I *do* have this sneaky feeling we're being watched.'

'Terrific,' Jeff muttered.

'I'm all shivery.'

'You and me both.'

'Yeah?' She slid her hands behind Jeff and scraped her fingernails lightly up his back. Goosebumps scurried over him. He trembled. Her hands stopped at his shoulder blades. Holding him there, she eased forward. Her belly pushed at his penis. Her nipples touched his chest. Her wet, open lips caressed the side of his neck.

She kissed him, licked him.

Jeff moaned.

Her mouth went away. 'Let me have the knife,' she whispered.

The knife felt hot and slick in his hand. He kept his hand shut. 'I don't know.'

'You're not gonna chicken out, are you?'

'Might be dangerous.'

'Of *course* it's dangerous. But not very. Not if we're careful. It won't even *hurt* much if we use the knife.'

'What about . . . diseases?'

'What've you got?'

'Nothing, I don't think, but . . .'

'Me, neither. Come on, you want to do it, don't you?'

He didn't much care for the idea of playing vampire, but he very much wanted to have Shannon touching him again. If it meant losing a little blood, fine.

'Sure,' he said.

'You don't *sound* very sure.'

'It's just . . . what if you hit my jugular vein, or something?'

'That's why we got our clothes out of the way, silly.'

With that, she had him laughing. She laughed along with him.

Then she said, 'You're pretty nervous about this.'

'A little.'

'I tell you what. Why don't *you* go first?'

354

'I thought that was what we were talking about.'

'I mean, you go first and suck *me*. I loved how it felt when you were doing it before. I wanted it to keep on going, but then I started to worry about our clothes. And I remembered about the knife – so now you can get to my blood without mauling me. Just a neat little slit or two. It'll be great.'

'I don't want to *cut* you.'

'I'll do it. Let me have the knife.'

He gave the knife to her. Holding it in front of her belly, she looked down and tried to pry open the blade. She seemed to have some trouble with it. 'My hands are shaking,' she murmured.

Jeff stared at her breasts. They were only inches from his chest. The dark nipples jutted out as if reaching for him.

'There we go,' Shannon said, swinging the blade out of the handle. It locked into place with a soft click. 'You want the left side?' she asked. She tilted her head to the right.

'I guess so.'

'Good.' With her left hand, she fingered the side of her neck. 'About here?' she asked.

'That'd be fine.'

'You don't sound too thrilled.'

'I'm thrilled, all right. Just nervous. I've never . . . drunk blood before. Just my own a few times. You know, when I've had a cut. Never someone else's.'

'Same here. Now we'll find out what all the fuss is about.'

'Yeah.'

Keeping her fingers against her neck to mark the place, she brought up her right arm. Elbow high, she swung her forearm across the front of her neck and touched the point of her knife to the area in front of her middle finger.

355

'How's this?' she asked.

She's really going to do it!

'Fine, I guess.'

'Ready?'

Jeff lowered his gaze from her hands, from the knife poised at her neck, and stared at her left breast. She was breathing hard. The breast was lifted by her expanding ribcage, then lowered, then lifted again.

'Jeff? Are you ready?'

'When you are,' he said, and raised his eyes.

'Here goes.' Her skin dented under the point, then enveloped it. The blade went in no more than a quarter of an inch, maybe less. When she pulled it out, a dot of blood grew and began crawling downward. 'How's that?' she asked.

'Fine.'

'No, wait. One more. Gotta make it official.' She poked the point into her neck again – cutting a fresh wound an inch from the other. Then she ducked, set the knife by her feet, and rose up again in front of Jeff. 'Okay,' she said.

By then, blood from the first cut had spilled over her collar bone and was sliding down her chest.

Jeff put one hand on her right shoulder, the other on her left side – just below her ribcage.

Shannon soon had two strips of blood rolling down her chest.

Jeff stared at them.

'Are you gonna do it?

Trying to sound like Lugosi, he said, 'Your blood, it is so beautiful to watch.'

'You wanta taste it, don't you?' Shannon asked, her voice trembling.

Jeff watched the narrow, dark trails slide out onto her left breast.

Shannon squirmed. 'It tickles,' she said.

356

One stream curved off to the side of her breast, while the other trickled to its very tip.

Jeff crouched slightly, leaned in and licked the blood off her nipple.

Shannon flinched.

He sucked her nipple into his mouth, swirled his tongue around it and tested it with his teeth, relishing its stiff, rubbery feel.

'Hey.' She pulled his hair. 'Don't.'

He took his mouth away. 'The blood,' he gasped.

'But no funny stuff.'

'Sorry.'

She let go of his hair.

He expected her to grab it again as he lapped the blood off the side of her breast, but she didn't. He licked the side and the bottom, and up from underneath to the front, briefly running his tongue over her nipple. She stiffened and moaned, but made no attempt to stop him.

Though he ached to suck on her nipple again, he figured it might be pressing his luck.

So he abandoned her breast and licked his way up her chest, following the strips of blood.

He followed them over the smooth curve of her collar bone, followed them to their source. As he latched his mouth against the wounds, he wrapped his arms around her and drew her tightly to his body. Her breasts pushed against his chest: the right was dry and warm; the left was moist and clammy. His rigid penis shoved against her belly and glided upward on splippery juices until its whole underside was snug against her.

He squirmed, rubbing her.

And he sucked.

Sucking, he felt her blood come into his mouth.

He wondered if he could make it *squirt*.

357

The harder he sucked, the more blood poured into his mouth. And the more Shannon groaned and gasped and writhed against him.

She's going *nuts*, Jeff thought. She *loves* it.

Bet she won't stop me now.

Keeping his right arm clamped against her back, he brought his left arm forward, turned himself slightly to make room for his hand to fit between their bodies, then slipped it in and took hold of her right breast.

It filled his hand.

The nipple pushed against his palm.

'Don't,' she gasped, still writhing.

She loves it.

He squeezed the breast. It felt soft, firm, springy, incredible. He sucked harder on her neck. Blood flooded his mouth. Shannon shuddered and panted.

'Stop it,' she gasped.

Okay, okay. Better do what she says.

He let go of her breast and put his hand behind her. Eased it downward. When he curled it over the smooth hump of her right buttock, she whimpered and squirmed against him.

Yes! This she likes!

'Jeff!' she blurted.

He slid his other hand down. He clutched her buttocks with both hands, digging his fingers in, pulling her more tightly against his body, rubbing himself against her, digging his teeth into her neck, sucking, swallowing.

'No!' she squealed. 'Stop! It hurts!'

Of course it hurts, I'm biting your neck.

I AM biting her neck!

SHIT!

He opened his mouth and pulled his head back. Above and below the tiny knife cuts on the curve of her neck were crescent rows of tooth-holes. Deep, distinct impressions as if he'd sunk his teeth into a block of cheese.

In the blink of an eye, they filled with blood.

He yelled, 'SHIT!'

And then Shannon chomped the side of *his* neck.

Pain blasted through his body. He cried out, flinched rigid, then lost his footing as Shannon wrapped her legs around him. He stumbled backward, clutching her tight against him by her buttocks.

Then he fell.

His back slammed the stone. His head, past the pedestal's edge, hit only air. He let it hang, too stunned to raise it.

He had lost his hold on Shannon's buttocks. His arms lay by his sides.

But she hadn't lost her hold on his neck.

She was on top of him, squirming as she sucked.

Grunting as she sucked.

He could feel her teeth buried in his flesh, feel the force of her suction, feel his blood squirting out.

Hear the sloppy wet sounds as she sucked and swallowed.

Then her teeth released him. Her mouth went away.

'No. Shannon. Don't. Don't stop.'

'Like it?'

'Christ. Yes. Please.'

'No more blood. Not tonight.'

'Please!'

'No, no, no. No more blood.'

On elbows and knees, she glided backward, lightly sliding her nipples against his chest and belly and thighs.

And kissed his rigid penis.

Slid her lips around it.

Sucked it deep into the tight, wet hole of her mouth.

Squirmed and grunted, licked, sucked, stroked the hard length of it up and down with the slick O of her lips . . . and finally swallowed.

Later, they licked each other clean. Then they jumped off the pedestal and hunted for their clothes. Wearing their shoes but carrying everything else, they hiked back to Jeff's car. There, they patched their necks with gauze pads from Shannon's purse. Then they checked themselves for blood in the car's overhead light. After removing the last traces, they hurried into their clothes and sped for Shannon's home.

'I'm afraid you're going to be late,' Jeff said.

'Who cares?' Shannon asked. 'This was the greatest.'

'Not only that,' Jeff said, 'but the vampires didn't get us.'

Shannon grinned at him. 'Think not?'

Stickman

We were on a forty-mile stretch of blacktop through the cornfields after taking in a double bill bloodfest at the drive-in movies over at Darnell, the County Seat. There were four of us in Joe's old convertible.

There was Joe Yokum at the wheel, of course. Up there next to him sat Windy Sue Miller, her feet propped on the dash, her hair blowing wild in the hot wind, a Hamms in one hand.

I sat in the rear next to Jennifer Styles.

She was Windy Sue's cousin from Los Angeles. She'd been in some TV ads, and figured she was mighty hot stuff. Too hot for the likes of me. I hadn't been in the car with her more than two minutes before I was wishing I'd stayed home. Then we finally parked at the drive-in, and Joe had no sooner got the speaker box hooked over his window than she narrowed her eyes at me and said, 'You just keep to your own side of the car, Spud, and everything'll be fine.'

For one thing, my name is Dwayne, not Spud. For another, I didn't need any warning.

It turned out to be a mighty long double feature, what with Joe and Windy Sue carrying on in the front seat, me stuck in the back with Jennifer the Great.

I couldn't even enjoy the films much. All the commotion in the front seat didn't bother me much except to remind me of what I was missing. But it bothered me considerably to be sitting next to a gorgeous thing who thought I was dirt. And then, just about every time I'd manage to put her out of my mind and get into the screen action, she'd let out a long, weary sigh.

She was plainly dying of boredom, and wanted us to know it. Not that the lovers were in any shape to notice. But I sure noticed.

Just once, near the end of the second movie, I looked over at her when she let loose with one of those sighs.

'What's wrong with *you*?' she said.

I sniffed a few times. 'Is that Obsession, sweet thing? Or did you cut one?'

'Fuck you, tractor boy.'

I decided to keep my mouth shut after that. Finally, the movies ended. I sure didn't look forward to the long trip home, but Joe pulled over just past the city-limits sign. He went around to the rear, opened the trunk, and came back with a cold six-pack of beer.

'You aren't going to drink with *me* in the car,' Jennifer protested.

'It's a long walk home, honey,' Joe told her.

'Don't you "honey" me.'

'Lighten up, huh?' Windy Sue said.

'It's more for the rest of us,' I said.

'Gawd,' said Jennifer as we popped our lids.

I wished Joe had broken out the suds back at the drive-in. Would've made things go a bit easier. But us being only sixteen and in a convertible, he'd likely figured it wasn't worth the risk. Anyway, it was good to have them now.

Jennifer took to sighing all over again, but put a different spin on the things so they sounded pissed off instead of bored.

She sure was a piece of work.

She kept herself busy sighing while the rest of us worked on our beers and Joe steered us along that forty-mile stretch of blacktop. The first beer tasted great. The second one tasted even better. When it was half gone, I rested the can on my knee and settled back in the seat. I felt the hot wind blowing against me. I smelled the fresh, sweet air of the cornfields. The sky was spread out overhead, all sprinkled with stars. The full moon made the night so bright I could read the label on my beer can.

I looked over at Jennifer. She sat crooked, her knees against the door, one arm on the windowsill, the other on her lap. Maybe she sat that way to enjoy her view of the corn, but I figured it was meant to show me her back.

She did look fine, the way her hair streamed out behind her in the moonlight, the way her arm looked so dark against the white of her blouse. The blouse was sleeveless, so I could see her whole arm, all the way from her shoulder down to where her hand lay on her lap. Her shorts were white, so I couldn't tell where her blouse left off and the shorts started. The one leg I could see looked as dark and nice as her arm.

'You sure look fine from way over here,' I told her. 'A real shame you're a snot.'

Up front, Joe laughed.

Windy Sue twisted around, reached down over the seatback and gave my knee a swat. 'Dwayne, you behave.'

'It ain't easy.'

She squeezed my knee, then took back her arm and mussed Joe's hair for him.

Up ahead, the road spit into a Y. Joe steered for its right-hand branch, then killed the headlights. The blacktop pretty much disappeared.

Now *that* got Jennifer's attention. She unglued herself from the door and faced front. 'What the *hell* are you doing! Turn those lights back on. Are you crazy? We'll crash.'

'We ain't gonna crash,' Joe said.

'Put them on *this instant*!'

Windy Sue looked back at her. 'Can't just yet. Stickman might get us.'

'What?'

'This time of night, Jen, we sorta gotta *sneak* through this section.'

I punched the back of Joe's seat. 'Hey. Stop the car. Jennifer doesn't know about Stickman.'

I grinned as Joe hit the brakes and swung over. He parked us between the roadside and the edge of a ditch, then shut off the engine.

'What are you doing?' Jennifer asked. She didn't sound curious, just peeved.

We didn't answer, but boosted ourselves up onto our seatbacks and gazed off to the right.

'There,' Windy Sue said, and pointed.

A second later, I spotted his straw hat and head. The rest was behind the cornstalks that reached up and hid him to the shoulders.

'He don't seem to be moving,' Joe said.

'Cut it out,' Windy Sue said. 'You're gonna give me the creeps.'

'Are we just going to sit here, or what?' Jennifer asked.

'You want to see him, don't you?' Windy Sue asked.

'See who?'

'Stickman,' I told her.

'Climb on up back there and take a look,' Windy Sue said. 'You've gotta. He's famous in these parts.'

Jennifer gave off a good, loud sigh. Then she pushed herself up and sat on the back of her seat. 'So where *is* this fabulous Stickman?'

Windy Sue pointed.

'See?' I asked. 'There's his head.'

'You see him?' Joe asked.

'In the straw hat?'

'That's him.'

'Why, that's nothing but an old scarecrow.'

'Stickman,' I said. 'He's not just *any* old scarecrow. The story has it that once a year – on what they call Stickman Night – he comes to life and wanders the fields, looking for someone to kill.'

'How terribly quaint,' Jennifer said. 'Can we go now?'

'What night's this?' I asked Joe.

'July twenty-fifth.'

'Is not,' Windy Sue said. 'It's past midnight.'

'Oh my God,' I said. 'Then this *is* Stickman Night!'

'I know that,' Joe said. 'Why do you think I killed the headlights?'

'You people are a riot.'

'Tell her about him, Dwayne,' Windy Sue said.

'Aaah, she doesn't care.'

'Right.'

'Tell her anyhow,' Joe said.

'*I* want to hear it again.' Windy Sue turned sideways to face me. She hung one leg down off the seatback and swung it. 'Go ahead. Joe, you keep your eyes on Stickman.'

'Well,' I began, 'it all started about a hundred years ago.'

'Is this *necessary*?'

'Shhhh. Let him talk.'

'Christ.'

'Like I was saying, it started about a hundred years ago. Darnell, the town we just came from, got itself a new undertaker by the name of Jethro Seer.'

'Jethro? Give me a break.'

365

'That was his name.'

'Keep interrupting,' Windy Sue said, 'and we'll be here all night.'

'And Stickman'll likely come after us if we hang around too long,' Joe added.

'Sure.' Jennifer turned toward me and folded her arms across her chest so she looked like she was cradling her boobs. Which were so big I judged they could use the extra support. 'Go on,' she said. 'Let's get it over with.'

It took me a minute to recall where I'd left off. 'Oh, yeah. Jethro. He was about six-three, and skinny as a rail.'

'Skinny as a skeleton,' Windy Sue added.

'And he was white. All white. An albino. With pink eyes. He always wore a black frock coat and top hat.'

'That didn't look like any top hat to me,' Jennifer said, thumbing over her shoulder toward the distant scarecrow.

'That's not Seer,' Joe explained.

'That's Stickman,' Windy Sue said.

Jennifer sighed.

'Top hat and black coat,' I went on. 'And he never went outside till after the sun was down. A real boogyman. *Everybody* was scared of him. I mean, he didn't just look so queer but he was the *undertaker*. There was talk of firing him, just to get rid of him. But nobody on the town council had the guts to do it. So he stayed on. And then people started to disappear.'

'Gals,' Joe added.

'Yeah. Just women. Young women. A few townies, but mostly they were gals who lived out on the farms around Darnell. They'd vanish in the night. Without a trace.'

'Let me guess,' Jennifer said. 'It was Jethro. Now can we go?'

'*Would* you shut up?' Windy Sue blurted at her.

She sighed. 'All right, all right. So sorry.'

'Anyway, they finally caught him one night when this gal got away from him. Mary Beth Hyde. Her folks had given her a young colt for her sixteenth birthday, and she went out to the barn by herself that night to pay it a visit. That's when he jumped her. Before she could let out a holler, he drugged her senseless with chloroform or something. She came to down in his embalming room. Flat on the table and buck naked. Jethro was up on the table, too, kneeling over her.'

'I suppose *he* was buck naked, too.'

'Yep. Except for his top hat. He had a scalpal in his hand, and was all set to open her throat, so Mary Beth hauled off and stuck her fingers in his eyes. Jabbed them right in. Glop came pouring out, and—'

'Spare me, okay?'

'Anyhow, that's how she got away. She shoved him off and ran screaming into the street. Nobody was around, it being so late. But there was plenty of action at Clancy's Bar, so she ran in there. Once they heard her story, every feller in that place raced over to the mortuary. They laid their hands on Jethro and made him talk. He confessed everything. He'd snatched every one of those missing gals, brought them to his embalming room and killed them. After they were dead, he . . . you know.'

'You're making this whole thing up.'

'It's all true,' I said.

'Right.'

'It is,' Windy Sue told her. 'Every word.'

'Anyway,' I went on, 'he'd kill them first and *then* he'd fool with them. He just wasn't interested in anything that wasn't dead. Now, he only snatched a

367

gal when there was a funeral set for the next day. Once he got finished with her, he'd haul her pieces out to the bone orchard and plant them at the bottom of the grave that'd already been dug. Nobody ever caught on. Next day, there'd be a funeral and they'd lower the casket and cover it up.'

'Two burials for the price of one,' Joe said.

'They had to dig up fourteen caskets,' I explained, 'to recover the remains of all his victims. That happened later, though. The night the guys from Clancy's got their hands on Jethro, first they made him talk, then they lynched him. Hustled him down Lincoln Street to the square. He was bawling and squealing the whole time, blood and goo running down his face from his eye sockets.'

'You are really disgusting.'

'He's just telling it like it was,' Windy Sue said.

'Anyhow, they got themselves a good strong rope and made a slipknot at one end.'

'That was so he'd strangle real slow,' Joe put in.

'Right,' I said. 'You take a genuine hangman's knot, it's supposed to bust a feller's neck. Like that.' I snapped my fingers. 'But they wanted Jethro to suffer for his crimes, so they used a slipknot so he'd strangle and choke.

'They didn't tie him, but just dropped that slipknot over his head, tightened it around his neck, and tossed the other end of the rope over the limb of an oak tree at the corner of the square. Then they hauled him up. Once he was off the ground, they tied off the rope on the trunk and just watched him. For a while, he danced and flapped around. He kicked and swayed and jerked. He pissed. He took a dump.'

'Lovely,' Jennifer muttered.

'Then he quit. He just dangled there, limp, and they figured he was dead. So then they started arguing.

Some wanted to leave him hanging so the whole town could enjoy the view, come morning. Others said they oughta cut him down in consideration of the ladies, since he wasn't wearing a stitch of clothes.

'They hadn't quite made up their minds, though, when all of a sudden Jethro let out a roar. His arms flew up. He grabbed that rope above his head and climbed straight up it hand over hand, going for the branch they'd hung him from. Some of the guys just freaked out when he did that. But one of them, Daniel Guthrie, who'd lost his daughter to the nut, ran hellbent and leaped and caught hold of Jethro's legs. The extra weight was too much. Jethro lost his grip on the rope. They both dropped. When Jethro hit the end of the rope, his head popped clean off. Then both guys landed on the ground. Guthrie, he scrambled off the body. Before anyone could stop him, he snatched up Jethro's head and ran off with it.

'They carted the rest of Jethro off to the mortuary. When the sun came up the next morning, the hanging branch was missing from that oak tree on the town square. Somebody had sawed it off during the night. It was Guthrie, of course. The next thing you know, he had himself a new scarecrow out in his cornfield. *This* cornfield,' I added.

Jennifer glanced over her shoulder. 'That one?'

I nodded. 'Yep. It looked just like any other scarecrow, dressed up in bib overalls and an old shirt, stuffed plump with straw, a straw hat on its head. But its bones were made of the branch from the hanging tree. And its head was the head of Jethro Seer.'

Jennifer's upper lip crawled away from her teeth. 'They didn't let him keep it, did they?'

'Are you kidding? Nobody was about to mess with Guthrie. So the scarecrow stayed put, and so did Jethro's head.'

369

'It's still . . . ?'

'Nothing left but an old skull,' I said. 'Guthrie's family still owns the farm. They tend to the scarecrow, keep it dressed and stuffed. I don't know who started calling it Stickman, but the name stuck.'

'No pun intended,' Joe said.

'And once a year – so the story goes – on the night of July twenty-sixth, the anniversary of the hanging, Stickman walks. He wanders the fields, searching for beautiful young women to kill.'

'Uh-huh.' Jennifer twisted around and peered back. 'That's actually supposed to be Jethro's *skull*?'

'It *is* his skull.'

'I'm sure.'

'Can't fool Jennifer,' Joe said.

'I'm not *blind*. That head out there's too big for a skull.'

'What you're looking at is a burlap bag,' I told her.

'There were too many complaints when you could see the skull from the road,' Windy Sue explained.

'Jethro's skull is *inside* the bag,' I said. 'But it's right where it's always been, jammed onto a stick from the hanging branch.'

'I'll just bet.'

'Go look,' I said.

'Right. What do you think I am, an idiot?'

'Scared?' Windy Sue asked her.

'Of what? An old scarecrow?'

'Stickman,' I said. 'You're scared the story's true and he'll grab you.'

'I don't *have* to go and look. I *know* it's all a big lie.'

'You don't know any such thing. Tell you what.' I hauled my wallet out of my jeans. I opened it, pulled out my twenty-dollar bill, and held it up in front of

370

her. 'I'll bet you this twenty that you haven't got the guts to go over and *see* if there ain't a skull under that burlap.'

'Go for it,' Joe urged her.

'Hey, come on, guys,' Windy Sue said. 'If anything happens to her . . .'

'Don't worry,' I said. 'She isn't about to do it. She's great when it comes to putting us down and calling us liars, but she's gutless.'

'It has nothing to do with guts,' Jennifer protested. 'The whole thing's silly.'

I waved the bill at her. 'What's silly about this? I know it ain't much for a big TV star like you, but twenty bucks is twenty bucks. Pretty good pay for a little stroll through the corn.'

'I don't want your twenty dollars.'

'What if we go with you?' Joe asked.

'*I'm* not leaving this car,' Windy Sue said. She gave Joe the eye. 'And *you're* not leaving me alone here.'

'*I'll* go with you,' I volunteered.

'Sure thing. Just the two of us? You'd like that, wouldn't you.'

'Not much.'

'Right.' She shook her head. 'This whole thing's probably nothing but a trick to get me alone with you.'

'Nope. I'll stay right here if that's the way you want it.'

'I won't do it for your measly twenty dollars.'

'Surprise, surprise,' I said.

'But I *will* do it.'

Now, that *did* surprise me.

'Don't,' Windy Sue warned her.

'I'll do it on one condition.'

'Name it,' I said.

'I'll walk over there all by myself. And I'll just *see*

371

if it's got a skull. Even though I already know there's nothing but straw inside that sack. I'll check anyway. Because I know your story's a lie and I'm not scared. And then, when I get back to the car, you keep your twenty dollars. But you get out and we leave you here and you have to walk the rest of the way home.'

Joe went 'Yah-ha!' and started laughing.

I figured we were about halfway between Darnell and Sackett. That would mean a twenty-mile hike.

If I lost.

But Jennifer was sure to chicken out before she ever got anywhere near Stickman.

'What do I get if you chicken out?' I asked.

'I won't.'

'Hey now. A bet's got to work both ways.'

'He's right,' Joe pointed out.

'Let's just forget this whole thing,' Windy Sue said, 'and get out of here.'

The corners of Jennifer's mouth curled up. 'I'll grab the scarecrow's hat. If I come back with it, Spud, you walk. If I come back without it, I'll let you take me to the drive-in tomorrow night. Just you and me.'

I laughed, but my heart was starting to pound a bit harder. 'Sounds like I lose, either way.'

'I'll pretend to like you.'

'That I've gotta see,' I said.

She raised her right hand. 'I swear. It'll be the best night you ever had.' She lowered her hand, and grinned. 'But it won't happen. Because I'll be back with the hat.'

'And if you chicken out, we've got a date for tomorrow night?'

'They're my witnesses.'

Joe pursed his lips and let out a low whistle.

'This is crazy,' Windy Sue said.

'Is it a bet?' Jennifer asked.

372

'It's a bet.'

We shook on it, and the way she squeezed my hand sent a hot current rushing all the way through my body. I could still feel her, even after she let go and scooted away and swung her legs over the side of the car.

'You shouldn't do it,' Windy Sue said as Jennifer hopped to the ground.

'Right. Stickman'll get me. Get real.'

Windy Sue's back stiffened. 'It's your funeral, hot shot.'

'Right.'

Windy Sue turned around, and the three of us sat perched on the seatbacks watching while Jennifer rushed down to the bottom of the ditch and climbed the other side. At the top, she glanced back at us. She shook her head as if she thought we were a bunch of real losers. Then she shoved her way in between a couple of corn rows.

While the stalks were only shoulder-high on Stickman, they were taller than Jennifer's head. She didn't take more than two steps into the cornfield before she vanished.

We could hear her, though. Crackling, rustly noises as she tromped along.

Joe grinned at me. 'Hope you've got your walking shoes on, good buddy.'

'She'll be back. Without the hat.'

'Think so, huh?'

'Yep.' Actually, I didn't think so. That girl would likely do just about anything to win the bet. She was a royal pain in the ass, for sure, but there was no doubt but what she had a whole lot of nerve. 'Either way,' I said, 'at least we've gotten rid of her for a while.'

'Nothing better happen to her,' Windy Sue said.

'What could happen to her?' I asked. 'Stickman Night's still two weeks off.'

'I know that,' she muttered. 'Even so . . .'

'Two weeks off!' Joe blurted. 'Hey, let's get real. There *is* no Stickman Night.'

'You don't have to tell *me* that,' I said. 'I'm the guy that made it up. But it's *supposed* to be August 10. That's the night they lynched Seer, so it has to be the night Stickman goes hunting.'

'But he *doesn't* go hunting.'

'I know, I know.'

'Glad to hear you say so. I was starting to worry about you. About both of you.'

'I still don't like her going off like that,' Windy Sue said.

We all went quiet for a while and studied the cornfield. I couldn't see any stalks moving about to show where Jennifer was. She must've made some distance, because I couldn't hear her, either.

For no good reason, I got a cold feeling in my stomach.

'She'll be fine,' I said. 'The worst that can happen is she actually gets to Stickman and sees the skull.'

'Yeah.' Joe chuckled. 'She *knows* it ain't there.'

'I'd sure like to see the look on her face if she lifts that bag and finds old Seer gaping at her.'

'Hope she don't wet her pants,' Joe said.

'Have you got a towel you can put under her?'

'Cut it out, guys. I'm worried.'

We stopped talking again and watched the cornfield. Still, no sign of Jennifer. I saw that Stickman, off in the distance, still wore his straw hat.

'She must be almost there,' I finally said.

'I think something happened to her.'

'Nothing happened to her,' Joe said.

'There's no telling who might be out in that field,' Windy Sue said. 'Maybe some sort of pervert or killer or . . . Thelma Henderson, she vanished without a trace last month. Nobody knows what—'

'Jeez, honey, don't get yourself worked up.'

'Well where *is* she?'

'I guess she might've gotten lost,' I admitted.

So Windy Sue began to shout Jennifer's name. She called out five or six times, but never got an answer. Then she frowned at Joe. 'You *still* think nothing's happened to her?'

'She's probably just having some fun with us.'

'Trying to get us worked up,' I added.

'We've gotta go and find her,' Windy Sue said. 'Come on.' She stood on her seat, planted a foot on the door sill, and jumped down. Turning to us, she jammed her fists on her hips. 'Well?'

'Shit,' Joe muttered.

We had no choice, so we both stepped across the seats and hopped to the ground. Joe took the lead. I took the rear. We made our way to the bottom of the ditch. Windy Sue slipped going up the other side. I had to catch her by the rump and give her a push, which was about the only good thing that'd happened to me so far that night. She had a mighty fine rear end.

I wondered how things might go at the drive-in tomorrow night. If Jennifer kept her side of the bet . . .

'Who wins if we find her before she gets to Stickman?' I asked as Windy Sue pushed her way into the cornstalks.

'Forget your dumb bet,' she told me.

'That bitch wouldn't have put out for you anyhow,' Joe said.

'Maybe not, but—'

'You don't want to mess with her,' Windy Sue said. 'Why would you *want* to?'

Joe laughed. 'That's a terrible way to talk about your cousin.'

'Dwayne's a sight too nice for her.'

'Yeah?' I asked.

'Well, you are.'

That made me feel really good, coming from Windy Sue. Of course, I knew she was Joe's girl. It was nice to hear, anyhow. My night seemed to be getting better and better, and I didn't mind at all that we were shoving our way through a forest of cornstalks. I was with my best friends. We were having our own little adventure, and I figured we'd stumble onto Jennifer sooner or later and it would all turn out just fine.

I even stopped caring about the bet. Damned if I would walk home after this, but it seemed that I would just as soon miss out on the trip to the drive-in with Jennifer.

I might get in some feels – at least if she kept her word – but they wouldn't be worth much. I've messed around before with some gals I didn't much like. Even though it was kind of exciting at the time, it left me wishing I hadn't.

So the hell with the bet. And the hell with Jennifer.

Then she screamed.

Somebody did, and it wasn't one of us.

Windy Sue gasped, 'Oh, my God,' then yelled, 'Jennifer!'

No answer.

'Guess she found the skull,' Joe said.

'Get going!' Wendy Sue snapped at him.

'Don't shove!'

'Move!'

I couldn't see what Joe was doing, but he must've put on some speed because Windy Sue started running. I rushed after her, keeping her back in sight and staying far enough behind not to trip her up. We crashed along for a while. Then Joe yelped. Windy Sue stumbled and flopped down on top of him. I couldn't stop in time, and fell sprawling onto her back. She was hot underneath me. Squirming and panting. But I couldn't enjoy it much, too worried that I'd hurt her. 'Are you okay?'

'Yeah.'

As I crawled off her, Joe gasped, 'Christ, you broke my ankle.'

'Did not,' Windy Sue said.

'You sure didn't *help* it any.'

'Why'd you slow down?'

'I didn't.'

They untangled themselves and stood up. Windy Sue bent over and held her knees and tried to catch her breath. Joe put a hand on her shoulder to steady himself, and tested his right foot. 'Guess it's okay. Just watch where you're going.'

'I didn't stomp you on purpose. Come on, let's move it.' She gave Joe a push.

We took off running again. Pretty soon, it started to seem like we'd gone too far. We'd set out on a line between the corn rows that should've led us directly from the car to Stickman, and as far as I knew we hadn't turned. So we should've gotten to him by now. But maybe we'd hurried right by him. He'd be easy to miss, even if he was just a couple of rows off to the side.

'Hey!' I called. 'Hold on.'

They stopped in front of me.

'We must've gotten off course.'

'Nah,' Joe said.

'We must've. Maybe after we fell. It wasn't this far.'

Nodding and breathless, Windy Sue grabbed Joe's arm. 'Down. Get down.' He sank to a squat. She stepped behind him and swung a leg onto one of his shoulders.

'You've gotta be kidding,' he muttered.

'You got a better idea?'

'Yeah. Let's give it up and go back to the car.'

'Not without Jennifer.' Windy Sue hooked her other leg over Joe's other shoulder. With his head clamped between her thighs, she took hold of his hair. 'Okay, all set.'

Joe sighed, then stood up, lifting Windy Sue above the tops of the cornstalks.

I thought how very much she looked like a kid perched on her father's shoulders to watch a parade go by. A large kid, but this was the only way she could see over the heads of the crowd. The crowd was cornstalks, a mob pressing tight around us so we couldn't see anything. I thought how lucky she was to be up there above it with a view.

Real lucky.

At first, she and Joe had their backs to me. She glanced this way and that.

Joe, holding her thighs, turned slowly.

I had a side view when it happened.

Way up there in the moonlight, Windy Sue looked from left to right. She shook her head. 'This is weird,' she said. 'I can't see either of them.'

'You *gotta* . . . be able to see . . . Stickman,' Joe gasped, straining under her weight.

'Maybe I gotta, but I can't.'

'Oh, for godsake. Open your eyes.'

'He's not . . .' Windy Sue's voice went still. Her back went rigid. Her mouth fell open.

Because she heard it. We all heard it. The rush of someone smashing through the cornstalks right in front of Windy Sue and Joe.

'Jennifer?' she asked.

Jennifer's arm jammed through the leafy wall of corn. I glimpsed a pointed stick – in her hand, I thought

378

– just an instant before she punched it deep into Windy
Sue's belly just above the top of Joe's head. Windy Sue
grunted like she'd been slugged.

I shouted, 'No!'

In my shock, I figured Jennifer had gone mad.

Then she yanked the stick out of Windy Sue and I
saw it wasn't gripped in her hand – it was where her
hand *should've been*. It jutted out from the stump of
her wrist.

Joe, making gaspy whines, staggered as Windy Sue
slumped forward and grabbed his face.

I threw a body block against him. It bashed him
aside, but put me in the way of Jennifer's next thrust.
The stick only ripped through my shirt and gouged my
arm. Then I slammed down on top of Joe. Even as I
landed on him, I heard Jennifer shove her way through
the cornstalks.

It isn't really right to call her Jennifer, I guess.

But I was still *thinking* it was Jennifer until I flipped
over and saw the thing coming at us.

It was partly Jennifer, all right. But it was mostly
Stickman.

I saw him plain as day in the moonlight, striding
toward us. Joe must've seen him, too, because of how
he shrieked.

The burlap bag was off the scarecrow's head. The
eyeless skull of Jethro Seer wobbled at the top of the
center stick. The shirt and bib overalls were gone, too.
And all the straw stuffing.

Stickman wore nothing but Jennifer.

Parts of her.

He wore her arms and legs, just as if he'd torn them
from her body, plucked off the hands and feet, and
skewered the remains onto himself.

He wore her torso, too.

It was stripped naked.

379

His middle stick came out at the top through the stump of Jennifer's neck a few inches below Seer's skull. It came out at the bottom through her pussy. Just under there, the branch forked and ran down to where her legs were spitted on.

It was a sight to make you sick. And to make you think you'd lost your mind.

Joe and I both yelled like a couple of lunatics as Stickman lurched toward us.

What I wanted to do was run like hell.

Instead, I jumped up and tackled him. His balance wasn't that terrific, as he was only standing like someone on stilts. I tried to dive at him low enough to miss Jennifer and just knock him off his pins. But my shoulders hit her shins. I grabbed the sticks under her ankle stumps, and slammed Stickman down on his back.

Then I scurried off. Joe and I hefted Windy Sue and shoved sideways through a few corn rows to get clear of Stickman. Joe carrying her by the shoulders, me carring her legs, we raced all the way back to the road.

We didn't look back till we got to the car.

No sign of Stickman.

We stretched Windy Sue across the backseat. I sat with her, her head on my lap, and pushed my palm against her wound to slow the bleeding while Joe sped us to the emergency room at Sacket General.

Nobody believed Joe and I, of course. I can't blame them. I couldn't really believe what'd happened, either, and I'd seen it with my own eyes.

We likely would've gotten nailed for murder, only Windy Sue pulled through. She hadn't seen much, but enough to convince the cops that she hadn't gotten stabbed by either one of us.

380

So they figured Jennifer must've been murdered by a stranger.

Their search didn't turn up any stranger. It turned up Stickman's overalls and shirt, his straw hat, the burlap bag with a face painted on it, and scattered clumps of straw stuffing. It turned up Jennifer's clothes, too. And her hands and feet. And her head. Nothing else.

All those things were found on the ground right where the scarecrow used to stand. Still, though, nobody would believe our story.

The county papers ran stories about the 'Cornfield Butcher.' They claimed he must've been a serial killer passing through.

Pretty soon, we gave up on trying to convince anyone otherwise. No point in making ourselves look crazy.

We never went back to the drive-in that summer, not even after Windy Sue got well. There was just no way to get there, not without driving the forty-mile stretch of road that passed through the Guthrie family's cornfield.

The search party hadn't found Stickman, but we knew he had to be out there. Somewhere. With what was left of Jennifer hanging on him and Jethro Seer's skull grinning in the moonlight.

Mop Up

Flophouse Droolers

A live one came after Mike Phipps when he shouldered open the door of 214. This kind of thing had happened plenty of times before, but it still turned his stomach to warm jelly.

The drooler hadn't been missed by the main force when it moved through. He'd been hit by something, all right. In the shimmering red fire glow from the tenement window, Mike could see that he was holding a bundle of his guts with one hand as he lurched past the end of the bed, raising a butcher knife that looked as if it had already been used on someone. '*Commmme* to papa,' the guy said, foam spraying from his mouth.

Mike groaned.

God, he hated this.

He gave the drooler a squirt.

The blast of fire from his flame thrower filled the room with light. The drooler, suddenly ablaze from head to toe, shrieked and staggered backward, dropping his knife, dropping his guts. His intestines spilled toward the floor, sizzling and snapping like sausage on a skillet. The end of the bed knocked his legs out from under him. He flopped onto the mattress.

By the light of the burning man, Mike scanned

382

the room. Over near the open closet was sprawled a naked woman. She'd been head shot, probably by the main force. And someone had been snacking on her.

Mike gave her a squirt, shrouding her with flames.

He looked back at the bed. The fiery body of the man seemed to be sinking into the mattress.

Backing into the corridor, he did a quick pivot to make sure there were no other live ones around. The smoky hallway fluttered with firelight from the doorways of the three other rooms where he'd already torched bodies. He ran past them, crouching low, eyes watering, the smoke bitter in his nostrils, dry in his throat.

His heart gave a sickening lurch as he started down the stairs and stepped on a drooler. He'd forgotten about this one. He'd passed it coming up, and planned to light it on the way out. But the damned thing had slipped his mind. When his boot came down on its shoulder, the body flipped onto its side, hurling Mike at the banister. The rail creaked and wobbled as his hip slammed against it. For a moment, he thought he was going over the top. But he rebounded off the banister and stumbled down several stairs, somehow missing the drooler's legs, grunting each time the fuel tank pounded his back. With a quick grab of the rail, he managed to stop himself.

When he had his breath again, he turned around and gave the corpse a quick burst.

He trotted to the bottom of the stairs. He was tempted to skip the ground-floor rooms. The last thing he needed was a run-in with another live one. Besides, the fire would take care of any leftovers down here.

You can't be sure of that, he told himself. One could get buried under the rubble and never be touched by the flames. Might pass it on to somebody sooner or later.

So Mike rushed down the dark, narrow corridor to its far end. Then he began working his way back toward the foyer, throwing open doors, charging into rooms, checking inside closets and bathrooms, behind furniture and under beds, finding plenty of dead droolers and torching each of them.

After the last room, he paused in the foyer. The top half of the stairway was a bright pyre. Its flames had already joined the conflagration at the opening to the second-floor hallway.

Feeling shaky but relieved, Mike pushed open the front door. He rushed out into the night.

Sarge, Ray and Stinger, already done with their buildings, stood by the Land Rover in the middle of the street. Only Stinger still carried his flame thrower. He was busy taking the tank off his back as Mike approached.

Sarge was lighting a cigar.

Ray was using the front of his open fatigue shirt to wipe the grime and sweat off his face.

Doug was missing.

Mike turned around slowly as he pulled the straps off his shoulders. The street, flanked by burning shops and flophouses, was a junkyard of charred cars, broken glass and rubble blasted from buildings. Several bodies were scattered around – black, misshapen heaps on the pavement, some still smoldering. Mike had fired a couple of them himself, during the Exterior Mop-Up Phase.

But he saw nobody moving about.

No sign of Doug.

He eased his flame thrower down, stretched, and rubbed his shoulders.

'Having fun yet?' Stinger asked.

'Take a leap,' Mike said.

Stinger's lean face grinned. 'Got me a couple of livies over at the pawn shop.'

'Made his day,' Ray muttered. Ray, a baby-faced kid of nineteen, didn't care for Stinger any more than the rest of them did.

'Yessir. They was both packin' heat. Not as much as me, though.' Chuckling, he nudged his flame thrower with a boot. 'Took out the fella, first. Gals can't shoot worth shit, anyhow. Shoulda seen the tits on this one. Out to here, y'know? Gazoombas. She's coming at me, butt naked, poppin' caps, missing by a mile, these big old headlights bobbin' around. So I let her have it, y'know? Zip, zip. A dash here, a dash there. She starts floppin' around with her tits on fire.'

'Shut up, huh?' Mike said. 'I'm getting pretty sick and tired—'

'Hey man, hang on, haven't got to the good part yet. So then I lay one right in her face.'

'Knock it off, Stinger,' Sarge said.

'Her fuckin' head explodes. *Explodes!* Can you dig it? Got some on me.' He wiped his hand across a gob of goo on his shirt and swept it at Mike's face.

Mike swatted the hand away.

'I *said* knock it off!' Sarge snapped.

Stinger laughed, shook his head, and rubbed off the mess on a leg of his fatigue pants.

'You're having such a high old time,' Sarge told him, 'suppose *you* go look for Doug.'

'Fuck that. Dickhead's a pain in the ass.'

Sarge scowled at Stinger, squinting through gray shreds of cigar smoke. Then he took a final suck on the stub, plucked it from his mouth, tapped off a load of ash, and shot the cigar at Stinger's face. Red sparks flew as the glowing tip shattered against the soldier's cheekbone.

'Hey! Ow! Shit!' Stinger cried out, slapping away the embers and ash.

'Do what I tell you,' Sarge said.

'Jesus! I was *gonna*. Jesus!'

'On the double.'

'Yessir!' Stinger hefted his fuel tank, swung it onto his back and shoved his arms through the straps. Crouching, he snatched up the squirter. 'Which way'd he go?'

'He took the Carlton Hotel.'

'Well no wonder he ain't back yet,' Stinger whined. 'Look at that place!' The hotel, at the end of the block, was a square brick structure four stories high.

Mike scanned its upper windows. He saw no trace of fire. Doug would've started at the top and worked his way down. That was SOP. If he'd made it to the fourth floor, he must've found no droolers to torch.

But maybe Doug hadn't made it that far.

Mike didn't like the way the squad was getting whittled down. If they lost Doug, they'd be down to four men. Scuttlebutt had it that they wouldn't be getting any replacements.

'Okay if I go with him?' he asked Sarge as Stinger headed for the distant street corner.

'Yeah. Go on. It'll hurry things along.'

Mike picked up his weapon.

'While you're in there, do the place.'

'Right.'

'Be careful,' Ray said.

'Bet on it.' He slapped the kid on the shoulder, then hurried to catch up with Stinger.

He joined the lanky soldier and walked beside him.

'Just don't fuck with me, Phipps.'

'I may kill you, pal, but I'll never fuck with you.'

Stinger laughed.

386

Mike followed him into the lobby of the hotel.

Sissy Suit

'Krugman!' Stinger yelled up the dark stairway. 'Krugman, you shit, answer up!'

'He isn't going to hear you,' Mike said.

'Oh, yeah. Worse pussy than you are.'

They turned on flashlights and started climbing the stairs.

Doug Krugman, who generally acted as if every other guy in the squad was no better than after-birth, had a fear of contagion that prompted him to continue wearing his protective gear – dubbed 'sissy suits' by Stinger – long after everyone else had tossed theirs. Mike had kept his suit longer than anyone except Doug. He didn't consider the garments to be sissy suits, but they were just too bulky and confining. And the head covering knocked out most of your vision. He'd decided he would rather take his chances with the virus than get himself blind-sided by a live one. Or fall down a flight of stairs.

Which I nearly did anyhow, he thought, remembering the last place.

Stopping at the second-floor landing, Stinger again yelled, 'Krugman!'

'Knock it off.'

'He mighta taken off the headgear, dipshit.

'Not Doug. So hold it down.'

'Scared I'll wake the dead?'

'It's not the dead I'm worried about.'

Mike heard a soft, nasal snort. 'Wouldn't be no fun, we didn't run into some livies now 'n' then. Know what I mean, sweetums?'

Mike didn't bother to answer.

387

As they climbed toward the third floor, Stinger said, 'Booger at twelve o'clock.'

'Hold fire.'

'Yeah yeah.'

They reached the landing and hit the drooler with their flashlight beams. He was a kid, maybe sixteen, slumped against the wall with an axe across his legs. He wore his Fruit of the Looms, and nothing else. Someone had stitched him with an M-16, poking a trail straight up his front from groin to forehead. As if for the fun of it, his eyes had been shot out.

Stinger laughed softly. 'Guess what? I'm not the only guy with a sense of humor.'

'Let's split up,' Mike said. 'You take this floor, I'll take the top.'

'Don't like my company?'

'Just don't go torching anyone till I'm down.'

'Can't make no promises. I run into a livie—'

'Use your pistol.'

'Where's the fun in that?'

'All depends where you shoot 'em,' Mike said.

'Ha! Good one!'

Mike stepped over the outstretched legs of the drooler, and shined his flashlight up the last flight of stairs. The area looked clear. He started to climb.

He felt a little guilty about his last remark to Stinger. Like stooping to the creep's level. Better that, though, than to leave him thinking it might be amusing to set the place on fire.

The bastard might do it, anyway.

Probably fire escapes up here someplace, Mike told himself.

Stinger'd better pray he doesn't make me use one.

Nearing the top of the stairs, Mike switched off his flashlight. He climbed the final steps, crept across the landing, and leaned through a doorway. As he'd expected, the corridor glowed faintly – light from the burning neighborhood that came in through the room windows. Several doors had been left open by the soldiers of the main force, so that patches of murky, rust-colored light trembled in the hallway. Not much, but enough to see by.

Mike clipped the flashlight to his web belt, glad he wouldn't need to use it.

He stepped into the hallway, took a shaky breath, and tried to decide whether to start here or at the far end. There were points in favor of both methods. If you torched them in the rooms as you went along, you took a chance of fire spreading into the corridor and blocking your escape. That was its downside. Its upside was that it pretty much removed the chance of a live one jumping you from the rear.

The first order of business is finding Doug, he reminded himself.

So he made up his mind to check each room as he went along, hold off on squirting any droolers he might find, and take care of them on the way back.

Where the hell *is* that guy?

He stepped into the first room. A female drooler lay spread-eagled on the floor at the foot of the bed, her face shot away.

Like most of them, she was naked.

All they wanted to do, once the virus nailed them, was fuck and kill and eat each other.

The damn germ must've been invented by a guy like Stinger, Mike thought.

He stepped past the sprawled body. He used his flashlight to check the bathroom and under the bed. No other droolers. No Doug.

As he headed for the door, glancing all around, the pale beam of his light swept across the body and his heart gave a kick when something moved down there. He whirled. He gazed at the corpse.

It *couldn't* have moved. The poor gal was as dead as dead can be. What he'd seen must've been a shadow cast by her body as the light passed over it.

Nothing more.

But he stared at her chest, half expecting it to rise and fall with her breathing.

If she sits up, he thought, I'm gonna throw a heart attack.

But her chest appeared motionless.

She had a small freckle above her left nipple.

The same as Merideth.

She *looked* like Merideth.

Feeling hot and sick, Mike realized that the dead woman appeared to be in her early twenties. Her hair, spread out against the floor, was long and blonde. She had Merideth's slim build, small breasts . . . and that freckle.

With the face demolished, there was no way . . .

It's not her, Mike told himself. Impossible. She was in Sacramento when Black Widow hit.

But she's just as dead as this woman. Probably sprawled out naked and shot in her apartment . . .

He knew that. She'd had no more chance than anyone else who didn't have protective gear when the strike took place. He'd been living with the knowledge, trying to do his job, trying to keep her death hidden in a back corner of his mind.

He wished he hadn't come into this room.

He wished he hadn't taken a closer look at this corpse.

His throat tightened. The body blurred as tears filled his eyes. Switching off his flashlight, he backed away. His shoulder bumped the doorframe. He staggered into the corridor, turned away and flinched as a dark shape moved through the shadows down the hallway.

He brought up his flame thrower.

Suddenly realized the vague figure was a man in a sissy suit.

'Doug!'

A gloved hand waved a greeting at him.

'Jeez, man, what've you been doing up here? We figured they must've gotten you.'

Doug didn't answer. The lenses of his headgear shimmered golden for a moment as he strode past the doorway of the next room down. The glow of distant firelight fluttered on the camouflage pattern of his suit.

He had no flame thrower. His gunbelt was gone.

'Where're your weapons?' Mike asked. 'What's going on?'

A muffled sound of laughter came from him.

Mike felt a chill spread up his back.

'Take that thing off and talk to me,' he said.

More laughter.

'Doug, stop being an asshole and . . .'

In a voice that sounded as if it came from inside a tight box, Doug said, 'Okay, okay.' A stride away from Mike, he halted. With gloved hands, he reached up and tore at the seal of his mask.

He lifted the hood off his head.

Grinned and laughed, slobber flowing down his chin.

Mike thought, *Quit kidding around.*

Then he thought, *He's turned into a drooler.*

Then he knew. *It's not Doug.*

A live one who just bore a vague resemblance to the guy.

He thought, *Shit!* and tried to swing up the muzzle of his flame thrower as the laughing drooler rammed

391

the headgear into his face and shoved him. He stumbled backward. He crashed to the floor, the tank slamming into his spine. The drooler kicked the weapon from his hands. It tumbled across the hallway until the fuel hose jerked it to a stop and it dropped. Mike tried to sit up, saw a kick coming at his face, and turned his head so the blow only clipped his cheek. It was enough to knock him back.

The drooler stomped on his belly. His breath blasted out.

The infected man flopped down on him, straddling his hips, ripping open his fatigue shirt. Mike went for his pistol, but a knee blocked his way. He landed a punch that snapped the drooler's head sideways. The guy didn't seem bothered, though. Chuckling softly, he rubbed and slobbered on Mike's chest. Then he clutched Mike's shoulders and lunged toward his face, the germ-rich saliva splashing a trail up his chest and throat and chin. Clamping his lips tight, Mike punched both thumbs into the man's eyes.

The eyeballs popped, splashing warm fluid down his thumbs and wrists.

The drooler shrieked.

Thumbs deep inside the sockets, Mike clutched the sides of the drooler's face and hurled him sideways. Scrambling to his knees, he jerked out his Beretta and put three 9 mm slugs into the man's head.

Hot Spit

Mike tried not to panic. Keeping his mouth shut and panting through his nose, he threw off the straps of the fuel tank and yanked his shirt off. With the back of his shirt, he scrubbed the foamy spittle off his mouth and cheeks, his chin, his neck and chest. He wiped spit and blood and viscous fluid off his hands and forearms.

I'll be okay, he told himself.

He didn't think he had any breaks in his skin.

If the stuff doesn't get into your bloodstream . . . What do they know? Maybe it only has to get in your mouth. Nobody knows shit.

Snatching up his sidearm, Mike glanced through the doorway at the body of the woman who looked like Merideth. He didn't want to go in there. So he ran to the next room. He fumbled the flashlight off his belt, switched it on and rushed in.

Looked empty.

He raced to the bathroom door and threw it open. A skinny, naked drooler lay sprawled over the side of the tub – feet on the floor, butt on the edge of the tub, back bent, shoulders and head resting on the bloody enamel of the tub's bottom. His arms were flung out, and a straight razor lay near his right hand. He'd been hit in the chest with something better than an M-16. Probably a 12-gauge assault shotgun.

Crouching beside the body, Mike twisted a faucet handle. Water splashed from the spout.

Works!

He grabbed the drooler by the ankles and yanked him out of the tub. The head made a nasty thump when it struck the floor. Mike dragged him from the bathroom, rushed back inside, and slammed the door. It bumped open. The doorframe was splintered, the latch plate hanging by one screw. Soldiers from the main force must've bashed the door open, coming for that guy.

Big deal, Mike thought. So you can't lock it. The bastard slobbered *all over you*!

He set his flashlight on the edge of the sink so its beam lit the partly open door. Bending over the tub, he turned the water on full force. No hot, but he didn't care. Lucky to have any water at all. He plucked up the shower knob. In seconds, a hard spray was rushing from the nozzle. He let it run to wash the drooler's blood down the drain. While he waited, he picked up the straight razor and tossed it into the sink. Then he hurled his shirt into the tub and climbed in.

The water felt icy on his hot skin. It splattered his face, sent cold rivulets flowing down his body, soaked through his pants and made them heavy and clinging.

With a bar of soap from the dish beside the tub, he lathered his body.

He left the shower curtain open. He kept the automatic in his right hand. He watched the lighted doorway. He wondered if the soap and water would do any good.

Or was he already a walking dead man?

Yesterday, a live one bit Ringo. The little guy had kept it quiet, explaining his torn and bloody sleeve away by claiming he'd been cut on a broken window. They went about their business. Two hours later, when he didn't come out of a liquor store, Ray had gone in after him. Ray returned looking as if the blood had been drained from his usually rosy cheeks. He'd found Ringo in the back room, humping a drooler. When he shouted, Ringo had turned his head and grinned, foam gushing from his mouth. One squirt took care of Ringo and the girl.

After Ray finished telling his story, Stinger had said, 'You get all the luck, Raygun.'

I'll blow my own brains out, Mike told himself, before I end up like Ringo.

I'll know one way or the other in a couple hours.

Thinking about that, heat seemed to pulse through his body and he had a hard time catching a breath.

I'm probably all right.

394

Jesus, what if I've got it?

He rinsed off the suds. Watching the door, he soaped himself again.

How do you know if you've got it? he wondered. All of a sudden, you just start feeling horny for no good reason?

When Stinger starts looking good to me . . .

He heard himself laugh. It sounded a bit mad.

Maybe it's when you start laughing at shit that isn't funny.

God, he thought, I'll be like one of *them*. When it hits, maybe I'll *like* it. Maybe I won't want to kill myself, just everyone else.

Mike let the spray wash the soap off his face, then turned his back to the shower. He raised his Beretta in front of his face. He could barely see it.

Go ahead, he thought.

But what if I'm not infected?

What if you are? You want to risk it? What if it hits you and you take out Sarge or Ray?

He tipped the barrel downward to make sure it had no water in it.

What, scared it'll blow up in your hand?

He opened his mouth wide. He inserted the muzzle. He clamped it between his teeth.

Oh shit, he thought. I don't want to do this.

Merideth's dead. And Mom and Dad. The whole country's fucked. Maybe the whole world, by now. Or pretty soon. Nobody around but droolers and soldiers. Even if you get out of this mess in one piece, what's left?

Come on, find one good reason not to blow your head off. Better make it a good one.

Okay. What about Sarge and Ray? Stinger can take a leap as far as I care. But what about Sarge and Ray? They're my friends. How're they going to feel, I go

395

AWOL on them? What if they run into some bad shit and need me?

I'll go back out there. Tell them what happened. Tell them to drop me if I turn haywire.

Mike eased the pistol out of his mouth. He slipped it into his holster and sagged beneath the cold spray, shivering and gasping for air.

The door crashed open.

Hider

Dropping to a crouch, Mike pulled his sidearm, pivoted and swung the gun toward the bathroom doorway where Stinger stood in the bright beam of the flashlight.

'It's only me from across the sea, dickbrain.'

Mike straightened up. He put away his pistol and bent under the spray to shut the water off.

'What the fuck are you doing in here?' Stinger asked.

'I got drooled on. Did you see the guy in the hallway?'

'Doug?'

'That's not Doug.'

'Could've fooled me. 'Course, there wasn't much face to go by.'

'Must've killed Doug and taken his suit.' Mike bent to pick up his shirt, then decided against it.

'And he gotcha, huh?'

'He didn't *get* me. It's not like Ringo. He just yucked me up, so I showered off.'

'Yeah?'

As Mike climbed out of the tub, Stinger unclipped his own flashlight and stepped the rest of the way into the bathroom.

The beam hit Mike's face. He squinted and turned away.

'Don't mind if I check you out, do you?'

'For what? Bite marks?'

'That. Broken skin.'

'What if you find something? You going to torch me?'

'Yep.' The beam swept slowly down Mike's body. 'Turn around.'

He did.

'Drop your pants.'

'Not for you, pal.' He turned around slowly and squinted against the glare of Stinger's light. The muzzle of the flame thrower was pointing at his chest. 'Maybe the guy did get me with his spit. I don't know. I guess there's a chance of it. So how about you keep an eye on me? If I start acting weird, take me down.'

'Maybe I oughta just do it now.' In the glow of the flashlight on the sink, Mike saw a grin lift the corners of Stinger's mouth.

'Maybe you should,' he said. 'No replacements coming, though. It'll just be you, Sarge and Ray. You three and the droolers.'

For a few moments, Stinger didn't move. Then he lowered the muzzle of the flame thrower. 'I can wait,' he said. He backed through the doorway.

Mike rinsed off his flashlight at the sink, dried it on a leg of his pants, and followed Stinger to the corridor. They made their way toward the far end, Mike checking the rooms on the left, Stinger taking those on the right.

Mike found plenty of dead droolers, but no Doug. He had two rooms to go when Stinger called, 'Got him.'

He rushed across the hallway. Stinger was standing over the body.

397

Doug lay on his back between the bed and an open closet. The top of his head was caved in. His shirt had been ripped open. His pants were down around his knees. Here and there, his skin was caked with white glop. Strips of his flesh had been torn off. Chunks of him were gone.

'Who says this ain't a picnic?' Stinger said.

'Shut up.'

Doug's flame thrower and gun belt were a few yards to the right of the body. They looked as if they'd been in the drooler's way, and he'd flung them.

Mike stepped over to the cast-off gear. With his flashlight, he checked for drool. Then he hefted the flame thrower, slung its tank onto his bare back, and worked his arms through the straps. He fastened Doug's web belt around his waist, just above his own belt, then slid the buckle to the rear so that the holster rested against his left hip.

'You're takin' all that stuff, go on and help yourself to his dog tags.'

'Why don't you.'

'I'm not touchin' that fucker. Be glad to torch him, though.'

'I'll do it,' Mike muttered. Stepping close to the body, he shined his light down. The dog tags were embedded in the bloody mess that was left of Doug's neck. Mike put his flashlight away and shifted the flame thrower to his left hand. Crouching, he took out his knife. He cut off a patch of Doug's shirt, sheathed the knife, and wrapped his hand in the fabric.

'What a pussy.'

With his covered hand, he fished the dog tags out of the gore and yanked, breaking the chain. He left them wrapped in the square of shirt. He shoved them into his pocket.

As he backed away, Stinger sent a stream of fire into Doug's bloody groin.

'You rotten . . .'

Laughing, Stinger hit the body with a full dose that wrapped it in flame. 'Happy trails, asshole.'

Mike, staggering backward, had his pistol halfway out of the holster when he thought, I can't shoot him for being a maggot.

He wondered if his urge to kill the son of a bitch was an early symptom. Jamming the pistol back down tight into the holster, he turned away and rushed from the room.

Seconds later, Stinger joined him in the hallway. 'You got a problem?'

Mike glared at him.

'Okay, let's move it. We got us four stories worth of droolers need squirting.'

They took care of the rooms at the end of the corridor, then made their way back toward the stairs, racing from room to room, entering those they'd already checked and torching the corpses. Mike came to the one with the body that looked like Merideth. He didn't focus on her, just fired a quick stream through the doorway.

He grabbed a strap of the flame thrower he'd discarded after nailing the drooler in the sissy suit. Hefting it beside him, he watched Stinger torch the guy. Then they rushed down the stairs.

At the third-floor landing, he dropped the spare weapon beside the dead drooler who had the axe. He raced down the hallway after Stinger. They split up and charged through the rooms, leaving fiery bodies behind. Mike lugged the extra flame thrower down the stairs to the second floor. He left it on the landing, and picked it up again after they'd flamed every body on that level of the hotel. He lugged it down to the first floor and left it near the foot of the stairs.

'You take care of the hall,' Stinger gasped. 'I'll see what we've got in the lobby.'

Mike didn't like that idea. Alone, it would take him twice as long to hit each room. Twice as long, with three stories of hotel above him. Ten to fifteen fires on each story. All of them growing.

But the lobby needed to be done. There was an area behind the registration desk. There were at least two doors that he could see at a glance. Maybe more, off in the shadows.

'Okay,' he said, and dashed for the end of the corridor.

Don't worry about the fire, he told himself. Right. Probably an inferno up there, by now.

But it won't spread downward all that fast.

You hope.

I'm on the ground floor, he reminded himself. I can always bail out through a window.

And the door at the end of the hall was probably an emergency exit.

He stopped short of that one and shouldered a room door hard so it slapped the wall behind it. Satisfied nobody was behind it, he entered. Nobody on the bed or floor. He pulled his flashlight and rushed to the bathroom. Clear. He dropped and shined the light under the bed. Clear.

He rushed across the hall and hit the next door. Male drooler slumped against the wall, one arm blown off, a pulpy chasm in the middle of his chest. Mike searched for others. None. He splashed the corpse with fire, and rushed out.

Ran to the next door. Hit it. Charged in. A pair on the bed. Still at it, obviously, when the troopers nailed them. An automatic had poked a large S into the guy's

400

bare rump and back. Mike couldn't see much of the woman. Just her spread legs on each side of the guy and one arm stretched across the mattress.

The floor around the bed looked clear. He checked the closet and bathroom. No one. No need to check under the bed. If a drooler was down there, it would go up when he torched these two.

Mike wondered about the woman, though. If she'd been under this guy when the troopers barged in, where was she hit?

Stepping closer to the side of the bed, he checked her with his flashlight. Her head was turned the other way, the guy's face resting on top of it. She had blonde hair, very short. No head wound was visible. Mike began to wonder if she might be a male, after all. But he saw that her armpit was shaved. A woman, all right. Not much of her showed, the way she was mashed between the body and the mattress. Just her bare side. Still, he saw no evidence of wounds.

Her skin, glowing softly in the firelight from the window, looked warm and smooth.

He considered throwing the guy off her.

You want to see how she got it? he thought. Or you just want to check her out?

Come off it! She's a drooler. She's dead.

He realized he *did* want to look at her. There was a tight, growing heat in his groin.

It's kicking in, he thought. Oh, shit! The bastard got me, all right. I'm a dead man.

All of a sudden, he didn't feel horny any more.

He felt as if his genitals were shriveling with cold.

Maybe there's hope after all.

He heard himself let out a weird laugh.

He raised the flame thrower.

Someone made a faint, high whimper.

Mike gasped as the man's head lifted.

401

A live one!

Before he could fire, he realized that the man hadn't moved his head. The head beneath it was already facing his way.

Wisps of golden hair across the brow. Big, terrified eyes. A bruised cheekbone. Lips pressed tight together. Chin trembling.

The mouth opened. No foam spilled out.

'What're you gonna do with that thing?' she asked in a tight, shaky voice.

She looked no older than twenty. She looked beautiful. She didn't look like a drooler.

'You're alive?' Mike muttered.

'So far. No thanks to the goddamn army.'

'Sorry. I . . .'

'You gonna kill me?'

'How can you be alive?'

'I'm a good hider.' She shoved the dead man. Mike stepped back fast as the corpse tumbled off the bed and hit the floor at his feet. He watched the woman sit up and swing her legs toward him. She had a slender body. One of her breasts had a smear of dried blood on it. There was another stain on her belly, just above the gleaming curls of her pubic hair. Another on her left thigh. Mike watched the way her breasts jiggled slightly as she stood up. She pushed his flashlight aside. 'You don't have to stare.'

'Sorry,' he muttered.

Crouching, she rolled the body away from the side of the bed. She got down on her knees and reached under the bed.

Mike gazed at the sleek curves of her back and rump.

He felt a hot swelling in his groin. This time, it didn't throw him into a panic. It's not Black Widow, he thought. Just healthy lust. Besides, it's too soon. With Roger, it took a couple of hours.

The young woman dragged a small pile of clothing out from under the bed, got up and sat on the mattress. As she drew pink panties up her legs, she looked at Mike. 'Come on, do you mind?'

He suddenly remembered something.

'Oh shit, we've gotta get out of here! The whole damn building's going up in smoke.'

R I P

He grabbed her arm and yanked her off the bed. She came up clutching some clothes to her belly. 'Take it easy!' she blurted. She jerked her arm, and Mike let go. Crouching, she snatched a pair of sneakers off the floor.

Mike raced to the door. The corridor was bright with fire from the rooms to the right. Some smoke, but not much. Should be no problem making it to the lobby.

He looked back. The woman, just behind him, was bent over and pulling her shoes on.

'Come *on*!'

She rushed up to him. He gave her a shove to help her through the doorway, then took a stride toward the corpse on the floor.

A good hider, he thought. Christ, how could anyone do that? Play dead under a drooler. Both of you in the raw.

He squirted the body, then turned to the doorway.

She was in the corridor, glimmering with firelight, a skirt or something clamped between her knees while she stretched up both arms and worked a T-shirt down over her head. Her face popped through the neck hole. 'What're we waiting for?' she asked, pulling the shirt

403

down. It was bloody, torn, and much too large for her. It hung off one shoulder. It draped her thighs like a short skirt.

Mike rushed past her, crossed to the next room and bashed its door open.

'I thought we were getting out of here.'

'I've got a job to do. Stay put.' He entered, checked the room, found no droolers, and returned to the hallway. Now, the woman had a skirt on. It looked like denim. Only a bit of it showed below her draping T-shirt.

She stayed beside him as he hurried to the next room. She waited while he went in. One drooler. He torched it. When he came out, flames were lapping out of the doorways down the hall.

'Shouldn't we get going?' she asked. 'I don't exactly look forward to getting cooked.'

'We'll be okay.' He left her and did the next room. Empty.

When he came out, the woman was gone.

He snapped his head to the left.

Spotted the faint white of her T-shirt. She was running. Almost to the lobby.

'Stop!' Mike shouted.

She kept running.

He raced after her.

So I let her have it, y'know? Zip, zip. A dash here, a dash there. She starts floppin' around with her tits on fire.

Mike ran as hard as he could, hands squeezing the flame thrower, tank pounding his back, lungs aching as he gulped the smoky air, eyes watering.

'No!' he yelled, and wondered if she could hear him over the noise of the roaring, snapping flames. 'Stop!'

Blinking his eyes clear, he saw the woman halt and turn around.

Not soon enough.

She was already beyond the start of the corridor, standing in the foyer.

Good as dead, Mike thought. If Stinger's there.

Dashing closer, he expected a burst of fire to squirt out of the darkness and engulf her.

'STINGER!' he shouted. 'DON'T HIT HER!'

Probably can't hear me, anyway.

But the woman heard. She looked away from Mike for a moment, then hurried toward him.

They met in front of the last room before the lobby.

'I told you to wait!'

'I'm sorry. But the fire . . .'

'I know, I know.'

'There's somebody else?'

'Yeah, a trigger-happy jerk. He'd zap you in a flash.'

'Oh.' She bared her teeth. A grimace as if she knew she'd done something stupid and wanted to kick herself for it.

'Get behind me and stay close.'

She nodded. Then she followed him into the lobby.

There was no sign of fire except for the glow behind them and brightness near the top of the stairs. The lobby looked just the same as when Mike had left Stinger there. Except for a door behind the registration counter. It had been shut. Now, it stood open.

'Stinger!' Mike yelled.

No answer. He heard only the roar of the fire at their backs and above them.

'Maybe he went outside,' the woman said.

Or ran into trouble, Mike thought. Doug's kind of trouble.

Then a dim shape filled the upper part of the doorway that was visible beyond the counter. Fire

405

bloomed. In its light, Mike saw Stinger back out of the room and turn around.

He wondered what Stinger had been doing in there before torching someone just now. Must've been at it a long time.

Better if I don't know, he thought.

'It's me,' he announced. 'I've got a survivor with me, so take it easy.'

'You *what*?' The lean soldier braced a hand on the counter, swung himself up, scuttled across the top and leaped to the floor. He raised his flame thrower.

'She's okay. She's not a drooler.'

'Step aside.'

'I told you, she's okay.'

'I'm not infected,' she said from behind Mike.

'Then you're the only one, babe.' Striding closer, he said, 'Let's see ya.'

'Don't even think about torching her, man.'

'Shut your face. Over here, hon.' He gestured with the muzzle of his flame thrower.

The woman stepped out from behind Mike and stood beside him. Her arms were raised high as if she knew how to behave like a prisoner.

Stinger blew through his pursed lips. Holding his flame thrower on the woman with his right hand, he used his left to unclip his flashlight.

From somewhere above them came a wrenching crash. Mike felt the floor shake under his boots. 'The place is coming down,' he said. 'Let's get out to the street and—'

'Go on and get. She stays.' The beam of his flash-light roamed up the woman's body. She squinted and turned her head away when it hit her eyes. 'A real cutie. Open up, cutie.'

She opened her mouth wide.

'Say "ahhh".'

406

'For Godsake, Stinger! You wanta play doctor, wait'll we're outa here.'

'And let Sarge spoil the fun?'

'You bastard.'

'What's your name, hon?'

'Karen.'

Fire began to lap around the doorframe behind the registration counter.

'She doesn't *look* like a drooler,' Stinger said. He sounded amused. Stepping close to her, he slipped his flashlight under the bottom of her T-shirt. Its beam seeped out through the thin fabric. He moved the flashlight upward, lifting her shirt.

'Leave her alone!' Mike snapped.

'Stay out of it.'

He could see Karen trembling as the bastard raised her shirt above her breasts. She made quiet gasping sounds.

'Just checking for open wounds,' Stinger said.

With the rim of the flashlight, he rubbed her right nipple.

Karen swept an arm down. She knocked the flashlight aside.

Stinger smashed her jaw with it.

Crying out, she stumbled backward. She fell to the floor.

Stinger pointed the muzzle of his flame thrower at her.

Mike put a bullet in his head.

The 9 mm slug came from Doug's pistol, held low in Mike's left hand. It punched through Stinger just above his right ear, kicked his head sideways and came out the top throwing up a tuft of hair, gobs of brain, chunks of bone, and a thick spray of blood. Stinger stood there while the mess rained down. Then his legs folded. His rump hit the floor. He flopped onto his side.

407

Mike gazed at him, stunned.

My God, he thought.

I didn't have any choice. He was going to torch her.

I killed one of our own.

He realized Karen was holding him, pressing her warm body tight against his, pushing her face against the side of his neck. He could feel her harsh shaking. And the racing of her heart.

'You okay?' he asked.

He felt her head nod.

Am I? he wondered.

He flinched as he saw a fiery beam crash down at the top of the stairway. With a shower of sparks, it slammed against the banister. The railing shook, but held. The heavy beam, weirdly balanced, rode it down, lopped the knob off the top of the newel post, and dropped to the lobby floor.

On top of Mike's discarded flame thrower.

He yelled, 'CHRIST!' He shoved Karen back, holstered Doug's gun to free his hand, grabbed her wrist, and ran. They raced past the beam's burning end. He threw open the front door, tugged Karen outside, and dashed with her into the street.

At the far curb was the charred husk of a station wagon.

Behind its rear fender, Mike clutched the back of Karen's neck and forced her down flat against the pavement. He sprawled on top of her.

'What're you doing?'

He didn't have the breath to answer.

'You're mashing me.'

An explosion pounded the night. A few seconds later, debris started coming down. Mike lifted his face off the back of Karen's head and saw splinters of wood and glass striking the pavement alongside the car. A

408

few bits of something clinked against the tank on his back. But he felt no jabs.

He felt Karen shaking and flinching beneath him. Soon, the flinching stopped. But she continued to tremble.

Through the ringing in his ears, he heard her say, 'Holy cow.'

'Yeah.'

'Can we get up?'

'Not just—'

A second explosion boomed in his ears. That would be Stinger's fuel tank. Not as close to the front of the hotel. The blast wasn't quite so deafening, and none of the debris came down anywhere near Mike and Karen.

'Okay,' he said. He crawled off her, lifted his flame thrower by its forestock, and got to his feet.

Karen stood up.

He rested a hand low on her back.

Side by side, they gazed over the roof of the car at the blazing hotel. The brick walls were still intact. Fire flapped and fluttered from the demolished doorway and most of the windows.

'I'm sorry about your friend,' Karen said.

'He was no friend.'

'I'm sorry anyhow.'

He rubbed her back, and she leaned against him.

He looked up the street. The Land Rover was gone. Sarge and Ray were nowhere in sight.

The Survivor

Mike led Karen out to the middle of the street – a canyon walled by burning buildings. The squad had been working its way through the slum from west to east. Maybe Sarge and Ray had gone on ahead to the next block. Nothing beyond the cross-street appeared to be on fire, though. Mike couldn't see the Land Rover, but it might be there, blocked from sight by the numerous abandoned vehicles.

'I was with two other guys,' he said.

Karen looked at him.

'Don't worry, they're not like Stinger.'

'Where are they?'

'Must've moved on. I don't know.' He took off his flame thrower. Crouching, he checked the tank's fuel gauge.

Still has some juice, he thought. But not much.

He stood up and faced Karen. 'About what happened back there.'

'I'll back up whatever you say,' she told him.

'Thanks. A drooler got Stinger, that's all. We didn't see it happen, just found the body.'

Gazing at him with solemn eyes, she nodded.

Mike reached behind his back and unhooked Doug's web belt. 'Put this on.'

She took the belt from him. She swung it around her waist and fastened it in front, the holster low against her right hip. Mike saw how the belt pulled the T-shirt taut over her breasts and how the wide neck hole, stretched shapeless, drooped off her right shoulder. The shirt was smudged with grime and dry blood, torn here and there. A small flap hung down, showing the smooth skin just below her collar bone. Her belly showed through a sagging rip that looked like a big, grinning mouth.

She finished adjusting the belt and looked up at Mike. 'Not much,' she said, 'but at least I've got one.'

'Huh?'

A smile turning her mouth, she reached out and patted his chest. 'A shirt.'

410

'Mine got wrecked,' he said.

Her smile vanished. 'Mine got taken. This one's borrowed.'

He nodded. 'Do you know how to use the pistol?'

'I'll manage. What's your name?'

He was surprised she didn't already know it. He felt as if they'd been together for a long time. 'Mike,' he said. 'Mike Phipps.'

'Karen Hadley.' She offered her hand, and he shook it.

This is strange, he thought as he said, 'Nice to meet you.'

'Same here.' Her smile returned. 'Boy, is *that* the truth. An honest-to-God human being who doesn't want to rape, murder, and gobble me up.'

'I just wanted to burn you.'

'Well, you didn't. And you saved my life.'

'Glad to be of service, ma'am.' He looked over his shoulder. 'I guess we'd better try and find the others.'

They started walking up the middle of the street. 'You're not taking your flame thrower?' Karen asked.

'It's almost empty,' he said. 'Anyway, we've got some extras in the Land Rover. If we can find it.'

'Think the guys ran off and left you?'

'Probably just on the next block. We were in there a long time.'

'*I* was in there for days.'

Mike wrinkled his nose. Unable to look at her, he asked, 'Under that guy?'

'Lord, no.' She took hold of his hand. 'He was on me for maybe ten minutes. When I heard you guys, I . . . *Ugh!* I don't like to think about it.'

'Must've been gross.'

'I've been through worse.'

'Can't imagine that.'

'Then you're lucky.'

He looked at her. She turned her face toward him. Her jaw was slightly swollen where Stinger had struck her with the flashlight. Her eyes glimmered in the glow of the nearby fires. Somehow, they looked both vulnerable and tough.

'Want to tell me about it?' Mike asked.

'Not much.'

'That's okay. I know it must've been pretty bad.'

'Yeah. If it wasn't the sickies, it was the soldiers. It's a miracle I'm still alive.'

'Why *are* you still alive?'

'Darn good at playing dead, for one thing. As you saw.'

'But the Black Widow?'

'Is that what they're calling it?'

'It's what *we* call it, anyway. Because of how it makes people act.'

'Iraq do it to us?'

'That's what we've been told. Who knows. They tell us whatever they want. But I haven't heard of any other survivors. I mean, as far as I know, the thing nailed everyone who was exposed to it. We were told there *weren't* any civilian survivors.'

Karen looked up at him with something of a smirk, her head tilted to one side. 'That's 'cause they didn't know about me.'

'You weren't exposed to it?'

'Oh, you've got to be kidding.' She turned her face away and peered straight ahead, her eyes narrow. 'For starters, the strike caught me outside. So I got . . . what do they call it? "Primary exposure." After that . . . I had some intimate contact with sickies. A *lot* of it.' She glanced at him, a fierce hurt look in her eyes, then lowered her head.

'I'm sorry, Karen.'

412

She squeezed his hand. 'Anyway, I've probably had enough of that virus in me to kill off the planet.'

'But you're okay?'

'Peachy,' she muttered. 'But I don't have the foaming crazies, if that's what you mean.'

'Why not?'

'It's 'cause I'm pure of heart.'

Mike felt a smile stretch his face. 'Maybe that's it.'

'Either that,' she said, 'or I've got some kind of a natural immunity.'

They stepped around the charred heap of a body. He saw Karen turn her face aside.

'If you're immune, there might be others.' He thought of Merideth. Maybe she . . .

'Won't be,' Karen said, 'by the time the army's done. They're dropping everyone in sight.'

'God,' Mike muttered. Survivors being cut down by the military. Maybe only a few here and there. But if Karen was immune, there almost had to be others. 'They think everyone's a drooler,' he said. 'We've got to let someone know . . .'

'Sure. Phone the White House.'

'The Land Rover has a transmitter. We can radio a message to—'

'But where is it?'

Mike halted, and Karen stopped beside him. They were in the middle of the intersection. On the block ahead, no fire seemed to be coming from any of the buildings. But there was plenty of light from the burning block at Mike's back to reveal corpses littering the street. Most were naked. None had yet been torched. There were some abandoned vehicles: a taxi at the curb, its windshield shot up; an overturned clunker with a body hanging out the driver's window; a bullet-riddled VW Bug resting crooked on the center

413

line, doors on both sides open; a few others. Halfway down the block, faint but visible in the ruddy glow, was a bus that had crashed into a parked car. The bus, angled sideways, blocked a lot of Mike's view.

He didn't see the Land Rover. He didn't see Sarge or Ray.

'Hope nothing's happened to them,' he muttered.

'Maybe they're behind the bus,' Karen said.

'Could be.' He glanced to the right and left. The cross-street didn't catch as much firelight as the area straight ahead. Not far beyond the intersection, the glow faded to moonlit darkness. From what Mike could see, however, it was no different from every other street in this section of the city. It looked desolate. He saw the dim shapes of scattered bodies. Trashed vehicles. Debris he couldn't recognize.

Nothing moved out there.

He saw no Land Rover. No Sarge or Ray.

'Let's go straight,' he said. 'I don't know why they'd take off, but that's the way we were heading.'

They started walking again. Karen held his hand tightly. They cast shadows on the reddish pavement in front of them.

Even though the night was warm, he felt a chill on his sweaty back as they left the fires behind.

Twin bright lights suddenly broke through the darkness beyond the rear of the distant bus.

Headlights!

He grinned. 'We're in business.'

He heard the faint, familiar sound of the Land Rover's engine turning over.

The headlights started to move, pushing their pale beams through the night.

'I guess they've seen us,' Karen said. She sounded a little nervous.

414

'Don't worry,' Mike told her. 'These guy's are okay.'

The vehicle picked up speed. It swerved to dodge the VW, but didn't bother to miss a body. A front tire bumped over the corpse, tipping the headlight up for a moment.

Somebody let out a merry whoop.

Mike said, 'Uh-oh.'

He drew his automatic.

The Charge of the Night Brigade

'Your guys?' Karen asked.

'Isn't them.'

Then the vehicle was close enough for Mike to make out the shapes of people above the glare of the headlights. A woman rode the hood, feet on the bumper, bare skin dusky in the fire glow, hair blowing, arm waving a bayonet as if she were leading a cavalry charge. A man behind the windshield. Someone in the passenger seat, mostly blocked by the gal on the hood. Two or three in the cargo bed, one standing.

The standing one, a bald man with a beard, raised a handgun as the Rover bore down.

Mike put two rounds through the windshield. One of them caught the driver's face. The vehicle swerved, throwing out the drooler with the gun. It sped by, fishtailing, tires screaming, and spun around. The one who'd fallen out stopped flipping over and lay motionless. Mike heard the engine die and watched the Rover skid until it came to rest near the far curb, some fifty feet down the street, headbeams pouring through the remains of a shop's display window.

He and Karen opened fire. Droolers leaped and scurried from the vehicle, ducked behind it. Someone shot back at them. A bullet whined off the pavement near Karen.

Mike slapped her arm. She looked at him. 'Come on!' He whirled around.

Side by side, hunching low and weaving, they dashed across the pavement. Behind them, gunshots crashed. They leaped the curb, crunched across the glass-littered sidewalk, and lunged through a dark doorway. They crouched and leaned against the front wall. Karen was huffing loudly.

'You okay?' Mike gasped.

'Peachy.'

'Christ.'

'At least . . . you got two of them.'

He duck-walked past Karen and she followed him toward the display window.

'How many more?' he asked. 'Did you see?'

'Four, maybe. I don't know.'

'Where'd *they* come from?' The damn troops, Mike thought, were supposed to nail these fuckers. How in hell did they miss so many? And how come these droolers had bunched together instead of going at each other?

He wondered if they'd killed Sarge and Ray.

Likely.

But there were other mop-up squads around the city. The Land Rover could've been taken from one of them.

Then where's ours?

Stopping at the edge of the smashed window, Mike leaned sideways until he could see out.

Nobody coming.

There were some droolers behind the Rover, keeping low, heads backlighted by the fires on the next block.

They all there? he wondered.

'Do you see them?' Karen asked.

416

'They're still at the Land Rover.'

'What're we going to do?'

'Take 'em out.'

'You're not into hiding?'

He laughed softly. 'Not when I have a choice. Besides, I want to get my hands on that radio.'

'We could sneak out the back,' she said. 'There must be a rear exit.'

Karen's comment reminded him of the store at their backs. He'd been too concerned about the droolers in the street to worry about others. Unclipping his flashlight, he turned away from the window. 'Keep an eye on 'em,' he whispered.

Karen crept past him, squatted beneath the window and peered out.

Mike swept his beam across the room.

They seemed to be in a small grocery market. A checkout counter to the left of the door. Beyond that was a refrigeration unit, probably the meat section. In the middle of the room stood three rows of shelves, the floor cluttered with fallen cans and packages. Over to the right was a liquor section. There, the shelves he could see were almost bare. Some broken bottles on the floor, but he supposed that most of the booze had been taken by looters – droolers, or soldiers from the main force.

He saw no bodies.

He saw no live ones.

Karen was right, though. There had to be a delivery door at the rear.

'Mike?' she whispered.

Stowing the flashlight, he twisted around and looked out the window.

The droolers were inside the Land Rover again. Its lights had been shut off, and it was slowly backing away from the curb. It came across the street at an angle, rear first, swerving slightly from side to side but making steady progress toward the market. And picking up speed.

One drooler was driving. Two seemed to be watching, their faces pale blurs just above the tailgate.

'We got trouble,' Mike muttered. 'Tailgate's armored.'

'Does that mean we can't shoot them?'

'Not unless you're Annie Oakley. Let's try for the driver.'

Mike shuffled sideways until his shoulder met Karen's. Then they opened up, their automatics roaring, jumping in their hands, ejected brass flying. The moment the shooting started, the droolers in the back dropped out of sight. Bullets sparked off the tailgate. Others slammed through the windshield. The driver slumped out of sight.

The Rover kept coming. Faster and faster.

Karen's gun went silent.

Mike fired his last round. He jerked Karen's sleeve. 'Let's go!' he shouted as the vehicle sped across the center line.

They lurched up and staggered away from the window.

Mike expected the Rover to keep on coming and try to ram through.

But it skidded to a halt at the curb. Two faces rose above the tailgate. A third drooler stood up behind them.

Time seemed to slow down as that one came to her feet in the cargo bed, as Mike rushed backward with Karen, as his hand worked fast to release his empty magazine.

The rising drooler was the one who'd been on the hood when the vehicle first came at them. Her right side shimmered with the distant firelight, and her left side was dark. She looked magnificent standing there

418

– tall and slim, her shoulders broad, her right breast glowing like polished gold, pubic curls glistening. Magnificent and awful. She had the bayonet clamped in her teeth. Slobber flowed down her chin. The shoulder Mike could see bore the dark strap of the fuel tank she wore on her back. Clamped between her arm and ribcage was the stock of the flame thrower. Its muzzle swung toward the store window.

Mike hurled himself sideways, slamming against Karen. They hit the floor rolling as a gust of fire rushed by. He kept tumbling until he saw Karen scamper up. He thrust himself off the floor and followed her. Glancing back, he saw a path of fire that led from the windowsill across the floor to the first section of standing shelves.

The woman came through the display window like a hurdler.

Before she landed, shelving blocked Mike's view. He kept his eyes on Karen's back. She was a few strides ahead of him, her shirt a pale, jolting blur.

As he ran, he shoved a full magazine up the butt of his pistol. He slapped it home. He jacked a cartridge into the chamber.

Karen still had an empty gun. He wondered if she knew how to reload. Probably not.

They were almost to the rear of the store. He glanced back. The drooler'd had time to reach their aisle, but she wasn't there. Probably in a different aisle, planning to get them as they cut across the back. He was about to warn Karen, but she let out a small yelp and lurched to a halt. Mike dodged, missed her, and stopped.

Just in front of them was a refrigerator unit that ran along the back wall. It had sliding glass doors. Instead of soft drinks and beer, it held a drooler. Mike couldn't see much. But he saw plenty. The naked guy was spread-eagled so tight against the glass that it pressed his skin flat. His nose and erection looked mashed. He was writhing, licking the glass, gazing out at them.

One arm stretched out farther. He hooked a rim of the door with his fingertips and the glass started to slide.

Mike put a bullet in his forehead.

He stepped around Karen, holding a hand up to keep her still, and leaned past the end of the shelves. In the fluttering red light from the fire, he could see that the back aisle was clear. The rear exit ought to be just beyond the end of the refrigeration unit.

If they went for it, they'd be exposed to anyone lurking between the next two rows of shelves.

Though he heard nothing except the crackle and snap of the fire, he knew that the gal with the flame thrower had to be nearby. And the other two or three droolers were probably in the store by now, sneaking through the aisles. One of them, at least, had a gun.

He didn't want to go out there.

Maybe sneak back to the front and try to . . . ?

He heard a quiet skidding sound – the sound that a door of the cold-drink compartment might make, sliding open. The skin on his back crawled. He snapped his head around.

The body of the drooler toppled out as Karen, gripping the handle, leaped out of the way.

'What're you doing?' Mike whispered.

She didn't answer. Crouching over the feet of the body, she reached forward with both hands, lifted up on a wire shelf rack inside the refrigerator and shoved it. Mike heard a few cans tumble and roll. The rack clamored, apparently dropping to the floor behind the unit. Karen raised and pushed the next shelf up. More falling cans. Another clatter.

Mike checked the rear aisle. Still clear. He scooted

420

backward and glanced around the way they'd come. Okay there.

Where are the fucking droolers!

As another rack rang against the floor, he crawled past the end of the shelving for a glance down the next aisle. He eased his face around the corner and looked straight at the belly of a drooler. A skinny old thing. A woman. Squatting there, grinning and slobbering. 'Hi-ya, honey,' she whispered.

Mike was on his hands and knees, his automatic pressed against the floor. As he started to bring it up, the hag dropped toward him, grabbed his hair with both hands and twisted his head, flipping him onto his back. He clamped his mouth shut tight.

Foam spilled onto his lips and chin.

Just like last time.

If the other time didn't infect me, he thought, this won't either.

Her tits slapped the side of his chest. Her hair draped his face. He jammed the muzzle of his automatic against her ribs. Her open mouth was inches above his face when a shoe shot in from the side, caught her in the eye, knocked her head sideways and Mike pulled his trigger three times.

He shoved the drooler. She tumbled off him. Karen grabbed the wrist of his gunhand and pulled as he staggered to his feet. She kept his wrist. Crouching, she guided him toward the open refrigerator. He stumbled as he stepped on the rump of the drooler who'd been in there. He fell to one knee between the guy's legs.

Something to the left.

He snapped his head that way and jerked his hand from Karen's grip as she ducked into the compartment.

Beyond the last section of shelves stood the gal with the flame thrower.

Bayonet still in her teeth. Tawny skin shimmering. Thick suds of drool flopping off her chin and flowing like lava down between her breasts.

Mike triggered four rounds at her. The first seemed to miss. The next pounded her hip. One got her square in the chest, shaking her breasts and splashing out a thick spray of drool and blood. One punched her under the nose. She flinched as each bullet struck her. As she staggered backward, Mike knew she was dead on her feet. Her back hit the far wall. She dropped to her knees. And flame bloomed from the muzzle of her weapon. Straight at Mike.

He sprang for the darkness. His hip scraped the edge of the sliding door. The back of his head struck a wire rack. Cans above him bounced and clinked. He landed belly first on the floor of the refrigerator compartment, sliding, kicking up his feet. Karen grabbed him under the armpits and dragged him the rest of the way through.

He looked back. His boots weren't on fire, but the aisle back there was ablaze.

He stood up, Karen holding him steady as cans and wire racks teetered under him. They were in a storeroom stacked with cartons.

Apparently, the stock people loaded the shelves from back here. Karen must've known that.

It looked like the looters had missed this area.

'You okay?' she whispered.

'You're a genius,' he said.

'That's me. Used to work in a 7-Eleven.'

Things Can Only Get Better

Mike wanted to hug her, but he realized his face was still wet with the slobber of the drooler.

422

No shower handy, this time.

'What happened out there?' Karen asked.

'I bagged the babe with the squirter.'

'All *right*!'

'Gotta clean my face,' he muttered.

Karen put a hand on his shoulder. 'Bend down,' she whispered. 'You think we got them all?'

'One or two left, maybe.'

When he was squatting in front of her, she tugged her T-shirt free of her belt, put a hand inside it, and lifted the fabric toward his face.

'You don't want to get this on you.'

'I'm immune, remember?'

With the front of her shirt, Karen rubbed the saliva off his cheeks and lips and chin.

'Thanks,' he muttered. He straightened up. 'Give me your pistol.'

She handed it to him.

'Over here.' He stepped around a stack of cartons, and she followed. They crouched down.

'Do you think we hit the driver?' Karen asked.

Mike dropped the empty magazine into his hand. 'I don't know.'

'Me neither.'

'There ought to be one more, plus the driver if we didn't get him.' He took a fresh magazine from the pouch on his belt, slammed it up the pistol butt, and worked the slide. 'Maybe they can't get back here,' he said, giving the weapon back to her. 'That gal laid a path right across the rear. They'd have to come through it.'

'So you think we're safe?'

'Well, we might burn up.'

He heard a soft laugh come from Karen.

After reloading his own Beretta, he said, 'What we'll do is take the back way out. Work our way around to the front and get back to the Land Rover. Then head for battalion.'

'What about your friends?'

'I don't think they're alive any more. These creeps must've taken 'em out.'

Mike stood up and turned around. Most of the storeroom was in shadows. Here and there, firelight shimmered on the sides of stacked boxes. He saw no one. 'Looks okay,' he said, holstering his sidearm as Karen rose beside him.

He ripped open the top of a carton, reached in and pulled out a can. In the gloom, he couldn't see what it was. 'Thirsty?' he asked.

'You bet.'

He popped the can open and gave it to Karen. As she drank, he took out another, and shook it hard.

'Hey, that'll . . .'

'I know,' he said. Tipping the can toward his closed mouth, he flipped its tab. With a *whish*, warm soda sprayed his face. Some went up his nose, but most of the liquid splashed his lips and cheeks. It spilled down his chin, ran down his neck and chest. He rubbed it around with his left hand.

'That's a crazy way to drink Pepsi,' Karen said.

'I can't stand having that stuff on me. I know it's not supposed to give you the Black Widow, but . . .'

'No harm being careful.' Karen set her can on the box. She pulled off her T-shirt, turned it around, and used its back to mop the soda off Mike. 'You're going to be sticky.'

'You too, now.'

'I'll survive,' she muttered.

He wanted to reach out and touch her, slide his hands up her smooth sides. But one hand was wet and the other held the Pepsi can. Besides, she might

424

not appreciate it. God knows what had been done to her by droolers before he came along.

She finished drying him, shook open her shirt, and lifted it overhead to put it on. He watched her breasts rise slightly. The ruddy light trembled on them. Her nipples were dark and jutting. Then they were out of sight beneath the filthy, torn shirt.

She picked up her can, and drank some more.

Mike rubbed his wet hand on a leg of his fatigues. He shifted the can to that hand, and drew his pistol. He took a few swallows of the Pepsi. He wished it were beer. He wished it were cold. But it tasted sweet and good. He finished off the can, and set it down inside the carton.

'Maybe we can latch onto some food,' Karen said.

'When was the last time you ate?'

'I don't know. The army came through here this afternoon. Yesterday, I . . .' She shook her head. 'Must've been day before yesterday. Didn't get much, though. I got into the kitchen of some diner, but then a couple of sickies came after me. The whole place was crawling with them before the soldiers showed up.' She made that '*Ugh*' sound again.

'Come on,' Mike said. 'Let's see what we can find. But we'd better hurry.' Though the fire hadn't yet penetrated the storeroom, smoke was coming in and the temperature seemed to be rising fast. 'Keep your eyes sharp,' he said.

Karen took another swig of Pepsi, then set the can aside.

They made their way across the floor. They passed the double doors that led into the shopping area. Tongues of flame were lapping through the crack at the bottom. Rushing by, they came to more stacks of boxes. Karen started ripping them open while Mike stood guard.

'Chicken soup,' she muttered. She tore open another box. 'Mayo. Darn.'

'Hurry.'

She ripped into another. 'Ah-ha! Oreos! Do you like Oreos?'

'Fine.'

'Double-stuffed, too.' She hugged them to her belly. 'All set.'

'That's all you want?'

'It'll do for now.'

He led the way to a large metal door at the back of the storeroom and shouldered it open. 'Wait a second,' he said. He stepped out.

An alley.

He checked both ways. Dark back here. Walled in by brick buildings. To the left, the alley stretched into darkness that seemed to have no end. To the right, the distant opening at the cross-street glowed from the block that Mike and the others had left burning. He saw trash bins here and there along the walls. Most of the buildings had rear doors. Some had loading docks. He saw no droolers.

'Looks okay,' he said.

He braced the door wide with his back and Karen came out, followed by a few shreds of smoke. He stepped away. The door swung shut with a heavy clank.

Side by side, they walked down the middle of the alley toward the ruddy light. The plastic wrapper crackled, and Mike watched Karen take out a cookie. 'Open up,' she said. He did. She pushed the cookie into his mouth. As he chewed, he peered past her at a loading dock to the right. The bay door beyond the platform was open.

We could go straight through to the street, he thought. We'd come out by the Land Rover.

426

But the area beyond the door looked black.

God knows what might be in there.

Here in the alley, at least he could see what was coming.

Karen used her lower teeth to pry her cookie in half. She chewed, then scraped off the white filling with her teeth and moaned softly as she savored it.

Mike switched the pistol to his left hand. He put his right hand low on Karen's back. Her shirt was damp. He thought about drooler germs, but told himself that the real slobber was on the front of her shirt. This was mostly Pepsi. So he caressed her back through the moist fabric.

She turned her head and smiled at him, the bottom half of the Oreo wedged between her teeth.

Looking at her, Mike felt warm and achy in his chest. He smiled. 'You're something else,' he said.

Karen crunched the cookie.

He moved his hand higher on her back. Up between her shoulder blades, the shirt was dry. He slid it against the smoothness of her skin.

'I came real close to blowing my brains out, earlier tonight.'

'I'm sure glad you didn't,' she said.

'I thought I might be infected,' he explained. 'And there didn't seem to be much point in going on, anyway. Everything's . . . gone.'

'Not everything. There's still Oreos.'

Mike laughed softly. 'Yeah. And there's you.'

Karen shifted the package of cookies to her other arm and eased closer. Her hip touched the side of his leg. Her arm went around his back and she caressed his side. 'I'm awfully glad we found each other,' she said. 'Things were looking pretty bleak, all right. Not that I ever considered suicide, but . . .'

'You're a survivor.'

427

'I just like things, you know? Food . . .'

'I noticed.'

'Sunsets, baths, friends, lovers.'

Mike curled his hand over her bare shoulder.

'You name it. There's always enough good stuff to make up for everything that's rotten. Besides, I figured things could only get better, you know? Turns out, I was right.' She squeezed his side.

Mike realized they were nearing the cross-street. And he realized he'd forgotten about their peril. He quickly looked over his shoulder. In the shadows behind them, nothing stirred.

We're doing just fine, he told himself.

But there's got to be droolers around. Don't let your guard down again.

At the mouth of the alley, he glanced from side to side. There was good light from a blazing tenement at the corner across the street. He saw debris, bodies, abandoned cars. Nobody moving.

He turned Karen toward the right, took a few steps, then stopped and faced her.

She looked up at him.

'I don't want to lose you,' he said.

She nodded slightly.

'If we join up with the main force . . . I'll be in it all again. They'll probably ship you off somewhere.'

'I wouldn't like that,' she murmured. She caught her lower lip between her teeth. She had a cookie crumb at the corner of her mouth.

'When we get to the Land Rover . . . How would you feel about heading west? I don't know what we'll find. Just dead people and ruins, probably. But there won't be any troops. We'll be on our own.'

'That sounds good to me.'

'I can radio battalion headquarters from the Rover to

pass on the word that there are survivors. Then we'll just head the other way.'

'You'll be a deserter, Mike.'

'They'll just think I'm a casualty. Hell, our whole squad's bit the dust. I'll just be one more guy the droolers got.'

'Are you sure you want to do this?'

'Do you?'

'You bet your ass. Let's get to that Land Rover and head for the coast.' Breaking away from him, she hurried up the sidewalk. She had a bounce in her step. Her short hair shimmered golden in the firelight. The tail of her T-shirt, rounded over her small buttocks, shifted and swayed with each step. She looked over her shoulder and smiled at Mike.

His bowels seemed to freeze.

The naked drooler that lurched around the corner of the building twenty feet in front of Karen was a fat bald man with a hard-on and an automatic.

'NO!' Mike shrieked.

The drooler fired.

Gunplay

Karen's head jerked as the slug hit her. She twirled like a clumsy ballerina, her arms swinging out, cookies flying from their package as it tumbled through the night, her legs doing a weird jig until she stumbled off the curb, tripped over her own ankles, and flopped onto the street.

Mike watched. Numb.

A bullet zipped past his ear, and he focused his mind long enough to empty his Beretta into the drooler.

He staggered toward Karen's body. She was sprawled on the pavement, her face turned away from him. One of her sneakers had come off. The bottom of her bare foot looked clean and pale. Her foot seemed very small, almost like that of a child.

Mike sank to his knees beside her.

The tail of her T-shirt had come up. It lay rumpled and crooked against the seat of her denim skirt. He holstered his pistol. Leaning forward, he rested a hand on the back of her shirt. It was damp from when she'd used it to dry the Pepsi off him in the storeroom.

A sob wrenched Mike's chest. He hunched over and clutched his face with both hands and cried.

'I'm not dead yet,' Karen muttered. 'No thanks to you, Quickdraw.'

'Oh God!' He wiped his eyes and tried to stop crying as she rolled slowly onto her back.

The right side of her face was torn and bloody. She kept that eye shut, but it didn't look damaged. There was a pulpy furrow just in front of her ear. Her cheekbone was laid bare. A corner had been knocked off the tip of her nose.

'Won't win any more beauty contests, huh?'

Mike sniffed and wiped his nose. 'You will if I'm the judge,' he murmured. 'Does it hurt much?'

'I've hurt worse.'

He unsnapped a satchel at the side of his belt and took out his first-aid kit. As he opened it, he checked around. The area looked clear.

He remembered that he'd emptied his pistol into the drooler.

He lifted the front of Karen's T-shirt above her waist and pulled Doug's pistol from the holster. He set it down on her belly.

For the next few minutes, he worked on her face. She flinched and gritted her teeth as he fingered the wound, gently prodding some torn flesh back where it seemed to belong. The bullet had carried plenty off

430

with it, but enough remained to fill in some of the gouge and cover most of her cheekbone. When Mike figured he could do no more to improve the situation, he bandaged her, taping down the gauze pads as firmly as he dared.

'That should hold you,' he said, 'till I can get you to a field hospital.'

'Field hospital?'

'You need real doctors.'

'We're going west, remember?'

'I can't take the chance. The wound might get infected. You could die.'

'Not me. I'm the survivor, remember?'

'Pure of heart.'

'Damn right. We're heading west, just like we planned.'

'I don't know.'

'I do.' She started to sit up, and groaned.

'I'd better carry you,' Mike said.

'Yeah, you'd better. I'll ride shotgun.' She reached down to her belly and picked up the pistol. She raised its barrel toward the reddish sky, twirled a little curlicue with it, and said, 'Let's go.'

Mike pushed one arm under her back. He slipped the other behind her knees.

'I think I'm missing a sneaker.'

'Okay.' He left her for a moment. He picked up the small shoe. She wiggled her toes as he started to put it on her. He felt his throat thicken.

'You don't have to tie it,' she said when he was done.

'Thanks.' He returned to her side, squatted low, and lifted her.

Instead of taking Karen to the sidewalk, he made his way to the middle of the street.

No more surprises, he told himself.

It felt wonderful to be holding her. To feel her warmth and movement as he walked.

He stepped past the corner, continued to the center of the intersection, and turned to the right. Some distance up the street, the Land Rover was just where he'd last seen it – stopped a few yards from the front of the market. The store was blazing. Though flames were gusting up from the display window, none reached as far as the Rover.

Karen's head was turned. She was looking, too. The pistol, tight in her grip, rested on her belly with its muzzle pointed that way.

'Spot any sickies,' she told him, 'just say the word.'

'If I spot any, I'll put you down and take the gun.'

'Don't trust me?'

'I've never seen you hit anything,' he said.

'Doesn't mean I can't.'

Mike smiled down at her.

She was cradled against his chest, the bandaged side of her face upward as she watched the area ahead. Her right arm was pressed against him. It was bent at the elbow, forearm angled across her belly, the barrel of the pistol resting on her left wrist as if ready for whatever might come at them from the front.

Her left hand lay curled between her upraised legs. The denim skirt, bunched around her hips, left her thighs bare. They gleamed in the firelight.

Mike knew he should be watching for droolers, not admiring Karen.

But she was keeping watch.

So he looked at her breasts. They were just below his face, very close. The loose T-shirt hung lightly over them. It took on their shape. He could see the way her nipples pushed the fabric out. The motion of his walking made her breasts shake and tremble just a bit.

She's so beautiful, he thought.

If he lifted her higher, he would be able to kiss her right breast. He imagined the turgid, springy feel of the nipple in his mouth. The shirt would be in the way.

'Looks like we got him,' Karen said.

Mike raised his eyes, then halted. They were only a few strides from the Land Rover. The driver was slumped forward, head against the steering wheel. The exiting bullet had splashed gore against the pocked and webby remains of the windshield.

Mike carried Karen closer to the Land Rover. A single flame thrower remained in the cargo bed. No droolers.

He leaned over the side and started to lower her.

'Hey, I want to ride up front with you.'

'You should be lying down,' he said. Gently, he set her down.

'No, I mean it. I don't want to ride back here, Mike.'

He pulled his arms out from under her. She started to sit up. With a hand on her bare right shoulder, he eased her down.

She strained against it for a moment, then seemed to relax. As if giving up, she let her legs go out straight.

'How am I going to ride shotgun for you if I'm back here?' she asked.

'Won't be for long,' he said.

'Promise?'

'Yeah.' He slid his hand away from her shoulder. He curled it over her breast. Through the T-shirt, he felt the heat of her skin, the push of her stiff nipple. Karen covered his hand and pressed it down more tightly.

Mike's heart raced. He had to swallow, but his throat felt tight. His penis felt like a hot iron bar jamming into the front of his fatigues.

He freed his hand.

He climbed over the side of the Rover, and Karen scooted sideways to make room for him.

'Mike,' she said softly. 'I don't know.'

'It'll be all right.' He crawled onto her, knelt above her.

'My face . . .'

'I know, but . . .' Shaking his head, he lifted the T-shirt above her breasts. The nearby fire felt hot and good on his back, but he wished his shadow wasn't in the way. He caressed her breasts. So smooth. They felt even more wonderful than he had imagined.

Karen writhed a little. In a low, husky voice, she said, 'We'll be in an awful fix if some sickies show up. Shouldn't we wait?'

'I can't.'

'Okay. I want you, too, but . . . Okay.'

As he gently explored her breasts, Karen set down the pistol. With both hands, she unhooked Doug's belt and spread it away from her waist. She unbuttoned her skirt, lowered the zipper.

Mike crawled backward, pulling the skirt down her legs. He slipped trembling fingers under the elastic of her panties. As he drew the flimsy garment over her sneakers, Karen sat up slightly. She crossed her arms and lifted the T-shirt over her head.

Kneeling beside her feet, Mike no longer blocked the firelight. Karen's naked body was bathed in the russet glow. As he gazed at her, she lifted a foot, gently rubbed his thigh with the sole of her sneaker, then swung her leg past him.

She was sprawled before him, open, waiting.

Mike unhooked his web belt and tossed it aside.

'Come here,' she said.

He crawled forward. Her thighs felt like warm satin

434

under his open, fluttering hands. Between them, she was hot and slick.

Karen guided his hands to her breasts. And while he caressed them, she opened his pants. She tugged them down his thighs. She drew the band of his shorts away from his belly. She dragged the shorts down.

Suddenly free of the confining garments, he let out a shuddering breath.

He had never known such desire. His penis felt solid, huge, monstrous.

Karen's fingers slipped around it. They glided downward.

Gasping, he squeezed her breasts. She whimpered quietly, squirmed, but didn't tighten her grip. She slid her hand slowly upward. And then it was gone. Mike sank onto her. He kissed one of her breasts. He tongued the nipple. He filled his mouth with the breast, and sucked. Hard enough to make her cry out softly and flinch.

He wondered how it would be to bite it.

Karen clutched his hair with one hand. She gave it a sharp pull.

She can't take any more, either, he thought.

He scurried up her body. He licked drying blood from her lips, savoring its coppery taste, then thrust his tongue into her mouth. He pushed his erection slowly into her slippery, tight warmth.

Karen writhed under him. She raised her legs, and he felt himself sink in more deeply.

He felt buried in her.

Then he felt a cool steel ring against his temple.

He pulled his tongue from Karen's mouth. He raised his face, but the muzzle stayed tight at his head. He stared down into her eyes.

'I hope to God you don't have it, Mike.'

'Huh?'

435

'But I think you might.'

'No!' he blurted, panting for air. 'It's just you! I haven't got the Widow!' A string of saliva spilled from his lips and dribbled onto Karen's chin. He swallowed hard. 'It's just . . . I want you so bad!'

'I'm sorry,' she said. 'God, I'm sorry.'

He shouted, *'DON'T!'* sprayed her, and a hot blast kicked through his head.